ONE NIGHT WITH HIS EX

KATHERINE GARBERA

SEDUCTIVE SECRETS

CAT SCHIELD

MILLS & BOON

First Published in Great Britain 2019
by Mills & Boon, an imprint of HarperCollinsPublishers,
1 London Bridge Street, London, SE1 9GF

One Night With His Ex © 2019 Katherine Garbera
Seductive Secrets © 2019 Cat Schield

ISBN: 978-0-263-27196-6

1019

MIX
Paper from
responsible sources
FSC® C007454

This book is produced from independently certified FSC™ paper to ensure responsible forest management.

For more information visit: www.harpercollins.co.uk/green

Printed and bound in Spain
by CPI, Barcelona

ONE NIGHT WITH HIS EX

KATHERINE GARBERA

This book is dedicated to
happy couples everywhere and to
those still searching for the one.

Acknowledgments

I know I'm always thanking the same people but,
when you live in a different country than all of your
friends and they are willing to video chat with you once
a week, I think it deserves some thanks. Eve Gaddy and
Nancy Thompson, I honestly don't know what I'd do
without you both. You make me laugh, let me whine,
talk plots and do sprints with me. Basically, you keep
me going and I love you both!

One

Hadley Everton both loved and hated living in Cole's Hill, Texas. To be fair, the town had been growing ever since the joint NASA-SpaceNow training facility had opened on its outskirts, but those small-town minds weren't keeping up. Today, she had dodged several well-meaning society matrons from the upscale Five Families neighborhood who were all concerned about her lack of a man. Since this was her sister's engagement party, everyone in her mother's circle of friends had fixed their eyes on her as the next one to finally wise up and land herself a husband.

It wasn't as if Cole's Hill didn't have its share of eligible bachelors for her to pick from, as her parents' neighbor Mrs. Zane had pointed out with her usual blend of sweet bluntness. Hadley could choose from any of them. Though in her infinite wisdom, Mrs. Zane advised her to stay away from the Velasquez brothers, especially after her recent breakup with Mauricio.

Seeing two more of her mother's friends, Mrs. Abernathy and Mrs. Crandall, making a beeline toward her, Hadley faked a sneezing fit and ducked into the country club's kitchen. The waitstaff were busy living up to her mother's exacting standards, preparing the trays of food for circulation, so they didn't care if Hadley had broken up with her "one good prospect" and seemed doomed to a life as a single woman.

She stood in the corner near the door to be out of the way of the staff, which unfortunately left her in earshot of her busybody pursuers.

"I heard she told him if he didn't put a ring on her finger, she was out of there," Mrs. Abernathy said.

"And he just said see you later. What is wrong with young people these days? He should have asked her then and there. He's almost thirty and it's not like anyone else is going to be interested in him if he couldn't make Hadley happy," Mrs. Crandall added.

Hadley turned to leave the kitchen via the back door but bumped into someone. She glanced up with an apology on her lips, but froze when she saw it was her sister, Helena.

Helena was the pretty sister, with a heart-shaped face, naturally thick eyebrows and blue eyes that Hadley had always envied. She stood a few inches taller than Hadley, as well. Today she wore a slim-fitting sheath that showed off her curves in a subtle way. Normally, her sister was very low key and laid back, but Hadley noticed she seemed tense.

"What are you doing in here?" Hadley asked.

"Same as you," Helena said. Reaching up, she tucked a strand of Hadley's hair behind her ear where it had escaped from her low chignon.

Hadley pulled the tendril back down to frame her face. Her older sister was forever acting like Hadley was still an eight-year-old and Helena was the more sophisticated ten-year-old.

"Hardly. This is your party," Hadley said, moving away from the door and the women who were still talking about her and Mauricio.

"Girls. What are y'all doing?" their mother asked as she entered the kitchen. Candace Everton was the spitting image of Helena, just twenty-one years older. She kept the grays at bay in her natural strawberry blond hair with bi-weekly appointments at her hair salon and kept her figure by playing in a women's tennis league at the club.

Their mother had always had it all together and there were times when Hadley wished she had just a tenth of her mom's ease when it came to dealing with the social pressures of living in Cole's Hill. But she never had.

Candace inspected a tray of canapés that one of the uniformed waiters was about to take out and wrinkled her nose at him. "This looks sloppy. Please get a clean tray before you serve my guests."

The waiter turned around as their mother walked toward them. Hadley found herself standing a little taller and tucked the tendril that Helena had been messing with earlier back behind her ear.

"Just enjoying a moment of quiet," Helena said. "I asked Hadley to help me with my zipper. It felt like the hook had come undone."

"Let me see," Mother said.

Helena turned around and their mother checked the hook and eye before wrapping her arm around both of her daughters' shoulders. "Ready to get back to the party?"

No, but clearly that wasn't the answer their mom wanted. She urged them both toward the door that led out of the kitchen.

When she got back out into the living room, Hadley

came to a stop as she saw Mauricio Velasquez standing there. Of course, he looked like he'd stepped out of her hottest dreams. That was the thing no one had warned her about with breakups and broken hearts. She might be ready to move on, but her damned subconscious kept churning him up in the middle of the night and giving him a starring role in her sexiest dreams.

He had what she'd heard the old biddies in town refer to as a chiseled jaw; his neatly trimmed eyebrows framed eyes that were as black as her favorite dark chocolate. When he looked at her, she always felt like he could see straight past the layers she used to keep the world at bay to the very heart of her. But she knew that was a lie. Had he been able to do that, he wouldn't have invited Marnie Masters, the femme fatale of Cole's Hill, into his bed, while he and Hadley were taking a break in their relationship. She had believed they were going to get back together up until the moment she found out about Marnie.

"Hadley, what are you doing?" Mother said, putting her hand on Hadley's shoulder.

"Sorry, Mother, I just saw Mauricio."

"So?"

"I'm not ready to talk to him," she said.

"This is Helena's day, sweet child, so you will straighten Grandma's pearls and walk over there and greet him like he's an old friend," Mother said.

She took a deep breath and looked over at Helena. "You're right. Sorry, Hel."

She'd known he'd be here. Mauricio and her sister's fiancé were best friends and had been since high school. It wasn't as if she could ask everyone she knew to stop socializing with him. Helena had even taken her to brunch at her favorite place to break the news that Mo would be in the wedding party. The picture of him walking out of his bathroom in a towel with the town flirt Marnie Masters right behind him had flashed through Hadley's mind. But it didn't matter. She had to be there for her sister.

"It's okay," Helena said. "I did warn you he'd be here today. Malcolm asked him to be a groomsman so you're going to see him at all the pre-wedding events."

"She's got this," Mother said. "I raised you girls to have steel in your backbones. And manners."

"That's right, you did," Hadley agreed. She wished it were that easy, but when she saw Mauricio, he stirred to life so many different emotions. Anger she could understand, and sadness of course; it was hard to move on. Then there was guilt. But another feeling entirely came into play when her gaze drifted down his body, to that tailor-made suit that emphasized the width of his broad shoulders, the jacket buttoned neatly at his waist showing off the slimness of his hips, the pants displaying those long legs to perfection.

She groaned but Helena pinched her in warning. She straightened her shoulders and realized that Jackson Donovan had come in behind Mauricio. Jackson was Hadley's date for the event, and as he waved at her, Mauricio turned to greet him.

"He better not make a scene at my baby's party," Mother said.

"He won't," Hadley said with a confidence she was far from believing as she headed off to run interference between her ex-lover and her new boyfriend.

Mauricio had taken care to arrive late at the engagement party, even though Malcolm Ferris was one of his best friends. He'd known today was going to be a challenge and he'd never been one of those men who could just smile when he was pissed off. His twin brother always said it was the reason they were so good at speculative business ventures. They weren't afraid to fight for the underdog or walk into a bad situation and make the best of it. Though Mo had his doubts, Alec had found a way to make that work. For Mauricio it was real estate, for Alec it was technology and social media. Frankly, Mo didn't understand his brother's multi-million-dollar business but there was one thing he did understand… No matter how many months passed, he still couldn't look at Hadley Everton and not feel his blood start to flow heavier in his veins.

She looked like a perfect Southern lady today. Her dress was a beautiful navy blue that hugged her slim torso, drawing his eyes to her delicate neck encircled with her heirloom strand of pearls. Damn if there wasn't something sexy about seeing a lady all dressed up and knowing what she looked like naked.

He cursed and started to turn to leave the party. He wasn't going to be able to keep his cool. But just then Jackson Donovan walked up next to him. The two of them had always rubbed each other the wrong way. Ever since their school days, Jackson had been a goody-two-shoes. The only thing that had changed was that back then he had been a skinny geek and now he was six foot five and muscular.

"Mo, good to see you," Jackson said, holding out his hand.

Mo shook it, keeping his grip light, but Jackson squeezed before letting go. "I didn't know you knew Malcolm."

"I don't, well, not really. I'm here with Hadley."

Mo saw red. Sure, they were broken up and it felt final this time, but Hadley could do better than this—

"Hello, boys," Hadley said, joining the two of them. She gave Jackson a kiss on the cheek before turning to smile at Mauricio.

Mauricio took a deep breath. "Hiya, Had. You look gorgeous as usual."

"Thank you," she said, with a tiny nod. "I hope you'll excuse us, Mauricio. I promised Mother I'd bring Jackson over to meet her cousin."

"Of course."

She slipped her hand into the crook of Jackson's elbow and Mo watched her walk away, unable to tear his eyes from the curves of her hips. Had her legs always been that long?

"Mo, I was surprised to see you chatting with Jackson," his brother Diego said as he handed him a longneck Lone Star beer.

Mauricio brought the bottle to his lips and took a long pull. "Mama told me to mind my manners today. And I'm not going to give her another reason to be embarrassed after last fall."

"Glad to hear it," Diego said.

"Yeah?"

Diego nodded.

"Me too. I can't keep avoiding everyone from our life together."

"That's a good point," Diego said.

He hoped so. He was working his way back to *good*. A year ago, he'd been trying to manage his real estate business in the hill country, a reality TV show in Houston and a relationship with Hadley, who had been transferred to her company's Manhattan offices. She worked for a large design firm and was one of their top designers. He'd been barely hanging on and he'd crashed and burned, especially after what had happened with Hadley. It forced him to take stock of his life and narrow his focus to the things—people—who were really important. His family, his good friends like Malcolm and his other polo team buddies.

"Glad to hear it. Pippa's in London this week, so if you

want to hang out, I'm free," Diego said. His brother was in a long-distance relationship with Pippa Hamilton Hoff. His brother's fiancée was the COO of House of Hamilton, Britain's famous jewelers, and divided her time between London and Cole's Hill.

"Sounds good. I'm actually working on a project with Homes for Everyone this week. If you have some free time, we could use another set of hands. We're putting up some framing for the walls tomorrow night." Mauricio was heavily involved in the charity, which helped low-income families who were struggling to buy their own house. Mauricio usually provided tracts of land for the different projects that Homes for Everyone were doing in their part of Texas, and occasionally even joined in on volunteer days when they actually built the homes.

"I'll be there," Diego said as he turned his attention to Helena and Malcolm.

The engaged couple were opening presents, and everyone was watching them, but Mauricio couldn't keep his eyes off Hadley. She wore her thick dark curly hair pulled back in a low bun at the back of her neck. Several strands had escaped and framed her heart-shaped face. She chewed on her lower lip as she glanced down at the notepad in her hand, jotting down the details of each of the presents that her sister opened until she'd worried all of the lipstick from her mouth. Not that she needed to put on makeup to look like a knockout.

His gaze drifted down her body to the V-neck of her dress that gave a glimpse of her cleavage. *This was a bad idea.* He should have declined when Malcolm had asked him to be a groomsman but theirs was one of Mauricio's oldest friendships.

He stood up and Diego arched one eyebrow in question. "I need some fresh air."

He didn't get far before Malcolm caught up with him. They'd met in the third grade when they'd both been dropped off by their parents on a Saturday morning for the Hill Country Junior Polo League. They'd been close ever since. Malcolm's father died when they were in high school, and Malcolm had spent more time at the Velasquez house after his mom took on more hours at work to support the family. Now Malcolm was his partner in the real estate business and together they were determined to make sure that the growth of Cole's Hill wasn't too fast so as not to damage the community they both loved.

"Hey, Mo, I need you inside for a photo of all the groomsmen," Malcolm said. "I have a surprise for y'all that I think is pretty cool."

"I think most of us are just happy to see you in love and marrying the woman of your dreams."

Malcolm shook his head. "I still can't believe Helena said yes. I'm not nearly good enough for her, but I'm trying to make sure she'll never regret her decision."

"She's a lucky woman," Mauricio said, clapping his hand on his friend's shoulder.

"I saw you with Hadley and Jackson earlier."

"Yeah, that wasn't weird or anything," he said.

Malcolm laughed. "One of the cons to living in Cole's Hill is that it's hard to avoid past girlfriends."

"True."

"Helena already warned me I'd have to keep you in line. No fighting," Malcolm said. "Not with Hadley or Jackson or heck, even me."

"I'm not doing that anymore," he said. "That was just a bad spell."

"Glad to hear," Malcolm said. "Behind all their Southern charm, the Everton ladies aren't happy with you at all."

He didn't blame them. "I'll be on my best behavior."

"Mal, come on," Helena said. "Daddy wants to get the pictures taken so he can take off his tie."

"Coming."

Mauricio followed the engaged couple into a sitting room. There was a large picture window with a spectacular view of the hills behind the house, which were covered with bluebonnets in full bloom. Crissanne Moss, one of the newer residents of Cole's Hill, was acting as photographer today. She was engaged to Ethan Caruthers, who was related to Mauricio through marriage.

"I'm going to do a shot of the ladies first, then all of you guys and then a big group photo."

There was some grumbling especially from the men as they stood with their backs against the wall. The last time they were all together waiting like this was in high school when they'd gotten their yearbook photos taken.

He shook his head at the thought.

"I hate photos," Malcolm said. "I always look either like a creepy toothpaste ad or like I'm getting ready to be tortured."

"Just relax," Mauricio said. "Maybe look at Helena. You don't look creepy when you smile at her."

"Glad to hear it," Malcolm said sardonically.

"No problem, man."

"Guys, come on over," Crissanne said.

Mauricio walked past the bridesmaids and Hadley's floral perfume scent filled the air. He couldn't help taking a deep breath as he moved into the position that Crissanne directed him to. When she had everyone posed, she explained that they had to do a serious photo and a silly one. Mauricio realized that if he never had to be in another photo again, he'd be happy.

"Now let's mix it up," Crissanne said.

There was some jostling around Helena and Malcolm,

who were in the center of the group. Crissanne kept moving the men and women to get a good balance of something that only she could see with her photographer's eye.

Mauricio stood toward the back; being six foot five, he was pretty much always in the back of any group shot. When Crissanne repositioned two of the bridesmaids, it put Hadley right in front of him.

He stood a little taller and held himself back from her.

"Okay, guys, I need you to put your hand on the shoulder of the woman in front of you," Crissanne said.

He put his hand on Hadley's shoulder. As soon as he did, a tingle went through him. He noticed goose bumps on her left arm, and she shifted under his touch. Her breath become shallower and a slight flush spread down her neck. He felt a zing of awareness go through him, and he did his best to ignore it until Hadley glanced back over her shoulder at him and their eyes met.

They both might have decided to move on, that they weren't ever getting back together, but there was an undeniable sexual energy between them now; it hadn't been extinguished. He knew better than to think that this would lead to anything more than the most exquisite sort of torture, but he couldn't help rubbing his finger over the small bit of flesh exposed by the thick strap of her dress. Her skin was softer than he remembered, and she shivered delicately under his touch.

Crissanne brought their attention back to her and snapped the photos. "Okay, you're all free to go."

Hadley bolted from under his touch and all he could do was watch her go.

Two

One touch and she was back where she'd been all those months ago. She glanced around the busy party. Jackson caught her eye and nodded toward the door leading to the parking lot. She made her way through the crowd, careful to avoid all the women who had well-intentioned advice for her, and finally stepped outside and took a deep breath. She hoped that it was just being inside in close quarters with Mo that had made her react the way she had. But the truth was, her skin still tingled from where his fingertips had been. The back of her neck was still sensitive where his breath had brushed over it.

"Hey, there. You look like the party was getting to be too much for you," Jackson said, coming up and putting his hand under her elbow.

His touch was nice. But it didn't cause a chain reaction in her body the way that one small brush of Mauricio's fingers had. That was the problem.

She looked at Jackson. He'd always been a good friend to

her, starting back in high school when they'd both been in the International Baccalaureate program and study groups together. He'd been skinny and small and worn those glasses that were too big for his face. Of course, he'd changed. Matured into the kind of man she would have said was her type if not for that damned Mauricio messing with her body.

She wondered if she should just go home with Jackson and sleep with him. Maybe the fact that Mauricio had been her only lover was the reason why she still reacted to his touch. She toyed with the idea of sleeping with Jackson only until their eyes met. He was a good guy. He didn't deserve to be dragged into her mess with Mo.

"When you look at me like that I know this doesn't mean anything to you," he said.

The sun was shining brightly, and it was the kind of late summer afternoon where the heat was so oppressive that being outside was a chore. She was just thinking that when she glanced past Jackson's shoulder and saw Mo standing there on the patio outside the country club.

She shook her head. It was over between them, had been for longer than either of them wanted to admit.

"It could," she whispered to Jackson, not sure if she was talking to herself or him. "It's just…"

"I'm not Mauricio," he said with his usual bluntness. "I never will be. And I'm not about to apologize for that."

"I wouldn't ask you to, and I don't think you want to be Mauricio," she said. "I like you, Jackson."

He laced their fingers together and pulled her toward the willow tree that had been planted decades ago and now had large branches that cascaded down to the ground. He held the willow branches to the side as they stepped underneath them into the relative coolness of the shade provided by the tree. She could hear the melodic sound of the fountain in the nearby water feature.

He let her hand drop and then shook his head. "I like you too, Had, but not enough to play second fiddle to a Velasquez or any other man. There was a time when I might have considered it—"

"No, there wasn't. You've always been such a strong, confident guy. That's one of the things I've always admired about you."

"But you've admired me as a friend, right?"

"Yes. But I thought that's what you wanted from me," she said.

"It is. I mean it would be a major cosmic F you to Mauricio if you and I had clicked and ended up married," Jackson said. "But I wouldn't do anything to mess with our friendship."

"Me neither," she said, putting her hands on the sides of his face. He had a strong jaw with only a hint of five o'clock shadow. His eyes were gray, so unlike Mauricio's with their dark power. Jackson was the kind of man she'd always thought she'd fall in love with and end up marrying. But the heart didn't work that way. "I'm sorry."

"Don't be," he said, before pulling her close and bringing his mouth down on hers. He angled his head for the kiss and she closed her eyes as their lips rubbed against each other's. She opened her mouth and his tongue brushed against hers. He tasted of mint and it wasn't an unpleasant experience but…

There was no spark.

Not a single bit of attraction. There was no way she could hook up with him to get over Mo. Not when all she could think was how one single brush of Mauricio's fingers against her skin had set her on fire.

No matter how much she wanted there to be a spark with Jackson, there just wasn't.

He pulled back and shook his head. "Well, hell. I guess we are meant to just be friends."

She smiled at the way he said it. "I was hoping for something more too."

"I bet," he said. "You going back in? Want me to stay with you?"

She shook her head. She'd had enough of being the proper Southern lady her mama wanted her to be. She was done standing in the same room with a man she didn't want to lust after and pretending that she was cool with every society matron gossiping about her lack of prospects. "I'm not going back in. I think I've done my sisterly duty."

"Then I guess I'll see you around," Jackson said. As he walked away, she stood there in the shade of the willow tree and felt her hands clench into fists. She wanted to punch something or someone... Mauricio Velasquez, who had ruined her for other men, it seemed. She felt a scream rising up in her throat and realized she needed to get out of there. Go somewhere far away from engagements, her parents and the man she was thinking way too much about.

Mauricio went straight to the bar, ignoring his brother who lifted a beer toward him. He needed the hard stuff if he was going to be able to drive the image of Hadley and Jackson holding hands out of his mind. He knew he had no claim on her, and thought he had made his peace with that until he'd touched her.

Touching her had proven that all of his growth since they'd broken up had been for nothing. The spark was still there. Maybe what they needed was one good lay to get it all out of their systems. But he somehow didn't think that Hadley was going to be too interested in that.

He ordered Jack Daniel's neat and downed it in one swallow, and then forced himself to turn and move away before he started that slide back down to the out-of-control-guy he'd been last fall.

They'd broken up when she'd moved to New York but had kept in touch with texts and video chats. Mo had missed her but he had been casually dating and hooking up as well. He'd texted her a few times saying he wanted her back in his life permanently without realizing that she was coming back to town the very weekend he'd sent his last text. Then she'd used her key to let herself in and surprise him at his place early one morning after he'd hooked up with someone else. She'd caught them together.

Until that moment he had never realized what an ass he'd been. He had wanted Hadley back but he'd also hated to be alone so he'd been playing both sides. He shouldn't have done that. He'd regretted it since then but he was too stubborn to admit that at first.

He noticed Helena watching him with one eyebrow arched. He put his hands up and walked away from the bar, but as he turned, he knew he needed to sort this out. He was in the wedding party and had to spend the next nine months with this group. Helena deserved some reassurances that he wasn't going to ruin her wedding with some sort of brawl.

He walked over to Hadley's sister. "I'm not going to F this up."

"Good," she said. "Your mom reassured my mom that you were over Hadley."

"She did?" *For fuck's sake*, he thought. His mom was going around making sure that everyone knew he'd behave? That was messed up. Like really messed up. He didn't need her doing that.

"Yup. You know what it's like living here. It doesn't

matter that we're the fastest growing small town in Texas, the attitudes are slow to change," Helena said.

He sighed. "Believe me, I know. You should be in real estate if you want to see slow attitudes. No one wants to pay full market value for anything."

"I've heard you have a way of charming them into paying the going rate," Helena said.

Real estate was a nice safe topic and one that he had no problem discussing. Anything to keep from talking about Hadley.

"Your fiancé isn't that bad at it either," Mauricio said.

"Good to know…" Then after a long pause, she asked, "Has he made any investments lately…big ones?"

"Not that I know of. Why?"

"It's probably nothing," she said.

But he knew Helena. She wouldn't have brought it up if it were nothing. "Want me to talk to him about something?'"

She shook her head. "I'm not even sure if there is anything to talk about. It's just he's been acting odd and we have some funds unaccounted for."

Helena was notorious among their group of friends for her tight purse strings and keeping Malcolm on a budget. Or trying. It wasn't that Mal didn't earn a decent salary, but that he tended to be frivolous and impulsive in his spending habits. And Helena was a save-for-a-rainy-day girl.

"I haven't noticed any big new toys at work, but we are playing cards tomorrow night with my brothers, so I'll see what I can find out."

"Thank you," she said. "I don't want to make a big deal out of anything, but I had to ask my parents to put a down payment on the flowers for the wedding and you know my mother. She thinks that means she's in charge of the planning now."

He did know. His parents were the same way. If they

were paying, they micromanaged every detail, which was why he hesitated to ask them to invest in any of his projects. "You're welcome. It's the least I can do for causing you stress today."

"I knew you'd behave."

"Right, because of my mom."

"Nah," she said over her shoulder as she started to walk away. "Because you don't like hurting Hadley."

Of course, she'd lobbed that as a parting shot so he couldn't argue or defend himself against it. But it was the truth so who was he to argue.

He noticed Diego watching him and just shook his head. He needed to get out of here. Now. He'd done his part to support his friend and even been pretty damned polite to Hadley's new boyfriend, so he figured he could call it a day.

He left the country club and the party, but once he got outside, he didn't fancy going home to his empty penthouse apartment. He had always liked the place because Towers On The Green had been the first big development he'd done on his own in Cole's Hill. And he'd claimed the penthouse that overlooked the square for himself.

But he'd also lived there with Hadley for a short time and it had been where she'd come home from Manhattan to find another woman in his bed.

"Mo, wait up," Alec called from behind him.

He turned toward his twin and stopped. Growing up, they'd gotten into a lot of good-natured fun switching places with each other and pulling pranks on friends and their parents. But these days Alec was busy running his tech company and Mauricio didn't see him often enough.

"Thanks," Alec said. "I need a ride to the airport. Just got an email and I need to get to Los Angeles to take care of a problem."

"Sure."

"Want to come with me?" Alec asked. "A few days out of town would be nice and we could hang out. I feel like I haven't spent enough time with you lately."

He shook his head. "I can't. I have a meeting tomorrow with Homes for Everyone. It's one of my bigger projects. I agree we haven't been hanging out enough. When are you back in town?"

"Ten days," Alec said.

"For the polo match that Diego set up?"

"Yes. I can't wait. Should be a good game," Alec said.

Diego and Mauricio had been working on a new horse stable closer to town and had added a field that was big enough to host charity polo matches. Diego ran the Velasquez ranch, Arbol Verde, which had been in the family for generations.

Mo dropped his brother off at the airport and took the long way home, stopping by the old warehouse district where Hadley's loft was. He told himself he was checking out the land because it might be a good development project. But he knew a lie when he told one to himself, and as he stared up at the corner loft unit and noticed that the lights were on, he had to force himself not to call her.

Hadley spent a restless night trying to forget that one little touch from Mauricio. She went for a run and then showered and pretended that her week was starting like every other one. She had this. Of course, she'd broken up with Jackson and now had to find something to fill her hours, which made her feel exactly like the old biddies who thought she needed a man to be complete. It was just… Her sister was engaged and most of her friends were in long-term relationships, and it was hard being the third wheel all the time.

She went into her shop and took a moment to look

around. The best part of coming back to Cole's Hill was opening this place. She'd always known she wanted to do something artistic as an adult. After college, her career had taken her into brand marketing and graphic design, which was challenging and rewarding but had too many restrictions. She'd quickly realized she didn't mind following a brief but hated having someone tell her exactly how to design a project.

But here at her art studio, she was finding her true calling. She still had a few clients in New York that she was working with until she could make this studio start to pay. Her sister, who was a CPA, had designed a long-term investment strategy for Hadley and so far it was going pretty well.

She had designed some lithographs of the surrounding Cole's Hill area and had a commission to do the Abernathy ranch.

The bell on the door to her shop rang and she glanced over her shoulder to see Helena coming toward her with two thermal coffee mugs and a pastry box from the Bluebonnet Bakery. "I brought breakfast."

Hadley leaned her hip against the back counter, eyeing her sister. "What do you want?"

"What makes you think I want something?"

"It's not even nine and you're in my shop with a bribe."

"Maybe I just love my little sister," Helena said, putting the box on the counter in front of Hadley and handing her the thermal mug that was emblazoned with *#BRIDETRIBE*. She took the mug and inhaled the aroma. A skinny vanilla latte. Her sister definitely wanted something.

"You could, but I haven't known you to get out of bed this early unless you needed something," she said. Helena was famous in their family as a late sleeper and ridiculously hard to wake up under normal circumstances.

"Well, I might need your help to run interference with Mother."

Hadley took a sip of her latte and reached out to open the box. There were two cheese Danishes and a chocolate cake doughnut inside. Of course, Helena had brought her favorites so this must be serious.

"With what?" she asked.

"I had to ask Mom and Dad to put the deposit down on the flowers and now she's trying to take over. I mentioned that you were the artsy one and had already designed the flowers for the church and the reception…"

"That doesn't sound bad. I'm not sure you needed to bring the latte and the pastries to ask me to do your design. I was already planning to do it," Hadley said.

"Great. Glad to hear it. Mom is going to be over later to give you some notes on how she'd like the church to look. You will need to make some time to go and visit with the pastor, as well as with Kinley. Now that Mom is on board, we're going to have Kinley plan it."

Kinley Caruthers was a local girl who'd moved to Vegas and landed a primo job with Jaqs Veerland. *The* Jaqs Veerland, who planned weddings for A-listers and European royalty. Kinley had come back to Cole's Hill to plan former NFL bad boy Hunter Caruthers's wedding. Kinley had a complicated history with Hunter's brother Nate and after they got engaged Jaqs opened a satellite office here in town so Kinley could work in Cole's Hill.

"What?" Now the pastries were making a bit more sense.

"Sorry, sis," she said.

"There aren't enough cheese Danishes at the Bluebonnet to make this okay. Mom is going to be a complete tyrant about this," Hadley said.

"I know. I'm sorry, but I had no choice."

"Why not? I thought you'd budgeted to make sure you didn't have to ask them for any money," she said.

"I did, but something came up unexpectedly and we didn't have enough for the deposit, so I had to ask Daddy."

"That doesn't sound like you."

She shrugged. "You know how it is with brides."

"Actually, I don't. But I do know you and you have a backup for everything," she said. She put her coffee mug on the counter and walked around to her sister. "What's going on?"

Helena chewed her lower lip and turned away from Hadley, which made her even more concerned.

"Hel, whatever it is, you can tell me," she said.

She put her arms at her sides and shrugged. "That's just it. I don't know what the problem is. Malcolm withdrew the money and I can't ask him about it without it seeming like I'm checking up on him."

"Uh, yes you can. It's your wedding fund," she said.

"I know, but I took out a large amount to buy him a wedding present and I asked him to trust me and he did...so now I have to give him the same trust," she said.

"Did he say he bought you something with it?" she asked.

"No, he just said he'd have the money back in our account soon."

"Soon? That doesn't sound like Malcolm. When did he say that?"

"Six weeks ago," Helena said.

"Uh...that doesn't sound right."

"I know. I asked Mauricio to see if he can find out what's going on," Helena said. "He was really sweet after you and Jackson left the party."

Of course he was. She'd rather he was a jerk so she could go back to hating him and forget about how sexy he was, which she hadn't been able to do since she'd left the party.

"Anyway, thanks for working with mom on this. How's things with Jackson? He's really cute. You two make a good couple."

She shook her head. "I broke up with him."

"What? Why?"

"For a reason I'm not sharing with you," she said.

"No spark?"

"Yeah," she said. She wasn't planning to elaborate or let her sister know that Mauricio was still turning her on with a barely-there touch.

"So about the money…" Hadley said.

"I'm going to see if anything else comes of it from Mauricio. Otherwise, I just don't know. Am I wrong to trust him?"

Hadley hugged her sister close. "I don't know. My track record with trusting guys isn't great. You know him the best."

"I do," Helena said, hugging her back. "You're right. He's fine. We're fine. And you're handling Mother so everything is good."

She was glad she had her sister's wedding to help design instead of focusing on her own non-existent love life. Of course, after Helena left the studio, all she could think about was that she'd said Mauricio had been sweet to her. She hated when he wasn't a total douche because it made her remember how good things had been between them.

Three

Closing a deal in Houston, picking Alec up at the airport a few days earlier than expected and then driving back to Cole's Hill hadn't been what he'd planned for Friday, but Mauricio was hopeful that after the long day he'd fall into an exhausted sleep and for once not be tormented by dreams of Hadley.

But his youngest brother, Inigo, was back in town due to some downtime on the Formula One circuit and their father was in a rare mood, treating them all to dinner at the Peace Creek Steak House. His father loved it when he had all of his sons and his only grandson to himself. To be honest Mo liked these times too. Then they'd dropped the old man and Benito off at home in the Five Families neighborhood and headed out to the Bull Pit for shots of tequila and a grudge-match pool game.

"Twins versus the baby and the favorite," Alec said, coming back to the high table with a round of Lone Star longnecks.

"Works for me," Mo said. He and Alec had been a team since the womb, and they were pretty unstoppable once they got playing.

"Or as I like to think of it, the wusses versus the awesomes."

"Awesomes? That's not even a word. No wonder you're a driver. You're not smart enough for anything else," Alec said, winking at Inigo.

"I'm plenty smart for you," Inigo said. "Who gets paid to drive fast and who has to sit in an office in front of a computer? I think we both know who's the smart one."

"Touché," Alec said, lifting his beer toward his little brother as Diego set up the balls and they tossed a coin to see who would go first.

As Mo listened to his brothers josh with each other and tossed the coin in the air, he felt a shiver go down his spine. He looked toward the jukebox and saw a pair of skintight jeans encasing an ass he'd never forget.

Hadley.

She had her hair loose, hanging over her shoulders, and was wearing a flimsy blouse and her hand-tooled leather boots. She threw her head back to laugh at something her sister said. Mo felt every part of his body tense and come alive at the same time. He could tell himself that he'd just imagined his reaction to that one touch at the engagement party, but he knew he would have been lying.

The coin fell to the floor and he cursed but didn't bend down to pick it up.

"Dude...damn. Is it too late to change teams?" Alec teased.

Mauricio gave him the finger and bent to pick up the coin. "It was heads. We go first."

"You're going to need every advantage as long as Hadley is here," Inigo said.

"Doubtful," Mauricio said. "I was distracted by something else."

"Really?" Diego asked. "What was it that caught your eye?"

His brothers were going to be asses and not leave this alone, and unless he wanted to turn a friendly Friday night into fight night and get himself kicked out of the Bull Pit again, he needed to shrug it off.

But that was his problem. He'd never been able to just shrug off anything where Hadley was concerned. He knew it and his brothers seemed to, as well. He was screwed. He'd moved on. Or had until that damned photo session. He should never have agreed to be a groomsman. Then he could have stayed away from Hadley until he found another woman. Someone who could push the last of the lingering sexual attraction he felt for her out.

"Dude, stop staring at her," Alec said.

"Shut it, Alec. I'm not looking at her."

"Whatever," Alec said. "It's your turn. Don't screw up."

He made a face at his brother and leaned over the table to line up his shot. The sound of the jukebox playing loud country music on a Friday night made it easier for him to focus on the game. He took a deep breath and broke the balls. Though he knew this was a friendly rivalry amongst his brothers, he didn't want to lose.

He took his next shot, sinking a ball in the corner pocket, and then moved on to line up his next shot. He had a pretty good run of three balls before it was Diego's turn. Mauricio went to lean against the high table next to Inigo, who was posting to one of his social media accounts. His youngest brother was a hot up-and-coming driver who had been on the Formula Two circuit for a few years before making it to the big leagues of Formula One.

"Not bad, Mo. I'd hate to see what would happen if you were really concentrating."

"I am concentrating," he said.

"Sure you are. Like you didn't notice Hadley on the dance floor," Inigo said, drawing his attention to the small wooden floor set to one side of the jukebox.

He cursed under his breath as he saw her dancing with a group of her girlfriends, and was unable to tear his eyes away from her. He tried to remind himself that he was over her, but when she moved to the music, her arms in the air, hips swaying, his body reacted like she was still his.

Maybe one more night together was what he needed to clear her out of his system for good. Of course, Hadley deserved better than that. She deserved an apology, not because he wanted something from her but because he never should have slept with Marnie when he was still…hell, while he still liked Hadley.

If losing her had taught him anything it was that he hadn't wanted things to end so horribly between them.

He took another long swallow of his beer. That kind of thinking was dangerous, because he knew if he let himself dwell on it too long, he'd start believing that it was a viable option. That sleeping with his ex would be the solution to finally getting over her.

The music changed to a slow song—"Night Changes" by One Direction—one of her favorite songs. Mauricio watched as most of her friends left the dance floor, Hadley following behind them. Without thinking, he put his beer down and walked to the dance floor.

"Do you want to dance?" he asked. "I realize I'm not your first choice but I know you love this song. And I'm sorry."

"Sorry for what?" she asked.

"How I behaved. We never really talked about it."

"I don't want to talk tonight," she said.

"Then how about a dance?" he said.

She hesitated then put her hand in his. "One dance."

"That's all."

He pulled her into his arms and she put her hands on his waist. He told himself this was just another part of moving on but his body didn't agree.

Hadley hadn't had the best week. Her mom was an exacting perfectionist when it came to any event she was planning but the added element of it being her sister's wedding had pushed her to extremes. Hadley felt safe saying there wasn't enough tequila in Texas—maybe even the entire South—to take the edge off her nerves. But dancing with her girlfriends was helping until she saw…him.

Mauricio.

Of course, she'd noticed him when she came in. It was impossible not to when he was with his brothers. They drew the eye of every woman in the bar. Seen together, they made you wonder what kind of deal with the devil Elena Velasquez had made to get four such good-looking boys. They were the kind of eye candy that made this part of Texas famous.

Mauricio smelled good too.

She shook her head. "How've you been?"

She wanted this to feel normal. Surely, the thing with Jackson under the willow tree had been a fluke. There was no way that she still wanted Mo. Not after everything he'd done. She wanted something nice and steady like Helena and Malcolm had. But she'd always felt this heat around Mo. He made her restless like heat lightning on a summer's night. Just ready to go off without any provocation.

"Good. Busy," he said. "You?"

His voice was a low rumble but easy for her to hear despite the music. She'd always liked the way he sounded. She put her head on his shoulder for a second and closed her eyes, pretended that this wasn't the bad idea she knew it was, and then made herself stand up straight and step away from him.

"Good, Mo. Really, good," she lied, but then "fake it till you make it" had been her mom's mantra for her and her sister growing up so she figured that was okay. The song ended and she started to leave the dance floor. "Thanks for the dance."

She walked away without looking back and forced herself to put on a smile as she climbed onto the high bar stool at the table where her friends were.

"Girl, what are you thinking?" Josie asked.

"That I did it. I danced with him, played it cool and nothing happened," she said.

Zuri shook her head. "You're full of it, but we're good friends so we'll let you get away with it. Another round of shots to celebrate you keeping your cool."

Hadley drank another round with her friends and ordered nachos as they talked about the men in the bar. Manu Barrett, the former NFL defensive end who now coached football at the local high school, came over with a tray of shots for Josie. Her friend was the art teacher at the high school and Manu had been asking Josie out for the last month or so, but he was a player. Josie and Manu hit the dance floor, and Zuri and Hadley just watched their friend for a minute.

"She's smitten," Hadley said.

"Who's smitten? Remind me again why we came to the Bull Pit tonight?" Helena asked as she slid onto a bar stool next to Zuri and reached over to take one of the shots that Manu had brought.

"Josie is smitten and we are here because you set Mom on me. It's been a long-ass week," Hadley said.

"And, girl, you've been working too hard," Zuri said to Helena. "You need a night out. Where is your other half?"

"He's in Houston to close a deal. He won't be back until tomorrow, which is why I suggested book club," Helena said.

"This is better than book club because we don't all have to discuss something that we've only read the back cover of," Hadley said with a laugh.

"True. But the book I recommended is getting really good buzz over at the Paperback Reader. Teddi expressly recommended it because she thought we'd all love it," Helena said. "It's about an undercover prince."

As a CPA, Hadley's sister did the accounting for a lot of the bespoke small businesses in Cole's Hill. Teddi had been the bookworm in Helena's class in high school, so no one had been surprised when she'd opened a bookstore after college.

"I'm going to read it next week," Hadley said. She needed something to take her mind off Mauricio and a prince in disguise sounded right up her alley.

"So you and Mo?"

"There is no me and Mo, Hel," Hadley said.

"It didn't look that way when you were dancing," Zuri said.

Hadley shook her head. "You know the worst part about breaking up?"

"No, tell us," Zuri said wriggling her eyebrows at Hadley. "You're the expert."

Her friend had clearly had too much tequila, she thought as she shook her head. "I was just going to say that all the feelings don't just disappear. I mean anger should burn away all the other stuff…"

"What brought this on?" Helena asked. "Is it because things didn't work out with Jackson?"

"You let Jackson go?" Zuri asked. "I'm out of town for a few days and I missed everything. When did this happen? You two looked pretty cozy at the engagement party."

"Ugh. We were but then we decided we'd be better off as friends," Hadley said. Maybe she'd had too much tequila. She should never have brought this up.

"Friends… He friend-zoned you? Dude better check himself. It's not like we don't all remember he used to be a total nerd."

"No, it was the other way around," Hadley protested.

"He's hot now," Helena said, signaling the waiter and ordering another plate of nachos and margaritas for the four of them.

"He is," Zuri said. "I wouldn't kick him out of my bed."

"No one would," Helena added. "Except for Had."

"I didn't do that. Here comes Josie," she said. Thank God. She was tired of discussing how she let Jackson slip away and she definitely didn't want to talk about Mauricio, who was over by the pool table laughing with his brothers. She couldn't help watching him as he lined up a shot. Of course, he had to wear those skintight Levi's tonight, making matters worse.

"I think we know why it didn't work with Jackson," Zuri said.

"What?" she asked, turning back to her friends, her sister and Manu, who were all watching her stare at Mo and his brothers.

"Y'all are crazy. So, Manu, are you joining us?"

Everyone turned their attention to Manu and Josie, and Hadley forced herself to focus on the nachos and margarita, but a part of her was listening for Mauricio's laugh. Which was the last thing she needed to be doing right now. She was moving on...except now that she'd danced with him, she wasn't sure she had.

Helena smiled and laughed with her friends, and for the first time since she discovered the money missing from the wedding account felt like herself again. Her mom had told her that marriage was a million little compromises. But Helena had never really been someone who could just let things go. She was a control freak when it came to money, though she didn't know why. Their family had always had more than enough when she and Hadley were growing up.

But she'd never been someone who could waste money just because she had it and that's what this thing with Mal felt like.

"You are looking way too serious," Hadley said, handing her a shot of tequila. The nachos were long gone. Josie was on the dance floor pressed against Manu, and Zuri had decided to see if she could tempt one of the astronaut trainees from NASA into having a bit of fun.

That left the Everton sisters, who were sitting at the table like two spinsters.

"Can't help it," she said, doing the shot and then turning the glass upside down on the tabletop.

"Don't worry, I'm handling Mom," Had said.

Helena smiled and nodded at her sister. She was the eldest and she had always taken her job as the big sister seriously. She wasn't about to cry on Hadley's shoulder because she didn't know where Malcolm was tonight or where that money had gone. She was going to keep it together, keep her smile in place and fix whatever was going on with Mal privately.

"Thanks for that," Helena said.

"Be right back. Want another shot?" Hadley asked.

"Water would be better," she said.

Hadley nodded and danced her way to the bar as Mauricio came over to the table. "Hey, Helena, I wanted to let you know that I haven't been able to get anything out of Malcolm. He's shut me down every time I tried to bring up finances."

She sighed. It figured. "Thanks for trying. Do you know where he is tonight?"

Mauricio tipped his head to the side and shook it. "No. I thought he was here with you."

"No. He texted me earlier to say he was busy," Helena said. "Do you think he's having an affair?"

Mo put his arm around her shoulders. "I can't believe he would do that. He loves you and whatever this is, it's not that."

It was somehow easier to talk to Mauricio than her sister because she knew that he wouldn't talk to anyone in her family about what was going on.

"She's taken," Hadley said, coming up and putting a large glass of water in front of Helena.

"I'm trying to reassure your sister that I'm not going to screw up things for her wedding," Mauricio said.

She didn't know what had happened, but it was obvious to Helena that there was still a spark between these two, no matter how hard they tried to move on from each other. Thinking that she was casting a pall over the evening with her Malcolm worries, she nudged Mo toward her sister. "You are going to have to dance together at the reception. Better practice."

Mauricio gave her a hard look, which surprised her. He seemed so easygoing when it came to her sister but it was clear that he wasn't as cool as he pretended to be.

"Sure. Why not?" Hadley said.

Mauricio took Hadley's hand and led her to the dance

floor. She could handle herself despite what their mother thought. Helena sipped her water and turned her attention to her phone. She clicked on the friend finder app but didn't see Malcolm's icon. She was starting to worry that he was having second thoughts about getting married.

She sighed and kept refreshing the app to try to make him appear, but he was still unavailable. Waiting had never really been one of her strong suits so she finally texted him.

Where the hell are you?

She saw that the message was delivered and kept staring at the screen as if that was going to make him respond to her. But nothing.

What was going on with Malcolm? They'd always been on the same page with their relationship. She'd counted herself lucky that she'd fallen in love with a man who wanted the same things out of life that she did, but now she didn't know if she'd been fooling herself.

That's what Hadley had said about Mauricio when they'd broken up last year, that she'd fooled herself into believing he was a different man than he really was. As Helena shoved her phone into her handbag and looked up at her sister, dancing way too close to the man she'd said she was over, she realized that they all did that. Hadley was just like her, fooling herself into believing she was in control of her emotions when in reality they were all prisoners to them.

Her phone pinged and she scrambled to get it out of her purse. It was Malcolm. Finally! His phone had died and he was at home waiting for her.

Four

The Bull Pit crowd had thinned out, but Hadley and Mo still alternated between doing shots and dancing. As the night wore on, she couldn't remember why she'd been so mad at him.

When the DJ announced last call and then played Eric Church's sensual song "Like a Wrecking Ball," it seemed natural to press herself against him, her hands on his lean hips, her head on his shoulder as he held her and they swayed along to the music. She looked up at him and he was watching her.

He lowered his head but she ducked away from him.

"Not feeling it?"

"Yes and no," she said.

"Should we talk about this?"

"Yes," she said. "I know we were on a break, I mean, I get that. But why text me how much you wish I was there with you and then hook up with Marnie?"

He shook his head and stepped back. She had thought she'd dealt with everything that happened but when he'd almost kissed her, she had wanted to cry. For most of her adult life she'd believed Mo would be her man for the rest of her life and then…well, he'd hurt her more deeply than she wanted to admit.

"I don't know. I wanted you. Just you. But you weren't here and I wasn't sure you were ever coming back and I hated that feeling of wanting you and feeling…"

Vulnerable, she thought. But that didn't excuse him or take away what he'd done.

"I'm sorry. I never meant to hurt you like that. I honestly wasn't thinking about anything," he said, leaning even closer. She felt his lips brush over hers and closed her eyes. She knew that she should walk away. Sure, she'd regret this in the morning but tonight there was nowhere else she'd rather be. She'd been alone for way too long and she was horny.

For him.

This could be that farewell hookup they'd never had because of the way things had ended. Maybe then she could move on with a nice guy like Jackson or someone else.

He cupped her butt and lifted her more fully against him so his groin nestled into the notch at the top of her thighs. She parted her legs slightly, rocking against him.

He lifted his head, and she noticed his lips were wet from kissing her and his eyes were heavy-lidded. She felt the ridge of his erection against her so she knew he was as turned on as she was.

"Uh…that wasn't what I intended to do," he said, stepping back. She did the same.

"Me neither, but honestly, Mo, I think we both need it," she said. "Ever since Sunday when you put your hand on my shoulder, I've felt it."

"Me too," he said.

That was all she needed to hear. She took his hand and stopped by the deserted table where she'd left her handbag and then led him out of the Bull Pit. The night air was cool and fresh as they stepped outside. She tipped her head back and looked up at the big Texas sky dotted with a few stars and a half moon.

She heard him sigh and looked over at him.

He had his hands on his hips and his head was tipped back. The way his legs were parted, she knew he still had a hard-on, and when he glanced over at her, she saw… Well, she thought she saw him hesitate.

"Changing your mind now?" he asked.

"Are you?" she returned.

"Not a damned bit but I don't want this to be something I forced on you," he said.

She turned and closed the small distance between them, rubbing her hand over the ridge of his erection and putting her other one on the back of his neck as she went up on tiptoe and kissed him hard and deep.

"I'm exactly where I want to be tonight," she said.

He lifted her off her feet, into his arms. "That's all I wanted to hear."

She put her arm around his shoulder as he carried her toward the parking lot but she stopped him. "We can't drive."

"Uber?" she suggested.

"The only driver out this late will be someone we know," he said.

"That's true," she said. "So…"

He stopped and set her on her feet. "The Grand Hotel is only a five-minute walk."

"Perfect," she said. "It's a nice night for a walk."

"Is it?"

"I think so," she said, slipping her hand into his. She'd

missed this. The way his big hand completely enfolded hers. She wasn't going to remind herself of all the reasons why she shouldn't be enjoying this. For tonight she wanted some good memories of Mo instead of the painful ones from the recent past, including their breakup and then Mauricio fighting with her date at the Bull Pit last fall.

"I thought you had book club on Friday night," he said as they walked to the hotel.

"Is there a question there?"

"Just wondering why you were at the Bull Pit instead of at Helena's place," he said as they headed down historic Main Street with its wide sidewalks to accommodate the pedestrian tourist traffic.

"We all needed a night out," she said. "You know Helena delegated the wedding flowers and interior design to me so I have to liaise with Mom on it."

"I didn't know that," he said. "She seemed pretty determined to do it herself."

"She was. She had to ask our parents to pay for some of it—" Hadley clamped her hand over her mouth. "Please forget I said that."

"It's okay, I knew about the problem. I've been trying to talk to Mal and figure out what is going on for her."

"You have?"

"Yes," he said, stopping to look at her with an arched eyebrow. "You sound surprised."

She was. "It just doesn't seem like your sort of thing."

"Why not?"

"There's nothing in it for you," she said.

"Fair enough. But there is something in it for me," he added as he started walking again. He'd dropped her hand but they were still walking side by side.

"What?"

"Your happiness," he admitted. "It's in my power to

help your sister out and to figure out what's going on with Mal, and I know how much you love her so in a way I'm doing it for you."

"Why would you do that?"

"To make up for being an ass, Hadley. We both know I handled things like the hothead I am, and I regret it now," he said.

They were in front of the Grand Hotel now and he stopped to turn to face her. "Have you changed your mind?"

She shook her head. Not in the least. This right here was the man she had fallen for. It wasn't often that Mauricio felt comfortable showing this side of himself, but she was happy he had tonight.

"I still want you," she said. "What about you?"

"I think I'd have to be dead not to want you," he admitted.

It was so quiet in the hotel bathroom except for "God Bless Texas" buzzing in her head, which was one of the songs she'd danced to earlier with Mo. He was being very cautious with her, which she appreciated. More than once he'd asked her if she was sure about this. But honestly, she wasn't sure about anything except that she wanted him and didn't want to think beyond tonight. Unlike stud muffin out there, she hadn't slept with anyone since they'd broken up a little over eighteen months ago, and though she'd never describe herself as sex crazed, she missed it. She leaned in to look at her face in the mirror.

She didn't look too bad; all the dancing had made her sweat a bit and she used a tissue to wipe at the mascara, which had left the faintest black marks under her eyes. Then she smiled at herself in the mirror and winked before turning to go back into the bedroom.

Mo had switched on the lamp atop the nightstand, turned

down the bed, and was now standing at the window looking down on their once sleepy Main Street. He'd taken off his shirt and she couldn't help but let her gaze drift down his muscled back to his lean hips. His jeans were tight, showing off his physique.

She had removed her shoes earlier and the carpet was rich and soft against her feet as she approached him as quietly as she could. She wrapped her arms around his waist from the back, kissing his shoulder blade as she hugged him from behind.

He put his hands over hers where they were joined on his rock hard stomach. He lifted one of his arms and pulled her into the curve of the side of his body. "Hey, lady."

"Hey, you," she said, looking up at him, wishing more than anything that they only had this craving between them and not all of their past baggage. Shaking her head, she lifted her thigh, wrapping it around his hip. He turned and cupped her butt, lifting her off her feet so that she could grind her center against the ridge of his erection.

She tipped her head back and felt the heat of his breath moments before his lips touched her neck. He nibbled on the length of her neck and she felt a shiver run down her spine. His kiss was deep and hot and left molten lava in its path. The kind that was slowly turning her from a woman who could rationally analyze this into a creature of need. He lifted her higher in his arms, turning and moving until she felt the wall at her back. He pinned her in place with one thick thigh between her legs and she felt his hand moving up and down on her butt, his finger tracing over the seam of the jeans right there in the middle of her cheeks.

She arched against him, her head tipped back against the wall, and then she felt his mouth moving down the vee of her blouse into the valley between her breasts. Her nipples tightened as she lifted her arms up to his chest, ran her hands over his pecs, then down the center of his body. Mo had a smooth hairless chest, his skin soft over rock hard muscles that she knew he worked hard to maintain.

She ran her fingernail over his skin, and then with the pads of her other fingers felt the gooseflesh spreading out from her touch. His erection grew against her thigh as she slowly drew her hand down between their bodies, undoing the button at the top of his jeans and pushing the zipper down. She slipped her hand beneath the front of his boxer briefs, wrapping her hand around his shaft and stroking him up and down, taking care to run her finger over the tip with each stroke.

He groaned and grunted her name. "Had."

She smiled as she continued to work him with her hand, felt him getting bigger with each stroke. He tangled one hand in her hair and pulled her head back as he brought his lips down with the perfect amount of pressure on hers. His tongue thrust deep into her mouth, taking control of her and distracting her from her stroking.

His kiss left no room for anything but the aching need in her core. It was an emptiness that was begging to be filled by him. She felt his hand moving between their bodies as it dipped into the top of her blouse, his fingers seeking out her nipple through the fabric of her lacy bra.

She groaned as he stroked it until it pebbled under his fingers, and then he pinched lightly, which made her moan in pleasure and arch against him, her hand tightening on his erection.

She let go of it and reached for the hem of her blouse, pulling it up and over her head, tearing her lips from his. He reached behind her with one hand, undoing the clasp of her bra, and she shifted her shoulders so that the straps fell down her arms. Mo pulled the lacy material away from her body and tossed it aside. He backed away slightly so he could look down at her naked breasts.

Her breath was coming in faster than she would have liked, making her chest rise and fall, and the more he stared at her, the harder her nipples got. He brought his finger to her lip and she kissed it. He drew it down the center of her neck, caressing her chest and tracing the globe of her breast, drawing his finger up one side, around the areola and then back down the other side. He slowly moved his hand to her other breast and did the same thing. She moaned and felt the liquid heat between her legs. The emptiness in her center was growing with each touch of his finger. He brought his mouth back down on hers as he continued to fondle her breasts.

He reached between their bodies and undid the fastening at the top of her jeans, then shoved his hand down the back of them. She had worn a thong so his hand encountered her naked backside. His hand was large and hot as he cupped her butt cheek and lifted her so that her back arched, the tips of her breasts brushing against his chest as he ran his finger down the furrow between her cheeks. He gripped her and she moaned, stroking her hand up and down his shaft until she realized this wasn't going to be enough.

She pulled her mouth from his. "Let me take my jeans off."

"Not yet," he said, kissing her again, his tongue thrusting deep into her mouth.

She sucked on it and drew him deeper. Using the edge of her nail, she trailed her finger up the side of his cock and felt his hips jerk forward as she ran her nail delicately around the tip. She did it again and he cursed as he pulled his mouth from hers.

He stepped back and she slid down the wall as he pulled his thigh back from between her legs.

"Take 'em off," he said, his voice a low gravelly sound that turned her on even more.

She shimmied out of her jeans but they were skinny jeans and got stuck around her ankles. She finally got them off and then pushed her underwear down her legs. Mauricio took his pants off, as well.

He stood there totally naked and completely turned on, his erection standing out as if begging for her. She reached for it, took him in her hand again and this time he caught her around her waist and lifted her off her feet. She wrapped her legs around his waist as he wrapped a strand of her hair around his hand; the other one was at the center of her back, his arm holding her up.

His chest was flush against hers and she put her hand on his shoulder as he dropped open-mouthed kisses against her jaw and then down the side of her neck. She shoved her hand into his thick black hair and held his head as his mouth moved down her neck. She felt the edge of his teeth, which made her core tighten, and she shifted so the ridge of his erection was nestled against her clit.

He moved his hips slightly and she shivered as sensations spread up through her body. She ached for him to be inside her and shifted around, trying to get him where she yearned for him. But he moved his hands down her back and slowly stepped away from her until she once again felt the carpeted floor under her feet. His mouth took hers again and then she felt one of his hands moving down her body, over her stomach, tracing her belly button and then lower, caressing her. Then he was moving his finger slowly between her lower lips, lightly rubbing against her engorged clit. She clawed at his shoulders as he pushed his fingers down until she felt the tip of his forefinger penetrating her, his thumb tapping on her clit.

Her hips moved against him, trying to take him deeper,

but Mo kept his touch light and only allowed her to take the very tip of his finger. She dug her nails into his shoulders as that delicious sensation continued to build between her legs.

She thrust her hips forward, needing more, and he still wouldn't let her have what she needed. Instead he kept teasing her until she thought she was going to explode but didn't.

She took his shaft, working her hand up and down its length as she leaned up on her tiptoes, which inadvertently pushed his finger deeper into her. She smiled as she caught his earlobe between her teeth and then whispered into his ear dark sexual yearnings, telling him how good he felt inside of her and how she couldn't wait for his cock to fill her.

He cursed and shoved his finger deeper into her and she moaned in satisfaction, letting her head drop back. Her hair brushed against her shoulder blades as her orgasm started and spread out from his fingers between her legs, tightening her nipples even more and making her legs weak.

He caught her to him, held her up as his mouth came down on hers. She rode his hand until her orgasm started to die down. She was hungry for more and as he broke the kiss and looked down at her and their eyes met, she felt a wave of emotion go through her that was hard to ignore. Saying goodbye in the morning would be harder than she had expected.

She was tempted to get her clothes and walk out right now but she wasn't done with Mauricio Velasquez. Not yet. She was going to squeeze every bit out of this night they had together.

She took his hand in hers and drew him over to the bed, pushing him down on the edge. He pulled her onto his lap and she felt the tip of him at her entrance. She started to sink down on him before she realized what she was doing.

"I'm not on the Pill," she said.

"Shit," he said. He lifted her off his lap and turned away.

"Don't you have a condom?"

"I might. Let me check my wallet."

He got up and she leaned back, her body so full of sensation all she could do was watch him.

"Found one," he said, coming back.

She took the packet from him and opened it up as he came closer to her. She took her time pushing it down his length and he shuddered under her touch. She put his hands on her waist, lifting her and pushing her back on the bed before coming down between her legs. His hips nestling between hers. She felt the tip of him at her entrance as he took her wrists in one hand and stretched them over her head.

She arched her back, her nipples brushing against his chest, his hardness pushing against her center.

He pulled his hips back and then thrust deep inside her. She moaned as he pushed into her. He was always bigger than she remembered, and once he was fully seated, he pushed, giving her body a moment to adjust to his width. She tipped her head back and their eyes met.

"I've missed you," he admitted.

She bit her lip, not wanting to admit the same was true for her. She wondered if he knew that because he sighed and brought his mouth down on hers as he started thrusting in and out of her. With each thrust, she felt the tip of his cock hitting her in just the right spot. She lifted her legs up against his side and he let go of her hands to lift her leg higher on his right side, leaning more heavily onto her as he continued to thrust.

His rhythm was building and driving her higher and higher until she was out of control, making noises she only made when she was having sex with Mauricio. She wrapped her arms around his shoulders and lifted her upper body against him, tucking her face into his neck. He pulled her closer, holding her tightly to him while he drove into her again and again until her orgasm washed over her.

He continued thrusting into her a few more times and then groaned her name as he came. She felt him inside of her as he collapsed onto her, careful to keep his weight on his arms on either side of her body as he rested his forehead against hers. Their breath mingled, and she hugged him to her with her arms and legs as if she never wanted to let him go.

But he'd already let her go. She had to remember that. This was one night only. This was a chance to move on without the anger and hurt. But this was also Mo. Her first lover and her first love and that was harder to distance herself from than she'd have thought.

He rolled to his side, bringing her with him. He held her close as their breathing slowed and she rested her head on his chest, thinking how nice it was to have his arms around her. She put her thigh over his hip and found the notch between his neck and shoulder for her head. He pulled the comforter up over her, and she felt all the tension that she'd been carrying around with her for what seemed like forever melt away as she drifted off to sleep.

Five

Mauricio swept his hand idly up and down Hadley's back as she slept in his arms. It had been too long since he'd held her. He was realistic enough to realize this changed nothing between them, but he hadn't realized how much he'd missed her. How much he'd missed making love to her. While sex with other women had been satisfying, Hadley and he seemed to have a special chemistry that never failed to make him feel like he'd given her a piece of his soul.

She wasn't going to just forgive him for his behavior. Maybe if he'd apologized sooner. But it had taken him a long time to realize what he'd lost when she'd left. He'd used anger as a shield to pretend he hadn't royally screwed up.

He shifted a little, wanting to dispose of the condom before he fell asleep. He pulled away from her, felt the wetness on his shaft and looked down.

"Shit," he said, standing and pulling off the broken condom. This wasn't a good thing. They didn't need the complications of unprotected sex right now.

Hadley shifted on the bed, opening her eyes and smiling up at him with the sweetest smile he'd seen on her face in the longest time. For just a moment, the cowardly part of him didn't want to tell her about the condom. He wanted to just wash up, climb back into the bed with her and pretend that nothing had happened.

Chances were she wouldn't get pregnant from one time but he knew he owed it to her to tell her.

He wasn't sure how to say it. She was sleepy and would probably go right back to sleep… Maybe he could wait until morning.

"Mo, you okay?" she asked, lifting herself up on her elbow. The comforter he'd draped over her fell to her waist; his gaze was drawn to her breasts and he felt his cock stir for a moment. He thought about climbing back on top of her and taking her again.

"Yeah, um, Had, I don't know how to say—"

"Don't say anything. We don't need to talk at all tonight," she said. "This thing between us… I'm glad it happened tonight. I needed it and it seems like you did too."

He listened to her talking about their broken relationship with only half of his attention. He had to stop her and tell her what had happened with the damned condom, but he wasn't sure how.

"It's not that," he blurted out. "The condom broke."

"What?" She jumped out of the bed, staring down at her thighs. Her face got tight and that expression he'd come to see on her face all the time toward the end of their relationship was back. It was hard, a little bit angry, a little bit unforgiving, and he hated that.

"I don't know how it happened," he said. "I'm sorry."

"Don't be," she said, shaking her head. "This is what we get for not using our heads."

He wanted to comfort her, but when he reached for her, she shook her head. "I'll go to Pimm's Pharmacy in a week or so and get a pregnancy test—hell. No, I won't. Everyone will know if I go there." She rushed into the bathroom and shut the door.

She'd thought she'd wake up in the morning maybe feeling a little sad but this… No, she should have known better than to hook up with Mo. Things between them were always one step away from a full-on mud rodeo in the rain. Just a shit show waiting to happen. The problem as far as she could see it was that she had no willpower around him. Especially when it had been such a long dry spell…which she knew was a bad excuse.

She'd come here tonight because she missed him. There, she'd admitted it. She might not have wanted to deal with that particular truth, but she was tired of only having him in her hot sexy dreams.

There was a knock and she turned to look at the closed bathroom door. He probably wanted to get in here and wash up too. She opened the door and he stood there with a weighty look in his eyes. He put one hand on the doorjamb and the other on his chest. She saw his signet ring on his ring finger as he rubbed his hand over his chest.

"I'm sorry."

"It's not your fault. Honestly, you don't have to keep apologizing. We both came up here with our eyes open," she said.

He nodded.

She hated this. She hated the distance between them because they weren't in a relationship. No matter how much she wanted to pretend that Mauricio was just a Bull Pit hookup, she knew he wasn't.

She reached out and took his hand, threading their fingers together and squeezing before she walked by him and let him have the bathroom. They were going to have to figure something out. But it was—what the hell time was it?

She glanced at the digital clock under the TV.

Four in the morning.

Her mother had always said that nothing good happened after midnight. Of course, she was always right. Still, Hadley might not be pregnant… Maybe they could wait to find out?

She heard the toilet flush and then a few minutes later Mo came out. He hesitated, and she realized that even though she had said neither of them was to blame, she was acting like he was somehow to blame. If she hadn't been so hot for him, this wouldn't have happened, but she hadn't felt this spark with anyone else.

"Mo, it's okay. It's not like this is the first time we had the pregnancy scare," she said.

"You're right. Girl, you go to my head. Normally, this sort of thing never happens to me," he said.

"Same. I'm not going to be able to get a pregnancy test for a while, which I guess is fine since I can't take it for a week or two. I have an exhibit I'm supposed to start installing in my shop. I'm thinking I can go to one of the big box stores near Houston to get the test when I'm there next week."

He moved farther into the room and sat down next to her at the foot of the bed. He was close enough that she could feel the heat coming off his body and smell that cologne of his that she loved.

"Do you want me to go get one?" he asked. "I have a meeting with a supplier for Homes for Everyone."

She knew the charity was close to his heart. When they were still together, she'd gone with him to help build the homes and had even donated her time and artist talents doing murals in the children's rooms.

"It's okay. I think it will be better if I go and get it," she said. She didn't want him to be too involved unless…

"What are we going to do if I am pregnant?" she asked after what felt like an hour. The clock under the TV showed that only two minutes had gone by.

"We'll figure it out," he said. "I'm not the same man I was when you left me."

She nodded. She knew that. She had changed too. For a long time, she'd been defining herself by how she was seen in town… The younger Everton sister, Mauricio's girlfriend, that arty girl who went to Manhattan… The truth was, she hadn't ever taken time to figure out who Hadley Everton really was.

And she'd been slowly figuring it out. Apparently she still had a weakness for Mauricio's dark brown eyes and square jaw.

"Want to try to sleep some more or should I walk you back to your car and take you home?" he asked, breaking into her thoughts at just the right moment.

Mauricio had taken a few minutes to get his mind together in the bathroom. While he had wanted some resolution to their relationship and the breakup, and thought Hadley needed it too, this wasn't what he'd had in mind. For one thing, he wasn't sure waiting two weeks was going to be easy for either of them. Now all he could think about was the possibility that she was pregnant with his child.

And while he'd never thought of himself as a family man, he had to admit the image of her with her belly round, expecting his child, kept dancing through his mind and making him think things that he knew weren't possible. They were nowhere near ready for anything more than a hookup.

He'd apologized and he knew it would take a lot of time for her to truly forgive him. It wouldn't surprise him if Hadley thought he hadn't changed. All those fights last fall had wisened him up. He knew that it was going to take a lot of time to show her he'd changed. And she might not…she might not want more from him. She might never be able to forgive seeing him with another woman in his bedroom.

He didn't blame her. He wasn't sure he could forgive himself for hurting her that deeply.

But he was going to let Hadley take control of this situation. Whatever he felt, he was pretty damned sure that she was probably freaking out inside. She looked so calm and almost serene sitting next to him, but she kept tapping her left foot really fast and then she'd realize she was doing it and stop for a minute.

"Whatever you want to do is fine with me. I would like to come over when you take the test," he said.

"Of course," she said, then looked around the room. "I don't think I can sleep anymore tonight. Do you mind taking me home? I caught a ride with Zuri last night."

"Not at all. Do you want to wait here and I'll go get my car and pick you up?" he suggested.

"Yeah, that sounds good," she said. "I didn't drive tonight."

He put his shirt back on; it smelled like smoke and whiskey and the faintest trace of Hadley's body spray. He buttoned it up quickly, then stomped his feet into his boots. "I'll text you when I'm out front."

She just nodded and he got up and let himself out of the room. He'd had one-night stands in the past and yet he'd never felt like this. It wasn't exactly a nice feeling; he couldn't define it, didn't really want to. He wanted to get to his car, drop her off and then go home where he could try to figure this out.

One thought that plagued him as he walked toward the Bull Pit parking lot was how he always managed to screw things up with Hadley. Even in the beginning when they'd first started dating, he'd been trying so hard to make things perfect for her. It hadn't helped that she had certain expectations for the men she dated. She told him that on their first date. It had been kind of cute and he hadn't really paid attention to it until he'd hurt her the first time. Then he realized that she'd invested a lot in him as her boyfriend.

That pressure had made it harder for him to live up to her expectations and eventually he'd started to resent her. But that was on him. He'd always been the hothead. It had set him apart from his family, even his twin, since he was a kid. People who struggled to tell Alec and him apart based on their appearance could always tell in a fight.

There were only five cars left in the parking lot. He unlocked his car and drove on autopilot back to the Grand Hotel. He noticed that the streets were starting to get busy; it was nearly 5:00 a.m. and the commuters who drove to Houston were already getting a head start to beat the traffic. Then he saw a familiar Cadillac CTS turn onto Main Street from the Five Families area and cursed. His mother.

She was one of the morning news anchors for a local Houston affiliate. She did a double take as he drove by. He didn't want to stop at the hotel, which would just raise more questions from her, so he drove past it, down toward the apartment towers where he had his penthouse, waited ten minutes and then went back to the Grand Hotel, staying vigilant along the way for his mom.

He pulled around back in the guest parking lot and then texted Hadley his location. He was sweating and felt like he was sixteen years old instead of thirty. But he didn't want his mom to know anything. She had been upset when he'd broken things off with Hadley the first time; he knew that tonight wasn't about them getting back together, and he didn't want to have to explain that to his mom.

As much as he hoped that everything would sort of go back to the way it used to be, he knew those days were over. Hadley wasn't going to start trusting him again. Not this quickly. He knew he was going to have to show he'd changed.

That scared him. He had never wanted to need her more than she needed him.

When he saw Hadley come out of the hotel and walk to the car, he hopped out to open the door for her.

"That took longer than I thought it would," she said. "You okay to drive?"

"Yes... I passed my mom when I was coming back to pick you up and so I had to pretend to be driving to my place in case—"

"You don't have to explain. The less our moms know about this the better," Hadley said.

"Agreed," he said, then drove her home to her loft on the outskirts of Cole's Hill. He parked near the entrance to her shop, which was housed underneath her loft. She made no move to get out of the car and he turned toward her.

"I don't have any regrets," he said. "Well, maybe the condom breaking but otherwise I'm good."

Hadley nodded. "Me neither."

She leaned over and kissed his cheek, and then let herself out of the car. "I'll text you when I have the test and we can get together when I take it."

"I'll take you to dinner afterward," he said.

"You don't have to," she said, and he felt her pulling away even then.

"I know. But either way I bet we'll want to talk about it," he said.

She nodded and then turned away. He watched until she entered the building and then waited until he saw the lights come on in her loft. He hated leaving, felt like he should have tried harder to stay with her, but he knew that he wasn't in the right headspace to figure out anything right now.

<u>Six</u>

The coffee shop on Main Street was busy with the bloggers, would-be writers and freelancers who didn't have an office to take meetings. Mauricio hardly spared them a glance as he got in line behind someone he didn't recognize. As much as he professed to dislike small town living, there was something about knowing everyone in town that he liked. Then he heard the door open behind him and he immediately smelled gardenias.

Hadley's scent.

He glanced over his shoulder, removing his sunglasses, and their eyes met. She looked tired this morning. Of course, he had to acknowledge she also looked good. But he wondered if she'd slept as poorly as he had. Haunted by dreams of a "maybe baby" and how that would link their lives together.

"Morning, Hadley," he said.

"Mo," she replied, stepping up behind him, and his body

reacted. His blood flowing heavier in his veins, he stood a little taller and tightened his muscles before he realized what he was doing.

Preening in front of Hadley had never been enough to make amends for his screw-ups. And as far as last night went, he had a hard time in the cold light of day thinking it had been anything other than that. What had he been thinking?

He'd just started to get over her—*yeah, right*, his subconscious jeered. But he'd been trying.

"Stop staring at me like that," she said under her breath. "The biddies are about to come in and have their book club discussion. I don't want to give them more reason to talk about us."

"Darling, they don't need me looking at you to do that," he said.

The bell jingled again and Loretta, Alec's assistant, walked in. "You two! Makes me happy to see you together again."

"Uh, what?"

"It's all anyone is talking about this morning. Last night at the Bull Pit you were all over each other."

"It wasn't what it looked like," Hadley said. Her expression had completely shut down.

"Really? Even Alec didn't deny it this morning. He actually smiled before he realized I had forgotten to get the coffee," Loretta said.

"Alec is mistaken," Mauricio said, realizing that Hadley didn't want anyone to know about last night. He would follow her lead no matter how much he didn't want to hide anything about the two of them. "It was just two friends hanging out. Nothing more."

Nothing more. The words stuck in the back of his throat

and he wondered when he'd become so adept at lying. But then Loretta tipped her head to the side and shook it.

"Whatever y'all say."

"I think they're ready for your order, Mo," Hadley said, giving him a small smile. "I'll have a skinny latte and grab us a table at the back."

Us?

He didn't question it, just placed their orders and then waited for them, aware of the eyes of Cole's Hill on Hadley and him. Even the guy he hadn't recognized earlier seemed unable to tear his gaze away from her, though to be fair it could have been because of Hadley's good looks and not the gossip.

She wore a pair of pale pink trousers that tapered to show off her slim ankles and a sleeveless white top with black polka dots. Her hair was pulled up in a ponytail that emphasized her high cheekbones and heart-shaped face. He couldn't tear his eyes away.

Yeah, he'd really been almost over her.

The barista called his name and he grabbed the ceramic mugs with the Main Street Coffee shop logo. He moved through the tables, dodging toddlers who were playing a game of tag while their tired moms sipped coffee and chatted.

He finally got to the back and took a seat across from Hadley.

"So, that was…"

"Predictable," she finished. "I'm in town to talk to Kinley over at the bridal studio but ducked in here to avoid my mom. I saw her going into the bank, but this is almost as bad. What are we going to do?"

"Fake date," he said. "We should at least seem like a couple until we find out…what's going on." He knew it wasn't an ideal situation but the way she'd reacted to Loretta asking if they were together again had made him realize how hard it would be to win her back. And they were in a situation thanks to last night.

"Fake date?" she asked and then gave him a look that told him he was an idiot.

"Well, I'd love to really date you, Had, but you've been pretty clear every time but last night when you were full of tequila that you're over me," he said. Then realized he was being an ass. "Sorry. I shouldn't have said that."

"No, you're right. That is what I said," she admitted. "But maybe the tequila made me realize that I'm not over you."

"Don't," he said.

She quirked one eyebrow at him.

"I know I'm the insensitive, macho jackass but the truth is, getting over you was harder for me than I thought it would be."

She reached over and put her hand over the fist he hadn't realized he'd clenched. She rubbed her finger over his knuckles and a shiver went straight to his groin, making him shift his legs under the table.

"You're not a jackass all the time."

Their eyes met and for the first time since she'd walked out of his bedroom eighteen long months ago, with the possible exception of last night, he saw something other than anger in her eyes.

"Let's take this slow," he said. "Dinner tonight?"

She nodded. "Okay."

"Well, this is something I wouldn't have believed if I hadn't seen it for myself," Candace Everton said as she stopped next to their table.

"Mother," Hadley said, drawing her hand back from his and sitting up straighter. He saw her lace her fingers together and knew from the past that she was fighting the urge to tuck that one tendril of hair that never stayed in place back behind her ear.

"Ma'am," Mauricio said, standing. "I have to get back to work. But I'll see you for dinner tonight, Hadley."

She just nodded. "Peace Creek Steak House at eight. See you then."

Of course, she'd pick the most expensive place in town. But he didn't mind. He nodded at her and her mom and walked out of the coffee shop. If they were going to fake date, why not live it up?

Hadley wished she could just as easily escape her mother, but Candace sat down in Mauricio's vacated seat, waving over one of the coffee shop staff to clear away his mug and order herself a skinny mocha.

"Ma'am, I think you have to order it yourself at the counter," the teenage boy said.

"Son," Candace said with the sweetest smile she had, and Hadley hid her own smirk behind her hand. "I will more than make it worth your while to get my mocha and bring it to me. Don't I know your mama?"

"Yes, ma'am, Mrs. Everton," he said. "I'm Tommy Dunwoody."

"I thought I recognized that handsome face," she said. "I knew I could count on a Dunwoody man to do the right thing."

Tommy blushed and then nodded and turned away.

"Mother, you are something else," Hadley said as she took a sip of her now cold skinny latte. There were times when she missed the taste of real cane sugar in her coffee, but she didn't like to exercise so it was worth the sacrifice to keep her weight under control.

"I am, aren't I?" she said with a kind laugh. "Now we're going to talk about Helena's wedding, but first I have to ask… Do you know what you're doing with that Velas-quez boy?"

No. She had no clue. She was dating or fake dating him until she found out if she was pregnant and she had the feeling that it wasn't going to be as easy to walk away from Mo this time as it had been before.

"Of course, Mother. I have him exactly where I want him," she said. Lying to her mom about her personal life was an old habit, one she wasn't about to break right now in the middle of the coffee shop by divulging she might have gotten pregnant last night.

"Where you want him? That's not how relationships work," Candace said.

"Mom, please. It's Mo. You know how complicated it is. We have history and chemistry and I'm just trying not to make another mistake."

"Okay, Had. I won't pry, but I'm here if you need to talk," Candace said, taking a twenty-dollar bill from her wallet as Tommy walked back over with her mocha.

"Thank you, Tommy," she said, handing it to him.

"I'll get your change," he said.

"No need, son. Tell your mama I said hello and she's doing a good job raising her boys."

"Thank you, ma'am." He nodded and moved away.

"Now about Helena's cake. I saw the sketches you did. Hon, you really do have a lot of talent," Candace said. "I loved them. But we have to make sure we get Tilly at the bakery to work on this. Her assistants are competent, but they won't be able to do justice to your design."

"I'm sure whomever they give us will be fine," Hadley said. "Besides, isn't that up to Kinley to take care of?"

"I'm sorry?"

"Mother, don't do that. You know what I said—" she began.

Her mom shook her head. "I'm pretty sure I heard you suggest that I leave the details of my eldest daughter's wedding to someone else."

"It's not like Kinley doesn't know what she's doing," Hadley said. "She's planned plenty of weddings for A-listers."

"She's good, I'll give her that. But we know what we want. Maybe I'll go over to the bakery and chat with Tilly. Her daddy and I went to cotillion together," Candace said.

Her mother had notes about the flower arrangements that Hadley had designed and some suggestions for the bridal bouquet and the bridesmaids', as well. She gave her very detailed notes to pass on to Kinley. When she was done, she kissed Hadley on the cheek and left the coffee shop, stopping along the way to greet someone at almost every table. Hadley finished her drink a few minutes later and followed.

When she got to the door, she ran into Bianca Velasquez-Caruthers, Mo's sister and Derek Caruthers's wife, a preeminent heart surgeon in Cole's Hill. She'd been in Helena's class at the Five Families elementary school but had left Cole's Hill during high school to go to New York and become a model.

They'd reconnected in New York at Sera Samson's book launch. Sera was a lifestyle guru who had launched her tell-all book about life in the fast lane with her fiancé, Lorenzo Romano, a three time Formula One World Champion. It had been nice to see a friendly face from her hometown at the crowded cocktail party. Bianca knew Sera's fiancé from her days as the wife of the late Formula One Driver Jose Ruiz.

"Hi, Hadley," she said, holding the door for her to exit. "I bet your ears are buzzing this morning."

She shook her head. "You have no idea."

"You've got my sympathy, girl. You and Mo were all any of the moms at drop-off wanted to talk to me about."

She wrinkled her nose. "School moms? Really? I thought the gossip was confined to the old biddy book club meeting here this morning."

"Sadly, no," Bianca said.

Hadley sighed, stepping out of the way of customers trying to get into the coffee shop.

Bianca followed her away from the entrance. "Where are you heading?"

"To see Kinley," she said.

"Nothing like planning someone else's wedding when your own love life is all anyone in town can talk about, right?"

"Exactly, but I've got this. It's not like I didn't know what I was getting into when I started dancing with your brother last night," she said, finally admitting out loud what she'd been thinking all day.

"Why did you?"

"Sometimes even I can't resist him," she admitted. "Don't tell him that though."

"I wouldn't dream of it. He already thinks he's God's gift…though to be fair that's probably my mother's fault. She did tell those boys they were the best thing in town every day when we were growing up."

Of course she had.

Hadley said goodbye to Bianca and tried to focus on Helena so she wouldn't obsess about her upcoming date with Mo for the rest of the day.

Malcolm was already at work when Mauricio walked into the office. He nodded to his friend, who looked the worse for wear. He remembered what Helena had said last night and, though he had a strict rule not to mess around in other couples' business, he felt like Malcolm was dealing with something and wanted to see if he could help.

"Mal, you got a minute?" he asked.

"Sure, what's up?" he said, leaving his desk in the open plan area and coming over to Mo.

"Um, let's talk in my office," Mauricio said, leading the way toward his corner office. As a partner in the business, Malcolm had his own office but he liked being on the floor with the new guys. He said it kept him hungry to keep achieving.

But last month's numbers were in and Mal wasn't up to his usual standards. Mauricio needed to find out what was going on.

They entered his office and Malcolm walked over to the plate glass windows that offered a view of the square where the town held all of its major celebrations. His friend put his hand on the glass and leaned forward before cursing and turning away.

"What's going on with you?" Mo asked.

"Huh?"

"Listen, I'm not one to meddle but your numbers are down from last month, Helena is worried about you and, to be honest, you look like shit this morning," Mo said.

Malcolm cursed and shoved his hand through his hair, which explained why he looked so unkempt. "Hell. I don't know. It started with one deal that was sort of wonky."

"Wonky how?"

"Just the financing looked a bit odd to me and when I dug deeper I still couldn't find anything solid, but there was something that didn't feel right," Malcolm said.

"Bullshit."

"What?"

"I know you. You're solid when it comes to financing. So what's really going on?" Mauricio asked, leaning one hip against the side of his desk. He had worked hard to open his real estate business and to make it into the profitable company it was today. They were the best that this part of Texas had to offer and no one who worked here was taking any wonky financing deals.

"Fine. I bet too much on my fantasy football league. My team isn't doing that great and so last week I took a blind and lost," Malcolm said.

"Do you need me to cover you?" Mauricio offered.

"No, I got it," he said. "I've been trying to earn back what I lost but the harder I push here the more the clients feel it. It's like they know I'm desperate instead of just hungry for their business, you know?"

"I do know. How about this? I'll go with you to your next meeting and we'll close the deal together," Mo said. "You'll get back on top."

"Great," he said.

"Who are we waiting on?"

"The Tressor Group. They're the plastics manufacturers from Plano. They really want to be closer to Galveston and the port and I have them interested in the old Porter Warehouses."

"Damn, you're good. We haven't been able to get anyone near there in years," Mauricio said. It was a listing that he'd taken since old man Porter and his father were friends. They'd both come up together in school. But the property wasn't close enough to town to be part of the revitalized district. He'd tried to convince NASA to use it but they didn't need storage facilities in Cole's Hill when they had everything they needed in Houston at the Johnson Space Center.

"I haven't been able to convince them after the initial meeting. They're coming back today for lunch and then we're going to tour the location one more time," Malcolm said.

"I'll meet you after lunch. We can close it together. Just

turn on your usual Southern charm and don't mention the property during the meal, okay?"

Mal nodded. "Thanks, Mo. I know Helena spoke to you but I've got this under control."

"I know you do. You always come out on top."

Malcom nodded his head a bunch of times. "That's right, I do."

Damn. He'd never have thought that Malcolm would be this insecure, but he realized how falling in love changed people. There wasn't a man he knew who was better than Mal. He was one of the solid ones.

He let himself out of the office and Mauricio went to his desk, making a reservation at the Peace Creek Steak House for dinner and then ordering a bouquet of peonies to be sent to Hadley. He didn't want tonight to feel like they were just marking time until she took the pregnancy test. He wanted it to be...well, maybe the start of rebuilding something.

He messaged his assistant and asked her to notify him when Malcolm left the offices. In a way it was good that he had his friend to distract him from the fact that he was going on a date with Hadley tonight. It felt like it had been too long since he'd had something like that to look forward to.

But what if he ended up screwing it up? Doing something stupid like Malcolm had done?

After she'd left him, he'd been angry and out of control. This felt better. Right, even. Like he was in a place to actually be the man she needed him to be this time. Or rather the man he wanted to be.

His assistant pinged him when Malcom left and Mo went out to talk to the guys he knew who were in the office fantasy football league. They all posted their teams each week and bet against each other.

Todd, Alan and Rob were all in the kitchen having their mid-morning coffee break.

"Hiya, boss man, you want a coffee?" Todd asked.

"Nah, I'm good for now. I wanted to find out how the football thing is going," he said.

"Good. Our office is out ahead of everyone else in the league. Your boy, Malcolm, has been winning the most, but that's to be expected since he's been picking Manu's brain about the strengths of different players."

"He's winning?" Mauricio asked.

"Yeah. Like a lot. He even got a bonus a few weeks ago," Todd said. "You want in?"

"Nah. Not my thing," Mauricio said.

He chatted with his men for a few more minutes before he left. Why would Mal lie? And what was he hiding? Mauricio would have liked to let it go but he didn't want Helena to get hurt. And it wasn't just because he knew that Hadley would kill him if he let anything happen to her sister.

Seven

Hadley ran the wedding errands assigned by her mother and drove back to her shop just in time to meet the deliverymen who had brought the shipment of paintings from El Rod, an up-and-coming Western portrait artist whose work had recently been generating a lot of buzz. The paintings were raw and captured the wildness of the lives of the people who lived in southern New Mexico. He was from Taos and she'd only communicated with him via emails since he preferred not to use a phone.

She'd never considered herself a high-strung artist, but if she ever started selling her canvases for the amounts he was making, maybe she'd tell everyone not to call her. Too bad the one woman she didn't want to talk to—her mother— probably wouldn't be deterred by that type of edict.

She heard the bell on the door at the front of her shop jingle as she was opening the first crate. She put down the wedge she was using and looked over, surprised to see her sister standing there.

"What's up?"

"Um, shouldn't that be my question? I mean, I saw you dancing last night with Mauricio, but I thought you were smart enough to not let it go any further than that," Helena said.

"What makes you think that it did?" Hadley wasn't sure she was ready to talk to her sister about last night. Today she'd been trying so hard to focus on anything but that broken condom and the possible consequences.

All she'd been trying to do last night was get some closure with Mauricio. If she were a superstitious person, she'd probably assign some sort of greater meaning to what had happened.

"I was doing the books today at the Grand Hotel," Helena said. "The night manager saw me on his way out and told me how happy he was y'all had made up."

"Ugh. This is crazy. This morning half the people in the coffee shop thought the same thing," Hadley said.

Helena put her arm around Hadley and hugged her close. "Are you happy about whatever happened last night? Is this a good thing?"

"Oh, crapola," Hadley said. "It's complicated."

"That's what I thought. So, I brought lunch and figured we could talk," Helena said. "It's the least I could do after sticking you with Mom and the wedding."

Her sister squeezed her shoulder and showed her the insulated lunch bag from Famous Manu's BBQ. "Out here or in your office?"

Hadley started clearing one of the tables she used for her Wednesday night art classes and then drew over chairs for her and Helena.

"I really don't mind the wedding stuff. It's so much fun and different from the projects I normally work on," she said as she went to the little fridge under the counter and got out two sparkling waters.

Helena opened the bag of food and Hadley almost groaned. She had a weakness for the brisket from that place.

They sat across from each other eating in silence for a few minutes. When Hadley finally spoke, she dropped a bombshell.

"I might have gotten pregnant last night."

"Are you kidding me?"

"No. Mo's condom broke," Hadley said. "I'm going to get a pregnancy test but you know I can't buy one here or everyone will really lose their shit, especially Mom when it gets back to her."

"So, what are you going to do? You can't go to Dr. Phillips either," Helena said. She'd put her fork down and was staring at Hadley. "God, girl, when you do something, you don't do it by half measures, do you?"

"I don't. I mean, I never intend for stuff like this to happen, but it does. I really don't even know how."

"We'll figure this out," Helena said. "What does Mo think?"

"I don't know. We're having dinner tonight. He's apologized a ton but it's not like it's just his fault, you know?"

"I do know."

Hadley wiped her fingers on her napkin and put it down. "I'm going to Houston a week from Wednesday and I'll pick up a test there. I mean, until then it's not like knowing or not knowing is going to change anything."

Helena shook her head. "Not the outcome. But the truth is, just thinking you might be pregnant is probably doing something to your thoughts about Mo. And his about you. Leaving him was hard for you. Are you sure you don't want to consider other options?"

"Other options? No. That's not for me. It's not bothering me," Hadley said. "Why do you think it would?"

"Because having a man's baby is a big deal. Especially when that man is one that you can't seem to get over, even though you know there's no future with him," Helena said, sounding very much like a know-it-all older sister.

Hadley admitted Helena was saying the very thing she didn't want to acknowledge. "Whatever happens with that test, the truth is Mo and I have to figure out how to at least be friends again if we are going to both keep living here. I mean, if today is any example, then the town isn't ready for us to not be a couple either."

"I don't think the town cares who y'all are with as long as you're happy. But you're always going to be in the spotlight, so get used to it. There isn't a person in this town who isn't connected to Mother and Mrs. Velasquez in some way or another."

She remembered her mom using her old cotillion date as leverage at the bakery and knew that Helena was right. She and Mo had to figure out how to coexist and tonight would be a good first step toward figuring out how to be friends.

Just friends.

No matter how excited those crazy butterflies in her stomach were for her to see him again.

Mauricio helped Malcolm close the deal with the plastics people and they returned to the office. It was a little before five o'clock and quiet. A lot of his residential agents were out on appointments with clients who could only see the listings when they got off work.

He knew he should let Malcolm start the paperwork for the deal but he wanted some answers. It was one thing for Malcolm to not tell him about his money trouble, that he could understand, but lying about it? That wasn't like Malcolm at all. And put together with Helena's fears, it made Mauricio wonder what the hell was going on with his friend.

"So I had a chat with Todd today and he told me that our office is way ahead in the football league for the city," Mauricio said. "Now that's not what you told me, so I'm pretty damned sure one of you is lying to me. I don't give a crap about our football league standings, but if you felt the need to make something up, that does concern me."

Malcolm shook his head and leaned back against his desk, crossing his arms over his chest and his feet at the ankles. "Mo, it's not something I want to talk about. I'm sorry I lied to you about the league."

"Okay, fair enough. But if you hurt Helena because of this thing, I'm coming for you," he said.

"She's not yours to protect," Malcolm said, standing up.

"No, she's yours but you're clearly distracted," Mo said. "Get your shit together."

He turned and went into his office, closing the door behind him. He had no idea what kind of trouble Malcolm could be in, but for right now he was determined to do all he could to keep his friend safe and his engagement intact.

His phone pinged with a text message and he glanced down at it, hoping it wasn't Hadley canceling on him. Not that he'd blame her after the high-handed way he'd invited her to dinner.

But it was Diego reminding him he had polo practice tonight at six o'clock. He sent back the thumbs-up emoji and then texted his housekeeper, Rosalita, and asked her to bring a change of clothes and his toiletries bag to the polo grounds so he could shower and get dressed there.

Then he sat down at his desk just as the door to his office opened and his dad walked in. Domingo Velasquez took off his black Stetson as he entered Mauricio's office and leaned one hip on the corner of his desk.

Mo had that sinking feeling in his gut that this wasn't a casual visit because his father was being too casual.

"Poppy, what are you doing here? Don't you have a standing round of drinks at the club at this time of day?" Mo asked. *Play it cool*, he warned himself.

"You know I do," he said. "But your mother saw you on Main Street at 4:49 this morning so we need to talk."

"Wow, that's precise," Mo said.

"I know. She wants to know what you were doing out at that hour and asked me to remind you that she would rather hear it from you than from the gossips when she goes to the club for dinner tonight," Domingo said. "So I'm here to get the scoop."

He took a deep breath and shook his head. "I went out with the boys last night to play pool at the Bull Pit and Hadley was there."

His father went stiff and turned to look more closely at Mauricio's hands. He seemed to relax when he didn't see any swelling or bruising on his knuckles. *Damn.* He wished he'd kept better control of his temper last year. "I wasn't fighting, Poppy. I ended up dancing with Hadley and one thing led to another. We had a lot to drink, so we walked to the Grand Hotel and then I went back for my car to take her home. That's when Mom saw me."

His dad stood up and walked over to the plate glass windows that looked down on the park. He turned his hat in his hands and didn't say anything. When Mauricio had been in trouble when he was younger, he'd always kept talking to fill the silence. But honestly, he had nothing more to say to his dad. He wasn't sure what would happen next with Hadley.

"Was it a one-time thing?" his father asked, his voice low and gravelly.

"I don't know. I don't want it to be, but I'm not sure what she wants. I'm taking her to dinner tonight," he said. "Also I'm not sure she will ever be able to forgive me. Or if I can prove to her that I'm worthy of her trust."

"Dinner is a good place to start. I know how this town is, but you have to do what's right for y'all. So if you need time or if that was what you needed to move on, I understand," his father said.

"Thank you," Mauricio said. "I just don't want her to get hurt again because of me."

"No man does," Domingo said.

"Does it ever get easier?" he asked his dad.

"Not really, and just wait until you have kids. If you have a daughter, it gets even worse," he said.

After his father left, his words echoed in Mauricio's mind. What if he did have a daughter with Hadley? He hadn't thought beyond a baby and what it would mean if she was pregnant. But a daughter—one who looked like Hadley—that would be a challenge. He knew how men would react to her and he wasn't sure his temper was ready for that. Or if it would ever be. Also what if he let down his daughter? He wanted to believe he'd changed, but he wasn't sure he was ready for fatherhood.

The Peace Creek Steak House was just off Main Street. Hadley realized if they wanted to keep a low profile, she shouldn't have suggested this place, but it wasn't as though most of the people who knew their families hadn't already cottoned on to the fact that something was going on. And she'd always been more of a face-it-head-on kind of girl.

Mauricio had shaved and changed into a gray suit that

was clearly custom-made, paired with fancy leather boots. He held a Stetson in his left hand that perfectly matched his suit. His collar was open and she saw his St. Christopher medallion nestled in the hollow of his throat.

He put his hand on the small of her back as she followed their hostess to the table that was tucked into one of the alcoves near the back. She wished she'd chosen a wool dress instead of the light silk halter dress that left her back naked. But she'd wanted to look good for him and the touch of his hand on her skin did feel nice. Too nice.

They were in a nebulous no-man's-land and she wasn't sure what would happen next. But she'd promised herself no more free passes to hop into bed with Mo. She needed to be thinking with her head and not her vagina.

He held the chair out for her and then took a seat across the table as the waiter placed her napkin over her lap and then asked for their drink order. She started to order her customary glass of wine but then thought of why they were here. She could be expecting his baby. Better play it safe.

"Sparkling water with a twist of lime," Hadley said.

"Same," Mauricio said, and she heard the amusement in his voice. "On the wagon?" he asked once the waiter left.

"No. Just in case it turns out I'm…you know, I figure I'd better not take any chances," she said.

He sank back in his chair. "Good thinking. So, should we jump right into this discussion or what?"

"I think we should wait until we get our drinks, so we don't have any awkward waiter intrusions," she said.

He nodded again, and she realized that he was nervous, which was silly when she thought about all the dates they'd been on together. But the truth was, she'd always been hyper aware of everyone watching them, of trying to give the impression that they were the perfect couple. There had been so much pressure that, honestly, she couldn't remember a single meal where she hadn't been upset with Mo over something he hadn't done correctly.

"How was your day?" he asked after a minute of silence.

"Not too bad after you left me alone with Mother," she said, arching her eyebrows and sending him a look.

"Sorry about that. But Candace never really warmed to me, and I had a feeling if I stayed, it wasn't going to be a good experience for anyone."

"You're probably right," Hadley said. Her mother really had liked Mauricio when they'd first started dating, but she'd gotten frustrated with how they had always broken up and then gotten back together. "She just thought we were like oil and water."

"She's wrong there. We were always like fire."

They *were* like fire, something that she'd never been able to control. The passion had always been the easy part between the two of them and so she'd felt that she had to work harder on the other stuff. It made her realize how immature she'd been, trying to make them perfect to the outside world instead of perfect for each other.

"So, after you dealt with your mother, what did you do?"

"I got a shipment from an artist I'm exhibiting next week. He's really hot right now. And I'm lucky to have gotten him. There's an invitation-only showing next Friday. I sent out the announcement to all the big-time collectors in the state. Would you like to come?"

"I would. What if we aren't…"

She put her hands on the table next to her plate and looked over at him, seeing the same uncertainty in his eyes that she felt deep inside. "No matter what, I think you and I have to figure out how to be friends. Unless one of us is leaving Cole's Hill. But I don't think that's going to happen."

"How do we do that, Had?" he asked just as the waiter brought their drinks.

Luckily, it gave her a reprieve from answering because she had no idea what to say. She wondered if too much had passed between them for them to ever just be friends but she hoped not. They could surely figure this out. Especially if she was pregnant. They were going to have to do something more than just be polite to each other. She wanted them to be friends, at least.

But how could she trust him? Really trust him? She wanted to believe he'd changed but was it permanent or was it simply that he felt bad for hurting her? Was it at his core?

"Hadley?"

"Hmm?"

"Have you decided what you want to eat?" Mauricio asked.

She hadn't even looked at the menu tonight but had been here so many times over the course of her life that she knew what she was going to have. She ordered the four-ounce filet mignon with the chef's special sauce, which had a creamy peppercorn flavor. After the waiter left, she realized that next Mo was going to want to talk about what they should do if the pregnancy test was positive.

She didn't want that. She wasn't sure that she could talk about a hypothetical and honor whatever agreement they made before she knew if the pregnancy was real or not. She only knew that she wasn't ready to walk away from Mauricio and that she was going to do her best to figure out if that meant starting a friendship with him or something more.

"So…"

"Would you mind terribly if we didn't discuss this tonight?" she asked. She was sort of surprised that she'd blurted out what was on her mind instead of doing as she usually did, which was accommodating him. Trying to guess what he wanted.

"Not at all. I thought you wanted to talk about it," he said.

"Not until we have to," she said. "Now tell me about your day."

"It wasn't too bad. I'm working on a few details for a new charity project and I had a showing on the Dunwoody mansion."

"I love that house. Is it as gorgeous inside as it used to be?"

"It's still nice but everything is dated. They could probably use someone like you to update the interior," he said.

"I don't do houses," she said.

"Not professionally but what you did at the house we shared was really good. Relaxing and elegant."

"Maybe too relaxing," she said without thinking.

"Probably. Made me think I didn't have to worry about you," he said. "But I should have, Hadley. I'll be honest. I think I took advantage of you because you were always so accommodating."

"I think I let you," she admitted. "I wanted what my parents have and for some reason I thought if I made life easy for you, you'd do the same."

"I wish I had," he admitted.

She just nodded. "The food here is really good."

He let her change the topic and they talked about the high school football team and the new menu at Famous Manu's but she couldn't help noticing that Mo got quieter and a little tenser.

As the evening wore on, she realized that by relaxing and being herself, she was enjoying her time with Mauricio more than she had in the entire last year they'd dated.

She was able to concentrate on what he was saying and realized he was a really good storyteller. As the evening ended, she felt that no matter what the outcome of the pregnancy test, the two of them were setting up the bonds of a true friendship.

Eight

After dinner, Mauricio suggested they tour the new polo grounds and stables that he and Diego had recently opened on the outskirts of Cole's Hill. He was happy when she said yes.

"Diego and Bartolome Figueras are both the experts when it comes to horses and polo but I still wanted to invest and be a full partner in the facility," he said as they drove through the quiet town. Bart was a famed polo player and model from Argentina. He'd been friends with the Velasquez family for years.

"I'm glad you are. You always wanted to be more than the man who makes the real estate deals," she said.

His ego perked up that she remembered that tidbit about him. But he knew that was simply because she tended to listen when he talked. He wished he could say the same about himself. He didn't know as many details about her from their time together.

"What about you?" he asked. "I know you have the exhibit, and Bianca mentioned you do some sort of class once a week."

Hadley rested her head against the leather seat and turned to stare out the window at the passing landscape.

"Yes, I have the Wednesday night drawing class for serious artists and I'm thinking of adding a Mommy-Daddy-and-Me art class either after school or on the weekends," she said. "I'm still trying to figure out what I want the shop to be. I don't need to make a profit at this moment in time because I'm still working with one of my bigger clients in Manhattan so that covers the bills, and I own the property where the shop and loft are outright—thanks to you. I never would have thought to invest in real estate if you hadn't made me."

He couldn't help the chuckle that escaped him. "Darling, no man on this planet has ever made you do anything. The word *stubborn* was invented for you."

He glanced over to see her smiling to herself. "You are just used to women taking one look at your muscles and charming smile and giving in to whatever you suggest. I'm…discerning."

He had been used to that. From the very beginning, Hadley had been different and he liked the challenge of her. She kept him on his toes.

"You are certainly that," he agreed, turning off the main FM road toward the polo grounds.

He pulled up to the main building containing the stables and put the car in Park. "I need to text Diego and let him know I'm here so he doesn't come out if the alarm goes off."

"Sure," she said. "I'm going to walk over there by the fence. I've been wanting to see the new grounds."

He nodded. As she got out of the car, he followed her, texting his brother, who simply told him to have fun and make sure he locked up when he left. Then he caught up to Hadley where she leaned against the fence. The breeze caught her hair, pulling at it and drawing it away from her face. She had her head tipped back and his breath caught in his chest. She was too good for him, but he still wanted her more than anything in this world. She'd always made him a better man and he'd never realized that until he'd lost her.

He raised his phone, snapped a picture of her and then pocketed it. He knew himself well enough to guess he'd screw this up again and he wanted a record of this moment when they were getting along perfectly and nothing else had intruded.

She glanced over her shoulder at him as he approached. "Did you get permission, or do we have to keep an eye out for Johnny Law?"

"When have you ever had to worry about the cops?" he asked. If there was a poster child for being a good girl, Hadley was it. She was a rule follower and stickler for doing things properly.

"Never," she admitted. "It doesn't even make me embarrassed. I hate that feeling I get when I know I'm doing something I shouldn't."

"Like what?"

"Dancing with you," she said.

"Touché."

"I'm just saying you feel dangerous to me. You make me… Well, that's not fair. It's not you making me do anything. Around you, I just forget my normal self and the things I do to make my life comfortable… I'm just making it worse, aren't I?"

"No, you're not. I think I like that something about me makes you uncomfortable, unless you meant it in a negative way. Did you?"

She turned around, leaning back against the fence with her arms on the top railing. "No, I didn't. Most of the time I like being the good girl, the one who knows all the rules of etiquette and how to act in public. But with you, I also feel edgy. Like I should throw all of that out and just be… different. Just take a chance."

He wanted her to take a chance—on him. He'd been thinking about her a lot since they'd broken up. He knew they'd been young when they'd first hooked up. They both came from good families so everyone thought they were a good match but, honestly, he'd never really taken the time to find out what it was they had in common beyond upbringing.

And it was an opportunity he wasn't going to waste again.

Hadley hadn't meant to be as honest as all that with Mo. Not tonight and maybe not ever. There was something that made her feel vulnerable when she stepped out of the shadow of her very proper mother and let her real self shine through. She wasn't ever going to be fully comfortable with that. But with Mo, who had seen her at her best and arguably at her absolute worst, she sort of had no choice.

"What about you?" she asked. "Do I do anything to you?"

"Other than turn me on?" he asked.

She glanced away. Of course, he'd bring it back to the physical. She bared her soul and he wanted to talk about the ridiculously hot passion that had always been between them.

"Hey," he said, coming over and putting his hand on her upper arm. "I'm sorry. I guess what you do is make me feel vulnerable. Like I have something that I don't want to let go of, and instead of reacting like a grown-up, I fall back to being a teenage boy with the hots for the prettiest girl in Cole's Hill."

She felt her heart soften a little toward him. She didn't know if he was playing her right now but she was going to take him at his word. "I'm not the prettiest, I can tell you that. I mean, Helena is gorgeous, your sister was a super-model—"

"You are to me. I don't know about either of them. Since they're sisters to us, I don't see them the way I see you. And truthfully, it's not just those two, Had. I don't see other women the way I see you. Something about you is just... perfect for me."

"Then why was Marnie in your room?"

"I missed you," he said. "I wasn't sure you were ever coming back. You know I had texted you and you never responded."

"I didn't," she admitted. "I was afraid we'd just continue the rest of our lives breaking up and getting back together... but then I was in Cole's Hill and I had to see you. I know that part of this was my fault—"

"No. It was me," he said. "I cared about you back then and I still do today. I shouldn't have slept with anyone else."

The evening breeze stirred around them and she tipped her head back, taking in the moon and the seriousness in his eyes.

"Do you mean that?"

"I do," he said, drawing his hand down her arm and leaving gooseflesh in its wake. He linked their fingers to-gether and started walking across the paddock toward the main building. "Remember when we first started dating and I used to always look at you?"

"Yes. I think I said stop staring at me, creeper," she said with a laugh.

"You did," he confirmed. "But a part of me couldn't believe you were mine, that you'd picked me out of all the other men you could have chosen. I kept looking at you to see if you had regrets, and I'm pretty sure that's where our troubles started. I never felt like I was enough for you."

She stopped walking and looked over at him. "Mauricio Velasquez, million-dollar deal maker, son of one of the most prestigious Five Families…you were enough. Sometimes more than enough. You can be very intense."

He dropped her hand. "We should have talked about this, shouldn't we have?"

"Probably, but we weren't ready for that. I had this image in my head of what kind of couple we should be, you had something you wanted us to be too, and we are both very competitive when it comes to our careers. I think talking would have been hard when we were together."

He turned away and started walking again and she fell into step beside him until they got to the barn where the horses were kept. He entered a code and then held the door open for her as she walked inside. She realized that something she'd said bothered him, and as he moved silently past her to turn on the light, she wished she knew what it was. They were never going to be one of those totally in sync couples like Helena and Malcolm were or like his sister, Bianca, and her husband. Was it her?

"Listen, I'm sorry if I said something that upset you," she began.

"Stop. I'm a man, not some wuss. I don't get upset," he said.

"What do you get then?" she asked, because he was clearly out of sorts. When her daddy got like this, her mother would send him out to his man cave until he could be *decent*, to put it in her mom's famous words.

"Pissed off. And I'm not pissed at you, darling, but at

myself for thinking I'm even worthy of you, that we could be rebuilding a relationship."

She realized they needed to talk. She wasn't sure what she wanted from this. Friendship, of course. That was a must, no matter how much further it went.

She went over to a stall where one of the horses had come and put its nose over the railing. She held her hand out for the horse to smell her first, and then once it seemed to accept her, she pet it.

If there were only some way of doing that with Mo. Some signal he could give her of what he wanted.

"I'm not sure what's going on between us," she began, her own voice low in part not to startle the horse but also because she wasn't sure of what she was saying. "Today I realized that we're going to have to be friends. Then tonight as we talked at dinner and I had a really good time, I hope it's the start of a new phase for us."

She looked over at him where he stood in the middle of the aisle with his hands on his hips just watching her. She wanted to trust him. The lights made his black hair look darker than midnight. It was so thick, she wished she could reach out and thread her fingers through it like she was doing to the horse's mane.

"If I'm pregnant, that will force us into making choices we might not have made. But if I'm not, I still want to work on our friendship."

He wanted that too. But he felt like he was already letting her down. He didn't do conversations about emotions well, and the only emotions he'd ever really felt at ease with were anger or passion. But he knew that wasn't going to be enough. Not with Hadley. Not this time.

There was a reason why they kept breaking up each time they tried again. And she was so right when she said that the baby—if there was one—would complicate things.

"I want that too. I'm not going to pretend I don't want to sleep with you and that I'm not thinking about last night every time I look at you. I mean, I'm smart enough to know that's not what either of us needs right now, but that doesn't mean I don't want you."

She smiled at him. It was the sweetest smile he'd seen on her face in a long time, like the one she'd worn last night when she'd been sleeping in his arms and he thought he'd done something right. Like he'd said the right thing. But what the hell was it?

"I want you too. But I think that's gotten in our way over the years. It's so easy to fall into each other's arms instead of talking things through. For both of us," she said. "But if you're on the same page as I am, why don't we try the friends thing, no matter what the outcome of the test—which I will go to Houston and pick up."

Friends.

"Is this you friend-zoning me? Or are you saying if we're friends first, we'll be a stronger couple if we get to that stage later?" he asked.

"The second one. I want you too, Mo. That's never been an issue. I really want to figure out how to live together in this small town of ours, and if we have a kid to raise together, we have to know how to do that. That's got to be the first thing."

What she said made sense. Even though he had been hoping to get her into his arms again tonight, he could wait if it meant that this time if they got back together, it would last.

He was getting to the age where a crazy roller-coaster relationship wasn't what he wanted. Maybe it was seeing his brother getting married or spending so much time with

his nephew, but he knew he wanted something more substantial for this next phase of his life. His thirties…that's
when his dad had always said it was time to grow up.

"Okay," he said. "Let's do this friend thing."

"Okay…so what do we do now?" she asked.

"Don't ask me. I'm still trying to stop thinking about
kissing you again. And how much I want to pull you into
my arms."

"Stop that," she said, wagging her finger at him. "Now
you've got me thinking about it too."

"Good," he said with a wink. "Want to go for a ride? Or
should I take you home?"

"Home, I think," she said after a pause. "But I do want
to come back and tour the polo grounds. When is your
next match?"

"Two weeks," he said. "We're doing a charity match
against Bartolome and his team. It will be for fun, but you
know we don't want to lose."

"When have you and your brothers ever approached a
sport as just *fun*?"

"Never. We picked a date when Inigo wasn't going to
be racing and could come home to play with us. He's tech-
nically not allowed to do anything high risk, which is why
we're just saying this is an informal match." She shook
her head and he just shrugged. "We're all rule breakers."

"I know that, Mo, believe me. For some reason it's one
of the things I like about you."

"I'd never do anything to put anyone in danger," he said,
as he led her out of the stables and turned out the lights.
They walked over to his car in silence and when he opened
her door for her, she brushed past him and then she stopped.

Her breath caught between her parted lips as a shiver
of sensual need went through him. He leaned down before
he could stop himself and brushed his lips over hers. Then

he felt her hands on either side of his face as she kissed him back before she broke the contact between them and got into the car.

He closed the door and turned to walk around behind it, stopping for a minute to take several deep breaths to center himself. How was he ever going to manage being just friends? He couldn't think of a time when he was next to her that he didn't want to reach out and touch her, kiss her, pull her into his arms and never let her go.

But he had to.

If he wanted her to stay in Cole's Hill for good this time, he had to figure it out.

Did he want her to stay for good?

He was pretty damned sure he did.

He got into the car. When he started the engine, she reached over and fiddled with the radio until she found a country western station. The music filled the car on the drive home and he did a pretty good job of forgetting he wanted her until Eric Church's "Like a Wrecking Ball" came on.

He almost thought that Hadley wasn't affected until she reached over and pushed the button to change the channel to a Top Forty station. But the damage had been done. He remembered her pressed against him last night at the Bull Pit, dancing so close that he felt every inch of her.

When he finally pulled into her parking space at her loft, she looked over at him.

"Thanks for a nice night," she said, dashing out of the car before he could say anything more.

Nine

Hadley woke to her phone pinging and someone knocking on her door. She groaned and rolled over to look at the clock. It was eight in the morning. Not exactly early but she hadn't slept well last night, dreaming of Mauricio and regretting not taking that kiss further than she had.

The knocking continued, and she grabbed her phone as she hopped out of bed. Her Ravenclaw boxers and *Also, I Can Kill You With My Brain* T-shirt were respectable enough for whoever was trying to wake her up.

She glanced at her phone and saw that her sister was texting and as she glanced in the peephole, she remembered it was Tuesday.

Tuesday morning.

She was supposed to meet her mother at Kinley's to help her and Helena finalize the floral bouquet choices. Hadley had done a few design sketches and sent them over to Kinley, who was having samples made for them to look at.

She opened the door and stepped back as her mother brushed past her into the apartment. It had an open floor plan, and though her bed had two decorative screens that blocked it from the view of the living room, her mother went straight to it and then came back out as Hadley moved into the kitchen area, starting a pot of coffee. She had a feeling she was going to need at least ten cups to face her mother this morning.

"I'm not interested in excuses. I thought you were dead," Candace said, setting her Birkin bag on the table near the front door before coming over and standing next to the kitchen island.

"I had a long night working on my project for the company in New York. I slept through my alarm, Mom. No excuse, but I'm sorry," Hadley said, going over and giving her mom a hug that she immediately returned, squeezing Hadley close.

"I really thought something had happened to you. You are never late and then I couldn't get you on the phone," Candace said. She kissed Hadley's temple and then stepped back, blinking as she reached up to touch her chignon.

Hadley hadn't realized at first how much it had freaked her mom out when she hadn't shown up. But then she was the reliable sister. The one who never said no and was always there. "Again, I'm very sorry. Why did you check the bedroom?"

"Mavis Crandall saw you out with Mo last night and I was just checking to see if he was why you were late," she said.

"No. We're trying to get past the breakup and be friends," Hadley said, checking the glass coffeepot and seeing there was already enough for a mug of coffee. She grabbed two earthenware mugs that she'd gotten from a local artist on Main Street and put one under the drip while pouring out the coffee into the other one.

"Want a cup?" she asked her mom.

"I can't. I already had one today," she said. "I'd love some juice if you have it."

"I do. Have a seat and let me get it for you," Hadley said. "Did you reschedule for today?"

"I tried to but Kinley isn't available until Thursday," her mother said in a tone that told Hadley she was put out by the fact that Kinley wouldn't reschedule her other clients.

Hadley wasn't surprised by that. Kinley wasn't one to back down and was used to dealing with bridezillas who made her mom look like a saint.

"How about I make it up to you by taking you to brunch?"

"Sounds good. I'll text Helena and ask her to join us," Candace said.

"She might be working, Mom," Hadley pointed out.

"Nonsense. She's her own boss. She can take a break and have brunch with us. I'll call the club while you shower and make sure they have the table I like by the window. Oh, this is going to be so nice," she said.

Hadley got her mom her juice, then took her coffee into her bedroom area to get ready. She heard her mom on the phone being as sweet as could be but not hesitating to coerce first Helena into joining them and then the maître d' at the club into reserving her favorite table.

Hadley took a quick shower, got dressed and applied a light bit of makeup to cover the evidence of her sleepless night. Then she rejoined her mother, who looked perfectly at ease moving around the apartment fluffing pillows.

"I think it's time you redid your place," Candace said. "It looks like you just threw everything in here. I know that when you moved out of Mauricio's you didn't really have the time to pick out nice pieces, but now that it looks like you're staying, we should get you some good furniture."

Her mom had a point. No matter what happened with her and Mauricio, she was going to need to make this place her home. And her mom was right: she'd simply looked at the loft as temporary. It had been a stopgap after she'd moved back from New York, unsure of what she was going to do next.

"I might need to take a trip to the antique markets," Hadley said.

"I'll reach out to my contacts and see what's available," Candace said. "There's nothing I love more than shopping for my girls."

Hadley smiled as they both grabbed their handbags and left the apartment. She'd been so busy thinking about the baby in terms of how it would impact her and Mo that she hadn't considered what it might be like to be a mom...like her mother.

She followed her mom's Audi as she drove through town to the Five Families Country Club, but her mind wasn't on the drive, it was on the child. What if she was really pregnant? She'd have a baby of her own. Someone she could dote on the way her parents always had.

For the first time since she'd looked at that broken condom, she had the thought that maybe being pregnant wasn't the worst thing to happen. Sure, she and Mauricio could be closer, but they were working on that. And a child...of her own? Someone who was hers? That was one thing she'd never realized she'd been missing.

Brunch with her mom and her sister was the last thing that Helena wanted to do today. For one thing, Malcolm's behavior was getting more and more erratic and she would have a difficult time fooling either of them that she wasn't stressed out. She could put it down to wedding jitters. Yeah, she thought, that was the excuse she'd use if one of them brought it up.

She used some undereye concealer and highlighter on her cheeks to try to make herself look peppier, but to be honest, when she looked at her reflection in the rearview mirror, she knew she hadn't really hidden her inner turmoil.

Her mom and sister were already inside the country club. Even if Hadley hadn't been texting Where are you? every thirty seconds for the last ten minutes, she knew they were inside thanks to their cars parked side by side in the lot. She had asked her assistant to text her after thirty minutes and say there was an emergency so she wouldn't have to stay the entire time.

"So you weren't dead," Hadley said to Helena as she joined her mom and sister at their usual corner table near the large windows that overlooked the golf course.

"I wasn't," Helena said.

"I told you," Hadley said, giving her mom a pointed look.

"You girls have no idea what it's like to be a mom. When I text or call you and get no response, my first reaction is to run through a long list of everything that could be wrong, starting with kidnapping and ending with death."

Helena reached over and squeezed her mom's hand. "We know you worry but you need to remember we're your daughters. Anyone who comes for us better be ready for a fight."

"I know. Doesn't stop me from worrying," her mom said. "Hadley was just telling me she has to run to Houston for a client next week and I asked her to go back to the flower district and speak to Manuel to find out what blooms will be the freshest in December for your wedding."

"Thanks, sis," Helena said. She should probably try to

get Hadley alone and see if she was doing okay with the whole might-be-pregnant thing.

"No problem. I'm pretty sure that Kinley will have some good ideas too," Hadley said.

"If she'd had time to talk to us today, then we'd know that," Candace said.

Helena fought to hide her smile. Her mother didn't like it when the world didn't bend to her demands. Their daddy had said more than once it was his fault for treating her like a princess when they'd been dating, but Helena didn't buy that at all. Her mother had always had a steel backbone and demanded excellence.

"She has other clients, Mom. It will be fine," Helena said.

"Of course it will. And it was our fault that we missed the first one," Candace agreed. "Now, what's going on with my girls? I'm so glad we're getting this time to catch up."

"Well, I had to rearrange my work schedule this morning," Helena said. "Apparently my sister was in mortal danger but everything is great now."

"You have your daddy's smartass humor, Helena. It's not as attractive as either of y'all believe it is," Candace said, rolling her eyes and then taking a sip of her sparkling water.

"That's one opinion. Had, what do you think?"

"I'm going to have to side with Mom on this one. It's funny to hear you joke about someone else but when you direct it at me, I'm not a huge fan," Hadley said.

"I'll try to remember that. So what were you doing last night?" Helena asked as the waiter placed an avocado salad in front of her. "Were you out with Mo again?"

"I was, as you know. We're trying to be friends," Hadley said, looking down at her plate and pushing the lettuce around. Helena felt a little mean for bringing him up.

"How's that going?" Candace asked.

"Well, we're taking it slowly. I invited him to the art exhibit I'm having next week at the shop, and he invited me to a polo match that he's participating in. He apologized for the other-woman thing. He's trying to show me he's changed."

"Relationships take work, but make sure you are both doing it."

"We are. I'm not going to just fall for him saying things are different."

"Glad to hear that," Helena said.

"Sounds like y'all are making a good second start," Candace said.

But to Helena it sounded like her sister was playing a careful game. Helena knew how hard it was to manage a man when there were variables out of her control. In her case, it was whatever the hell Malcolm was up to; in Hadley's, maybe a baby.

"Thanks, Mom. I think so too," Hadley said. "Helena, are you and Malcolm going to Bianca's baby shower on Saturday?"

"We plan to," she said, but who knew if her fiancé was going to be reliable? She needed to sit him down and force him to tell her what was going on, but the truth was, she was starting to think he'd changed his mind about marrying her and a part of her didn't want to know.

Of course, she didn't want to get left at the altar either. She was nervous about what it was that was taking up so much of his time and money and would eventually have to confront him about it.

"Good. I was going to send a present and my regrets, but since you're going, I think I'll attend."

The conversation drifted to Kinley Caruthers who rumor had it might have let her husband, Nate, out of the doghouse after he bought their four-year-old Penny a four-wheeler and let her sit on his lap and drive it around the yard.

Helena laughed but her heart was heavy. All she wanted was to be like Bianca or Kinley, starting a life with the man she loved, not sitting over here like Nancy Drew trying to solve the mystery of what was going on with him.

When Mauricio got home from work that evening, Alec was waiting in his apartment. His twin brother looked harried and not his usual self. Mauricio undid his tie as he walked through the living room where Alec was sprawled on the couch watching ESPN.

"Hope you don't mind if I crash here," Alec said. "I would have called first, but I came from the airport."

"I don't mind," Mo said. "What's up?"

"Today is the release of the latest update," Alec said. "This time I might have bitten off more than I could chew."

Alec was a software genius who wrote code that handled everything you could imagine. His house in the Five Families subdivision was completely automated. But each time his company had a new release, Alec, who was normally the most confident of guys, was nervous.

"Is it a tequila or beer night?"

"Tequila," Alec said. "But I promised to take Benito so that Bianca and Derek could go to their prenatal class, so neither."

His brother kept flipping between all the sports channels, finally stopping on one that showed the Formula One rankings. Alec turned up the volume as they both turned their attention to the stats. Inigo was in the top five. Not surprising since he was a determined competitor who'd been driving since he was a teenager.

When the rankings story was over, Alec turned the volume down. He knew that Alec needed to be distracted. Otherwise, he'd just sit here worrying about the reaction to his latest release, which would be happening on the West Coast this evening at four o'clock…so any minute now.

"I'll drive. Let's get Beni and go play some polo. Text Diego and tell him to meet us there," Mauricio said.

"I'm not sure I'm up for—"

"You're not. So, I'm going to suggest you play on Diego's team," Mo said with a wink. He and Alec had never been those twins who felt each other's exact emotions, but they were empathetic with each other. Both of them knew when the other one was dealing with something bigger than normal.

"Ha. Okay. You're right. Sitting here stewing isn't going to help," Alec said. "Which makes me wonder how you knew that. You're not normally the intuitive twin."

He shrugged at his brother. What could he say? He could relate to needing a distraction. He'd been keeping as busy as he could until Hadley let him know if she was pregnant or not. Then it occurred to him that he hadn't told anyone about it. But what would he say to them if she wasn't?

"What is it?" Alec said. "I've been having weird dreams again."

Damn.

The one thing that had always linked them was their dreams. Neither of them had ever been comfortable talking about it to their other brothers.

"Hadley might be pregnant," he said. "We won't know until she has a chance to go get a test."

"Wow. Okay, I wasn't expecting that. Do I need to give you the protection talk? I thought Dad covered it pretty well when he said no one likes using a condom but always use one."

Mauricio shoved his hands in his pockets and shook his head. "I did. It broke."

"Well, hell," Alec said.

"Exactly. And we aren't really in a place that I can say we're a couple, which I know isn't good. Why do things like this always happen with Hadley?"

Alec studied him for a long moment. "We never talked about your breakup. I mean, I know the details of what happened...her walking in on you with Marnie. But what I mean is how it affected you. I never understood why you both broke up the first time."

Mauricio ran a hand through his hair. "I'll tell you while we go pick Benito up. If we're late, Bianca won't be very happy with us."

"True," Alec said. "I'll drive. I have the prototype of an electronic sports car that I designed the engine for."

"That's yours? I saw it in the garage. Me likey."

"Me too. They are going to go into production in the fall. Want me to put you down for one?"

"Hell, yeah," Mo said. They took the private elevator to the garage and Alec got behind the wheel. For a few moments, they listened to the radio and Mauricio thought his brother had forgotten about their conversation.

"So what happened with her?" Alec asked when they were headed toward the Five Families subdivision.

Mauricio took a deep breath. "I want to say I don't know, but the truth is, I think I started to take her for granted. You know Hadley. She looks nice all the time, she scheduled all of our social events, she has a good career and she made our place really comfortable. And I thought that she'd keep doing all of that and I'd just be me."

Just be me. Like he was such a prize that she'd keep on giving her all to a man who wasn't really checked in to the relationship.

"She just got tired of asking me to be a part of the couple and said we needed a break. Instead of seeing it as a wake-up call, I thought it was my chance to be a single guy until she came to her senses and returned to me."

"Damn. I know I'm the smart one, but I never thought of you as dumb until you said that," Alec said.

"I know. I hate that part of myself," Mo admitted. "But you know me. I always think I'm God's gift."

"You're being too hard on yourself. I'm sure there is more to it than what you've said. But now that you know what's wrong, you can fix it," Alec said. "Don't discount yourself, Mo. I know you, and you've always adapted when you need to. If you want Hadley back for good, you'll figure it out."

He hoped so. Because as he'd been vocalizing what had gone wrong, he realized that he wasn't the same man he'd been eighteen months ago when she'd left. He'd changed. And partying and his image as a player used to seem so important weren't compared to having Hadley in his life.

Ten

Hadley got back from Houston later than she expected thanks to the traffic, which was no one's fault but her own thanks to her dawdling at one of the large shopping centers on the outskirts. At least she had the test; there was no more putting it off. She could take it and find out the results. But Mauricio wanted to be there when she did. She picked up her phone and sent him a text.

Back from H. Do you still want to come over when I take it?

He responded right away.

Yes. I can't be there until after nine.

Okay. Text me when you are on the way.

She put the test on the counter in the bathroom and walked away from it. It was six o'clock. That meant she had three hours to kill. Helena was working late since their mom had hijacked her workday earlier.

She texted Zuri and Josie to see if either of them wanted to meet for dinner or go to the gym.

She heard back from Josie first.

Dinner. I need to talk.

Then Zuri replied.

Gym? Who are you kidding? We aren't the gym type.

Hadley laughed as she typed.

Wanted to give you options. So where for dinner? I think I can get a table at Hinckleman's on short notice.

Her friends thought the farm-to-table restaurant was the perfect choice, so she texted the head chef who was a friend of hers and got them a table. Then she touched up her makeup and headed out. Hinckleman's was near the highway, which made it more convenient for the ranchers and farmers who didn't always like coming into town for dinner.

Josie was already seated in a highbacked booth when Hadley arrived.

"What's up?" she asked after they exchanged pleasantries.

"Z said if we talked without her, she'd shoot me. And you know, I think I believe her," Josie said.

"That's right. I did," Zuri said as she slid into the booth next to Hadley, hugging her and reaching across the table to squeeze Josie's hand. "Now spill. Is it about Manu? It has to be."

Hadley thought it was about the football coach, as well. Of all of them, Josie was the most cautious when it came to men and dating. Her mother had remarked one time that it was no doubt due to all the books that Josie read. They gave her higher standards when it came to the men she wanted to date.

"Yes, it is. He asked me to go with him to the Hall of Fame dinner this year. His team is getting an award," Josie said.

"I think there is only one answer and that's hell, yes," Zuri said with a toss of her head. As her long silky black hair swirled around her, the fragrance of roses wafted toward Hadley.

"No, there isn't. We've all seen what famous football players' wives and girlfriends look like and I don't fit the mold," Josie said.

The waitress arrived and they all ordered a glass of wine and their entrées. When she left, Josie didn't say anything.

"Okay, so do you want to go?" Hadley asked, realizing how grateful she was to have her good friends here tonight. When she'd moved to Manhattan, she lost touch with them, and when she came back, and everything had happened with Mauricio, she hadn't wanted to reach out with a problem. But they had both come to her when they'd realized she was back in town. It made her realize how lucky she was to have these women as friends.

"I think I do," she said. "It's an important night for him and I want to help him celebrate, but I don't want him to see me with other women and…"

"And what?" Zuri asked. "Because, girl, I know you're not trying to say that he might reconsider. That's an insult to you and to him."

"Don't you think I know that? I feel stupid even thinking that I might not be able to fit in with that group. I mean, I know that Ferrin is going to be there and she's super sweet and nice."

Ferrin Caruthers was the wife of former NFL bad boy Hunter Caruthers—Mo's brother-in-law. Hunter and Manu used to be teammates.

"Then it's not about who's going to be there, is it?" Hadley asked. "It's you. You're afraid that if you go, you're not going to be able to keep things casual with him."

Josie nibbled on her bottom lip. "I think you're right. I mean, we've both been very careful at school and it's not like dating is prohibited between teachers. But what if it doesn't work out?"

"What if it does?" Zuri asked. "You're one of the most solid people I know. You really know what you want and how to go after it."

"I do?" Josie said.

Hadley knew exactly how her friend felt. Once emotions were involved, it was harder to trust that she was making a smart decision. "Definitely. We've known each other since Brownies. Z and I know you better than you know yourself at times. I think you're hesitating because once you commit to this, you'll be risking your heart."

Wow. It was so much easier to see it from the outside. But this was why she'd been reluctant to take the pregnancy test. She hadn't realized it until this moment. Taking the test meant things between Mauricio and her would change—one way or the other—and she wasn't completely sure she was ready for that.

"I agree," Zuri said. "When did Hadley get so smart?"

"When she got her heart broken," Josie said. "That's wisdom tempered by experience."

"Yes, it is. No reason y'all can't benefit from my mistakes," she said, but she wasn't sure she'd classify her time with Mo as a mistake.

"No reason at all. But I don't think it was all bad for you," Zuri said. "I mean, I'm pretty sure you guys are moving forward now, right?"

"Maybe," Hadley said. She wanted to see what happened tonight before she committed in front of her friends. "Josie, are you going to go to the awards dinner?"

The waitress dropped off their wine and some pimento cheese and crackers before Josie answered.

"Yes, I think I am."

After Alec had dropped him back off at his penthouse, Mauricio almost texted Hadley using the lateness of the hour as an excuse not to stop by. But of course, that wasn't an option.

He'd changed.

Alec's launch had gone very well, which hadn't surprised any of them, and they'd ended up at their parents' house celebrating the good news. Mo felt better than he had in a long time. The breakup with Hadley had unmoored him, shaken the very foundations of his life. He'd been drifting for a while, even though he was keeping his business on top of the real estate market, working with his charities. And then last fall, he'd given into the jealousy and anger that came from seeing Hadley moving on, while he was stuck.

But tonight, he saw the seeds of his future, the man he was regardless of whether or not Hadley was pregnant. And that made him feel content. Which was something that had eluded him for way too long.

He was parked behind the retail shops where the entrance to Hadley's loft was located. He was sitting there in his Bugatti, letting the engine run, trying to decide if he should text first or just go up, when his phone pinged.

When are you going to be here?

I'm here. Was just fixing to text you.

Come on up, I'll buzz the door.

He got out of the car and walked to the security door Alec had designed. It had a camera and intercom for visitors, but for residents it had a retinal scan in case they forgot their key.

The door buzzed and unlocked as soon as he was in sight of the camera, which meant she'd been watching for him.

He took the elevator up to the residential area. There were only six loft apartments in the building. He was still hoping to develop another plot of land opposite this one with a similar structure. Hadley owned the adjoining land, so maybe that was a project they could work on together.

He knocked on her door when he got to it and she opened it, stepping back for him to enter. He realized she was in an odd mood. And he totally got it. He wasn't too sure what he wanted the outcome of the test to be.

"How was your day?" he asked, trying to be chill.

"Okay. I slept through my alarm. My mom thought that I was dead and came over here banging on the door to wake me up," Hadley said. "But otherwise not bad."

He had to laugh at that. "Moms always think the worst."

"They really do. I pointed out that I'm pretty tough, but she said she can't help panicking."

"I get it. I think I'd probably react the same if I couldn't get in touch with you. You're usually so reliable."

"That's me," she said. "Reliable."

There was a sadness… Maybe that wasn't the right word, but there was something in the way she said it that made him realize she was in a funk.

"Hey, there's nothing wrong with being reliable. I like that about you. In fact, it's probably one of the things that I took for granted when we were together. Like because you were solid I didn't need to be. I'm sorry about that."

She went into her living room area and took a seat in the large armchair, crossing her legs underneath her. He sat down on the matching couch. Her apartment was a hodge-podge of furniture that seemed to come from one of those furniture places that sold pieces by the room. It was nice, but it wasn't Hadley with her artsy eclectic taste.

"Thank you for apologizing for that," she said after a minute. "I think I sort of wanted us to be this picture-perfect couple too, so I was forcing both of us into things that weren't really us."

He didn't know about that, but just nodded. "So…"

"I guess I should just go do it," she said.

"If you want to," he said. "Do you want to talk first?"

"I don't know," she said at last. "I mean, chances are really slim that I'll be pregnant, you know?"

"I do. But that hasn't stopped me from thinking about a baby with you, darling," he admitted.

"And what do you think?"

"I keep coming back to the fact that I have rotten timing when it comes to you," he said. "I don't want anything to complicate this new thing you and I have going."

She nodded. "Me neither."

"So whatever happens, I don't want to go back to living separate lives," he said.

"Okay. Whatever happens, we won't," she agreed. "Let me go pee on the stick now. I'll let you know when it's done."

When she stood up, he did, as well. Reaching out to catch her hand, he drew her into his arms, wrapping them around her until they were pressed together. He rubbed his hands down her back and then leaned down to kiss her long and slow, because this was a moment that they'd never have again. One where they were on the cusp. He wanted to remember it forever.

She returned his kiss, her hands tunneling through his hair and holding his head so that she could deepen the embrace as she came up on tiptoe. Then slowly she pulled back and stepped away.

He watched her walk toward the large screens that concealed her bedroom and her bathroom. He followed her after a minute, sitting down on her bed, feeling more awkward than he had before. At least the last time they'd thought she might be pregnant, they'd been living together and thought they had a future together.

This time was so different. They already knew they could screw up a relationship and that made it harder to believe they could make it work this time.

She stared at the negative result for too long. The ache in her gut was a mix of relief and regret. Bittersweet, like so many things with Mauricio. Well, at least it would be much easier on both of them to not have to figure out a baby in the midst of everything.

When she opened the bathroom door, he took one look at her face and stood up, coming over to her.

"No?"

"Yeah," she said, feeling an odd burn of tears at the back of her eyes. She blinked a few times to keep them from falling. It wasn't as if she wanted to be pregnant. Really. Or was it?

"Well, hell," Mo said. "I'm not as relieved as I thought I'd be."

She nodded. She wasn't sure what she felt. He pulled her into his arms, hugging her close. She hugged him back and realized that there was something solid about Mauricio. She felt like she could count on him and that was new. There was so much familiar between them but this new thing, well, it made her realize how much he'd changed.

"Obviously, this was for the best," he said, but it felt like…well, like they'd missed a shot at having an excuse to get back together. Not just to be friends like she'd suggested, but as a real couple.

He stood back, realizing that when it came to Hadley, he always hesitated. And maybe that was why they'd always been on again, off again.

"I'm going to lay it on the line, Hadley," he started, and she looked up at him with one of those expressions that always kept him guessing about what she was really thinking.

"Okay."

"I'm disappointed, but more because if you'd been pregnant, I'd have had a reason to call you and be with you and I don't think we would need an excuse to be together. I want to start over. I know I screwed up—"

"You weren't the only one," she said.

"Either way, I want a second chance. A real one. Not one where we just try to become friends, but the whole shebang," he said.

She didn't say anything but just stood there with her arms around her waist. In a pair of faded jeans and a T-shirt, she looked lost and confused to him.

Damn.

Maybe his timing was off again. Should he have kept quiet and then…what? He wasn't subtle. He never had been. He was blunt and quick to say what was on his mind.

"Sorry if that isn't what you want to hear, but I'm tired of pretending I don't want you. I was doing an okay job of it until we slept together, and that night made me realize what was important…and it's you."

She nodded.

"Stop nodding and say something. Tell me to go to hell or you need time to think or you're relieved that you're not—"

She closed the distance between them and put her fingers over his lips to stop him from talking. "Enough options. I'm sad because a baby would have been something special we had between us, even if we never figure out how to make a relationship work. I'm confused because part of me wants what you want but another part of me isn't sure we can do it. And because I'm already sad that makes me more hesitant."

He kissed her fingers before drawing her hand into his and leading her over to the bed. He sat on the edge and drew her down on his lap. She easily sat on it and he held her like she was his. And for a moment everything was clear to him.

It was just Hadley and him. That was all he needed in this moment. It might change at some other time but right now it was all about her.

She cuddled closer to him and he held her tight. There was nothing sexual in the moment and she wasn't making him laugh or doing anything to make him feel like a man, but he didn't need that. He simply needed to be here for her and he knew that he was.

He finally knew what she needed from him.

He was realistic enough to know this moment wasn't going to last forever but right now with her in his arms, it was enough.

He was enough.

And that tight knot that he'd felt lately when he was around Hadley completely melted away. He just held her close, rubbing his hand up and down her back. She rested her head right over his heart and he knew that this was what he wanted.

He wanted to find a way to do this.

To be what she needed because it made something inside of him that had always been empty feel sort of full. Not like that aching knot that he usually carried around.

Eventually they ended up lying back on the bed, her cuddled against his side, and realized that she was spent. He used his smartwatch to turn on some music, the soundtrack from an old movie that she liked, and held her until she went to sleep.

As he watched over her, he knew that Hadley's not being pregnant was probably about the best damned thing to ever happen because now he had a chance to do things right this time. To woo her as a man and not as a frat boy. And that was exactly what he was going to do.

He could be subtle. It would be hard, but he would do it. For her.

And for him. Because the old Mo had been out of control and it was time to grow up and start adulting for real.

Eleven

One week later, Hadley walked into the Jaqs Veerland Bridal Studio just off Main Street fifteen minutes before she was due to meet her mother and Kinley. She wanted to apologize to Kinley for her mother's autocratic behavior and hang out for a bit before they got down to business.

"Hello?" she called out. The door was open and some soothing Mozart was playing in the background. Hadley drifted over to the portraits of brides and bridal parties that hung on the wall. She recognized a lot of the famous A-list clients but also the locals. Ferrin Caruthers looked absolutely stunning in her simple and elegant Givenchy dress, which had caused a stir when she'd worn it at her wedding. It was all anyone had been able to talk about around town.

She glanced around. It was odd that Kinley hadn't come out to welcome her. The shop usually had an assistant during busy times, but it felt like it was completely abandoned.

Hadley moved toward the private hallway that led to the offices and heard the sound of someone throwing up.

She ran down the hall, stopping at the open bathroom door just as Kinley stood up and groaned.

"You okay?"

Kinley nodded and went to the sink to rinse her mouth out and wipe her face. Hadley handed her one of the monogramed towels that was in the handbasket and then stood back while Kinley composed herself.

"Please don't mention this to anyone," Kinley said when she turned around.

"I won't… I'm guessing you're pregnant?"

"Yes. Nate has been on me to have another kid and even got Penny in on it. At first I was hesitant because of our history, you know?" Kinley said as she opened one of the drawers in the cabinet next to the porcelain washbasin, took out a cosmetic bag and touched up her makeup. Kinley and Nate had first met on a wild weekend in Vegas. After he'd gone back home she found out she was pregnant, and he didn't find out until she came back to Cole's Hill for her job—with the child.

"I do know," Hadley said, thinking about Mo and her, and how she'd sort of wanted a baby but was also very relieved when she found out she wasn't pregnant. "How did you handle it the first time on your own? I mean that had to have been hard."

"I had no choice. And this time I wanted it to be perfect."

"Isn't it?"

"Well, Penny is going through a new phase and really testing our temper. Nate's trying to be the doting daddy, but he also doesn't want us to raise a brat. In the middle of all this, I went off the Pill without telling him because I thought it'd be a nice surprise, but then last night in bed he let it drop that he thought it was good we only had one kid because they're a lot of work..."

Hadley walked over and hugged her friend. "Worst timing ever. Men are so good at that."

Kinley nodded. "They are. The thing is, I know it's a phase and he'll be back to pestering me about having another one in a week or something, but it did drive home how much work it is and it never seems to get easier. I mean, I thought once Penny could walk and pee by herself I had the motherhood thing in the bag, but it's always something new."

Hadley hadn't even considered any of the things that Kinley was talking about when she'd thought about being pregnant and having a child. She'd thought it might bring her and Mo closer but now it sounded like that might not be the case.

"I had no idea parenting was that hard," Hadley said.

"It's also the best damned thing that ever happened to me. I was a straight up mess before I had Penny and I'd probably still be partying and moving from job to job if I didn't have her. But enough about me. Why are you here early?"

Hadley took a deep breath and looked into the mirror to make sure she didn't have lipstick on her teeth. "I came early to apologize for my mom. She's going to be difficult today."

"It's not like I haven't experienced mothers of the bride before," Kinley said. "I can handle her. My mother might not be Texas-raised but she knew enough about Southern charm to teach me how to deal with the good women of Cole's Hill."

Hadley shook her head. "You're going to need all that learning today. She called your boss on Monday and wants to conference her in on this meeting."

Kinley just smiled as both women left the bathroom and went down the hall to the bridal showroom. "Oh, I know about that. Jaqs is going to be at the meeting this morning. I asked her to come."

Hadley couldn't help but laugh at that. Kinley did indeed know how to handle the women of Cole's Hill. Marrying into one of the Five Families meant she had to deal with them on a daily basis. Her family weren't part of the original five who founded the town but her mom was part of Cole's Hill society so she knew all about the importance the townspeople placed on status.

"Nicely played," Hadley said.

"Like you mentioned, I have to be able to hold my own and I knew she was going to demand to speak to my boss so I saved her the hassle. Also, Jaqs gets off on going toe-to-toe with the *tough cases* as she calls them. Between the two of us, we will make sure she gets everything she wants from the meeting."

Hadley was impressed that her friend was ready to do whatever it took, but then she guessed that was why Kinley and Jaqs were so successful. "I way underestimated you."

"Happens all the time," Kinley said with a wink. "Want a coffee while you wait? Jaqs ordered a new machine and I'm dying for someone to try it out since I'm not having caffeine while I'm preggers."

"Sure."

Hadley watched her friend as she left the showroom and went to make the coffee. Today had been a revelation on a couple of levels. She realized that when she was at home, she fell back into the behavior of a good Cole's Hill daughter. Talking to Kinley this morning had reminded her that she had been also a total badass when she was in Manhattan and she needed to find a way to blend those two personas.

* * *

Mauricio started the morning with a run and then headed into the office. When he got there, he was surprised to see Malcolm waiting by the front door. He was kind of slouched over and leaning against the building. When he got closer, it was plain to see his friend was sleeping standing up.

He looked like a mess but didn't smell of booze.

"Malcolm."

His friend's head lolled to one side, and when he looked up, Mauricio could see his eyes were bloodshot and there was a cut on his cheekbone.

"Dude, are you okay?"

"Yeah…"

Then Malcolm shook his head as he stood up. "Fuck. I'm not. I thought I could handle this but everything is spiraling out of control."

Mauricio squeezed his friend's shoulder. "Let's get out of here. You need breakfast and a shower and then we can talk and figure this out."

For a split second it looked like Malcolm was going to argue but he just conceded, showing none of his usual determined spirit. That worried Mauricio. He led him to his sports car, and once Malcolm was seated, he drove toward Arbol Verde. His brother Diego lived there but he was in London with his wife for the next few weeks, and Mauricio had the feeling that getting out of town would be good for Malcolm.

His friend drifted off as Mauricio drove to the ranch. When they arrived, he parked the car, texted his assistant and told him that he and Malcolm were taking the day off, and then woke his friend and directed him to the guesthouse where he'd be able to shower and change into some clean clothes.

Diego's housekeeper was visiting her family in Dallas

while he was gone, so Mo had the place to himself as he went to make breakfast in the main ranch house. He texted Diego to let him know he'd come out to check on the place, something that Mo had promised to do, and that he and Malcolm were going to take a couple of horses for a ride.

His brother called instead of texting back.

"What's up? Why are you at my place on a workday? Is anything wrong?" Diego asked in that spitfire way of his.

"Mal is in a bad place. I figured riding would help him sort some stuff out. Otherwise, things are fine here," Mauricio said. "How's London?"

"Cold and wet," Diego said. "But Pippa is launching her new product line of Classic H jewelry for House of Hamilton on Friday and she's so excited that the weather doesn't matter."

"Of course, it doesn't. When your woman is happy, all is right in the world," Mauricio said. He wished that he'd learned that lesson a bit sooner. Maybe then he wouldn't have to work so hard to get Hadley back.

"That sounds very mature coming from you. Are you back with Hadley?" Diego asked.

"We're still working that out," he said. "But I'm hopeful this time I won't screw it up."

"You're too hard on yourself," Diego said. "Sure, you've had some issues, but you always owned them."

He tried. But there had been times in the past when he felt like all he did was fail. "Thank you for saying that."

"That's what big brothers are for," Diego said. "I'll be home this weekend for the polo match. I'd like to make this an annual event."

"I've been doing some work around that," Mauricio said, then caught his brother up on the corporate sponsors he'd reached out to. A lot of them he worked with in conjunction with his housing charity work. Diego was impressed and Mo, who'd always been happy being the hothead, realized that he liked getting attention for doing something that was good. He liked not always being the brother who was in hot water. He thought that was Hadley's influence and he realized how much she was changing him...or maybe helping him to change. He doubted she'd even realize just how much she had.

"See you on Friday, Mo," Diego said. "Love ya."

"Love ya too," he said ending the call as Mal walked into the breakfast room.

His friend still looked like crap but his eyes were clearer.

"Are you using?" Mo asked without preamble.

It was the only thing he could think of that could explain how messed up Mal looked and the money that had disappeared from the wedding account he and Helena had set up.

"No. I'm not. Why do you think that?"

"You look like shit, you still haven't paid back your wedding account, your fiancée is freaked and you aren't manning up. Something is definitely up with you. And I'm not about to go all Dr. Phil but you need to fess up and get straight."

Mal turned one of the breakfast chairs around and straddled it. He put his elbows on the ladderback and his head in his hands. "God, when you say it like that I can see how out of control my life has gotten."

"Yes, it has. So what the hell is going on?"

Mal rubbed the back of his neck but still wouldn't look Mo in the eyes. He honestly feared for his friend. This wasn't the man he'd known. This person was evasive and there was something, almost a desperation to him.

"I can't..."

"Just say it. You know I'm going to find out," Mauricio said. "You were the one who found me at the Bull Pit and told me if I got into one more fight, Sheriff Justiss was going to put me in jail on a thirty-day hold. You said *don't screw your life up*."

"I did say that," Mal said, looking him in the eye for the first time in weeks. "I guess it's easier to give advice when you see your best friend crash and burn than to take it yourself."

"Definitely. I thought drinking and fighting was the way to get over Hadley, but it wasn't. And I don't even know what demon you're battling."

He put a mug of black coffee and a plate of food in front of his friend before sitting down across from him.

"It sounds stupid when I say it out loud," Mal said.

"Fair enough, since you've been acting like an ass."

His friend gave him a faint smile. "I started thinking about the future. My in-laws have a really nice life and I knew I had to provide at least that level of comfort for Helena. And you know me. I work hard, but I play hard too."

"Nothing wrong with that. Helena loves you, not your money."

"You think?"

"Of course! It's an insult to Helena and yourself if you think otherwise. If she wanted a trust-fund man, she could have found one. She loves you."

Mal rubbed the back of his neck. "Well, I had a line on a sure-thing bet that would double our wedding fund and give her the extras she'd been scrimping on so I took the money and placed the bet…"

"And lost," Mauricio said. "Who did you gamble with?"

"No one you know. Anyway, I've been working extra hard to try to make back the money, but we saved for two years to afford our wedding and I lost the money in one night… I mean, if I lost it in one night—"

"No. Stop. You're never going to win it back like that. Damn. Why didn't you come to me?"

"Why would I? This is my problem," Mal said.

"Well, screw you too. I thought we were friends."

"Sorry, Mo. I didn't think of it that way. I just was damned mad at myself. I don't know how to get out of this. I've been working odd jobs around the area—not in Cole's Hill—to try to make up the money. I told Helena I'd get it back in our wedding account before we had to make all the payments, but I'm not sure I can," Malcolm said, pushing his plate away. He stood up and walked over to the French doors, putting his hands on his hips and staring out at the rolling hills.

"I'll help you. Alec is really good at investing and together the three of us can figure out a way that doesn't involve gambling to get your money back."

"Really?"

"Hell, yes. But you have to do something first," Mauricio said.

"What?"

"Come clean with Helena. She's freaked out, and I think only by being honest will you be able to fix this. She needs to know what's in your head and your heart."

"I thought you weren't going to go all Dr. Phil," Malcolm said wryly.

"I can't help it. I'm the wisest of our group."

"You keep telling yourself that," Malcolm said with a bit of humor in his voice.

Mo felt like he was seeing his old friend come through for the first time since the engagement party.

Mal reached over and awkwardly hugged him. "Thank you."

"No problem. You call Helena. I'm going to text Alec and maybe we can get something going with your investments."

Thirty minutes later Helena was at the Arbol Verde. Mauricio stayed in the house while his friends went for a horseback ride.

Helena had been surprised to get the call from Malcolm. He hadn't been home in two days and she hadn't slept in that time. She was worried, angry and edgy. Her mom was in a power play with Jaqs Veerland, and honestly at this point she wasn't sure she even wanted to get married. But there was no way she was backing out of the wedding of the year unless she was sure that Malcolm was truly gone.

So this call… Well, it was exactly what she'd been both hoping for and dreading. Whatever was going on with him, it sounded like he was going to come clean. She hoped it wasn't another woman. She knew she wouldn't be able to handle that. Or at least she thought she wouldn't.

"You haven't said a word since we left the barn," Malcolm said.

She wasn't going to lie, she was afraid to start this conversation. She shook her head. She was the strong sister, the one everyone could pile stuff on and she'd deal with it, but here she was riding next to Mal, pretending he didn't look like hell. None of it made sense. The knot in her gut got tighter.

"I don't know what to say. I'm scared," she said, pushing her sunglasses up on her head and glancing over at him. He had on a straw cowboy hat and dark glasses so his face was pretty much hidden from her. But she'd seen his bloodshot eyes earlier.

"I'm sorry, Hel. I never meant to do this to you," he said.

"What have you done? I mean, I know the money is missing. Is it gone? What did you do with it?" she asked.

He pulled his horse to a stop and dismounted. She did the same. The horses at Arbol Verde were trained to stay when their leads were on the ground so she dropped them and went over to him.

Suddenly all the anger she'd been pushing down since she'd first seen that low balance in their account exploded and she couldn't help it—she shoved him hard on the shoulder. "What the hell are you doing? If you don't want to get married, just say that. Don't dick around and screw up everything so I'm the one who has to be the adult and break things off. You were never a douchebag before."

He stood there and let her rant at him, which made her stop. She hated losing her cool, so she stepped back, wrapping her arms around her waist, and just waited.

"I'm sorry. That wasn't ladylike."

"I deserve it," he said. "The truth is, I know I'm not the man your family wishes you'd fallen for. I can't keep you in the same style as your parents. I saw a chance to change that, to give you what you needed and it didn't work out."

"What I needed? Let's deal with that BS first. When have I ever said I needed more than you?" she asked. She wasn't going to be able to keep her cool, especially if he was trying to play this like it was all her fault.

"Never. You've never made me feel like I wasn't enough. But you are… Well, you are my heart, Helena, and I want to give you the world, but I can't. And I wanted more for you and for me. For us," he said.

Damn.

Of course, he wasn't making it about her. Malcolm always had big dreams and a big heart, which was why she'd fallen for him. "I don't need more. We don't. What did you do?"

He sighed, shoving his hands through his hair, which knocked the cowboy hat to the ground. They both ignored it.

"I took our money and placed a very large bet on a sure

thing and lost it all," he said. "I've been trying to get the money back—"

"By gambling?"

"No. Not that. I don't have a large enough stake to make it work," he said. "I've been doing odd jobs all over the county, working nights to try to get some of it back."

"Malcolm, you should have said."

"I couldn't. I felt dumb enough that I lost all of our wedding money and then you had to go to your parents, which I know you didn't want to do," he said. "And I made the mess so I had to fix it."

She walked over to him and wrapped her arms around him. He hugged her close and the tension in her stomach started to disappear. "We can fix this. We're partners for life, Mal. We can do this together. The money doesn't matter as long as we are together."

"I love you," Malcolm said.

"I love you too."

He told her about reaching out to Mauricio and how they had a plan to consult with Alec and invest the money to rebuild the funds from the wedding account. Helena offered her advice, but she knew that Alec was better with investments than she was. She felt like they were on the right track. She knew that all couples had tough times and maybe they were having theirs now so that they'd be stronger once they were married.

Twelve

When Hadley arrived at the large Five Families mansion where Mo's parents lived, she stood outside for a moment and reflected. Going to a polo match brought back so many memories of her relationship with Mauricio. Now his mother was hosting a brunch before the game and, of course, all of the extended Velasquez family would be there. Hadley wondered if she was really doing this, if she was really going to jump back into a life with him.

But the last few weeks had been...well, what she'd always hoped things could be between them. While there were still some areas that neither of them seemed to want to delve into, she did feel that this time they were making changes that would make them stronger as a couple.

"Nervous?" Mo asked, coming up beside her and putting his hand on the small of her back. A shiver went down her spine, making her wish they'd made love one more time before they came here.

"Yes. Your mom never thought I was good enough

for you, and when we broke up, she probably was very happy."

Mo leaned down and kissed her. It was one of those deep passionate kisses of his that made her feel like she was going to melt into a puddle at his feet. This was exactly why she'd been struggling to believe that they were real. This incendiary passion that always exploded between them felt like an addiction, one that would leave her strung out if she couldn't get her daily hit of him. Actually, she knew what that felt like.

The stakes were higher this time. She knew that if they couldn't make this work, he'd be gone from her life forever. They were both too smart to keep hitting their heads against the wall.

"She thought *I* wasn't good enough for *you*," he corrected, as he lifted his head and brushed a strand of hair behind her ear. "She knew you'd hurt me when you finally realized it."

She shook her head. "Did I hurt you?"

"I got drunk for three months and then started fights with every guy you tried to date… What do you think?"

"That you don't like to lose," she admitted.

He shook his head. Wrapping both arms around her, he pulled her close in a tight bear hug and leaned down, whispering into her ear, "I never thought I could hurt like I did when we were apart, darling. I never want to feel that way again."

She hugged him back, twisting her head so that she could rest her cheek on his shoulder. "Me neither."

"Yo, bro, maybe save the making out for when you're alone. Mom definitely doesn't approve of PDA."

Hadley lifted her head and stepped back as Alec came up the walk.

Mo shot him the bird, then draped his arm around Hadley's shoulder and turned to walk toward the front door with his twin following them. Her nerves were gone as she entered the house, giving her handbag to the Velasquez family butler and following Mo into the drawing room where they were announced.

Mrs. Velasquez was deep in conversation with her group of friends. Diego called Mauricio over to the group of men Hadley recognized from pictures on the polo club walls. These were the other investors in the new development, some of them world famous players and horse breeders.

She excused herself, knowing that she didn't want to be the only woman in a group of men talking about horses, and made her way down the hall toward the living room. The door to the hall bathroom opened as she walked by and Bianca stepped out with her young son, Benito. He was dressed in jodhpurs, riding boots and a polo shirt. He smiled when he saw her.

"*Buenos días*, Hadley."

"Hiya, Benito. Are you riding today?"

"*Si*, during the… What's it called, Mama?"

"He is going to be riding with Diego during an exhibition," Bianca said. Bianca was several months pregnant and glowed with an inner beauty. But she also looked a bit tired.

"That sounds like fun. Want to tell me all about it?" she asked the little boy. She'd known him since he was born, and as he tucked his tiny hand into hers, she realized how intertwined her life and Mauricio's were and how much she'd missed his family.

She followed the pair back down the hall toward the backyard where the brunch had been set up. Everyone else had come out from the living room. She stood there to the side for a short time, just watching Mo with his family, and she couldn't help noticing that he seemed way more relaxed than he'd been in a long time.

When someone came up beside her, she glanced over to see it was his mother. "I didn't think you'd give him another chance."

"I… We…"

"It's okay. I know that love is complicated. I've been married to Mauricio's father for a long time and it still isn't easy. I'm glad to see you with him. He's different now. More relaxed with everyone. I like it."

"Me too," Hadley said.

"Come on, let's have a Texas Sunrise cocktail and join the men," Mrs. Velasquez said, and just like that Hadley felt like she was part of the family. Part of this group that she'd wanted to be a part of ever since she and Mo had first started dating. But she'd always been trying to be perfect, trying to prove to herself and to everyone else that she and Mauricio were the perfect couple. It had never been real, and had put distance between her and Mo's family.

As she followed his mother and joined him, she knew that this time Mauricio wasn't the only who was different. She was too. It was humbling to realize that she hadn't been as mature as she'd always thought she was.

When she got to Mo, he leaned down to kiss her cheek and whispered, "See, I told you she liked you."

She just laughed and shook her head.

Mauricio was tired by the time the charity polo match was over. But he knew that this was what he wanted. He was grateful that Malcolm had shown up for the game and had played well. Even Helena was there, standing next to Hadley in the viewing area and cheering them both on. He couldn't help but think that as the hashtags on Instagram always put it, he was living his best life in this moment.

That thought made him feel anxious, like a major screwup was just around the corner, and he knew that was because in the past he'd never been able to simply let himself be content. Part of it was that he'd always been hungry for more, trying to fill that emptiness deep inside of him with something, but never really finding the right thing.

Hadley... Well, he hoped she was it, but he knew it was dangerous to put that on her. The fact was he had to be content in himself before he could be totally committed to their relationship. If helping Malcolm deal with his own shit had shown him anything, it was that very fact.

Malcolm was running and trying to do something to impress his fiancée instead of realizing that he was enough for Helena.

Mauricio had to wonder if he was enough for Hadley. That was always the question, and it had never been answered between them. They both had spent a lot of time looking outside of the relationship, but that pregnancy scare had bonded them, made them a team. Since that moment he'd felt like...well, almost like they were a couple once more.

He rubbed the back of his neck. Okay, he was overthinking this. But he didn't want to lose her again. He didn't want to jeopardize the second chance he still wasn't sure he deserved but that he wanted more than anything.

He showered and changed and met up with Alec. "I forgot how much I like playing."

"I know. When we were kids I always resented being forced outside to ride and practice polo with Dad but now, I'm glad I was," his brother said.

"No one would have believed we were twins if you'd stayed inside... You were getting too nerdy."

"Nerdy? You wish, bro. Women like my smarts," Alec said.

"Is that what they tell you?"

"Trust me. I know they do."

"What do you know?" Hadley asked as they approached her.

"That brains are sexier than brawn," Alec said.

"Good thing Mo has both," she said with a wink that sent a shot of pure desire straight through him.

"You think so? He's not as smart as me."

"No one is as smart as you," she said.

"True," Alec said.

When Alec drifted over to the bar, Mo stood there in front of Hadley, realizing how much he wanted her to be right here by his side for the rest of his life. But he couldn't say that. They were taking it slow, not making the same mistakes again. But there was a part of him that was afraid to pump the brakes. He had that feeling...the one that told him to grab her with both hands before he lost her again.

"You were pretty impressive today," she said, after Alec had left.

No doubt his brother was going to try to woo some women. Alec had been different lately, and it was only now that Mauricio was noticing it because he'd been busy trying to keep Malcolm from imploding and losing the only woman he'd ever loved.

"Thanks. I try," he said wryly. "I noticed Helena was with you earlier. Where did she go?"

"To find Malcolm. She told me what you did for him. Well, for them. That was really nice," she said.

"Thanks," he replied. He watched as she looked around at the crowd.

"Being here is strange," she finally said. "I mean, this is the first time we are together with our families. Your mom was nice earlier. Helena commented that she was glad we were back together. But this involves our families and friends, and that scares me."

He pulled her into a quiet corner and turned so she was blocked from everyone's view by his body. He looked down into her brown eyes that always hid her real thoughts and feelings from him, but in this moment, he had no doubt what she was thinking. She was nervous just as he was, afraid that now that they'd gone public with this second chance that everyone would be second-guessing them.

"I don't care what anyone else thinks about us," he said, realizing that it was the truth. "You're the only one I care about."

"Mo."

She just said his name but there was so much in that one word. So much emotion. She was trying to make sense of this the same way he was.

"We got this, darling. I'm not going to let any outside pressure contribute to bringing us down. Not this time. If the past has taught me anything, it's that I'm much better with you by my side."

She tipped her head to the side, studying him in a way that made him realize how vulnerable he was to her. He stood a bit straighter, knowing he wanted her to see whatever it was she was searching for.

"I am too," she said at last.

She leaned up to wrap her hands around his shoulders and kissed him, and in that moment, he realized that if he lost her this time, he might not recover. That Hadley had somehow made her way into that empty part of his soul that he'd never realized had been waiting for her to fill it.

Helena left the others and went to find Malcolm. Mauricio had been a godsend in helping her figure out something was wrong with her fiancé. But she still wasn't sure if the problem was fully solved. Did Malcolm have a gambling problem?

Or was it what he'd told her—that he just wanted to give her a good life? As if they didn't already have one. After meeting him at Arbol Verde, she'd taken him back home with her and they'd had a good long talk. Today was the first time since the engagement party when she'd realized the money was missing that she felt like things were back to normal. But a doubt still nagged at the back of her mind.

Malcolm was talking to Diego and Alec, and she saw how relaxed he looked. It gave her hope that they were finally over the rough patch that had threatened their marriage.

"Hey, Hel, you okay?" Hadley asked as she slipped her arm around Helena's shoulders.

"Yeah, I think I am," she said, sneaking a cocktail off the tray of a passing waiter while her sister did the same. "Love is so dammed complicated, you know?"

Hadley nodded and then took a sip of her drink. "Wouldn't it be nice if it were like those stories we read as teenagers, and once the girl fell for the guy all the problems sort of magically disappeared?"

Helena had to smile at her sister. "Yes. Especially when I'm in the middle of planning a wedding. I used to think there was no difference in living together and being married, but honestly, knowing that we're going to be a couple for the rest of our lives is enough to freak me out sometimes. I get that it could do the same to Mal, but there are moments when I still can't figure out why he can't just…"

"It's okay," she said. "We're allowed to expect the men in our lives to step up when we need them to."

"Is that what's going on with you and Mauricio now? Is he stepping up?"

Hadley chewed her lower lip and looked across the room at him as he talked to his parents and someone Helena didn't know.

"Yes, I think so. We've been dating—well, hooking up for the last couple of weeks—and this is the first time we're out as a couple. It's scary and exciting. How can it be both of those things?"

"I don't know. But I get it. So, you've been hooking up?"

"He's the one guy I can't get over," Hadley admitted. "Even when I was dating other guys, I always compared them to Mo. I thought that was crazy until I realized that there was something between us that I couldn't explain and now… Well, I think we're both really committed this time."

Helena wrapped her arm around her sister's waist. "Good. I'm glad to hear that. I think you both needed to grow up a bit."

"Of course, you did," Hadley said, pulling away. "It's not like you and Mal are any more normal than we are."

"Don't I know it. Maybe we are all just bumbling along," Helena said.

"Yeah, I think we are," she said, then groaned. Helena followed her sister's gaze and noticed her mom was walking toward them.

"I thought Mom was going to lose it the other day before Jaqs walked into the meeting," Helena said.

"I did too. She really wants your wedding to be perfect," Hadley said. "I don't know if perfect is ever possible though."

"Of course it is," their mother said as she joined them. "You two look beautiful today."

"Thanks, Mom," Helena and Hadley said at the same time. Their mother seemed more chill today than she had been at the last meeting with the wedding planner, and maybe that was because Helena was more at ease, as well.

She hadn't wanted to tell her mom about any of her problems with Malcolm, but Helena knew she'd been broadcasting her worries by her behavior and it hadn't made the wedding planning sessions with Kinley any easier.

"Both of your men played well today," Mom said.

"They did," Helena said.

"Are you okay with me and Mo?" Hadley asked, sounding a little nervous.

Her mom reached out, tucking the strand of Hadley's hair that always wanted to be free back behind her ear. "If you are."

"Really?" Helena asked.

"Yes. You girls think I have some dream guy in mind for you both and the truth is, I do. I want a man you love, a man who loves you and treats you right. That's it. Malcolm makes you happier than I have ever seen you before, Helena. And for some reason, Hadley, Mauricio is the one guy you have never been able to walk away from."

Helena glanced at Hadley and easily read the surprise on her face. Their mom had been vocal and judgy about every guy they brought home in the past.

"What brought on this change?"

"Something your father said to me the other day," Mom said.

"What was that?" Helena asked. Daddy did have a way of making Mom see sense and not act like the queen of the world.

"Just that you girls wanted something different from life than I did. And he told me to stop trying to force my ideals on you," Mom said. "He had a point. I want you to have the man of your dreams, not the guy I imagine you'd like."

Helena reached over and hugged her mother and Hadley did the same. It made her realize that love was always complicated, even when it was between a parent and child.

Malcolm and Mauricio joined them, and for a moment Helena felt like everything was perfect in her world. She was happy with the man she loved, and her baby sister had finally figured out how to make things work with the man she wanted.

Thirteen

The text message from her client in New York wasn't one she was looking forward to reading. The client had exacting standards, and like her mom always said, if someone was paying for something, they wanted it to be the best. But Hadley felt like no matter what she did, it was never good enough for this client.

"You're frowning at your phone," Mauricio said.

"I know. It's an email from Jenner," she admitted to him. They were sprawled on her couch. Mo had put the Spurs game on and she was sitting with her feet in his lap, alternating between looking at her email and checking out bridesmaids dress designs on the private website Kinley had sent her.

"Isn't that job over?"

"I thought so, but this email means he probably needs one more tweak to his marketing campaign, which I designed."

"You'll never know if you don't open it up."

She stuck her tongue out at him. "You don't say."

"Open it. Whatever it is, not knowing is worse than whatever he wants. Plus, I don't want it to ruin our entire Sunday."

She leaned her head back against the couch and studied him. They had spent the entire weekend together and she was starting to get used to living with him. Everything was different this time. He was different. Before he would have been on his phone or taking calls or rushing out to meet a potential buyer. Instead, he'd been dedicated to making this time together quality time.

She tossed her phone on the coffee table and straddled his lap.

He pushed his hands up under her T-shirt and with the snap of his fingers undid the clasp of her bra.

"Do that thing you do," he said.

She quirked her head to the side. "What thing?"

"That thing where you take your bra off without removing your shirt," he said, his voice dropping a decibel and rumbling through her, turning her on.

She reached under the sleeves of her T-shirt, slowly drawing the bra strap down her left arm, taking her time as she pulled her hand from underneath the elastic. He was watching her as if she were performing some sort of complicated task and it made her smile. She loved seeing him so serious about her. She slowly drew the second strap down her other arm and then tugged her lace bra out of the sleeve and dropped it on his chest.

"Was it as good as you remembered?" she asked, arching one eyebrow at him.

"Better," he said, putting his hands on her waist and then pulling the hem of her T-shirt until it was tight against her body. "That's what I wanted to see."

She glanced down at her chest and saw that he'd made

it so her light colored T-shirt was pressed against her chest and her nipples were visible through it.

She put her hands on his shoulders, kneading them as she shifted on his thighs, pushing her shoulders back so that her breasts were thrust toward him.

"Are you just looking tonight?"

He made a sort of rumbling noise that didn't really answer her question, but then she felt his arm moving up behind her back, holding her as his head came forward. She felt the heat of his breath on her nipple before his mouth closed over it, sucking her through the fabric of her shirt.

She closed her eyes and let her head fall back, pushing her fingers into his hair and holding him. But then he lifted his head, moving to her other breast and doing the same thing to her other nipple.

The wet fabric clung to her skin and she shivered. He shifted back, undoing the button fly of his jeans, and she glanced down to see the firm ridge of his cock pressing against the fabric of his boxer briefs. She reached down to stroke him, and he smiled as she ran her hand up and down his length, feeling him grow underneath her touch.

"That's better," he said.

She leaned over him, using the hand that was in his hair to urge his head back as she brought her mouth down on his. He opened his lips under hers, his tongue thrusting up into her mouth, and she couldn't help but bite it. He turned her on like no one else, and though she'd started out with a slow burn in mind, there was no way that was going to happen with him now.

She pushed herself off his lap and stood next to him, watching as he pushed his underwear down to free himself. Then he took his length in his fist, stroking up and down.

She melted a little and shifted her legs. He watched her with narrowed eyes as she slowly undid the buttons on her jeans and lowered them down her legs, swiveling her hips and thrusting her breasts forward as she did so. She paused and looked up at him when her jeans were at her knees. He stared at her pointed nipples, then his gaze slowly moved down to her white lace bikini panties.

"Like what you see?"

"You know I do," he said. "I wouldn't mind seeing you disrobe from the other side."

To be honest, she knew that. Mauricio liked her butt. It wasn't as though she was extra curvy or anything, but he liked the way she looked from all sides. He'd told her more than once, and tonight, with the new knowledge that they were stronger as a couple, she wanted to make this hotter than it had ever been before.

She turned around and slowly drew one leg from her jeans and then the other. As she stepped out of them, she bent over so he could see her backside and glanced at him over her shoulder. His cock had gotten so hard that she was pretty sure it wouldn't take much to push him over the edge. And that was exactly what she wanted.

She wanted him so on fire for her that he forgot the past and the future, and thought of nothing but the two of them in this moment.

She turned around and pulled at the hem of her shirt, slowly pulling it up over her head. As she tossed it aside, she felt his hands on her breasts and his thigh between hers. He rubbed his leg against her center and she arched her back, feeling one of his hands move around to hold her to him.

She let her head fall back, trusting him to hold her up. His mouth was on her breast and his other hand slowly moved down her body, tracing her ribs, then dipping into her belly button and then lower, skirting over the top of her mound. He palmed her, rubbing his hand over her, and then slowly she felt his fingers parting her.

She reached for him. Taking his long length in her hand, she stroked him up and down, and she used her grip on his cock to rub the tip of it against her clit. It felt so good, pulses of pleasure rushed through her.

He bit her nipple lightly and then he fell back on the couch with a bounce. He maneuvered her until she lay on the sofa cushions and he came down over her. She rubbed his chest; he was still wearing his shirt.

"Mauricio," she said.

"Yes, darling," he responded.

"Why are you still wearing your shirt?" she asked.

"You like it," he said.

"I like it when I can feel your skin better," she said.

The soft sound of her voice, the teasing tone and husky timbre, inflamed him and made it hard for him to think about anything other than driving his cock deep inside of her and taking her over and over again until they were both exhausted. This was what Sundays were made for, he thought. Making love to Hadley.

He took her hand in his and kissed it before bringing it to the buttons on his shirt. She slowly undid them. He held himself over her body. Each brush of her fingers against his skin drove him closer to the edge, to the moment when all this teasing was going to be too much and he was going to just thrust up into her. Hell, he didn't even care that his condoms were in her bedroom.

But he knew he should. They were rebuilding their trust and he couldn't expect her to trust him if he didn't use protection.

"Dammit. The condoms are in your room," he said.

"Then take me there," she said.

"Wrap your legs and arms around me," he said.

She did, her center pressed against him and her breasts

against his chest, her arms underneath his shirt holding him tightly to her.

He groaned, knowing if he shifted his hips the tiniest bit, he could enter her. But he didn't. He sat up and pulled her close to him with one hand as he stood up and walked across her loft to her bedroom, not stopping until he reached the bed. He sat down on it and she straddled him, dropping a kiss on his mouth that made him harder than he'd been before.

She shifted, her breasts brushing against his chest as she reached for the nightstand and the box of condoms he'd put there earlier. She grabbed the box and handed it to him.

His entire body felt too hot. Like he was going to explode if he didn't get inside her. But he shoved his own need down. He didn't want to waste a moment of this second chance with her. Putting his hand on her waist, he felt her brush over his erection. Her nipples were beaded and hard.

She arched her back, which thrust her breasts forward, and a growl escaped him. He put his hands on her waist as she leaned forward, the tips of her breasts grazing his chest. Her mouth was on his neck, kissing and nibbling up the length of it until she reached his ear. Scraping her teeth down the column of his neck, she suckled the pulse that beat there and then lightly bit his skin.

He groaned, "Woman, I can't take much more."

"Good."

He shifted his hips to rub the ridge of his erection against her center.

She bit him again with a little more force and then shifted back to put her hand between their bodies, rubbing his cock.

She scratched his chest with her nail, tracing the thin line of hair that ran down to his stomach and lower. He shuddered. He wasn't going to make it much longer. He brought his hand to hers and held her hand to his pecs for a moment, placing it over his heart. It was then that he realized how much she meant to him. That this was more than he'd expected to find with any woman. He wished he could tell her, but he didn't have the words and he wasn't sure she'd believe him.

"Hadley."

"Don't," she said, putting her finger on his lips. "Don't talk. Just take me, Mo. Make me forget everything but you."

He nodded. He wanted her and in this moment that was all that mattered. Her other hand was on his erection, rubbing him, and he shifted his legs. His mind was no longer on talking; it was on her sex. He needed her naked.

He needed to be buried inside her. Talking could wait for later. He lowered his mouth to hers. Her lips met his and he thrust his tongue deep inside, taking her the way he wanted to take her.

She sucked on his tongue and drew it deeper into her mouth. He shifted back on the bed until he felt the headboard against his back. Putting her hands on his shoulders, she leaned down and kissed his chest. He saw her tongue dart out and brush his nipple.

She traced each of the muscles that rippled in his abdomen and then slowly made her way lower. His cock was so hard he thought he couldn't get any harder. He felt his heartbeat with each pulse through his shaft. He wanted to take control and get inside of her. But another part of him wanted to just sit back and let her have her way with him.

Her hand went to his erection, brushing over his straining length. He wrapped his arm around her back, holding her so that his forearm was aligned with her spine and he could tunnel his fingers into the back of her hair. Then he brought their chests together so that her nipples were poking his torso.

Blood roared in his ears. He was so hard, so full right now, that he needed her. To claim her. To make it so she never left him again.

Skimming his fingers down her body, he found her center. It was warm and wet and he parted her, tapping her clit lightly. Her hands tightened on his shoulders as she arched her back, her head falling to the side as he rubbed her sensitive flesh.

She bit her lower lip as she shifted her hips, moving until he was touching her in the exact right spot. He wanted more. Needed her to come for him. He slipped one finger lower and traced the opening of her body, and then when she moaned, he pushed two fingers up into her.

He worked his fingers in and out of her, keeping one finger on her clit, rubbing and tapping against her as she began to rock against him with more urgency. She put her hands on either side of his face and drew his mouth to her breast. She brushed her nipple over his mouth and he sucked on it, drew it between his lips and teased the tip with his tongue.

He caressed her, bringing both of his hands down her back until he could cup her ass in his hands.

Then he went back to thrusting his fingers deeper into her. When he felt her body start to tighten around him, he bit her nipple, which pushed her over the edge. She called his name as she came and he held her until she quieted. Then he rolled over so that she was underneath him and he put his hands on her ankles and drew her legs apart, putting one knee on the bed between her spread legs.

He quickly put on a condom before leaning over her, placing his hands on the bed near her breasts, he lowered himself over her and rubbed her body with his, loving the feel of her underneath him. She reached for his cock again and he caught her hand, lacing the fingers of her left hand through his and stretching it over her head. She smiled at him.

He pushed his hips between her thighs and she wrapped her legs around his waist. He felt her hand on the right side of his chest and glanced down to see her tracing his tattoo of his family's crest this time. What did that mean?

But he couldn't think right now. Instead, he drew his hips back and entered her, taking her as deeply as he could. Her hand fell to his shoulder, her nails digging into his skin as he drove himself into her, her head tipping back and her eyes drifting closed with each inch he gave her. She took it all. All of him.

He leaned down and caught one of her nipples in his teeth, scraping it very gently. She started to tighten around him. Her hips were moving faster, demanding more, but he kept the pace slow, steady, wanting her to come before he did.

He suckled her nipple and rotated his hips to catch her pleasure point with each thrust. Her fists were clenching in his hair as she threw her head back and her climax ripped through her.

A moment later he followed her, coming hard and deep and feeling like he'd lost his soul to her. He cradled her close in the aftermath and held her to him. She opened her eyes and looked at him in a way he couldn't explain, and he wanted to believe that something had changed.

They spent the rest of the evening in bed, talking about her job and the fact that she had to go to New York. Mauricio had a pang at the thought of her leaving. He needed her by his side. Something had changed inside of him and he was afraid to say it out loud.

But he needed Hadley more than he had thought he would.

Fourteen

Manhattan wasn't as fun as Hadley remembered. She found the pace dizzying instead of invigorating. She missed her morning coffee from the new shop that had opened in the retail park near her loft and frankly, as she stretched out in the king-sized bed in her friend's guest bedroom, she missed Mauricio. When they'd made love on her couch before she left, she knew something had changed between them. That she was in love with him again. Had she ever really fallen out of love with him?

She was beginning to think she hadn't, but she was definitely in love now. And that scared her. She'd left him more than once and each time it had been harder than she'd ever imagined it could be. And they were back together but trusting him… Well, it was getting easier because he was so different from the man she'd walked in on with another woman. But the truth was, there was always going to be a little part of her that believed that it couldn't last.

She didn't know if it was her past experiences with Mo

or her sister being brutally honest about her problems with her fiancé. But something kept Hadley from letting go and just trusting Mauricio fully.

She felt like a mean girl for holding back though. They'd talked on the phone last night until 2:00 a.m. He was in Houston today. He was receiving a charity award at a ceremony later tonight, and he had been cute, trying to say that he didn't deserve the honor. But she had seen firsthand how hard he worked building houses for the underprivileged in Cole's Hill. While the economy of their small town was growing, there were always those who didn't benefit from the new industries, and Mauricio was doing his part to make sure as many families as he could help wouldn't be left behind.

She was proud of him.

She couldn't think of a time in the past when she had felt like that. He'd always been driven by success and trying to become a millionaire before he turned thirty. It was something he'd done many times over at this point, but it had driven him for so long that the man she knew had been lost.

And it made her happy to think that he had changed.

If only she could make herself believe the change was real. Her phone rang, and she glanced over to see it was Mauricio video calling her. She glanced around her friend's apartment to make sure she was alone, that Merri was still in her own room before answering the call. Merri and she had been cubicle mates in the office and after Hadley had gone freelance, Merri always offered her the guest room when she was in the city for business.

"Hey, you," she said as the call connected. She saw he was in the hotel bathroom, fresh from a shower—she could tell because his hair was still damp and he had shaving cream on his face.

"Hey, darling," Mo said, turning to face the screen. "Missed you this morning and thought you could get ready with me."

"I'd love to watch you get ready," she said.

He arched an eyebrow at her. "I was hoping I'd catch you before you were ready for your day, but I can see I'm too late."

"You are," she said. "I got up early to practice my presentation one more time. I think I'm ready."

"I know you are. You'll wow them like you always do," he said, turning away from the camera and leaning toward the mirror to shave. He had a white towel wrapped around his lean hips. She curled her legs underneath her body to watch him. "Thanks for that," she said.

"I set up an alert for Manhattan, Upper East Side, on my phone and there are a few places that might make a nice investment for us," he said.

"Us?"

He stopped shaving and turned to face her. "Isn't there an us?"

She nibbled on her lower lip. All those things she had wanted to say and to hear from him in return before she'd left for New York were coming out in the open now.

"Yes. I want there to be an us. Do you?"

"Had, I'm looking at real estate, so we can have a place to stay when your freelance business takes you to Manhattan," he said. "I thought that would make my intentions clear."

"I need the words, Mo. I need to know what you are thinking," she admitted. "I don't want to guess at what you want and hope that we're both on the same page. I did that before and it backfired."

"Fair enough," he said, rinsing his razor, then turning to face her and leaning toward the camera. "Let me make this clear, I want to share my life with you. Do you want that? Or do you still have doubts about me?"

She smiled, and mimicked his movements and looked straight at him through the phone's camera. "Let me make this clear. I want that too."

He smiled at her, that sweet smile that he saved for only a few people, and she felt her heart beat a little faster. She knew she loved him, but she didn't want to tell him that over a video call.

"Good. Now that we have that settled, should I text you the addresses? You can go by and check them out while you're in town," he said.

"Or we could come back for a weekend trip just for fun and check them out together," she suggested.

"I like that. I'll have my assistant make the travel arrangements. Send me your calendar," he said.

"I will. I think the only major things I have are Helena and Malcolm's pre-wedding stuff. Now that he's back to being normal, it looks like everything is going to move a little more quickly than previously."

"Good. Those two belong together," he said.

"I agree. Thank you for what you did," she said. To be honest, the old Mauricio was more about himself than his friends and his helping Malcolm and pointing him to a smart way to improve his finances had really impressed her. But more than that, she could tell Mauricio had started to look at the world beyond himself. He'd put his friend first and that was something the old Mo wouldn't have done.

That made her heart overflow with love.

Damn.

Love.

She had been pretending the entire time they were dating that she was being smarter this time, that she wouldn't

make the same mistake of falling for him until she knew—
what? There were no guarantees in love and she knew that
if she was going to have any chance at true happiness with
Mauricio, she was going to have to trust him and trust herself.

Why was that so hard?

Mo had convinced Alec to come with him to Houston today. The twins were sharing a hotel room, but Alec
planned to skip tonight's Houston Cares humanitarian dinner—it just wasn't his thing. Still, Mo appreciated the company.

Not that long ago he'd have gone by himself and found
someone to keep him company after the dinner and the reception. But of course, that was the old Mauricio, one who
hadn't realized just how much having the right woman in
his world enhanced it. He'd spent a lot of time buying million-dollar houses and selling them, thinking that he would
have his own and the perfect woman to be his hostess. But
he had never realized that those properties were always
going to feel empty without the right woman in them.

"Bro, you look too serious right now. What's on your
mind?"

On his mind? He wanted Hadley to be his. Not his girlfriend but his wife. He wanted her by his side as his partner
for the rest of his life. And…he wasn't sure she was there
yet. That she'd forgiven him for past mistakes and saw the
changes he felt he'd made.

"I'm thinking about Hadley. I miss her," he said to Alec
because he wasn't sure how to put into words everything
else he was feeling.

"That's good," Alec said.

"Good? How do you figure?"

"I just remember when she took the job in New York

and you guys were sort of cooling off, you couldn't wait to go out, remember? She'd barely cleared the city limit sign before you were on the phone to me and we were making plans to go out. This time…it's different," Alec said.

So the inner changes were reflected on the outside…at least to his brother. "It is different. I want more with her, but I'm not sure…"

"You know my track record with women is pretty much three dates and then it all goes to shit, so I can't really offer you any advice," Alec said. "Diego would probably have some."

"Yeah, but I don't want him to give me big brother advice, you know?" Mauricio said.

His brother just clapped a hand on his shoulder. It wasn't that they had some tingly twin sense, but they both just understood each other better than anyone else ever could. Or at least Mo would have said that was true before Hadley. Before this time with her. By letting down his guard, he'd shown her his true self and now she knew him better than anyone else, possibly even Alec.

"What are you going to do about Hadley?"

Mauricio knew he wanted to ask her to marry him, but he was hesitating. He never hesitated. Not about anything. So why now? Did his gut know something his heart and his head didn't?

Was he missing something?

"Seriously, dude, you have to stop making that face," Alec said.

Mo shot his brother the finger. "She makes me…"

"Crazy?"

"Ha. I just want everything to be perfect."

"Honestly, Mo, I think that was the problem with you two the first time. Life isn't perfect, it's messy and it's complicated, and that's what makes it worth living."

"Are you kidding me right now? That sounds like something Bianca would say," Mauricio said as he glanced at his brother.

"She did say it when our sweet nephew painted on my Brooks Brothers jacket. To be fair, it was a picture of him and me on a horse, but it was Brooks Brothers."

Mauricio laughed. His brother might spend most of his time at his computer writing code, analyzing algorithms and making sure his high-end clients' social media presence enhanced their brand and message, but Alec was also a clotheshorse. He always was faultlessly dressed. Not that Mo and his other brothers were rocking the grunge look, but Alec paid special attention to his image.

"I feel ya. So do we think Bianca is right about this? That we should embrace the mess?"

"Yes. I'll deny this if you repeat it, but she's damn smart, probably smarter than any of the rest of us."

"Probably?"

"I was trying to give us the benefit of the doubt."

Mo smiled. "Thanks. How do I apply that to me and Hadley?"

Alec shook his head. "I don't know. But we both have experienced things that were supposed to be perfect or a sure thing that didn't work out. I think with you and Hadley, there's some kind of connection that only works with the two of you. Don't screw it up."

He was trying not to. But he wondered if by focusing on all the things he'd done wrong the last time, he was missing some of the moments he'd gotten right, and that wasn't what he wanted.

He needed to trust his heart and his gut when it came to Hadley. He knew that if he didn't, he'd always be on guard and that wasn't the way to move forward. That was just as bad as pretending to want a relationship the way he had the first time. The scary part was that this time he wanted everything he'd treated so lightly the last time he was with her. It would serve him right if she just wanted to keep being friends with benefits.

But Hadley had never been easy to predict, and it seemed to him that she wasn't the kind of woman who would be satisfied with anything less than a full commitment.

When Zuri and Josie texted her to see if she could hang out, Hadley texted them back that she was in New York. She was surprised that they were together. Josie had been spending pretty much all of her free time with Manu.

Her phone buzzed, and she answered the video call to see both of her friends sitting on the front porch of Zuri's townhouse with glasses of iced tea.

"Why didn't you tell us?" Zuri asked. "We thought you'd be in Houston with Mo."

"I'm sorry. It was a last-minute trip," Hadley said. "I had been planning to go with Mo to the gala though."

"It's okay. We were hoping for some gossip from you about Scarlet O'Malley."

"How would I have gossip about her?" Hadley asked. Scarlet was from a famous—or maybe notorious—family. They had more money than Midas and scandal and tragedy seemed to follow them wherever they went. Scarlet had a reality television show that was in its seventh season. She'd started it the year her sister had died of a drug overdose.

The tabloids were always speculating that she was searching for a father figure, as her normal type was twenty years her senior and into the jet set party lifestyle that was her world.

"She's going to be at the gala tonight," Josie said. "Which I only know because she was linked to Manu last week on TMZ."

Now Hadley remembered. Scarlet was going to hand out one of the awards. According to Mo, it was to show she'd turned over a new leaf. Hadley wasn't too sure about that, but she did know that Scarlet had recently donated a lot of money to a rehab center on the East Coast in her sister's name. So maybe she was trying to change.

"How was Scarlet linked to Manu?" Hadley asked.

"Apparently they were at a fundraiser in the Hamptons together," Josie said. "He invited me to go but the English department isn't as willing to give time off for a trip to the Hamptons as the athletic department is."

"How are things between you two otherwise?" Hadley asked, noticing that Zuri had turned to watch Josie, as well.

"I think they're good," she said. "I struggle a little with how busy his schedule is, but for the most part we're doing great."

"Good," Zuri said, putting her arm around Josie. "You'll get used to his lifestyle and he'll adjust to yours."

"I hope so," Josie said. "But back to Scarlet O'Malley... According to TMZ, she has to do some serious damage control on her image... There was a viral video of her—"

"Don't tell me. I don't want to know. She's famous because her family is rich. She hasn't done anything worth celebrating."

"I know," Zuri said. "But it's so much fun to watch the train wreck that is her life."

Hadley had to admit it was distracting to watch someone like that, whose entire life seemed like a runaway train. "Anything else happening in Cole's Hill?"

"The Five Families Country Club has a new COO and no one likes her."

"Who is it?"

"Raquel Montez. She wants to get rid of the old smok-

ing room that smells of cigars... You know, the one that all
the good old boys hang out in?"

"I do. That room is gross, but the guys all love it. I'm not
sure she's going to get the money from the board to do it."

"Apparently she doesn't need full board approval," Josie
said.

Hadley continued to chat with her friends, and when
she hung up with them thirty minutes later, she realized
that she missed Cole's Hill. She'd always wanted to get out
of there, get away from the small-town feeling. But now
she wanted to go back. She wanted to talk to her mom
and Helena, and find out their opinion on the new country
club COO. She was becoming that small-town girl she'd
always feared she would be and for some reason she was
okay with it.

Mauricio texted her a picture of himself in his tuxedo
with the caption How do I look? and she felt the sting of
tears as she realized how much she loved him. But she
wasn't going to text him that.

She wanted to see his face the next time they were together. Make sure that she was 100 percent sure of her
feelings.

She simply replied, Gorgeous.

A kissing face emoji flashed on her phone screen, followed by, Miss you.

Miss you too. I'm trying to change my flight to an earlier
one.

Good. Text me your details. Want to stay in Houston for
a few days when you get back?

Why?

Just figured it'd be nice to have a reunion without the distraction of our families.

Hadley laughed to herself. Their families were huge and could be intrusive without meaning to be.

That sounds perfect.

She put her phone away and fell asleep thinking about how unexpected this second chance with Mauricio was and how happy she was that she'd gotten it. She didn't dwell on the fact that it had come on the heels of a pregnancy scare, but instead saw it as fate stepping in to show her the kind of man that Mauricio had become.

She'd been struggling to leave him in the past and now she acknowledged to herself that it was because she had still been in love with him. She might have been able to get over him if she'd never gone to the Bull Pit that night. Never danced with him until the music had lowered her inhibitions and led her straight into his arms.

But she had.

And for the first time she embraced it. Maybe the drinks and the music had been like a beacon showing her the very thing she'd been afraid to go after: the man of her dreams.

Not a knight in shining armor, but a real man with faults and charms and so many things that made him just right for her.

Fifteen

Mauricio patted his pocket and the ring he'd purchased for Hadley earlier that afternoon. He had made up his mind that he could follow his gut and still not lose control of his temper and his actions. He'd changed. Now he had to start believing it himself. There was no way he'd be able to convince Hadley that he was a new man if he couldn't even convince himself.

He and Alec had room service delivered to his hotel suite. The food had been sort of questionable looking, but he'd eaten it all the same. Alec had left the room to take a call and hadn't had any of the fettucine Alfredo, which Mo was beginning to think was a good thing as his stomach started to feel like shit. He was violently ill in the bathroom, and when he returned to the living room, Alec came over, putting his arm around Mo's shoulders as he staggered into the room.

"You look like crap," Alec said, leading him to the couch and helping him sit down. "What's wrong?"

He shook his head as he swallowed hard, trying to keep from heaving again. "I think the dinner wasn't very good," Mo said. "Get me some antacids and I'll be okay."

Alec squeezed his shoulder and walked over to the kitchen area. Mo tried to swallow again but felt his stomach wasn't having it and he bolted for the bathroom. He felt weak and light-headed when he staggered back into the hallway and found his brother watching him with more than a little bit of concern on his face.

"Lay down, Mo. You're not going anywhere."

"Whatever, bro, I can't miss this gala tonight. It's a really big deal that they recognized our organization, and if I'm not there, it will reflect badly on us."

Alec pushed him toward the bedroom. "I'll go for you."

"You hate this kind of event," Mo said, but he was already toeing off his shoes as he sat down on the edge of the king-sized bed. Alec helped him out of his jacket.

"I do. But I love you, so I'll do this for you. I'm going to have to borrow your tux though. I don't even have a dinner jacket with me."

Mauricio undressed quickly and the ring box fell out of the pocket of his trousers as he handed them to Alec.

"I guess you figured out what you are going to do about Hadley," Alec said, picking up the box.

"Yeah, I love her, bro. I can't keep pretending that I'm casual about having her in my life. Damn, don't tell anyone that. I wanted her to be the first one I said that to," Mauricio said.

Alec just laughed. "My lips are sealed. Get your ass in bed and get to feeling better so you can tell her when you see her."

Alec finished getting dressed in the tux and then brought Mo a bowl from the kitchen and a damp cloth for his forehead. "Want me to call Mom and ask her to come check on you?"

"Don't do it. I'm not that sick," he said. Their mom tended to be full-on smother-mode when one of them was sick or seemed to need her. "I thought you loved me."

"I do, but you look really bad… We're talking *Walking Dead* shit here."

"I feel like it, but I think if I just lie here, the room will stop spinning and I'll be fine."

Alec put Mauricio's phone on the bed next to him. "Text me if you feel worse. Are you sure you'll be okay?"

"I'm fine, Alec. Thanks for doing this for me," Mo said. "I wrote a speech and it'll be on the teleprompter. Have you used one before?"

"Yes. When I was valedictorian," Alec said.

"Ass. Stop bragging. You only beat my GPA by .025."

"I still beat you," Alec reminded him.

His brother walked out of the bedroom and Mauricio lay in his bed, watching the ceiling spin around, wishing that Hadley were here with him. That stopped him in his tracks. He'd always needed to be strong and at his best in front of her but now he just wanted the comfort of Hadley.

He took his phone and texted her, even though he suspected she might be out to dinner with her friend Merri. Then he stopped. He didn't want to be that kind of guy who was always texting and not letting her enjoy her time with her friends. So he contented himself with a brief emoji text that just had the kissing face.

He drifted off to sleep, dreaming of asking Hadley to marry him. He knew that he needed to not screw it up the way Malcolm had once he'd gotten engaged. And he had a plan. He glanced down and saw he was holding a piece of paper that just said, *Don't screw up.*

That was his plan. He needed a better one than that.

He woke with a start. His phone vibrated in his hand and he opened his eyes to see it was Alec. He'd texted a picture of the award they'd given him.

Congrats, bro. You okay?

Not dead.

Alec responded with a laughing face emoji.

Mo saw that Hadley had also sent him a goodnight text, as well as one that congratulated him on his award.

Saw you on the live feed. Your speech was great. Can't wait to see you tomorrow night.

She had seen the speech? Even though she was mistaking Alec for him, the fact that she had watched meant more to him than he knew it should. She hadn't been out with her friend; she'd been tuned in to the awards ceremony. He glanced at the ring on the nightstand and knew that tomorrow he was going to ask her to marry him.

Night, baby. Can't wait to see you too.

He felt better now, so he got up, got dressed and headed down to the bar. Because he always did his best thinking when he was surrounded by people.

Hadley woke up early and showered, knowing she was going home today. For once that wasn't the only thing that added a spring to her step. She'd spent the night thinking of Mo after their last text exchange and she had that feeling of rightness in her gut.

As she braided her hair for ease since she was traveling and put on a bit of light makeup, she glanced out the window of Merri's third floor walk-up. It faced a brick wall of the building next door. She had once thought that she was meant for life in the big city, but she now realized how much she loved the wide-open space of Texas.

And that made her feel better about her decision to stop her freelance work in New York and just concentrate on jobs in Texas. At first she'd thought it was because of everything going on with Mauricio but honestly, she'd just changed. The idea of waking up to this view every morning wasn't one she relished. And as much as she loved the big city amenities, Cole's Hill offered a lot of entertainment.

She packed her carry-on bag and then glanced at the clock. Merri was moving around the apartment and she grabbed her phone to text Mo before she went to talk with her friend and say goodbye.

There were a bunch of news notifications from her app. To be fair, most alerts she received were from TMZ, so when she clicked on this one, she was expecting to see something about one of her favorite celebs. Not a headline about Scarlet O'Malley and her Texas billionaire hookup. She almost dropped the phone when the image finished downloading and she saw that the Texas billionaire was actually her boyfriend, Mauricio Velasquez.

He was kissing Scarlet O'Malley.

Honestly, she couldn't see his face or much of his body but she saw the tux and his arms, his hair.

She tossed her phone onto the bed.

That jackass.

That big, dumb, lying sack of crap.

That... Oh, God. Was it true?

She didn't want to believe it could be, but she'd seen him in that very tux in a text he'd sent her earlier and it wasn't

outside the realm of possibility that he'd...hook up? Really?
Just yesterday he'd been talking about getting a place together in New York and then...

Her stomach seized up and she realized that anger was
giving way to hurt. She blinked several times to try to keep
from crying, but it didn't work. She sank to the floor with
the bed against her back, pulled her knees up and put her
head against them. She started to really cry as her thoughts
spun out of control in her head.

How could I have been so stupid?

What was he thinking?

Why had she let him back into her heart? She'd known
he wasn't the settling-down type. She'd known that Mo
was too much of a flirt and a partier to ever be alone. But
she'd thought he'd changed. She'd believed him when he
had shown her how different he was. But maybe she'd been
seeing what she wanted to see.

Wasn't that what Helena had said about Malcolm, that
she'd missed the signs of him freaking out because she just
was so happy that she saw him as settled and contented
with the engagement?

Hadley was a fool.

It was bad enough that she'd rushed back to him from
New York the last time and found a woman in his bed. This
time...everyone was going to see that picture; everyone
would know what he had done.

She knew how hard it was to stop loving him, but pride
was going to make it impossible to forgive this. Plus, how
many times did she have to see him with another woman
before she realized that that was the man he truly was?

There was a knock on the door.

"Hadley, you awake?" Merri called.

"Yes," she said, wiping her nose on the sleeve of her
shirt and going to open the door.

"Oh, girl, what's the matter?" Merri asked.

She started talking but even trying to get the words out made her voice shaky.

"Mo is all over the gossip sites this morning. It looks like he hooked up with Scarlet O'Malley last night."

"What? How is that even possible?" Merri asked.

Her friend pulled her own phone from her pocket, but Hadley wasn't paying attention anymore. She needed to stop being so emotional. She needed to have some backbone, because when she got back to Texas, she and Mr. Velasquez were going to have a chat. And then she was going to put that man in her rearview mirror for good.

No more second chances... Hell, this had been his second chance. Hers too, but she'd been wrong. She should have known when they'd had the pregnancy scare that it wasn't a good way to start over.

"I'm sorry, Hadley. Is there anything I can do?" Merri asked.

"No, I'm fine. Besides, you have to get to work. I'm going to catch an Uber to the airport. Maybe I can get on an earlier flight. I want to be back home, so I can end it with him and then—"

She had to stop talking because she was crying again. Merri hugged her close and held her.

"Maybe there's an explanation that we just don't know," Merri said.

Was there?

She picked up the phone, unlocked it and glanced down at the photo once more. How was he going to explain another woman wrapped around him like a cheap suit?

"I don't think so, Merri. But I will give him a chance to explain," she said. She couldn't wait to hear what he had to say. At least this time he couldn't say they were on a break.

* * *

The pounding on the door woke him. He sat up and glanced at the door as Alec walked into his bedroom, his hair standing on end, his shirt unfastened.

"I screwed up," Alec said.

"What did you do?" Mo asked as he got out of bed and walked over to his brother.

"I slept with Scarlet," Alec said. "I think the paparazzi that follow her might have gotten a picture or two of us."

"Okay, it's fine. I don't think it will affect your business," Mo said. "That's really more your area than mine but we can handle this."

"No, Mo, you're not understanding me. They don't think I slept with Scarlet, they think you did," Alec said.

Mauricio shook his head. "What? Why would they think that?"

"I was you last night," Alec said.

"Why weren't you just yourself?"

"It was easier to pretend I was you," Alec said. "Of course, now I totally regret it, but at the time it seemed easier than explaining your absence. And I never expected to end up with Scarlet."

"Fuck."

"I know. I'm sorry."

"Dammit," Mo said, grabbing his phone. He dialed Hadley's number but it went straight to voice mail like her phone was off. "This sucks, Alejandro. I can't believe you—"

"I'm sorry."

"Well, Hadley doesn't know that it was you. She's going to think that it's me."

"Maybe she doesn't know."

He sincerely doubted it. "Do you think that's the case?"

"Uh, no. I already saw the alerts on my phone. I don't

know what to do. Does it make you look worse to say that you didn't attend a reception in your honor or let the world think—"

"I don't give a flying fuck what the world thinks. It's Hadley whose opinion matters, and right now she thinks I cheated on her. Again."

"I know that. Listen, what if I call her and explain?" Alec said.

"No. You can't do that. I have to talk to her and… Hell, I don't want to have to explain this. She's the woman I want to spend the rest of my life with and I know her. She's not going to be in a listening mood when she sees me. She's probably going to deck me. And rightly so."

"Not rightly so. I'm the one who did this. Let me fix it."

Mauricio couldn't let Alec do anything of the sort. He had to be the one to talk to her. He should have told her last night that he loved her.

He could be worrying for nothing, but given their past, he knew that Hadley wasn't going to just think there was an innocent explanation for those pictures. He didn't blame her. He was already mentally switching his proposal plan to a grovel plan. Maybe she would see him and know immediately that he would never cheat on her. Not now. Not when they had come so far as a couple. But another part of him knew that she was still leery of trusting him and he didn't blame her.

He didn't really blame Alec either. Mo's past behavior was to blame—it had set Hadley and him on this path.

"I have to fix this," Mauricio said. His phone was blowing up with text messages from everyone who knew him. His mom, Malcolm, Helena and Diego.

He sat down on the bed and rubbed the back of his neck. He needed to fix this. With Hadley but also *for* Hadley. Sure, he could tell her that it was Alec and she could be-

lieve him, but he didn't want anyone in town to judge her
because of this.

He sent a group text to his mom and brother.

It isn't what you think. I will text more later.

Helena was harder to respond to because her texts were
a string of curse words and the final message just read, You
stink. She loved you.

"Order us something to eat. I'm going to shower and
then we're going to figure this out," Mo said to his brother.
Alec looked like he was going to try to explain or apologize
again but Mauricio didn't want to hear it. He just walked
into the bathroom, put his hands on the marble counter next
to the sink and bowed his head.

He hoped Hadley was on the plane and hadn't seen the
articles, but he suspected she had. He'd seen the story and
he wasn't even looking for it. His stomach felt like it had a
rock in the bottom of it. Unlike the time Hadley had walked
in on Marnie Masters in his bed, he didn't have mock in-
dignity to fall back on now. He knew no matter what the
explanation was and despite his innocence, this was going
to hurt her.

The last thing he ever wanted to do was to see her hurt,
and there was no easy way out of this. He could say he was
sick, but he knew there would be friends from Cole's Hill
that had seen him in the bar late last night while he'd been
making his plan to propose to Hadley. There were so many
places where she would be able to pick apart his story.

If he were in her shoes, would he believe his own story?
Would he be able to just say, oh, that makes sense?

He knew he wouldn't. He'd lost his cool when she'd
kissed Jackson.

Finally he took out his phone and called her number.

This time he left a voice mail. He hoped she'd listen to it and it would help her to see his side in this mess. That he'd changed. She mattered to him in ways that he couldn't really explain but that he needed her to believe.

He showered, dressed and then started making calls. Alec looked hung over but was focused on figuring out the best options to fix the PR mess he'd created. Meanwhile, Helena wouldn't take Mo's calls, so he had to resort to using Malcolm as a go-between to try to figure out how to win Hadley back.

Sixteen

She'd always heard that old chestnut about how you can't go home again, but she had never really understood it until now. Until she saw that voice mail notification from Mauricio and realized that somehow he'd become tied to her idea of home.

The tears that she'd done a pretty good job of keeping at bay burned the back of her eyes and she blinked until they disappeared.

She ignored the voice mail, keeping her large-framed dark sunglasses on as she towed her carry-on bag through the Houston airport. Once she was outside, she didn't know what to do. She didn't have a car with her, and an Uber to Cole's Hill would cost the moon. Should she rent a car?

She felt like she was going to cry again but this time she kept it together. She was stronger than this. Stronger than a broken heart. She knew she needed to get past the sadness to anger if she was going to be able to get over this, but she had no fire in her. Not right now.

Never had she believed that loving someone was a negative thing, even when she and Mo had broken up the last time. She'd seen it as her chance to find herself as a woman and to move on, which she'd done. But now... Well, now she just felt wounded and vulnerable.

And stupid.

And sad.

Damn.

She had to do something.

She'd rent a car, drive home and then figure out when to see Mo. She could just ignore him for a few days if she stayed in Houston, but she wasn't the kind of woman to run away from her problems and she knew it. She'd always been one to face them head on.

And she really wanted to hear what Mo had to say. Her phone pinged, and she glanced down, expecting to see another text from Helena or her friends, but it was from Mo.

Glad you're safely back in Texas. Please call me.

She sat there. Call him? What was he going to say? She'd forgotten they had each turned on the friend finding app on their devices.

She'd never know if she didn't respond to him and she knew it was past time that she did. So, she called him.

He answered on the first ring.

"Thank you," he said.

"Sure. So, what did you want to talk about?" she asked.

"The photo. It wasn't me," he said.

"It looked like you," she said.

"It was Alec."

Alec.

"Why would Alec wear your tux and go to a gala in your honor?" she asked.

"Because I was sick with food poisoning. He's here at the Post Oak Hotel with me. Would you at least allow me to bring you over here, so I can tell you what happened?" he asked.

Just hearing his voice sort of made her want to believe him. It was just like she'd suspected: she was never going to be able to just walk away from him. She wanted him to not be the man in that photo. And Alec and Mo had changed places before, but she'd always been able to tell the two of them apart.

"Okay," she said at last. This wasn't the kind of conversation she wanted to have on the phone. She needed to see his face, because for all his faults, the one thing that Mauricio always had was his honesty. He had never lied to her. Even when she caught him with Marnie.

"Thank you. I've texted the car service and they have someone at the airport. Where are you?" he asked.

She glanced up at the sign over her head and told him, and then felt her tears stirring again. She hated how reasonable and nice he was being. It had been like a knife to her heart when she'd seen that photo, and she didn't know if she would recover from it. Strangely that picture of the kiss hurt worse than walking in and finding another woman in his bed.

She knew it was because this time they'd overcome so much to be together. And it was Alec kissing the woman, not Mo. But in her heart she wasn't as ready to forgive. She realized how afraid of being hurt by him she still was.

Her hand was shaking so she ended the call, because she realized that she couldn't talk to him. Not now and probably never again if she wanted to keep her cool. Because she loved him.

Whatever had been between them when they'd had their old relationship, it hadn't been love. Not like this.

This was something that wasn't going to lessen with time. This was the kind of pain that was like an open wound, and talking to him, hearing him tell her it was Alec, hadn't fixed anything. Because she knew that she had no walls to hide behind. Not anymore. Not where he was concerned.

"Ms. Everton?"

She nodded at the driver who came over to her.

"I'll take your bag," he said, reaching for her suitcase. She let him take it. He opened the door to a Bentley by the curb and she slid into the back seat. She wanted to close her eyes and pretend that she was going to be okay, but she knew that was a lie.

And lying to herself wasn't something she intended to do. She took out her makeup bag, fixed her mascara and then decided to add some eyeliner. She looked so pale that bronzer was in order too. By the time she arrived at the Post Oak, she had a full face of makeup on and felt like at least to the outside world she didn't look like the hot mess she was inside.

The driver opened her door and she climbed out.

"Please check my bag with the valet. I'll get it after my meeting," she said.

He nodded.

She walked into the lobby with no real plan. Maybe she'd text Mo and have him meet her in the lobby and they could talk in the restaurant. She didn't want to go to his room. Didn't want to be alone with him where she'd be able to say all the things that were tumbling around in her head. Things she'd regret later and would burn all her bridges with him.

He didn't bother waiting in the room for Hadley to come to him. He knew that he was on the back foot and needed to take the initiative. He could justify in his head that he was the innocent party, but he'd hurt this woman too many times in the past to sit in his room and wait for her.

The driver texted to alert him that he was pulling up to the hotel and Mo took the elevator down to the lobby. He stood to the side of the entrance and waited.

Hadley walked in with large sunglasses on her face. She pulled them off and scanned the lobby, and when their eyes met, she started blinking.

His heart broke. Right then. There was no need to ask if she was going to forgive him.

How could she?

How could she reconcile herself to being in a relationship with a man she didn't trust? And it was clear to him now that she still didn't trust him. If he were honest, he'd have to say that she probably hadn't forgiven him for hurting her all the times he had in the past.

And he knew that he didn't have the words to convince her that he was a changed man. *Hell.*

Hell and damn.

He walked over to her and she blinked even more rapidly. He knew she was trying to hold back tears, but a few leaked out and started to fall down her cheeks. He didn't care that she was mad at him or about anything but comforting her because she needed it.

He reached for her, but she stepped back, putting her hand up. "Don't. I'll lose it if you touch me."

He hated that, hated that the one thing he felt like he could do had been taken from him. From them.

"Come on. Let's go to my suite and we can talk."

She nodded. He reached out to put his hand on the small of her back but then dropped it before he touched her. He wasn't sure if one innocent touch was going to push past the fragile control she was using to hold herself together.

He used his card to access the concierge level where his

suite was located and then led the way down the hall to his room. Alec had left earlier, and the room was empty.

"Can I get you something to eat or drink?"

"No," she said. Her voice had the husky lower timbre it only had when she was biting back tears.

"Let me say again, it wasn't me with that woman."

She nodded. "I know. I believe you, Mo."

He nodded. "So, what's the problem?"

She shrugged, then turned her back to him and walked toward the window. She stood in front of it with her head bent, and he wished he couldn't see her reflection in the glass. Couldn't see that lost look on her face.

"I just realized a few things today. Well, first I thought it was you. And you know that really floored me because what does that say about us as a couple that I thought you couldn't go to one party without hooking up?"

He cleared his throat. "I don't know. Not anything good."

She turned around.

And he wished she hadn't. If he thought she looked lost in the reflection from the window, seeing the expression on her face directly was a thousand times worse.

"Exactly. That photo made me face something that I wasn't aware I was ignoring," she admitted. "I'm not sure I ever really forgave you for anything."

"Fair enough," he said. "But now that we know there's a problem, we can work it out and move past it."

Please, God, let us be able to do that.

She chewed her lower lip and wrapped her arms around her waist, and he knew.

They were never going to be able to move past this.

Fucking hell.

A litany of curses all directed at himself rained through his mind. He'd tried so hard to fix the problems his quick temper and selfish behavior had created. He'd fooled himself into believing that he could fix everything but now he knew. He saw on her face that he was never going to be able to fix the wounds he'd carved so deeply on her soul.

"I guess that's a no."

She shook her head as she started to cry, and he saw her throat work as she swallowed.

"I want to say yes," she said in that voice that made him feel like the worst sort of monster, because he was the one responsible for her hurt and her tears.

"Then say yes. I'm different, Had. You know I am," he said, coming over to her because his arms were starting to ache from not holding her. "I've made huge leaps in the last few months. Losing you showed me all the things about myself that I didn't really like, the stuff I needed to change."

She nodded, and he reached for her. She let him hug her, but she was stiff and the embrace wasn't enough. He didn't know how to get through to her.

She had to at least meet him halfway. Or be open to meeting him.

She rested her forehead on his chest, and he felt her arms snake around his waist, holding him tightly to her. Then she let her arms drop and stepped back.

"I wish I were a different woman, but I'm not. I don't think I can be what you need because of our past. I wish that we'd waited to get together until now, but we didn't, and I can't forget how you hurt me before. I thought I could. I thought I'd moved past it and forgiven you, but then I woke up to that photo and knew I hadn't.

"This is on me, Mo. The man you are becoming is so much stronger than the guy you used to be, and I wish you nothing but happiness in your life," she said.

Then she moved past him, heading toward the door.

* * *

Mauricio knew that if she walked out that door, she wasn't going to come back, and he couldn't just let her go. He thought of the ring in his pocket and the plan he'd developed last night in the bar but all of that meant nothing.

"Hadley!"

She stopped but didn't turn around. She just stood there, shoulders bowed, and he knew that whatever he did next was going to be the difference between having her by his side for the rest of his life and living with regret and pain.

"I love you."

The words weren't what he had planned to say but there they were, hanging in the room between the two of them. *Dammit.* He'd never felt so defenseless before. He'd never felt so scared of anything as he was of that she wouldn't respond and just keep walking away.

She turned to face him.

"What did you say?" she asked, but her voice was different now. Not that deep timbre that scraped across his soul and made him feel like he was going to break.

"I love you," he repeated, meeting her eyes and standing up taller.

He was proud of the affection he had for her. She'd made him realize that life wasn't just a race to have the biggest bank account or beat everyone else to the top. That life was sweeter with her in it.

Tipping her head to the side, she asked, "Why?"

"Hell, woman. I don't know why. If I did, then I wouldn't feel like this. I'm a mess thinking that you might leave, and I'll never be whole again. All I know is I love you," he said.

She nodded and then started walking toward him. "I love you too, Mo. I don't know how to stop this. When I saw that picture, I was broken, not angry. There was no anger because you own my heart and my soul, and I didn't want to believe that I could feel that deeply about you and it would mean nothing to you."

"It means everything to me," he said. "I'll do whatever you need me to in order to make this right."

"Loving me is all I need," she said.

"Well, then, we're good, woman, because I love you so damned much," he said, closing the gap between them and lifting her into his arms. She wrapped her legs around his waist and he stared down into her eyes.

He saw the truth of her emotions and knew that they'd have to sort out the photo and how to handle it with the wider world, but the two of them—the people who really mattered—knew the truth and they were together.

He'd never felt so relieved or happy in his life. She wrapped her arms around his shoulders. "I love you so much."

He laughed as joy coursed through his blood. He spun them around in the middle of the suite, holding her to him.

"Me too, darling."

He carried her into the bedroom and set her on her feet. Blood rushed through his veins, pooling in his groin and hardening him as she started unbuttoning his shirt. Her fingers were cool against his skin as she worked her way down his body. When she finished unbuttoning the shirt, she pushed it open and he shrugged out of it.

He growled deep in his throat when she leaned forward to brush kisses against his chest. Her lips were sweet and not shy as she explored his torso. Then he felt the edge of her teeth as she nibbled at his pecs.

He watched her, his eyes narrowing. His pants were feeling damned uncomfortable about now. Her tongue darted out and brushed against his nipple. He angled his hips forward and put his hand on the back of her head, urging her to stay where she was.

"I missed you," she said.

She had one hand braced on his chest as she leaned over him. He shifted under her and lifted her in his arms so that she straddled him. He leaned up and kissed her lips. "I missed you too. I thought I lost you."

"I'm sorry," she said, wrapping her arms around his shoulders and burying her face in his neck. "I can't believe how much I love you."

"Me too."

He tugged at the hem of her blouse, pulling it up over her head and tossing it aside. She was wearing some kind of bralette thing; when he couldn't figure out how to get it off, she laughed, pulling it over her head but not all the way off. Her breasts fell free and he cupped them, rubbing his fingers over her nipples. His cock, which had been hard since she'd jumped in his arms, strained against his trousers.

She shivered in his arms and rocked against him. His cock responded by twitching against her core. He rubbed his hands over the length of her naked back. He enjoyed the feel of Hadley in his arms and it was especially poignant now since he'd almost lost her forever.

She put her hands on his shoulders and eased her way down his chest. She traced each of the muscles of his stomach and then slowly made her way lower. He could feel his heartbeat in his erection and he knew he was going to lose it if he didn't take control.

When she reached the waistband of his pants, she stopped and glanced up into his eyes.

Her hand went to his erection, brushing over his straining length. He reached up and removed the bra she still wore and then lifted her slightly so that her nipples brushed his chest.

She nibbled on her lips as he rotated his shoulders so that his chest rubbed against her breasts.

Blood roared in his ear. He was so hard, so full right now, that he needed to be inside her.

Impatient with her leggings, he lifted her off his lap and tugged them down her legs. She bent over to take them off and he couldn't resist moving around behind her. He caressed her ass and then let his hands move down her thighs. He positioned her so she could lean on the side of the bed. She moaned as he touched her center and then sighed when he brushed his fingertips across the crotch of her panties.

The lace was warm and wet. He slipped one finger under the material and hesitated for a second. She looked over her shoulder at him.

Her eyes were heavy-lidded. He felt the minute movements of her hips as she tried to move his touch where she needed it.

He pushed the fabric of her panties aside and lightly traced the opening of her body. She was warm and wet and so ready for him. It was only the fact that he wanted her to come at least once before he entered her that enabled him to keep his own needs in check.

She shifted against him and he thrust into her with just the tip of one finger. He teased them both with a few short thrusts.

"Mo…" she said, her voice breathless and airy.

"Yes, darling?" he asked, pushing his finger deep inside of her.

Her hips rocked against his finger for a few strokes before she was once again caught on the edge and needing more. He reached for a condom and put it on.

"Take me, Mo."

He pulled his finger from her body and traced it around her clit. She rocked her hips frantically against him. Her hips pushed back toward him and he reached around her to take the tip of one breast in his hand.

He lowered his mouth to the base of her spine and then slowly licked his way up her back, kissing the nape of her neck and biting it. She shuddered in his arms, her hips pushing back against him again. He swiveled his hips and found the opening of her body. She moaned as he brushed the tip of his cock against her humid center.

He scraped his fingernail down her back as he thrust into her. He took her hard and deep, thrusting into her again and again until she called out his name. Then he felt his orgasm rock through him. He drove into her until he was empty and then wrapped his arm around her waist and fell to the bed, drawing her with him.

She curled against his side, her hand moving over his chest as their breath slowed and he looked over at her.

She was his.

Now and forever.

"I have something for you," he said, shifting around to reach for his pants.

"You just gave me something," she said, wriggling her eyebrows at him.

"I'm going to give it to you again after I recover," he said, "But I have something else for you right now."

He took the box out of his pocket and shifted to his side so he could look down into her eyes.

"You know I love you more than life itself, Hadley, and you might need more time. But I want you to be my wife. I want to spend the rest of our lives together. Will you marry me?"

She sat up as he held out the box. He realized he might have planned this better, but if he'd learned anything in his relationship with her, it was that he couldn't wait for perfection. He had to seize the moment when it came along.

He opened the box and took the ring out of it, while he waited for her answer.

"Had?"

"Yes, Mo. Yes, I will marry you. I love you."

He put the ring on her finger and then made love to her again.

Having Hadley in his arms made him realize that all the posturing and fighting he'd done his entire life had been to hide the pain of not feeling complete. He'd been so afraid to let his guard down and let her in but he knew he was better for having her by his side.

Epilogue

Helena and Hadley were waiting outside of the Jaqs Veerland Bridal Studio for their fiancés and Hadley couldn't help smiling at her sister. "I can't believe we're both getting married in the next nine months."

"Me neither," Helena said. "Malcolm is really doing so much better and I'm almost afraid to believe how happy we are at this moment."

"I know what you mean. After that photo of Scarlet and Alec appeared, I wasn't sure that Mo and I would ever be here. But I love him so much, Helena. I never thought I would."

"I know, sweetie. It's hard to believe that we both have found true love."

"Is it?" Hadley asked. "I think we both found what we were looking for, or at least I did. Mauricio has turned into the man I always knew he could be."

"Well, we were all ready to tar and feather him when

that photo showed up online, but once we saw him with you, well, even Mom said there is no way that he could kiss someone else and look at you the way he does."

"Of course, there isn't," Mauricio said, coming up behind them and hugging Hadley. "She owns me body and soul."

* * * * *

SEDUCTIVE SECRETS

CAT SCHIELD

One

Paul Watts entered the hospital elevator and jabbed the button for the fourth floor with more force than necessary. In two hours he was leaving Charleston to attend a week-long cybersecurity conference. His gut told him this was a mistake. His eighty-five-year-old grandfather's medical situation wasn't improving. Grady had been hospitalized six days earlier with cerebral edema, a complication arising from the massive stroke he'd suffered three months earlier that had affected his speech and left one side of his body paralyzed. In the midst of this latest medical crisis, the family worried that Grady wouldn't last much longer. Which was why Paul was rethinking his trip.

Despite the excellent care he was receiving from the doctors, the Watts family patriarch was failing to rally. At first the doctors and physical therapists had agreed that the likelihood of Grady making a full recovery was better than average given his excellent health before the stroke and his impossibly strong will. But he hadn't mended. And he hadn't fought. The stroke had stolen more than his voice and muscle control. It had broken Grady Watts.

Although he'd stepped down as CEO of the family shipping empire a decade earlier and turned over the day-to-day running of the corporation to Paul's father, Grady had remained as chairman of the board. Not one to slow down, he'd kept busy in "retirement" by sitting on the boards of several organizations and maintained an active social life.

Accustomed to his grandfather's tireless vigor, stubbornness and unapologetic outspokenness, Paul couldn't understand why Grady wouldn't strive to get well, and thanks to the strained relationship between them, Paul was unlikely to get answers. Their estrangement was an ache that never went away. Still, Paul refused to regret his decision to pursue a career in cybersecurity rather than join the family business. Stopping bad guys satisfied his need for justice in a way that running the family shipping company never would.

The elevator doors opened and Paul stepped into the bright, sterile corridor that ran past the nurses' station. He offered brief nods to the caregivers behind the desk as he strode the far-too-familiar hallways that led to his grandfather's private room.

His steps slowed as he neared where Grady lay so still and beaten. No one would ever accuse Paul of being faint-hearted, but he dreaded what he'd find when he entered the room. Every aspect of his life had been influenced by his grandfather's robust personality and Grady's current frailty caused Paul no small amount of dismay. Just as his grandfather had lost the will to go on, Paul's confidence had turned into desperation. He would do or support anything that would inspire Grady to fight his way back to them.

Reaching his grandfather's room, Paul gathered a deep breath. As he braced himself to enter, a thread of music drifted through the small gap between the door and frame.

A woman was singing something sweet and uplifting. Paul didn't recognize the pure, clear voice and perfect pitch as belonging to anyone in his family. Perhaps it was one of the nurses. Had one of them discovered that his grandfather loved all kinds of music?

Paul pushed open the door and stepped into his grandfather's dimly lit room. The sight that greeted him stopped him dead in his tracks. Grady lay perfectly still, his skin gray and waxy. If not for the reassuring beep of the heart monitor, Paul might've guessed his grandfather had already passed.

On the far side of the bed, her back to the darkened window, a stranger held Grady's hand. Despite her fond and gentle expression, Paul went on instant alert. She wasn't the nurse he'd expected. In fact, she wasn't any sort of ordinary visitor. More like someone who'd wandered away from an amusement park. Or the sixth-floor psychiatric ward.

Pretty, slender and in her midtwenties, she wore some sort of costume composed of a lavender peasant dress and a blond wig fastened into a thick braid and adorned with fake flowers. Enormous hazel eyes dominated a narrow face with high cheekbones and a pointed chin. She looked like a doll come to life.

Paul was so startled that he forgot to moderate his voice. "Who are you?"

The question reverberated in the small space, causing the woman to break off midsong. Her eyes went wide and she froze like a deer caught in headlights. Her rosy lips parted on a startled breath and her chest rose on an inhalation, but Paul fired off another question before she answered the first.

"What are you doing in my grandfather's room?"

"I'm…" Her gaze darted past him toward the open door.

"Geez, Paul, calm the hell down," said a voice from behind him. It was his younger brother, Ethan. His softer tone suited the hospital room far better than Paul's sharp bluster. "I heard you all the way down the hall. You're going to upset Grady."

Now Paul noticed that his grandfather's eyes were open and his mouth was working as if he had an opinion he wanted to share. The stroke had left him unable to form the words that let him communicate, but there was no question Grady was agitated. His right hand fluttered. The woman's bright gaze flicked from Paul to Grady and back.

"Sorry, Grady." Paul advanced to his grandfather's bedside and lightly squeezed the old man's cool, dry fingers, noting the tremble in his knobby knuckles. "I came by to check on you. I was surprised to see this stranger in your room." He glanced toward the oddly dressed woman and spoke in a low growl. "I don't know who you are, but you shouldn't be here."

"Yes, she should." Ethan came to stand beside Paul, behaving as if introducing his brother to a woman dressed in costume was perfectly ordinary.

This lack of concern made Paul's blood pressure rise. "You know her?"

"Yes, this is Lia Marsh."

"Hello," she said, her bright sweet voice like tinkling crystal.

As soon as Ethan had entered the room her manner had begun to relax. Obviously she viewed Paul's brother as an ally. Now she offered Paul a winsome smile. If she thought her charm would blunt the keen edge of his suspicion, she had no idea who she was dealing with. Still, he found the anxiety that had plagued him in recent days easing. A confusing and unexpected sense of peace trickled through him as Grady's faded green eyes focused on Lia Marsh. He seemed happy to have her by his side, weird costume and all.

"I don't understand what she's doing here," Paul complained, grappling to comprehend this out-of-control situation.

"She came to cheer up our grandfather." Ethan set a comforting hand on their grandfather's shoulder. "It's okay," he told the older man. "I'll explain everything to Paul."

What was there to explain?

During the brothers' exchange, the woman squeezed Grady's hand. "I've really enjoyed our time together today," she said, her musical voice a soothing oasis in the tense room. "I'll come back and visit more with you later."

Grady made an unhappy noise, but she was already moving toward the foot of the bed. Paul ignored his grandfather's protest and shifted to intercept her.

"No, you won't," he declared.

"I understand," she said, but her expression reflected dismay and a trace of disapproval. Her gaze flicked to Ethan. A warm smile curved her lips. "I'll see you later."

Embroidered skirt swishing, she moved toward the exit, leaving a ribbon of floral perfume trailing in her wake. Paul caught himself breathing her in and expelled the tantalizing scent from his lungs in a vigorous huff. The energy in the room plummeted as she disappeared through the doorway and, to his profound dismay, Paul was struck by a disconcerting urge to call her back.

Now just to get answers to the most obvious questions: Why was she dressed like that and what was she doing in Grady's room? But also why had she chosen to tattoo a delicate lily of the valley on the inside of her left wrist? He wondered how his brother could be taken in by such guileless naïveté when it was so obviously an act.

This last point snapped Paul out of whatever spell she'd cast over him. Grabbing his brother's arm, Paul towed Ethan out of the hospital room, eager to get answers without disturbing Grady. Out in the hall, Paul closed the door and glanced around. Lia Marsh had vanished and he noticed that didn't bring him the satisfaction it should have.

"Who is she?" Paul demanded, his unsettled emotions making his tone sharper than necessary. "And what the hell is going on?"

Ethan sighed. "Lia's a friend of mine."

Paul dragged his hand through his hair as he fought to control the emotions cascading through him. He focused on his anxiety over his grandfather's condition. That feeling made sense. The rest he would just ignore.

"You've never mentioned her before," Paul said. "How well do you know her?"

A muscle jumped in Ethan's jaw. He looked like he was grappling with something. "Well enough. Look, you're seeing problems where there aren't any."

"Have you forgotten that Watts Shipping as well as various members of our family have been cyberattacked in the last year? So when I show up in Grady's hospital room and there's a strange woman alone with him, I get concerned."

"Trust me—Lia has nothing to do with any of that," Ethan said. "She's really sweet and just wants to help. Grady has been so depressed. We thought a visit might cheer him up."

Paul refused to believe that he'd overreacted. And Ethan was transitioning into the CEO position at Watts Shipping, replacing their father who planned to retire in the next year. Why wouldn't his brother take these various cyber threats seriously?

"But she was dressed like a…like a…" It wasn't like him to grapple for words, but the whole encounter had a surreal quality to it.

"Disney princess?" Ethan offered, one corner of his mouth kicking up. "Specifically Rapunzel from *Tangled*."

"Okay, but you never answered my question. Where did you meet her?" Paul persisted, making no attempt to rein in his skepticism. Ethan's persistent caginess was a red flag. "What do you know about her?"

When meeting people for the first time, Paul tended to assess them like it was an investigation and often struggled to give them the benefit of the doubt. Did that mean he was suspicious by nature? Probably. But if that's what it took to keep his family safe, then so be it.

"Can you stop thinking like a cop for two seconds?" Ethan complained.

Paul bristled. It wasn't only Grady who hadn't supported his decision to join the Charleston PD after college and several years later start his cybersecurity business.

"What's her angle?"

"She doesn't have one. She's exactly like she seems."

Paul snorted. A cosplay fanatic? "What else do you know about her?"

"I don't know," Ethan complained, growing impatient. "She's really nice and a great listener."

"A great listener," Paul echoed, guessing that Lia Marsh had taken advantage of Ethan's distress over their grandfather's illness. "I suppose you told her all about Grady and our family?"

"It's not as if any of it is a huge secret."

"Regardless. You brought a complete stranger, someone you know almost nothing about, to meet our dying grandfather." Paul made no effort to temper his irritation. "What were you thinking?"

"I was thinking Grady might enjoy a visit from a sweet, caring person who has a beautiful singing voice." Ethan gave him such a sad look. "Why do you always go to the worst-case scenario?"

Paul stared at his brother. Ethan behaved as if this explanation made all the sense in the world. Meanwhile, Paul's relentless, logical convictions prevented him from grasping what sort of eccentricities drove Lia Marsh to parade around as a storybook character.

"She was dressed up. I just don't understand…"

Ethan shrugged. "It's what she does."

"For a living?"

"Of course not," Ethan countered, showing no defensiveness at all in the face of his brother's sarcasm. In fact, he looked fairly smug as he said, "She dresses up and visits sick children. They love her."

Paul cursed. Actually, that was a damned nice thing to do.

"How did you meet her?"

Ethan frowned. "I'm a client."

"What sort of a client?"

"None of this matters." Ethan exhaled. "Lia is great and your trust issues are getting old."

A heavy silence fell between the brothers as Paul brushed aside the criticism and brooded over Ethan's caginess. He hated being at odds with his brother and wasn't sure how to fix the disconnect. With less than a year between them in age, he and Ethan had been tight as kids despite their differing interests and passions. Paul was fascinated by technology and could spend hours alone, turning electronic components into useful devices, while Ethan was more social and preferred sports over schoolwork.

Both had excelled through high school and into college. And while they'd never directly competed over anything, once Paul decided against joining the family business, a subtle tension started growing between the siblings.

"You might as well tell me what's going on because you know I'll investigate and find out exactly who Lia Marsh is."

Lia Marsh blew out a sharp breath as she cleared the hospital room and fled down the empty hallway, noting her thudding heart and clammy palms. While Ethan hadn't glossed over his brother's suspicious nature, she hadn't been prepared for Paul's hostility or the way his annoyance heightened his already imposing charisma. Unaccustomed to letting any man get under her skin, Lia studied the phenomenon like she would a fresh scratch on her beloved camper trailer, Misty. Unexpected and undesirable.

Usually her emotions were like dandelion fluff on the wind, lighter than air and streaked with sunshine. She embraced all the joy life had to offer and vanquished negativity through meditation, crystal work and aromatherapy, often employing these same spiritual healing tools with her massage clients. Not all of them bought into new age practices, but some surprised her with their interest. For instance, she never imagined a businessman like Ethan Watts opening his mind to ancient spiritual practices, but his curiosity demonstrated that it was never wise to prejudge people.

Someone should share that warning with Paul Watts. He'd obviously jumped to several conclusions from the instant he'd spotted her in his grandfather's hospital room. The unsettling encounter left her emotions swirling in a troubling combination of excitement and dread, brought on by a rush of physical attraction and her aversion to conflict.

Distracted by her inner turmoil, Lia found it impossible to sink back into her role of Rapunzel as she stole along the corridor lit by harsh fluorescent lights. Her gaze skimmed past gray walls and bland landscapes. Recycled air pressed against her skin, smelling of disinfectant. She longed to throw open a window and invite in sunshine and breezes laden with newly cut grass and bird song. Instead, she dressed up and visited sick children, offering a much-needed diversion.

Heading down the stairs to the third-floor pediatric wing, Lia collected her tote bag from the nurses' station.

Since signing up to volunteer at the hospital these last few months, she'd been a frequent visitor and the children's care staff had grown accustomed to her appearances. They appreciated anything that boosted their patients' spirits and gave them a break from the endless rounds of tests or treatments.

The elevator doors opened and Lia stepped into the car. She barely noticed the mixed reactions of her fellow passengers to her outfit. Minutes later Lia emerged into the late afternoon sunshine. She sucked in a large breath and let it out, wishing she could shake her lingering preoccupation with her encounter with Paul Watts. Lia picked up her pace as if she could outrun her heightened emotions.

The traffic accident that had totaled her truck and damaged her beloved camper had compelled her to move into a one-bedroom rental on King Street until she could afford to replace her vehicle. Her temporary living arrangement was a twenty-minute walk from the hospital through Charleston's historic district. She focused on the pleasant ambience of the antebellum homes she passed, the glimpses of private gardens through wrought iron fencing, and savored the sunshine warming her shoulders.

Caught up in her thoughts, Lia barely noticed the man leaning against the SUV parked in front of her apartment until he pushed off and stepped into her path. Finding her way blocked, her pulse jumped. Lia had traveled the country alone since she was eighteen and had good instincts when it came to strangers. Only this was someone she'd already met.

Paul Watts had the sort of green eyes that reminded her of a tranquil pine forest, but the skepticism radiating from him warned Lia to be wary. Despite that, his nearness awakened the same buzz of chemistry that she'd noticed in the hospital room.

He wasn't at all her type. He was too obstinate. Too grounded. Merciless. Resolute. Maybe that was the attraction.

"You were hard to find," Paul declared.

Ethan had told her Paul was a former cop who now ran his own cybersecurity business. She suspected his single-minded focus had stopped a high number of cybercriminals. Her skin prickled at the idea that he'd do a deep dive into her background where things lurked that she'd prefer remained buried.

"And yet here you are," she retorted, dismayed that he'd run her down in the time it had taken her to walk home.

She wasn't used to being on anyone's radar. To most of her massage clients she was a pair of hands and a soothing voice. The kids at the hospital saw only their favorite princess character. She relished her anonymity.

"Is everything all right with Grady?"

"He's fine." Paul's lips tightened momentarily as a flash of pain crossed his granite features. "At least he isn't any worse."

"I didn't know him before his stroke, but Ethan said he was strong and resilient. He could still pull through."

"He could," Paul agreed, "except it's as if he's given up."

"Ethan mentioned he'd become obsessed with reuniting with his granddaughter these last few years," Lia said. "Maybe if you found her—"

"Look," Paul snapped. "I don't know what you're up to, but you need to stay away from my grandfather."

"I'm not up to anything," Lia insisted, pulling her key out of her bag as she angled toward the building's front door. "All I want to do is help."

"He doesn't need your help."

"Sure. Okay." At least he hadn't barred her from connecting with Ethan. "Is that it?"

She'd unlocked the door and pushed it open, intending to escape through it when Paul spoke again.

"Aren't you the least bit curious how I found you?" he asked, his vanity showing. Given her minimal electronic footprint, tracking her down left him puffed up with pride. No doubt he wanted to brag about his prowess.

Despite the agitation making her heart thump, Lia paused in the doorway and shot him a sidewise glance. While Paul exuded an overabundance of confidence and power, she wasn't without strengths of her own. She would just have to combat his relentlessness with freewheeling flirtation.

While teasing Paul was a danger similar to stepping too near a lion's cage, Lia discovered having his full attention was exhilarating.

"Actually." Pivoting to face him, Lia summoned her cheekiest smile. Everything she'd heard from Ethan indicated that Paul was ruled by logic rather than his emotions. Challenging the cybersecurity expert to confront his feelings was bound to blow up in her face. "I'm more intrigued that you wanted to."

Two

King Street melted away around him as Paul processed his response to Lia's challenging grin. Her expression wasn't sexual in nature, but that didn't lessen the surge of attraction that rocked him, demanding that he act. He clenched his hands behind his back to stifle the impulse to snatch her into his arms and send his lips stalking down her neck in search of that delectable fragrance. Frustrating. Intolerable. This woman was trouble. In more ways than he had time to count.

What was her endgame? Money, obviously.

Based on the fact that she'd chosen to live in one of downtown Charleston's priciest neighborhoods, she obviously had expensive taste. After meeting Ethan, she'd obviously targeted him, using their grandfather's illness to ingratiate herself. Was she planning on getting Ethan to pay off her debt or to invest in some sort of business?

"Ophelia Marsh, born March first—" he began, determined to unnerve her with a quick rundown of her vital statistics.

"Fun fact," she interrupted. "I was almost a leap-day baby. My mom went into labor late on February twenty-eighth and everyone thought for sure I would be born the next day, which that year was February twenty-ninth. But I didn't want to have a birthday every four years. I mean, who would, right?"

Her rambling speech, sparkling with energetic good humor, soured his mood even more. "Right." He had no idea why he was agreeing. "Born March first in Occidental, California…"

"A Pisces."

He shook his head. "A what?"

"A Pisces," she repeated. "You know, the astrological sign. Two fish swimming in opposite directions. Like you're a goat," she concluded.

Paul exhaled harshly. Horoscopes were nothing but a bunch of nonsense. Yet that didn't stop him from asking, "I'm a goat?"

"A Capricorn. You just had a birthday."

He felt her words like a hit to his solar plexus. "How did you know that?"

Her knowing his birthday filled him with equal parts annoyance and dismay. *He* was the security expert, the brilliant investigator who hunted down cybercriminals and kept his clients' data safe. To have this stranger know something as personal as his birth date sent alarm jolting through him.

"Ethan told me."

"Why would he do that?" Paul demanded, directing the question to the universe rather than Lia.

"Why wouldn't he?" She cocked her head and regarded him as if that was obvious. "He likes to talk about his family and it helps me to picture all of you if I know your signs. You're a Capricorn. Your mother is a Libra. She's the peacekeeper of the family. Your father is a Sagittarius. He's a talker and tends to chase impossible dreams. Ethan is a Taurus. Stubborn, reliable, with a sensual side that loves good food."

This quick summary of his family was so spot-on that Paul's suspicions reached even higher levels. Obviously, this woman had been researching the Wattses for some nefarious purpose. What was she up to? Time to turn up the volume on his questioning.

"You don't stay in one place for very long," he said, remembering what he'd managed to dig up on her. "New York, Vermont, Massachusetts, now South Carolina, all visited in the last twelve months. Why is that?"

In his experience grifters liked to work an area and move on when things became too hot. Her pattern fit with someone up to no good. She might be beautiful and seem to possess a sweet, generous nature, but in his mind her obvious appeal worked against her. He knew firsthand how easily people were taken in by appearances. He was more interested in substance.

"I'm a nomad."

"What does that mean?"

"It means I like life on the road. It's how I grew up." She paused to assess his expression and whatever she glimpsed there made her smile slightly. "I was born in the back of a VW camper van and traveled nearly five thousand miles in the first year of my life. My mother has a hard time staying put for any long period of time."

Paul was having a difficult time wrapping his head around what she was saying. For someone who belonged to a family that had lived within ten square miles of Charleston for generations, he couldn't fathom the sort of lifestyle she was talking about.

"Was your mother on the run from someone? Your father? Or a boyfriend?"

"No." Her casual shrug left plenty of room for Paul to speculate. "She was just restless."

"And you? Are you restless, too?"

"I guess." Something passed over her features, but it was gone too fast for him to read. "Although I tend to stay longer in places than she did."

Follow-up questions sprang to Paul's mind, but he wasn't here to dig into her family dynamic. He needed to figure out what she was up to so he could determine how much danger she represented to his family. He changed subjects. "Where did you and Ethan meet?"

"He's been a client of mine for about a month now."

"A client?" Paul digested this piece of information.

"I work for Springside Wellness," she said, confirming what Paul had already unearthed about her. The company was a wellness spa on Meeting Street that operated as both a yoga studio and alternative treatment space. A lot of mind, body, soul nonsense. "Ethan is a client."

This confirmed what Paul had gleaned from his brother's explanation about how he knew Lia. Still, Paul had a hard time picturing his brother doing yoga and reflexology. "What sort of a client?"

"I'm a massage therapist. He comes in once a week. I told him he should probably come in more often than that. The man is stressed."

Her answer took Paul's thoughts down an unexpected path. "Well, that's just perfect."

Only it wasn't perfect at all. A picture of Lia giving Ethan a massage leaped to mind but he immediately suppressed it.

"I don't understand what you mean," she said, frowning. "And I don't have time to find out. I have to be at work in an hour and it takes a while for me to get out of costume. Nice to meet you, Paul Watts."

He quite pointedly didn't echo the sentiment. "Just remember what I said about staying away from my grandfather."

"I already said I would."

With a graceful flutter of her fingers, she zipped through the building's front door, leaving him alone on the sidewalk. Despite her ready agreement to keep her distance, his nerves continued to sizzle and pop. Logic told him he'd seen the last of Lia Marsh, but his instincts weren't convinced.

Paul shot his brother a text before sliding behind the wheel, urging him to reiterate to Lia that Grady was off-limits. Thanks to this detour he was going to have to hustle to keep from being late for his charter flight.

Ethan's terse reply highlighted the tension between the brothers that seemed to be escalating. The growing distance between them frustrated Paul, but he couldn't figure out how to fix what he couldn't wrap his head around.

Pushing Ethan and the problem of Lia Marsh to the back of his mind, Paul focused his attention on something concrete and within his control: the upcoming conference and what he hoped to get out of it.

As much as Ethan had thoroughly enjoyed seeing his brother utterly flummoxed by Lia in a Rapunzel costume, as soon as Paul headed off to dig into her background, Ethan's satisfaction faded. Leave it to his brother to chase a tangent rather than deal with the real problem of their grandfather's condition. In the same way, Ethan's brother had neatly avoided dealing with Grady's disappointment after Paul chose a career in law enforcement over joining Watts Shipping and eventually taking his place at the helm of the family business. Nor had Paul understood Ethan's conflicted emotions at being the second choice to take up the reins.

While Ethan recognized that he was the best brother to head the family company, he wanted to secure the job based on his skills, not because Paul refused the position. Also, it wasn't just his pride at issue. Ethan was adopted and in a city as preoccupied with lineage as Charleston, not knowing who his people were became a toxic substance eating away at his peace of mind.

Although no one had ever made him feel as if he didn't belong, in every Watts family photo, Ethan's dark brown hair and eyes made him stand out like a goose among swans. Not wishing to cause any of his family undue pain, he kept his feelings buried, but more and more lately they'd bubbled up and tainted his relationship with Paul.

He'd shared some of his angst with Lia. She was a good listener. Attentive. Nonjudgmental. Empathetic. Sure, she was a little quirky. But Ethan found her eccentricities charming. That Paul viewed them as suspect made Ethan all the more determined to defend her.

Clamping down on his disquiet, Ethan reentered his grandfather's hospital room and noted that Grady's eyes were open and sharp with dismay. Had he heard the brothers arguing in the hallway? Although Grady never shied away from confrontation, before the stroke, he'd confided to Ethan that he was troubled by his estrangement from Paul and also the growing tension between the brothers. Ethan knew Paul was equally frustrated with the rift, but none of them had taken any steps to overcome the years of distance.

"Sorry about earlier," Ethan murmured, settling into the chair between Grady's bed and the window. "You know how Paul can get."

He didn't expect Grady to answer. In the weeks following the stroke, Grady had made some progress with the paralysis. He still couldn't walk or write, but he'd regained the ability to move his arm, leg and fingers. It wasn't so much his body that had failed him, but his willingness to fight.

Grady's lips worked, but he couldn't form the words for what he wanted to express. For the first time in weeks this seemed to frustrate him.

"He worries about you," Ethan continued. "Seeing Lia

here was a bit of a shock." He couldn't suppress a grin.
"Did you like her Rapunzel costume? The kids down on
the pediatric floor really loved her."

Grady started to hum a toneless tune Ethan didn't recognize. And then all at once he sang a word.

"Ava."

Ethan was shocked that Grady had spoken—or rather
sung—his daughter's name. "You mean Lia," he said, wondering how his grandfather could've confused his daughter
for Lia. Blonde and green-eyed Ava Watts bore no resemblance to Lia, with her dark hair and hazel eyes. Then Ethan
frowned. Had Lia ever come to visit as herself or was she
always in costume? Maybe Grady thought she was blonde.
And then there was the age difference. If Ava had lived,
she'd be in her forties. Of course, the stroke had messed
with the left side of Grady's brain where logic and reason
held court. Maybe he was actually mixed up.

Ava had been eighteen when she'd run away to New
York City. The family had lost track of her shortly thereaf-
ter. And it wasn't until five years after that that they found
out she'd died, leaving behind an infant daughter. The child
had been adopted, but they'd never been able to discover
anything more because the files had been sealed.

"Ava...baby," Grady clarified, singing the two words.
How had he learned to do that?

"You think Lia is Ava's daughter?" While Grady nodded as enthusiastically as his condition allowed, Ethan's
stunned brain slowly wrapped itself around this development. Grady was obviously grasping at thin air. With each
year that passed he'd grown more obsessed with finding
his missing granddaughter.

"Ava's daughter is here?" Constance Watts asked from
the doorway. "Where? How?"

Ethan turned to his mother, about to explain what was
going on, when his grandfather's fingers bit down hard

on Ethan's wrist, drawing his attention back to the man in the bed. Grady's gaze bore the fierce determination of old, sending joy flooding through Ethan. What he wouldn't give to have his grandfather healthy and happy again.

"Ethan?" his mother prompted, coming to stand beside him.

"Lia…" Grady sang again, more agitated now as he tried to make himself understood.

"Lia?" Constance stared at her father-in-law, and then glanced at her son for clarification. "Who is Lia?"

But when the answer came, it was Grady who spoke up. "Ava…baby."

After her run-in with Paul Watts the day before, the last place Lia expected to find herself was seated beside Ethan in his bright blue Mercedes roadster on the way to the hospital to visit his grandfather. Overhead, clouds dappled the dazzling February sky. Around them the sweet scent of honeysuckle and crab apple blossoms mingled with the sound of church bells coming from the Cathedral of Saint Luke and Saint Paul. It was a glorious day for driving with the top down, but this was no joyride.

"I'm really not sure this is the best idea," Lia said, shuddering as she pictured her last encounter with Paul Watts. "Your brother was pretty clear that he didn't want me anywhere near your grandfather."

"Paul's occupation makes him suspicious," Ethan said. "And Grady's illness has made him even more edgy. Add to that the fact that he doesn't like surprises and that explains why he overreacted at finding a stranger visiting his grandfather." Ethan shot her a wry grin packed with boyish charm. "And you were dressed like Rapunzel so that had to throw him off, as well."

Lia rolled her eyes, unmoved by his attempt to lull her

into giving up her argument. "Are you sure Paul will be okay with me visiting?"

She craved Ethan's reassurance. No one had ever treated her with the level of suspicion Paul Watts had shown.

"He wants Grady to get better just like the rest of us."

"That's not the same thing as being okay with my visiting," she pointed out, the churning in her stomach made worse by Ethan's evasion. Paul's bad opinion of her bothered Lia more than she liked to admit.

"Look, Paul's not in town at the moment so you don't need to worry about running into him. You just visit Grady a few more times and be the ray of sunshine that will enable him to improve and by the time Paul gets back, Grady will be on the mend and Paul will realize it was all due to you."

"I think you're overestimating my abilities," she demurred, even as Ethan's praise warmed her. Each time she'd visited Grady she held his hand and sung to him, pouring healing energy into his frail body.

"Trust me," Ethan declared, taking his espresso-colored eyes off the road and shooting a brief glance her way. "I'm not overestimating anything. Your visits have been transformative."

"But I've only been to see him four times," Lia murmured, determined to voice caution. If Ethan gave her all the credit for his grandfather's improvement, what happened if Grady took a turn for the worse? "I can't imagine I made that much of an impact."

"You underestimate yourself." Ethan spun the wheel and coasted into an empty spot in the parking garage. "He started communicating a little yesterday by singing the way you suggested. That's given him a huge boost in his outlook and he's growing better by the hour. You'll see."

In fact, Lia was excited to see Grady improve. She believed in the power of spiritual healing and trusted that she could tap into the energy that connected all living things and bring about change because she willed it. It didn't always work. Some concrete problems required real-world solutions. For instance, the broken axle on her camper trailer and her totaled truck.

Meditating hadn't gotten Misty fixed. She'd needed money and a mechanic for that. But after asking for help, the universe had found her a wonderful job, terrific coworkers and an affordable place to live. She'd been offered a solution at a point when she was feeling desperate.

Ethan shut off the engine and hit her with an eager grin. "Ready?"

"Sure." But in fact, she was anything but.

When they got off the elevator on the fourth floor, Ethan's long strides ate up the distance to his grandfather's hospital room, forcing Lia to trot in order to keep up.

As they neared Grady's room, Lia spied a familiar figure emerging. "Hi, Abigail," Lia said, as the distance between them lessened. "How is Grady doing today?"

For a moment the nurse looked startled that a stranger had called her by her name, but then she took a longer look at Lia and her eyes widened. "Lia! I didn't recognize you out of costume."

Lia gave an awkward chuckle and glanced at Ethan. "I'm not sure Grady will recognize me, either."

"Mr. Grady will know who you are." The nurse's reassuring smile did little to ease Lia's nerves. "There's a keen mind locked up in there." She glanced at Ethan and when he gave her a confirming nod, Abigail continued, "He's going to be so glad you've come today. Your idea to encourage him to sing has worked wonders. He's so excited to be able to communicate with people again."

Beside her, Ethan radiated smug satisfaction.

"That's great," Lia said, delighted that her suggestion had produced a positive result.

"His family and all the staff are so thrilled that things

started to turn around yesterday. He's doing so much better that the doctor thinks he'll be able to go in a few days."

"Wow," Lia murmured, "that's wonderful news."

"We're so glad she showed up when she did," Ethan declared. "She's worked a miracle."

"Please stop," Lia protested, the praise making her uncomfortable. "The credit really should go to all of you who've been taking such good care of him this whole time."

"There's only so much medicine can do when the will to keep on living is gone," the nurse said.

"Mind over matter," Ethan said. "People don't give it enough credit."

"They certainly don't," Abigail agreed before heading down the hall toward the nurses' station.

Ethan set his hand on Lia's elbow and drew her into Grady's hospital room. As soon as she stepped across the threshold, Lia was struck by the room's buoyant energy. The first time she'd visited Grady Watts, he'd been an immobile lump beneath the covers, unconscious and unaware that she'd taken his hand and softly sung to him. Today as she stepped closer to the bed, she noticed that he was wide awake and eagerly watching her approach. The directness of his gaze reminded her of Paul and she shivered. Ethan had mentioned his grandfather had a sharp temper and forceful manner when crossed.

Grady wiggled his fingers and she took his hand. His dry skin stretched over bones knobby with arthritis. She gave his fingers a light squeeze, shocked at the rush of affection for someone she barely knew. Yet was that true?

Usually she moved on every couple months and rarely got tangled up in people's lives. In this case, her accident extended her time in Charleston, leading to numerous massage sessions with Ethan where he'd spoken at length about his family. As the weeks turned into months, Lia had grown ever more invested in their stories until she almost felt like part of their circle.

"Hello, Grady," Lia said, her voice warbling as affection tightened her throat. "It's Lia. You probably didn't recognize me without my costume. How are you feeling today? You look really good."

Grady's fingers pulsed against hers as he acknowledged her with two sung words. "Ava daughter."

Ethan had explained how Grady had been desperate to reunite with his missing granddaughter before the stroke, even speculating that the patriarch's illness had been brought on by the crushing disappointment of a recent dead end. Since then, Grady had brooded nonstop about what had become of her and the family's failure to bring her back into the fold.

"That's right, Grady," Ethan said, beaming at Lia. His eyes held a wicked twinkle as he added, "Ava's daughter has come home at last."

Delighted by the news, Lia glanced at Ethan and noticed the way the handsome businessman was regarding her with purposeful intent. Her heart began hammering against her ribs as the import of what Ethan was saying struck her. She shifted her attention to the man lying in the hospital bed and she caught her breath to protest. But before she could voice her sharp denial, she saw the love shining in Grady's eyes for her. No. Not for her. For his missing granddaughter.

Head spinning, Lia turned her full attention on Ethan. "What's going on?"

"What's going on is that Grady knows you're his granddaughter." Ethan gripped Lia's elbow with long fingers while his eyes beseeched her to go along. "I explained how Paul located you through one of those genetic testing companies. It's long been Grady's dream to reunite you with your family. And now here you are."

Lia's mind reeled. The position Ethan had put her in was untenable, and to drag his brother into the mix was only going to create more drama. But the sheer joy in Grady's eyes tied her tongue in knots. This could not be happening. She had to tell the truth. She wasn't Ava Watts's long-lost daughter. To claim that she was the missing Watts grand-daughter would only lead to trouble.

"We need to talk about this," Lia growled quietly at Ethan. She put her hand on Grady's shoulder. "We'll be right back."

Leaving a confused Grady behind, Lia fled out into the hallway. To her relief, Ethan followed her. Worried that Grady might overhear their conversation, Lia grabbed Ethan's arm and towed him down the hall toward the wait-ing area near the bank of elevators.

"Have you lost your mind?" she whispered as soon as they reached the empty family lounge. "How could you tell him I'm his granddaughter? And why put Paul in the middle of it? He's going to be furious."

"Grady came to that conclusion all by himself," Ethan explained. "And the reason I gave Paul credit was to help repair the strained relationship between him and Grady."

"Your brother will never go along with this."

"He will when he sees the way Grady is recovering. Overnight his whole prognosis has changed. And it's all because he believes you're his granddaughter. It was his deepest desire to reunite with her and now he has a rea-son to live."

"But I'm not his granddaughter. Why would he think I am? I don't look like any of your family." Lia's heart twisted as she realized her protest might rouse Ethan's angst over being adopted.

"You could be Ava's daughter." Ethan lifted his hands in a beseeching gesture. "We've been trying for years to find her with no luck. I told you that after my aunt died, her baby was adopted and the records were sealed. Believing you're her has given Grady a reason to go on. Do you seriously want to go back in there and break his heart? He's been so depressed since the stroke. In less than a week you've brought him back from the brink of death."

Lia closed her eyes and spent several seconds listening to the pounding of her heart. This could not be happening. And yet it was.

"I just can't do this."

Besides being wrong, even if she agreed to a temporary stint as Grady Watts's missing granddaughter, there was no way Paul was going to let her take on the role.

"You can," Ethan insisted. "Making people feel better is what you do."

"Sure, but not like this," Lia protested. "And I don't want to lie to your family."

"I understand, but they aren't any good at keeping secrets. We've never thrown a successful surprise party or gotten into trouble without everyone in the family knowing about it. For this to work we need to leave them in the dark or else risk that someone will slip up and give you away."

From Ethan's aggrieved tone, this obviously bugged him, and Lia sympathized. Having been isolated from relatives all her life, she couldn't imagine having so many people in her business. Yet there was a flip side. Ethan could also count on his family to have his back.

"And what about Paul?" she quizzed. "Surely he's already dug up enough info on me to know I'm not your cousin."

"Let me handle my brother."

Lia slid sweaty palms along her jean-clad thighs. "Damn it, Ethan. You can't deceive your grandfather this way."

"I can if it means keeping Grady alive," Ethan said and his voice held genuine pain.

"It's a lie," Lia insisted, but she could feel her determination failing beneath the weight of Ethan's enthusiasm. "A big fat dangerous lie. And you know I wasn't planning on sticking around Charleston much longer. Misty is fixed. I almost have enough saved to replace my truck." While this was true, Lia didn't have enough to buy a quality vehicle she could trust. "It's time I got back on the road."

"All you need to do is stay a couple weeks until Grady's completely out of the woods and then we can reveal that a huge mistake was made with the genetic testing service." Something in Lia's expression must have betrayed her weakening resistance because Ethan nodded as if she'd voiced her agreement. "I've thought the whole thing through and I know this will work."

If she hadn't grown fond of the handsome Charleston businessman since he'd become her massage client six months earlier, she never would've agreed to hear him out, much less consider such a wild scheme, but the pain Ethan felt over his grandfather's illness had touched her heart. Plus, he'd made the whole scheme sound so reasonable. A couple of weeks of playacting and then she'd be on her way again. A bubble of hysteria rose inside her. What were more lies on top of the ones she was already telling?

"But I'll be lying not just to Grady, but your whole family. It's a cruel thing to do to all of them."

"I've thought about that, too, but if we do this right, they'll be so happy that Grady is healthy again that it will make the eventual disappointment of you not being family easier to bear." Ethan gripped her hands and hit her with a mega dose of confident charm.

Lia was rallying one last refusal when the elevator doors opened and a slender woman in an elegant suit the color of pistachios stepped off. Instead of immediately heading for the hallway that led to the hospital rooms, she glanced toward the family lounge. Her expression brightened when she spied them.

"Ethan," she said, coming toward them. "Glad to see you here."

"Hello, Mother." Ethan dipped his head and kissed her cheek. "This is Lia."

Constance Watts was every inch a genteel matriarch of the South with her blond hair styled in a long bob and her triple strand of pearls. Her keen blue eyes assessed the jeans and thrift-store T-shirt Lia wore and she braced herself for censure, but Constance only smiled warmly.

"Ethan told me all about you," Constance said, her captivating Southern drawl knotted with emotion.

"He did?" Lia hadn't yet agreed to the scheme and bristled at Ethan's presumption.

"Of course." Constance glanced from Lia to her son. "He said Paul found you through a genetic testing service."

"I'm really—" Lia began.

"Overwhelmed," Ethan broke in, closing his fingers around her hand and squeezing gently. He snared her gaze, his eyes reflecting both determination and apology. "And can you blame her? Finally connecting with her real family after all these years is pretty momentous."

Ethan's need and his mother's elation were a patch of quicksand, trapping Lia. To her dismay, she began nodding.

"Ava's daughter is finally home," Constance murmured, stepping forward and embracing Lia. "You are going to make Grady so happy."

Three

Paul was crossing the hotel lobby on his way to the first panel of the day when his phone buzzed. Incensed at Ethan for bringing a stranger into their grandfather's hospital room, Paul had been ignoring his brother's calls since leaving for the conference. He pulled out his phone and was on the verge of sending the call to voice mail when he spied his mother's picture on the screen. His first reaction was dread. Had Grady's health taken a turn for the worse? Is that why she was calling rather than checking in by text?

"What's wrong?" he demanded, shifting his trajectory toward a quiet nook opposite the reception desk. "Is Grady okay?"

"He's fine. In fact, he's doing better than ever." Constance Watts sounded breathless with delight. "I just wanted to update you that Grady is coming home from the hospital today."

"That's great news," Paul said, stunned by the upswing in Grady's progress. "So he's finally rallying?"

"Thanks to Lia."

"Lia?" Hearing that woman's name was like touching a live wire. The jolt made his heart stop. "I don't understand." Paul believed in cold hard facts not instinct, but at the moment his gut was telling him something bad was happening. "How is she responsible for Grady's improved health?"

"I can't believe you'd have to ask," Paul's mother said. "Ethan told me you found her."

"He did?" Paul responded cautiously. Obviously, his brother had neglected to mention Paul's suspicions about the woman. "Has she been visiting Grady?"

Constance laughed. "She's been by his side constantly for days. Having her there has made his recovery nothing short of miraculous. All the hospital staff are talking about it."

"Grady's getting better?" The volume of Paul's relief almost drowned out the other tidbit his mother had dropped. Lia was visiting Grady despite being told to stay away.

Obviously Paul had underestimated just how intent she was on interfering with his family. Well, he'd send her packing as soon as he returned home.

"…Ava's daughter back in the fold."

Who was back? His mother had continued to prattle on while Paul had been preoccupied. He shook his head to reorient his thoughts.

"I'm sorry, Mother, it's really loud where I am. Can you repeat what you said?"

"I said, Grady is thrilled that you found Ava's daughter," Constance said.

"I found…" Now Paul understood why Ethan had been working so hard to get in touch.

"When are you coming home? Grady's been asking to see you."

For the first time in his adult life, Paul Watts had no words. While his mother waited for his reply, Paul's brain worked feverishly to unravel what could possibly be going on back in Charleston. What sort of crazy stunt was his brother trying to pull? And why? Lia had no more Watts blood than Eth…

Paul shut down the rest of that thought. He and Ethan might not share a biological bond, but they were brothers and Ethan was just as much a Watts as any of them. The same could not be said for a drifter like Lia Marsh.

He hadn't been idle over the last few days of the conference. He'd taken the time to dig into her background and what he'd come up with only reinforced his suspicion that she was some sort of con artist.

"Mother, I need to go." Paul hated to be rude, but he needed to talk to his brother immediately. "Can I call you later?"

"Of course. When are you coming home?"

He was scheduled to return home in three days' time. "I'm going to cut my trip short and catch a flight today."

"That's wonderful."

Paul hung up with his mother and immediately called Ethan. He wasn't surprised when it rolled over to voice mail. Snarling, Paul disconnected without delivering the scathing smackdown his brother so richly deserved. He sent his personal assistant a text about his change of plans so she could organize a flight for him, and then he headed to his suite to pack.

An hour later he was on his way to the airport. A second call to Ethan went unanswered, but this time Paul left an icy message, demanding to know what was going on. The hours between liftoff and touchdown gave Paul plenty of time to check in with the rest of his family and get a feel for what had been going on in his absence.

The situation had progressed further than he'd anticipated. What really burned him was how happy and unquestioning everyone was with the arrival of a stranger claiming to be Ava's daughter. Lia had charmed his parents, aunt and uncle as well as his three Shaw cousins. Nor would any of them listen when he pointed out that they didn't know anything about this woman who'd abruptly appeared in their midst. All they cared about was that Ava's daughter had come home and Grady had magically become healthy.

Eager to get the whole messy situation sorted out, once he arrived in Charleston Paul headed straight from the airport to Grady's estate. He parked on the wide driveway at the back of the property, noting that Ethan's car was absent. The heated lecture Paul wanted to deliver would have to wait.

Paul's breath came in agitated bursts as he wound his way along the garden path and approached the back of the house where a set of double stairs ascended to a broad terrace. Taking the steps two at a time, Paul crossed the terrace to the glass door that led into the kitchen. The room had been remodeled a few years ago to include a massive granite island, abundant cabinets, professional appliances and an updated surround for the fireplace. Two doorways offered access to the interior of the home. Paul chose the one that led into the broad entry hall. Immediately to his left, a set of stairs led upward. Paul's tension rose as he ascended.

The home had been designed with spacious rooms off a wide main hallway. Upstairs, the broad space between the bedrooms was utilized as a cozy lounge area for watching television from the comfortable couch or reading in one of the armchairs that overlooked the rear of the property—as his grandfather's nurse Rosie was doing at the moment. Although Paul recognized that his grandfather didn't require her hovering over him at all hours of the day and night, seeing her whiling her time away over a cup of tea and a novel disturbed him.

"How's he doing?"

Rosie looked up from her book and shot him a wry grin. "Go see for yourself."

Paul approached his grandfather's bedroom, bracing himself for the same dimly lit, hushed space it had become since Grady's stroke. But the scene he stepped into was the utter opposite. Stuttering to a halt just inside the door, Paul gaped in confusion and alarm. What the hell was going on here?

Someone had pulled the curtains back from the windows allowing light to fill the large space. Elvis Presley's "All Shook Up" poured from a speaker on the nightstand, almost drowning out the soothing trickle of water from a small fountain situated on the dresser. The scent of rosemary and lavender drifted toward Paul. As the aroma hit his senses, he noticed a slight boost to his energy and felt a whole lot calmer than he'd been in months. He shook off the sensations and scowled at the source of all his internal commotion.

Paul realized it was Lia who'd transformed Grady's master suite from dark and bleak to bright and festive. And it did seem to be having a magical effect. For the first time since his stroke, Paul's grandfather was sitting upright in bed, propped against an abundance of pillows, his bright gaze fixed on the woman standing beside him. Lia was chattering away while her hands stroked up and down Grady's arm, working the muscles.

A bewildering swirl of emotions cascaded through him at the sight of his grandfather looking so happy and... healthy. Gladness. Relief. Annoyance. This last was due to Lia. She looked so utterly normal without all the theatrical makeup and princess clothing. Today she wore a plain gray T-shirt and black yoga leggings that showed off her lean hips and thighs. A silky ponytail of brown hair swept forward to cascade over one delicate collarbone, while long

bangs framed her narrow face with its pixie chin and bright
red lips. Silver hoop earrings swung against her delicate
jawline.

Paul's immediate impulse was to haul her out of the
room and away from his grandfather. He didn't trust her
despite finding nothing concrete in her background to support the warning in his gut. Just because she hadn't been
caught didn't mean she wasn't up to no good. Nor did it
help her case how swiftly she'd charmed his entire family
into embracing her as one of their own.

Even as he fumed in frustration, Paul became aware of
something hot and disturbing lying beneath his irritation.
It was as if his anger had awakened an insistent, instinctive
pulse of raw hunger. He cursed the untimely appearance of
this single-minded lust for Lia Marsh. Being distracted by
physical cravings was the last thing he needed.

As if alerted by his conflicting desires, Lia glanced his
way. Within their frame of sooty lashes, her eyes locked
on his. Pleasure roared through him as she bit down on her
lower lip. Color flooded her cheeks and for a second he pondered what might happen if his awareness was reciprocated.

Paul ruthlessly swept such musing aside. What did it
matter if she was attracted to him? But then he dialed back
his annoyance. Could he use it to his advantage?

His thoughts must've shown on his face because a wary
frown drew Lia's eyebrows together. Irritated that he'd
given himself away, Paul scowled in return. With a gri-
mace she shifted her attention to Grady. Her smile brightened with what appeared to be genuine affection. Paul's
gut clenched as he took in the tableau.

"Look who's here," she murmured, indicating Paul.

His grandfather turned his head and the warmth in his
welcoming smile filled Paul with blinding joy. It was as if
all the years of estrangement had been never been.

"Paul."

At hearing his name spoken so clearly by his grandfather, a lump formed in Paul's throat and stuck there. Because the stroke had affected Grady's speech, he'd struggled to make himself understood these last few months. Obviously, the reports of Grady's improvement hadn't been exaggerated. But to credit this interloper was going too far. Lost in his circling thoughts, Paul still hovered where he'd stopped just inside the room until his grandfather tapped out some rhythms on a small drum next to him on the bed.

"That means come," Lia explained.

Completely bewildered by what was happening, Paul crossed to his grandfather's side and gave his arm a squeeze. "How are you feeling today?"

The routine question was completely unnecessary. This man bore no resemblance to the invalid from a week ago. At that point, with Grady growing weaker by the day, Paul would've moved heaven and earth to see the return of a mischievous glint to his grandfather's green eyes, which had so recently been dull with defeat and grief. What he glimpsed in Grady's manner was the exact change he'd longed for. But at what cost?

"Happy." A distinct pattern of tapping accompanied Grady's singing. While his voice was breathy and tuneless, the word came out surprisingly clear. Yet despite his joy, Paul was disturbed by how his grandfather's gaze settled fondly on the young woman massaging his hand. "Lia home."

"What's with the drum?" Paul asked Lia, grappling with his shock at Grady's rapid improvement and his attachment to the stranger who had invaded all their lives. Discomfort formed a hard knot in his chest. Although thrilled by his grandfather's improvement, Paul could see nothing but trouble barreling down the road toward them and cursed his brother for doing something so radical and foolish.

"I did some research on stroke recovery and discovered that music and rhythm can help lift a patient's spirts, enable them to communicate and improve their speech." Lia smiled fondly at Grady. "Tomorrow we're going to learn breathing rhythms and also practice meditating to music."

"What's all that supposed to do?"

"The medical explanation didn't make all that much sense to me," Lia said. "But there was something about how the brain processes information and how music can affect that in a positive way. I think that's why Grady can't speak, but he can sing."

Paul's chest tightened as hope surged and he set his jaw against a blast of raw emotion. From the way his grandfather beamed at Lia, it was obvious what everyone had been saying. Grady's improvement had been inspired by the return of his long-lost granddaughter. Only Lia wasn't Ava's daughter and Paul hated the fraud she and his brother were perpetrating.

So, what was he going to do? Paul had never lied to his grandfather. Many times in the past when he was a kid growing up, he'd done something wrong and no matter how bad the punishment, he'd always told Grady the truth. It was a point of pride to Paul that his grandfather trusted him without question.

If he continued to let Grady believe his granddaughter had returned to her family, what sort of damage was he doing to his relationship with his grandfather? Yet Grady's will to live seemed to have been restored by Lia's arrival. Could Paul figure out a way to get rid of her without causing his grandfather harm?

"Do you have a couple minutes to talk?" he asked as she finished massaging Grady's arm and carefully placed it back on the bed.

"Grady has a session with his physical therapist in ten minutes."

With the number of relatives coming and going these days, Paul didn't want his conversation with Lia interrupted or overheard. "I'll meet you by the pool."

On the flight back to Charleston, he'd prepared a number of ways to extricate her from his family. Now, with Grady's improvement hanging on her continued presence, he wasn't convinced sending her away was the best idea.

While he waited for Lia to arrive, Paul paced the concrete deck, oblivious to the tranquility offered by the turquoise rectangle of water, the lush landscaping and the peaceful twittering of the birds.

This whole situation would be more cut-and-dried if anything suspicious had appeared in her background check. But Paul had nothing concrete to prove that she might not be as transparent as she appeared. While deep in his gut he was certain that she was keeping secrets, Paul was a man who acted on facts not feelings.

When Lia arrived, Paul wasted no time making his position clear. "When I told you to stay away from my grandfather, I had no idea things would get this out of control. I don't know what you and my brother were thinking, but this can't go on."

Because his entire family had embraced her, it fell to Paul to remain detached and keep his guard up. That would be easier if she didn't stir his body and incite his emotions. And if she hadn't worked miracles with his grandfather.

"You're right," she agreed. "I shouldn't have let Ethan talk me into lying to everyone. I'm sorry. It's just Ethan was so desperate to help your grandfather. And believing that I'm his granddaughter has made him better."

Paul watched her expression, determined to see past her guileless facade to the truth. "You've done a good job making sure everyone is attached to you."

Her lashes flickered at his deliberate accusation. "That's to be expected. They all think I'm their long-lost cousin."

She crossed her arms over her chest and lifted her chin. "Have you decided how you're going to break the news about me being an imposter?"

Paul forced air through his teeth in a soft hiss. "I'm not sure I can. The truth would crush Grady."

Her eyebrows went up in surprise. "What are you going to do then?"

"I don't know." He needed to discuss the situation with Ethan.

She narrowed her eyes in confusion. "So why did you want to talk to me?"

Why had he wanted to talk to her?

"I…"

What could he say? That she'd been on his mind the entire time he was gone? That he found her fascinating despite his mistrust? He wanted to know everything about her. And not just because her mysterious background and limited digital footprint awakened his curiosity. Some of her behavior didn't fall into easily explainable patterns. For example, why did she dress up and visit children in the hospital? Something so altruistic was contrary to how an opportunist would behave. Unless she played on the sympathies of parents with sick children to some end. He'd never know unless he got to know her better.

And then there was the pesky physical attraction she inspired in him. Even now, as his thoughts took him down a somber path, he caught himself admiring her long lashes and wondering if her full lips could possibly be as soft as they looked. Her casual outfit showed off a toned body with soft curves. He imagined framing her slim hips with his hands and pulling her close. Dipping his head and running his lips down her neck to the place where it met her shoulder. Hearing her groan in pleasure as he lifted her against his growing erection and plunged his tongue into her mouth…

"Paul?" she said. "Are you okay?"

His name on her lips shocked him out of his lusty daydream. "No, I'm not okay. You and Ethan have put me in the untenable position of having to lie to Grady." A slight breeze flowed toward them from the garden, bringing the sweet scent of honeysuckle and cooling the heat beneath his skin.

"I know and I'm sorry." She put her hand on his arm and the contact seared him through two layers of fabric. "But you won't have to worry about that for too long. In a couple weeks, as soon as Grady is firmly on the road to a full recovery, we'll explain that the genetic testing place made a huge mistake and I'll be gone."

That she and his brother thought they could just snap their fingers and undo the whole situation showed just how impulsive they'd been.

"Why are you doing this?" he demanded, badly needing to understand. "What do you get out of it?"

Something flickered in her eyes briefly before she composed her features into an expression of benign innocence. "Nothing."

Nothing? Paul's muscles bunched as wariness returned. That didn't ring true. Because what he'd glimpsed in that microsecond was all the confirmation that he needed that Lia Marsh was up to no good.

Lia could tell Paul wasn't believing her claim and decided she'd better elaborate. "I really don't want anything from your grandfather or any of your family. I just want to help." She infused this last statement with all her passion, wondering if anything she said would quiet Paul's suspicions.

Earlier when she'd looked up and spied Paul standing in his grandfather's bedroom, her first reaction hadn't been panic, but vivid, undeniable lust. The guy was just so gorgeous. For someone who made his living thwarting cyber-criminals he had an amazing physique. His broad shoulders and imposing height sent her heartbeat racing while his smoldering looks drove her desires into dangerous territory.

Now, as he frowned at her, Lia was struck again by his sex appeal. Sunlight teased gold from his dark blond hair and highlighted his strong bone structure. In those all too brief moments when he wasn't scowling, his features were almost boyishly handsome, and Lia caught herself wishing he'd smile at her. A ridiculous wish considering that he'd made his opinion of her crystal clear.

Before Paul could respond, his phone rang. He glanced down at the screen and grimaced. "I have to take this."

The instant his attention shifted to the call, Lia retreated toward the house. She wanted to check in on Grady before heading back to her rental. Now that Paul had returned home, she decided the less time she spent around him the better for both of them.

As Lia neared the house, she spied Paul's mother descending the wrought iron staircase from the back terrace. Constance's welcoming smile gave Lia an unfamiliar sense of belonging that left her tongue-tied and riddled with guilt over her deception.

"There you are," Constance said. "Isn't Paul with you? Rosie said he'd been up to visit Grady."

"He had to take a call."

"It's probably his office. I swear that son of mine does nothing but work."

"Ethan said he's quite good at what he does."

"He's exceptionally good with computers and dedicated to running down criminals." For a moment Constance's clear blue eyes glowed with maternal fondness, then she sighed. "It caused quite a stir in our family when he opted to go work for the police department out of college rather than join Watts Shipping, but he needed to follow his heart."

"Catching crooks seems to be his passion."

"Yes, but it's grown into more of an obsession these last two years."

"How come?" Lia cursed her curiosity. She should be fighting her interest in the elder Watts brother not delving into his psyche.

"His friend's network services company was hacked and implanted with a bug that affected four million domains, causing them to leak sensitive customer data, including credit card details, for six months before it was discovered. The resulting bad press led to the company losing nearly all their major accounts and forced them out of business."

"Did Paul catch the hackers?"

"Eventually, but not soon enough to stop what happened to Ben."

Although she regretted that the topic had distressed Constance, Lia couldn't stop herself from wanting the whole story. "What happened to his friend?"

"After losing everything, he died in a terrible car accident." Constance's expression turned grim. "Paul thought the circumstances were suspicious because there were no other cars involved. Ben lost control, went off a bridge and drowned. Plus, there was a cryptic email Paul received shortly before the accident. Taken together, he thought perhaps Ben killed himself."

"That's awful."

Constance nodded. "Ben's death hit Paul really hard. After that he became even more committed to shutting down hackers."

Sympathy for Paul momentarily pushed aside her wariness of him. At the same time she recognized this complex man had the power to turn her inside out.

"You know, I can't get over how much you look like your mother," Constance said, the abrupt shift of topic catching Lia off guard.

Lia knew her dark hair and hazel eyes set her apart from the blond and green-eyed Wattses, Ava included. She'd seen pictures of the woman. Yet on Ethan's word, the family had embraced her without question. At least most of them had.

"Tell me about her." Lia couldn't bring herself to say *my mother*.

"She was beautiful and talented." Constance's gaze turned inward. "She played tennis until she was fourteen at a level that she could've competed professionally."

"Why didn't she?"

"She had trouble staying focused on anything," Constance said. "By the time she hit her teenage years Ava was a handful. She grew up without a mother and Grady indulged her terribly. Everyone did because she could be charming when she set her mind to it."

"Ethan said after high school she headed to New York City to pursue modeling."

"She and Grady had a terrible row when he found out she didn't intend to go to college. He gave her a choice—get a degree or find a job. He had such high hopes for her future and wanted to motivate her." Constance sighed. "After years of no contact, Grady hired a private investigator to find her. That's when we learned she'd died. The police never contacted us because Ava did such a good job cutting her ties to Charleston. By the time we discovered Ava had given birth to you, you'd been adopted and the court records sealed."

"And my…father." The last word stuck in Lia's throat. Never mind her fake father—she knew nothing about her own father because her mother had refused to discuss him.

Constance blinked in surprise. "We don't know anything about him. Whatever your mother was up to in New York remains a complete mystery."

Both women lapsed into companionable silence, each occupied with her thoughts. Lia was wondering how to extricate herself without seeming rude when Paul's mother spoke again.

"It's so good to have you here," Constance declared with sudden vehemence. "I'm just sorry it took so long for us to find you."

"I had a good life." For some reason Lia felt compelled to defend her childhood. "A happy life."

"Of course you did," Constance said. "It's obvious that you're a loving, caring person. That sort of thing only happens if you've had the right upbringing. Your aunt Lenora and I were talking last night," Constance said, "and we think that you should move into your mother's old bedroom."

"Oh, well..." Overwhelmed by the thought of having to maintain her deception all the time, Lia scrambled for some polite way to refuse. "I couldn't impose."

"You're family. You wouldn't be imposing. And we have purely selfish reasons to suggest it. We all feel that the more time you spend with Grady, the faster he'll improve."

"Yes, but..."

"He's been without you for too long. You two have a lot of catching up to do."

"Well, sure, but..."

"What are you two talking about?" Paul asked, coming up the gravel path behind them.

Lia turned to confront him, bracing herself for the heat of his displeasure when he found out what his mother had suggested.

"There you are," Constance said. "Rosie mentioned you'd arrived. Have you been up to see Grady? His progress is absolutely amazing."

"Quite amazing," Paul echoed, his distrustful green gaze flickering in Lia's direction.

"And we have Lia to thank."

"So I keep hearing," Paul muttered, his tone neutral.

Seeming unaware of the tension between her son and Lia, Constance continued, "I was just telling her that Lenora and I want her to move in."

"And I was just saying that I don't think that's a good idea," Lia inserted, hoping that he would give her credit for keeping his family at arm's length.

"There's no need to spend money on a rental when there's so much room here," Constance said.

"It's only for a couple weeks," Lia protested. "Then Misty and I will be on our way."

"Misty?" Paul asked.

"She's my camper trailer." She and Ethan had decided to stick close to her original story to avoid slipups.

"You named your camper Misty?" Paul interjected, his lips twisting sardonically.

Lia glared at him. He could insult her integrity all he wanted, but disparage her home and she'd come out swinging. "She's vintage."

Before Paul could reply, his mother jumped in. "Everyone is coming here to have dinner tonight. I hope you can make it."

"I came here straight from the airport," he said, "so I need to run home first."

"Take Lia. I'm sure she'd love to see your home. She's been cooped up with Grady for days. A little sea air would be good for her." Constance turned to Lia. "And on the way back you can pick up your things and get settled in."

"Really, I'm not sure…"

"It will be much better for Grady if you're close by."

Lia caved beneath Constance's firm determination. "Okay."

"Dinner is at seven," Paul's mother said.

"We'll be back in plenty of time." Paul hard gaze flicked to Lia as he bent to kiss his mother's cheek before striding off.

Lia hustled to catch up to him. As soon as they were out of earshot, she said, "I want you to know I didn't put her up to that."

"I know you didn't. Everyone believes what you've done for Grady is a miracle."

"I haven't done anything."

Paul surveyed her for several silent minutes before replying, "On the contrary. You've done plenty."

Despite his rampant disapproval, Paul demonstrated pristine Southern manners by opening the passenger door on his Range Rover and waiting while she climbed in before closing the door and circling to the driver's side.

"I know you aren't interested in spending any time with me so if you want to just drop me at my place—"

"On the contrary, I intend to spend our time away from the estate getting to know the real you."

It took Lia several panicky heartbeats to decide whether to be alarmed or thrilled. Obviously, he hadn't yet decided to go along with Ethan's wild scheme.

"Awesome." She managed the comeback without a trace of irony. "Does that go both ways?"

Paul stopped concentrating on the road and glanced her way. "What do you mean?"

"You want to know everything about me." Something reckless had taken ahold of her. "Are you going to let me get to know you, as well?"

"Why would you want to do that?" While Paul's tone remained neutral, a muscle bunched in his cheek.

"Because it's what normal people do. They exchange information and feel each other out."

Feel each other out? The phrase sounded flirtatious, and heaven knew she'd give anything if he'd just smile at her, but Paul didn't seem to hear it that way.

"Is that what you did with Ethan?" The tightness in his voice took her aback.

"Why would you ask about him?"

"I still can't figure out your relationship with my brother. How much is he paying you for this little charade?"

Now she understood where Paul was going with his questions. "He agreed to cover what I'm losing in income for a couple weeks."

"How much?" Paul asked.

"I don't know." Lia scrunched up her face as she calculated. "No week is the same. I get paid by the client and that varies."

"Ballpark it for me."

"Including tips, it averages to about eight hundred dollars a week."

For the first time Paul looked taken aback. "That's it?"

Spoken like a man who drove a luxury SUV and lived at the beach. No doubt he couldn't fathom Lia's frugal ways any more than she understood paying more for a single pair of shoes than it cost her to eat for an entire month.

"That's it." Lia believed in the equitable exchange of money for goods or services. "All I want is what's fair."

Paul gave her a skeptical look. "What if I paid you fifty thousand dollars to go away and never come back?"

For several seconds Lia pondered the fancy truck she could buy with such an enormous sum. For six months she'd been stuck in Charleston while she saved enough to replace her wrecked vehicle. Accepting Paul's outrageous offer would enable her to return to her nomadic lifestyle in a few days.

"You said you wanted to get to know me better," she said. "Well, the first thing you should know is that I'm not motivated by money."

"Which is exactly what you'd say," Paul countered, "if your endgame would guarantee you a greater payout."

"Are you suspicious of me in particular or people in general?"

"You have to see that I have good reason to doubt you," he said.

"I really don't see it at all," she shot back, wishing that he'd stop toying with her.

Did he know about her past? Bile rose in her throat as she imagined his disgust. But if he'd dug up her secrets, he'd confront her directly. She studied his profile while her heart thundered in her ears and realized that fearing that he knew all about her background was making her come across as guilty. Lia breathed in for a count of four and released the air just as slowly. What did it matter if Paul knew her story? His good opinion shouldn't matter to her.

Paul studied her the whole time she was striving for calm. "You didn't answer me about taking fifty thousand to disappear."

Lia considered what her mother's reaction would have been to Paul's offer. Jen Marsh had a complicated relationship with money and many of her attitudes had rubbed off on her daughter. Lia lived frugally, avoiding debt, buying only what she needed, living with less stuff. But Jen Marsh took her disdain for spending one step beyond obsessive after what she'd experienced growing up.

"You don't have to pay me anything to drop this whole charade and vanish from your lives," Lia said, noticing a subtle easing in the tension around Paul's mouth. The desire to gain his trust prompted her to add, "Whatever you and Ethan decide is fine with me."

Four

"So you'd really go?" Even as he asked the question, Paul recognized exposing her would throw his whole family into chaos. "If I convinced Ethan that you should?"

"Yes." She cocked her head and studied him. "Frankly I'm surprised you haven't done so already."

"He's not taking my calls."

Paul gripped the steering wheel and contemplated Lia's declaration. Would she really leave the decision up to him and Ethan or would she act behind the scenes to win Ethan to her side?

"So you don't know."

"Don't know what?" Paul asked, wondering what else had gone wrong in his absence.

"How this whole situation came about."

Paul glanced her way. "And how's that?"

"Ethan put me in a position where the only choices I had were to go along and pretend to be Grady's granddaughter or tell the truth and risk that he might not recover from the blow."

Although he wasn't surprised that she'd blame the whole situation on Ethan, Paul asked, "Why don't you tell me what happened."

"Ethan set me up. I thought I was visiting Grady as myself. Instead as I stood beside his bed and held his hand, both he and Ethan ambushed me with this whole thing about being Ava's daughter."

"So you're blaming my grandfather for this situation, as well?"

"No. Yes. Sort of. Ethan told me Grady came up with the idea on his own."

"You didn't mention that Grady might be inspired to improve if his granddaughter miraculously appeared?"

Lia's mouth dropped open. "To what end?"

"The Wattses are a wealthy, old Charleston family. We wield both power and influence in this town. You might've liked the idea of being a part of that."

"Hardly," she sniffed. "In fact, it sounds stressful and intimidating. Not to mention having the threat of a simple DNA test hanging over my head all the time."

"Yet here you are." Distracted by their conversation, Paul almost missed the turnoff to Sullivan's Island. "And here I am. Damn it. I hate having to lie to everyone in my family, but most of all to Grady."

"I feel the same way. Your mom and aunt have been welcoming. And your cousins are really nice. It's horrible that I can't be truthful, but then I see how happy Grady is and watch him get a little better every day, and I think the whole messed-up situation might work out okay."

Paul refused to be persuaded by her feel-good justification. "I'm sure this is the logic you and Ethan have used to justify what you've done, but lying is wrong."

"A lot of the time it is, but not always. What about lying to protect someone's feelings? As long as the lie isn't malicious it doesn't do any harm."

It all sounded like a bunch of excuses to Paul, but he'd invited her on this trip to his house to gain insight into her and this conversation was teaching him a lot. "So you don't believe the truth can set you free?"

"Not always. Sometimes it can be painful."

"That doesn't justify lying."

Lia shrugged. "We will just have to agree to disagree."

Paul glanced her way and saw that she was staring out the passenger window at the passing landscape. Despite their opposing opinions, he couldn't shake his fascination with her.

"I guess we will."

An unrelenting silence fell between them that didn't break even as Paul turned the SUV into his driveway and stopped before his house. Switching off the engine, he glanced her way. Lia radiated disappointment and hurt, but Paul refused to be drawn in. Despite her positive effect on Grady, Paul couldn't shake the notion that Lia Marsh was going to cause trouble for his family.

She was working an angle. He just needed to figure out what it was. Which was why he'd decided to move into the carriage house, located near the back of the estate, for the next two weeks so he could keep an eye on her. He intended for Lia to understand that he wasn't taken in by her do-gooder act.

"I'll just be a few minutes," he said. "Do you want to wait here or come in?"

"I'm sure you'd prefer I stay here."

He dismissed her sarcasm with a shrug. "Suit yourself."

But as he headed up the stairs to his front door, he heard her footsteps on the wood boards behind him. The electronic lock on the entrance disengaged as he neared. He opened the door and gestured Lia inside. After suggesting she check out the view, Paul left Lia gawking at the beach beyond the towering floor-to-ceiling windows that made up one wall of his spacious great room. In his bedroom, he unpacked his luggage, swapping the tailored suits he'd worn to the conference for the slacks and button-down shirts he favored for the office.

Before he'd done more than replace his suits in the closet and dump his dirty clothes into the hamper, Paul's phone began to ring. He glanced at the screen, saw Ethan's name and the disquiet he'd been feeling at his brother's snub eased slightly.

Despite their family's expectations, it was Ethan and not Paul who was following in Grady's footsteps as family mediator and key decision maker. Ethan had always been the empathetic brother. Outgoing and social, he tended to be more in touch with the emotions. And despite being the younger brother, everyone turned to Ethan for advice and support.

In contrast, Paul was more comfortable as a lone wolf. He liked technology because of its logic and predictability and had chosen to become a cop because he thrived on the challenge of catching criminals. That doing so also helped people was a bonus, but it didn't drive him. No doubt Ethan would say this attitude made him a jerk.

Would Lia agree?

Paul couldn't imagine what made the question pop into his mind. Nor did he care about some interloper's opinion about him.

"It's about time you called me back," Paul said irritably into the phone, closing the master bedroom door in case Lia decided to eavesdrop.

"Before you go all big brother and start lecturing me about how much I messed up, tell me you don't see a huge change in Grady."

"Fine. I'll admit that Grady's better and that believing Lia is Ava's daughter is the reason, but why the hell did you drag me into it by saying I'm the one who found her?"

"I thought if you got the credit for doing something that would make Grady incredibly happy that it would repair your relationship."

"You're wrong to hope that will make me less furious with you for dragging me into your scheme." Yet even as he spoke, Paul's heart clenched. Despite the tension that had grown between the brothers, Paul appreciated that Ethan had his back. "Have you thought this whole thing through? He's going to be devastated when the truth comes out. And it will because there's no way I'm letting this go on."

"I didn't figure you would, but he'll be stronger in a few weeks." Ethan paused for a heartbeat. "Or she doesn't have to go anywhere." When Paul sucked in a breath to protest, Ethan jumped in. "Hear me out. She spends all her time driving around the country in a vintage camper picking up odd jobs wherever she goes. That's no life. Instead she could stay with us and be our cousin."

"Have you lost your mind?" Paul demanded, wondering what sort of madness had overcome his brother. "We don't know anything about this person."

"I do. She's genuine and kind. Everyone loves her."

"Even you?"

"What?" Ethan exclaimed, following it up with a rough laugh. "Hardly."

Unsatisfied by his brother's answer, Paul asked another. "Is she in love with you?"

"No."

Paul hadn't been entirely satisfied by Lia's denials and he sensed Ethan was holding something back. While it wasn't unusual for Ethan to champion something or someone he believed in, the level of trust he'd afforded Lia compelled Paul to take nothing for granted.

"Are you sure?" Paul pondered the amount of time Lia had undoubtedly spent with her hands roaming over Ethan's naked body. While she'd claimed to be a professional massage therapist, there was something overtly intimate about the experience. "Women tend to fall for you rather quickly."

"That's because I'm nice to them." Ethan's tone was dry as he finished, "You should try it sometime."

For a second Paul didn't know how to respond to his brother's dig. In truth, he had neither time nor interest in a personal life these days. His consulting company grew busier each year as criminals became increasingly bolder and more clever. Technology changed faster than most people could keep up and new threats emerged daily.

On the other hand, Ethan had taken on more responsibility since their grandfather's stroke compelled their father to pick up Grady's chairmanship duties. Although Ethan had been groomed for years to take over one day, having the responsibility thrust on him without any transition period had increased the amount of hours Ethan spent at the office by 50 percent. Yet he still carved out time for family and friends, dating and even attending their mother's endless charity events.

Paul just didn't want to put in the effort. He'd always been solitary, preferring intimate gatherings with his small circle of friends versus the active bar scene or loud parties. Her solitary lifestyle was probably the one thing Paul actually understood about Lia Marsh.

"Are you sure Lia didn't put the idea in your head that she should play the part of Ava's daughter?"

"Trust me—I came up with the plan all on my own."

Paul gave a noncommittal grunt. "She claims she's only planning on sticking around for two weeks." He paused, assessing how much damage would be done during that span.

"That's what we agreed to. I tried to convince her to stay

for a month, but she's determined to go. She doesn't like staying anywhere for more than a few months."

"What's up with that?"

"I don't know. She doesn't talk much about herself."

Paul considered his earlier conversation with Lia. "You don't think that indicates she has something to hide?" While he waited for Ethan to respond, Paul relived his joy in Grady's affectionate greeting. The thought of losing his grandfather's love and approval all over again filled Paul with dread. "Okay, I really hate the situation, but I agree that she's had a positive impact on Grady. As long as it's only two weeks, I'm okay if she stays around and pretends to be Ava's daughter."

"Thanks." Ethan released the word on a long exhale as if he'd been holding his breath. "And don't worry, we've figured out an exit strategy. It's all going to work out. You'll see."

"Both of you keep saying the same thing. I hope like hell that you're right."

"We are." Ethan's smile came through loud and clear. "And be nice to Lia. She's doing us a huge favor."

After he'd hung up with Ethan, Paul chewed over his brother's final statement as he tossed what clothes he'd need for the next two weeks into a duffel. No one would question his decision to stay at the estate. His office was a few blocks away. He'd slept in the carriage house often since Grady's stroke and even before that had utilized the cozy apartment to break for a nap during an intense case when an hour-long round-trip drive to his beach house was time he couldn't afford.

Paul dropped his overnight bag in the foyer and returned to the great room in search of Lia. He looked out the window and saw her standing beside the pool, her arms crossed over her chest, her attention fixed on the Atlantic Ocean. She'd freed her hair and the brisk wind off the water turned the dark strands into a fluttering pennant. He went out to join her.

"I've never been able to decide if I prefer the mountains or the beach," she said, her lips curving into a smile. "I guess that's why I travel so much. There are always new places to discover."

Her tranquil expression transfixed him. He surveyed the freckles dusting her nose and upper cheeks and wondered what about her captivated him. Was it the thrill of the hunt? He'd parlayed his passion for tracking down cybercriminals into a multimillion-dollar company. Lia presented the exact sort of mystery that drove him to work seventy-and eighty-hour weeks to keep his clients' data safe.

And yet here he was, compelled to accept a suspicious stranger as his cousin in order to save his grandfather. Despite Ethan's assurances, Paul knew Lia represented a danger to his family.

So with that foremost in his mind, why did he constantly find himself fighting the urge to touch her? To sample the warmth of her skin. To pull her tight against him and capture her rosy lips in a heated kiss. This unrelenting war between his body and mind was as exhausting as it was troubling.

Had she influenced Ethan the same way? From their earlier conversation Ethan made it clear he trusted Lia. Before she came along, Paul never questioned his brother's judgment. What was it about Lia that roused Paul's suspicions?

"I think my brother might be in love with you."

"What?" She tore her attention from the view and huffed out a laugh. "That's ridiculous."

"Is it?" Paul countered. "He's very protective of you."

"That's because he likes me." Lia turned and studied his expression for several seconds before adding, "I'm a nice person."

Paul's nostrils flared. "Are you sleeping with him?"

"He's my client," she shot back. "I don't sleep with clients."

"But you're attracted to him?"

"He has an incredible body," she mused, with reckless disregard for his escalating annoyance. "Great muscles. Shoulders to die for. Strong thighs." She paused as if taking stock of the impact her words were having. "And as a massage therapist I have to say it's nice when a man takes such good care of his skin."

"So you are attracted to him?"

Lia gave an impatient snort. "Ethan has impeccable manners, a deep, sexy drawl and an overabundance of charm. That I'm not the least bit attracted to him made my coworkers—of both sexes—question my sexual orientation. I'm a professional. I never would've kept Ethan as a client if he'd inspired even a trace of lust. That sort of thing crosses a line for me."

"You forget I've seen you two together. There's something between you."

"He's felt comfortable enough with me to share stuff," she murmured.

"There's more to it than that."

"No, there isn't," Lia declared impatiently before sucking in a deep, calming breath. "Look," she said, giving her shoulders a little shake to relax them. "I feel as if we're dancing around something."

"I don't dance."

"No," Lia muttered wryly. "I expect you don't. Look, for this to work, we really need to find a way to get along." She paused, giving him the opportunity to agree. When he remained silent, Lia chose not to wait him out. "How about if I confess something that's hard for me to admit?" She cleared her throat and gave a nervous half smile. "I find you attractive."

He should've regarded the admission as a clever manipulation and met it with skepticism. Instead, her confession lit up his body like a fireworks finale.

"Why would you tell me something like that?"

"It gives you a little power over me," she said with a sexy, sweet smile that sent an electric pulse zipping along his nerve endings.

"And you think I need that," he countered, bothered that she had him all figured out. Well, maybe not all figured out. But she had a pretty good idea of what made him tick. It served as a reminder that he needed to stay on his guard around her.

"Don't you?" Her presumptive manner bordered on over-confidence. "I think you crave being in control at all times and I'll bet it drives you crazy when things don't go according to plan."

"I don't go crazy," he said, stepping into her space, unwilling to consider his real motivation for what he was about to do. "I adapt."

Lia misjudged the reason Paul closed the gap between them and never saw the kiss coming. Being caught completely by surprise heightened the emotional impact of his soft breath feathering across her skin. An instant later, his lips touched hers and a million stars exploded behind her eyelids. He cradled her head with strong fingers, grounding her while the firm, masterful pressure of his mouth stole her breath and her equilibrium.

Paul's kisses were in a class all by themselves. Never before had she been so swept up in the magic of the moment. The perfection of his lips gliding over hers. The hitch in his breath as she shifted her weight onto her toes and leaned in to him. Lia never wanted the kiss to end, but couldn't explain why. What was it about Paul that called to her? He'd offered her nothing but skepticism and scowls. Yet the clean, masculine scent of him, the gentle sweep of his fingertips against her skin unleashed both joy and hunger.

When he sucked on her bottom lip, she groaned and gave him full access to her mouth. His tongue swept against hers and the taste of him only increased her appetite for more. Lia tunneled her fingers into his hair to keep their mouths fused as he fed on her lips and she devoured him in turn.

His arm banded around her waist, drawing her snugly against his hard torso. While she'd appreciated Paul's powerful body from a safe distance, pressed like this against the unyielding solidity of his strong abs sharpened the longing to feel his weight settle over her.

She'd been kissed enough to recognize she'd never experienced anything like this before. Where moments ago she'd been shivering in the cool breeze coming off the ocean, now her skin burned as fire raced through her veins and sent heat deep into her loins. Paul must've recognized the upward tick in her passion because his hand curved over her butt and squeezed just hard enough to send a jolt of pleasure lancing between her thighs. She gasped and arched her back, driving her breasts against him to satisfy their craving for contact.

His fingers tightened on her, the grip almost bruising, and then he was breaking off the kiss and relaxing his hold. Lia might've cried out in protest, but an icy lash of sea wind struck her overheated flesh, wrenching her back to reality. She shifted a half step back, surprised at the unsteadiness of her knees. Setting her hand on Paul's chest for balance, she noted his rough exhalation. Her own heart was pumping hard in the aftermath of the kiss.

She looked up and caught a glimpse of the twin green flames flickering in his eyes. A moment later all trace of heat vanished from his gaze. Had she imagined it? As much as it pained her to leave the warmth and comfort of his embrace, Lia needed distance to gather her thoughts and make sense of what had just happened. Paul had made it crystal clear that he didn't like her. So, what was he doing?

"Was that meant to determine whether I was telling the truth about being attracted to you?" Lia panted, scanning Paul's expression and hoping that wasn't what the kiss had been about.

"Why would you think I'd do that?" he countered, dragging his thumb over his lower lip.

Mesmerized by the action, Lia shivered as pleasurable aftershocks continued to rock her body. "Because you don't believe anything I say." The bitterness in her tone caught her by surprise. She wished Paul's good opinion wasn't so important to her. "So what's the verdict? Do you think I'm attracted to you?"

"Yes." He waited a beat for her retort. When none came, he raised his eyebrows. "Aren't you going to ask me if the feeling's mutual?"

Lia shook her head and forced her muscles to relax. "I don't want to play those sorts of games with you."

Paul's features looked carved in granite as he regarded her. "I told Ethan I will go along with your subterfuge for now."

"Great." Lia slumped in defeat, unsure why this news bothered her so much. Had she really hoped he'd call her out in front of his family and drive her away? Given who he was, what he believed in, he should. "I'm sure that made Ethan very happy," she murmured.

Paul scrutinized her for several seconds before nodding. "We should be getting back."

The ride to Charleston passed with little conversation between them. Lia needed to sort out her feelings about the kiss, Paul's abrupt acceptance of her temporarily posing as his long-lost cousin and what would happen if her reasons for playing the part ever came to light.

Already Lia suspected her strong attraction to Paul could

develop into an emotional attachment unlike anything she'd known before. She'd never experienced such an unshakable craving to be with anyone. The need scared her a little, but the compelling nature of her desire was impossible to ignore. She couldn't pretend that surrendering to temptation wouldn't have repercussions. Lia couldn't imagine this longing for him would just vanish one day. Even if Paul never found out where she came from and rejected her, she planned to get back on the road in a matter of weeks. For her future peace of mind, she needed to bottle up her feelings here and now.

Yet what was going on between her and Paul wasn't the only emotional time bomb ticking away. The way Paul's mother and aunt had welcomed her into the family had touched Lia in a way she hadn't expected. Despite her guilt at the fraud she was perpetrating on them, the love they'd shown for their missing niece left Lia pondering what her own homecoming might be if she ever reached out to the family her mother left behind in Seattle.

Jen Marsh had struck out on her own shortly after high school and never looked back. Reluctance to linger in any place for long meant she rarely formed any lasting attachments. And neither had Lia.

But even though she lacked experience with lasting familial support, sometimes Lia pined for a family to belong to. Not that she imagined fitting into a large, tight-knit group like the Wattses. The reality was slowly sinking in that she would soon be living amongst them and that they would expect her to share their limelight. Jen Marsh had gone to great lengths to escape her past and create an anonymous life for both her and Lia.

If Paul kept digging into her background, could he jeopardize that? Would a story about the granddaughter of a swindler interest anyone three decades after he went to jail?

Doubtful. But to be sure, she'd better avoid any public attention for the next two weeks.

After a brief stop at her rental to pack up her limited wardrobe, Paul drove straight back to the estate. Constance must've been on the lookout for them because she was on hand in the first-floor hallway to lead the way upstairs to the bedrooms, narrating as she went.

"The Birch-Watts House has six bedrooms and seven bathrooms," Constance said. "It was built in 1804 by Jacob Birch and his descendants lived here until 1898 when Theodore Watts bought it. The home's been in the Watts family ever since."

"Wow, that's a long time." Lia had been present when they'd brought Grady home from the hospital and had been too focused on getting him settled to take in much more than a cursory impression of the grand mansion. "And only Ethan's grandfather lives here?"

It seemed like a lot of empty space for just one person to rattle around in. A house with nearly ten thousand square feet and so many bedrooms should be full of people. And in its heyday, it probably was. But families were smaller now and not so likely to have several generations living under one roof.

"Grady's been alone since he lost Grandma back in the late 1960s," Paul added, "but the Shaw twins live in the caretaker's house on the back corner of the estate. And I spend the night in the carriage house here and there. More often since his stroke."

"He must like having you all close by," Lia murmured, realizing she might be inundated with family members over the next week.

"Both girls are so busy with their careers and social lives." Constance sighed. "Which is why it's wonderful that you've come to spend time with Grady. Did you bring a swimsuit? The pool was recently refurbished and switched to salt water."

"No, I didn't think it was going to be that sort of a visit." Seeing Paul's lips tighten, Lia suppressed a twinge of regret. No matter what he thought, she had no intention of treating her time with his family like a vacation. She intended to do her best to get Grady as healthy as possible in the next two weeks.

"This was your mother's room." Constance led the way into the room on the opposite side of the hall from Grady's master suite. "It's the best guest room in the house."

"Wow!"

The enormous, bright bedroom overlooked the gardens and side lawn with floral curtains framing the four tall windows set into the muted green walls. Lia's gaze darted from the view to the big bed with its matching comforter and the yellow fainting couch at its foot. A giant mirrored armoire dominated one wall and Lia knew without even opening the doors that even with the two bulky costumes she'd brought along, her clothes wouldn't take up half the space.

"You sound like you approve," Constance declared with a delighted smile.

"I've never stayed anywhere so nice. Or so big," Lia said. "It's more space than I'm used to."

Lia was a minimalist by necessity as well as desire. The friends she'd made during her travels marveled at how little she needed, but Lia had never known any other way to be. Traveling around the country in a nineteen-foot camper meant owning a bare minimum of essentials. The only deviation from that rule was her ever expanding collection of princess costumes.

Yet the moment she'd entered the bedroom, Lia had been blown away by the beautiful antiques, the intricate plasterwork around the ceiling and fireplace, the ridiculously comfortable-looking bed and the bathroom that was bigger than her entire camper. For several long seconds she imagined herself spending long hours soaking in the tub. Then reality intruded. She wasn't on vacation. A couple weeks from now she and Misty would be back on the road.

"Get used to it," Constance advised. "You're going to be with us for a long time."

"Um…"

Turbulent emotions rose up in Lia, tightening her throat and making it impossible to speak. Being thrust into the tight-knit Watts family highlighted the isolation in her lifestyle and brought her into direct conflict with her mother's attitude that just because someone was family didn't mean they gave a damn about you.

"Paul, can you go let Cory know he needs to bring up the rest of Lia's things?"

"This is all there is," Paul answered, setting the boxes containing her costumes on the bed.

"What do you mean?" Constance looked from the boxes to the small duffel that held most of Lia's wardrobe. "How is that possible?"

"Not everyone requires an entire room to hold every outfit they own," Paul remarked dryly.

His mother looked mystified. "But…"

"I don't have much room in my camper," Lia explained. "And I don't really need much."

"That was your life before. You are a Watts now and should dress the part." Constance cast a dubious eye over Lia's yoga pants and T-shirt. "We need to get you some new clothes. The twins can show you all their favorite boutiques."

"There's no need," Lia said, shooting a wary glance in Paul's direction. He would hate that his mother wanted to spend money on her. But his impassive expression tossed her no lifeline. "I'm sure Poppy and Dallas are too busy to take me shopping. Besides, I'm only going to be here a couple weeks."

"Nonsense. You simply have to stay longer than that. Because of you, Grady is getting better every day. No need for you to stay cooped up in the house all the time. The twins and Ethan can take you out so you can meet their friends. I have several events in the next two weeks that all of us will be attending. When word gets around all of Charleston will be dying to meet you."

As Constance spoke, Lia's anxiety ratcheted upward. Chest tightening, on the verge of a mild panic attack, she made another silent appeal to Paul. Why hadn't he spoken up? Surely he'd rather she stay out of sight between now and the time they broke the news that she wasn't a Watts after all. Once again, he remained utterly silent and aloof. Her eyebrows dipped as she realized his refusal to step in was deliberate. He was withholding aid in order to demonstrate the folly of Ethan's plan. As if she needed that pointed out to her.

"I'm feeling really overwhelmed at the moment," Lia protested. "I'm not used to so much attention. If you don't mind, I'd like to focus on helping Grady get better."

"Oh, well, of course." Constance looked surprised and then a bit abashed. "I guess I went a little overboard. We're just so overjoyed to have you home."

At long last Paul took pity on Lia. "Mother, why don't we leave Lia to unpack."

The grateful look she shot him prompted a frown. Honestly, there seemed to be no way to get on the man's good side.

"Of course," Constance said, her gracious smile returning. "Join us downstairs when you're ready." She'd taken several steps toward the door when she suddenly stopped and turned. "I almost forgot. There's a little welcome-home present for you on the nightstand."

Lia's first reaction after glancing at Paul's set expression was to protest that she didn't need any gifts. Then she realized that she could leave behind whatever they gave her. "That's lovely. Thank you."

Left alone, she started to fill the dresser drawers with her meager belongings, but then succumbed to curiosity about the gift. A small, flat box sat beside an elegant sheet of linen notepaper.

This belonged to your grandmother. We thought you should have it.—Constance.

Lia slipped the ribbon off the box and opened it. Nestled on a bed of black velvet was an antique locket. Her heart contracted as she opened the locket and saw that it contained a picture of Ava as a teenager. She sank onto the bed and stared at the photo, pondering all the events that had led her to this moment, wishing she'd done a dozen things differently.

"Hey."

Lia lifted her gaze and spied Ethan standing in the doorway. He looked authoritative in an elegant navy suit and lavender tie.

"Hi."

"Are you okay about staying at the estate for the next two weeks?" Ethan asked as he entered. "Both my mom and Aunt Lenora can be very determined and I don't want you to feel pressured."

Lia blew out her breath. "I plan to spend most of my time with your grandfather so I should be able to handle it for a couple weeks."

Ethan came over and took her hand in his. "I know this isn't what we originally planned on. I owe you a huge debt for helping out like this."

"You really don't," Lia said, some of her angst melting away. "I just want to bring your family some peace."

"You'll definitely be doing that."

"Can you please talk your mom out of introducing me all over Charleston as Ava's daughter, though? That's just going to end up complicating everything and I don't think you want your family to be the subject of gossip."

"Sure, that makes sense." Ethan tugged at the knot on his tie, loosening it. "I'll deal with it."

"Thank you because your brother was no help. I thought for sure he'd want to keep me out of sight."

"I know it's hard to believe, but I think that Paul will come around once he gets to know you."

"I hope so." The memory of their kiss sent heat rushing into her cheeks. Longing spiraled through her. "Because it's daunting how much he dislikes me."

Five

With the successful completion of a year-long investigation into a data breach of one of his company's clients, Paul knocked off early and headed to the estate to see how Grady was doing. Before Lia Marsh had entered their lives, Paul rarely worked a standard eight-hour day. He loved what he did and despite the number of bad actors he and his staff tracked down, there was always another puzzle to unravel, another hacker who'd stolen information. But these days he couldn't concentrate on his day-to-day activities.

When he wasn't following the trail she'd left all over the country, he caught himself ruminating over that stolen moment at his beach house when he'd surrendered to his desire to kiss her. At various times over the last several days, he'd have given anything to escape the distracting memory of how she'd felt in his arms. To forget the softness of her lips as they'd yielded beneath his. To stop imagining his hands gliding over her silky, fragrant skin.

He'd intended for the impulsive act to rattle her, but the

aftermath hadn't offered him any insight into her nefarious plans. Nor in the last week had she made any misstep to confirm she wasn't as genuine as she appeared. The dry facts that summarized her life gave him no sense of her character or her motivation for interrupting her life to act as Grady's granddaughter. He hadn't yet ruled out money, but nothing about the way she dressed or the things she talked about gave her away.

It also occurred to Paul that maybe he was concerning himself with the wrong thing. With only a week left to go in their arrangement, Grady continued to improve. But once they told everyone their story that a mistake had been made at the genetic testing service and Lia wasn't his granddaughter, would Grady's health fade once more?

There was no doubt that her presence had galvanized his recovery, but neither Paul nor Ethan could predict whether Grady's progress would slow or stop when she left the following week. Lia persisted in her belief that once she'd gotten the ball rolling, Grady would continue to improve on his own, but what if she was the oxygen that kept the flame burning on Grady's will to return to full health?

Paul stepped out of his SUV, intending to head straight to the carriage house for a cold beer and more brooding about Lia, when he spotted a flash of yellow coming toward him along the garden path. If he retreated without saying hello to whoever was coming, he'd never hear the end of it. Even as that zipped through his mind, he registered the sound of humming above the crunch of gravel and recognized the source.

Lia.

After that stirring kiss at his house, he'd avoided being alone with her, and he cursed at this untimely meeting. But the woman who emerged from the foliage had a completely different impact on him than what he was used to.

What the hell?

Before he could wrap his mind around her appearance, Lia spotted him and waved. Her infectious smile bloomed as she headed in his direction. His head spun as he took her in. She'd transformed herself into yet another one of her princess characters. Even her movement was different.

"What are you wearing?" he asked, regaining his voice.

"It's a ball gown," she responded as if it was the most ordinary thing in the world to be wearing a floor-length satin and tulle dress in bright yellow with three voluminous tiers, a red wig styled in a fancy updo with ringlets spilling over her bare shoulders and long yellow gloves. "I'm on my way to the hospital to visit the children's ward. I've been so busy with Grady that I missed last week and I can't disappoint them again."

Paul groaned inwardly. It was hard to maintain his skepticism about her when this woman kept proving him wrong. First, she'd brought his grandfather back from the brink of death. Now here was another reminder that she gave of her time to bring joy to sick kids. How was he supposed to resist her?

"Which princess are you today?"

"I'm dressed as Belle. From *Beauty and the Beast*," she explained with exaggerated patience. "The Disney movie about the prince who was turned into a beast and could only be saved by someone who loved him as himself." When Paul continued blankly regarding her, she rolled her eyes in exasperation. "I can tell you don't have children."

"Why do you dress like a Disney character?"

"Because the kids love it. Sure, they appreciate when I just show up to spend time with them, but when I visit dressed as Belle or Elsa or Cinderella...they are so thrilled." She grinned. "For a while they can forget how sick they are."

"How did you get started doing this?"

"I guess you could say growing up I wanted to be a

princess. I imagined that I was like Rapunzel or Sleeping Beauty, locked in a tower taken away from my parents. Hidden away. When I got older, I grew obsessed with getting a job at Disney as one of the princesses."

"So what happened?"

"I became a Disney character." She made a face that told him it had not gone well. "Only I didn't get to be a princess."

"A villain?" he asked, thinking that would be more fun.

"No," she said. "I was Dale." She waited a beat and when he didn't say anything, elaborated, "Of Chip 'n' Dale. They were chipmunks. I wore a big chipmunk head." She used her hands to indicate the costume's size. "It was hot and uncomfortable, but mostly worth it because the kids loved it."

"How did you make the transition from Disney character to massage therapist?" he asked, the thought of her massaging his brother once again flashing unpleasantly through his mind. He recognized that she'd been baiting him when they discussed it, but still he envied his brother.

"I think I mentioned it was hot and stuffy in that costume. Being a character wasn't as glamorous as I'd hoped it would be. One of my coworkers was taking classes in massage therapy and it sounded like a good idea. It was a way for me to help people and that's what I like to do."

"Well, you've certainly had a huge impact on Grady, so I guess you have a knack for making people better."

"Thank you for saying that," she said, showing her appreciation with a bright smile that kicked him hard in the gut.

"How are you getting there?"

"I'm going to walk." She shifted sideways as if to go around him. "It's only fifteen minutes away."

Paul stepped to block her path. "Why don't I drive you instead?"

"Really," she demurred. "It's no problem."

"I insist," he argued, faltering in his week-long battle to avoid being alone with her.

"I like walking."

"So do I. I could walk you there."

She set her hands on her hips and arched one eyebrow. "Don't you have evildoers to chase?"

"Nope. We just wrapped up a huge investigation so I took the afternoon off." Paul held out his arm to her in a gallant gesture that caught her by surprise. "I can't think of anything I'd enjoy more than to watch your performance as Belle."

"But I'm usually there for a couple hours. I'm sure you have better things to do."

"Stop trying to get rid of me," he growled. "There's nothing else I'd rather be doing." And much to his dismay, that was true.

Although she looked like she wanted to voice further protests, Lia gave a little shrug and took his arm. Her delicate grip made such a huge impression that Paul had a hard time concentrating as she told him the story of how Belle and the Beast fell in love.

Fifteen minutes had never gone by so quickly, and all too soon Paul was guiding Lia through the hospital's entrance. Gliding along the corridors, she paid little attention to the stir she caused. The staff greeted her warmly, but Paul couldn't help but notice the way many visitors goggled at her appearance or even laughed at her elaborate costume. He caught himself scowling at a number of them even as he recalled his own initial reaction when he first saw her.

"What?" he demanded, noticing her amused expression as they stood waiting for the elevator to arrive.

"I was just thinking that the way you're glaring makes me think you'd make an excellent Beast."

He forced his facial muscles to relax. "I don't suppose I'm Prince Charming material."

"You could be," she murmured, stepping into the elevator car.

"No," he corrected. "Ethan is Prince Charming." A now-
familiar pulse of irritation raised his blood pressure.

"Ethan?" Her snort was an indelicate sound at odds with
her royal appearance. "Do you really see him dressing up
in britches and a frock coat?"

Not in his wildest imaginings. Paul's lips twitched, but
he kept his tone serious. "Maybe for the right woman."

She gave another very unprincesslike snort. "I don't
think he'd enjoy playacting."

"I wouldn't, either."

She narrowed her glowing hazel eyes and shot him a
piercing glance. "You might be surprised."

Her knowing smile sent a wave of heat through him.
Before he could summon a retort, the doors opened and
Lia stepped into the corridor of what was obviously the
children's floor. She paused for a second, drew in a deep
breath, closed her eyes. A moment later, she exhaled and a
beatific smile curved her lips. Just like that she'd become
someone completely different.

The transformation robbed Paul of words. He trailed
after her as she approached the nurses' station and after
greeting everyone, introduced Paul. Several nurses accompanied them on the way to the lounge where some of the
children had gathered to play. The appearance of a beloved
princess in their midst electrified the children.

Mesmerized by the spectacle, Paul stood at the back of
the room with a cluster of parents and watched Lia work her
way around the space, going from child to child, spreading
joy as she went. Some of the kids she called by name, proving that she was indeed a frequent visitor. In every case she
lingered, answering questions, asking some of her own.

Nor was Lia's effect limited to the kids. Around Paul
several stressed-out mothers teared up at their children's

delight and tense fathers relaxed enough to smile. Once again, Lia was demonstrating the incredible magic she'd used to wrest Grady away from the brink of death.

Paul noticed a tightness in his chest and rubbed to ease it. This woman was too much. He recalled Ethan declaring that first day that Lia came off as completely genuine. Confident his brother had been hoodwinked, Paul had done whatever he could to unmask her. Now he was leaning toward her giving her the benefit of the doubt. This hospital visit was the whip cream, sprinkles and cherry on top of the ice cream sundae that was Lia Marsh.

Which made everything so much worse.

Keeping his attraction to her buttoned down had been way easier when he had reason to suspect her character and motives. Now, as she began to sing, Paul's spirits sank. Her clear, sweet voice captivated the children. Their parents looked beyond grateful to see their sons and daughters so happy. And some of the nursing staff were singing along.

Before her topsy-turvy world had intersected with his, Paul never would've imagined himself attracted to a free spirit like Lia. Her ideas about the rejuvenating effects of music and aromatherapies seemed more like wishful thinking than practical fact. Yet he couldn't deny Grady's marked improvement.

Or his own shifting opinion.

Over the next hour Lia demonstrated an extensive repertoire of familiar children's songs. When at long last she signaled the end of the performance with a princess-worthy curtsy and waved goodbye, Paul wasn't surprised at the sharp tug his heart gave when she shifted her full attention to him.

"Sorry that took so long," she said as they headed for the elevator.

"That was something," he remarked, struggling to sort out his muddled emotions as they stepped into the car.

She eyed him while they descended, letting the princess character drop away and becoming Lia in costume once more.

"From your tone I can't tell if that's good or bad."

"The kids really love you."

"Seeing their favorite princess come to life is a wonderful distraction for them."

"And you do this every week?"

Lia nodded. "I try to."

They reached the sidewalk and turned in the direction of the estate.

"Why?"

"You of all people should understand," she said, tugging at the fingers of one long yellow glove.

The movement snared Paul's attention and he noticed an immediate and sharp uptick in his heartbeat as he watched her slide the material down her arm. The practiced move wasn't at all provocative or sexy, but made his breath quicken all the same.

"Why do you think I should understand?"

"Because of all the charity work your family does."

"Philanthropy and wealth usually go hand in hand."

"There's a difference between writing a big check and giving time and energy to a cause. Your family actively participates because that's what's rooted in their personal values."

Yet part of those values was defined by the idea that because of their good fortune the Wattses owed something to those less fortunate. Lia had no largesse, so why was she driven to help others? What compelled her to dress up and sing to children or to help Grady get better?

Despite all the facts he'd gleaned about her, today's hospital visit demonstrated how little he actually knew—or understood—about her.

"Thanks for coming along today," Lia said, rousing Paul from his thoughts.

He noticed that they were nearing the estate and found himself suddenly reluctant to part ways. "Do you want to come in for a drink?"

For a beat she stared at him as if debating how to respond, and then she shook her head. "I can't figure you out."

"The feeling is mutual."

"All week long you've been avoiding me. Now today you come with me to the hospital and invite me for a drink. What's changed?"

What could he say? That he found her charming, her company invigorating? That avoiding her wasn't helping his peace of mind? He already knew their temperaments were completely different. Maybe if they spent more time together her eccentric ways and quirky beliefs would turn him off once and for all.

"Oh," she continued. "I'll bet you're scheming to get me drunk in the hopes I'll slip up and say something damning."

"Now who's the suspicious one," he retorted, wishing this was going more smoothly. As much as he didn't want to put his cards on the table, Paul realized he had to give her a peek at his hand if he hoped to entice her to extend their time together. "Maybe I enjoyed your company this afternoon and don't want it to end."

She blinked at him. "I'm sorry? Did I just hear you right? You enjoyed my company?"

"Do you want to join me for a drink or not?" he grumbled.

She tapped her finger against her lips, making a show of giving consideration to his invitation. "Well, since you asked so sweetly…sure. Let me change and check on Grady. It won't take me more than ten minutes."

"Need any help?" he asked, eyeing the gown's complicated lacings. "I've never undressed a princess before." The declaration came out of nowhere, surprising them both.

"If I thought you actually meant that," she said in a breathless rush, "I'd take you up on your offer."

Paul opened his mouth to either take back his remark or to double down, but before he decided which, Lia threw up both hands and shook her head vigorously.

"No. Don't say anything more." She began retreating toward the house. "I'll be back in ten minutes. That should give you plenty of time to figure out how to get yourself out of trouble."

Lia's buoyant mood lingered as she walked along the garden paths that led to the house. When she'd donned the Belle costume, she'd never imagined such a magical afternoon. She'd spent the last seven days anxious and miserable over Paul's pronounced disapproval, unsure how to cope with her body's irresistible response to his physical appeal or to manage the push and pull of apprehension and lust that kept her off-balance.

Before today, if asked to describe Paul, Lia would have used words like confident and authoritative. Yet at the hospital today he'd shown her a different side, demonstrating he could be reflective and more openminded than she'd imagined. This brief respite from his distrust was a welcome change.

To her relief she encountered no one on the way to her bedroom. Grady's door was closed, indicating he was resting, no doubt worn out from his latest round of physical therapy. Before leaving for the hospital, she'd popped in to show off her costume. His delight at her appearance had been nearly a match for the children.

Although Lia raced through her transformation she took longer than ten minutes. Because the elaborate wig and heavy gown left her feeling sweaty, she grabbed a quick shower and hastily reapplied mascara and red lipstick because she wanted Paul to see her as attractive. Reluctant to keep him waiting too long, she drew her wet hair into a sleek topknot, and just before she headed out the door, swept powder over her nose, obliterating her freckles. She'd noticed how often Paul's gaze focused on the imperfection. No doubt he found them unsightly.

By the time she reached the carriage house, Lia was trembling with anticipation. How many nights had she gone to bed in Ava Watts's old bedroom only to find sleep elusive? Over and over she called herself a fool for letting the cybersecurity specialist get beneath her skin. While the man treated her like a thief out to steal the heirloom silver, she was tormented by fantasies of him making love to her with all the passion and intensity of a man who craved closeness and intimacy. And today, all he'd had to do was show her a little kindness and she was all in.

"Sorry I took so long," she said, covertly scanning his expression in search of reassurance. Was the man attracted to her or not? She couldn't tell. "The wig and dress left me feeling grimy so I showered."

He stepped close and lowered his head, breathing her in. "Damn, you smell good."

A lightning storm of awareness electrified Lia's whole body. She leaned back and peered up at his expression. He watched her through half-lidded eyes, predatory hunger smoldering in their green depths. Her pulse accelerated as his lips took on a sensual curve. The last time she'd seen that smile had been that afternoon at his beach house. Heat raced through her veins, bringing lethargy to her muscles and sparking hope. Emboldened, she reached out and cupped his cheek.

"You are attracted to me," she murmured, awestruck and filled with delight. "What happened last time was real."

"Very real." He wrapped his arm around her waist and

pulled her close. "And something I promised myself would never happen again."

Crushing herself against his hard body, Lia breathed in his masculine scent. She wanted to burrow her hands beneath his clothes and slide her palms along his warm skin. "Why not?"

"You are pretending to be my cousin." His muscles tensed. "My first cousin."

"*Pretending* being the operative word." While Lia recognized that his argument held no water, she'd spent enough time in Charleston to understand that appearances were everything. "As long as we're careful and don't get caught…"

"Do you seriously think that's what I'm worried about?" He took her hands and eased them from his body, his grip gentle despite his frustrated tone. "Getting caught?"

"Isn't it?" She blinked at him in confusion as he set her free and took a half step back.

His bemused expression might have led her to ask more questions if her body wasn't aching with the sharpest longing. Day and night, she'd tormented herself with revisiting that kiss at his beach house, taking things past the moment when he'd stopped. She'd imagined a hundred variations. Them going inside and making love in his bed. Him drawing her into the hot tub and making her come while she floated on a raft of bubbles. Her dropping to her knees to pleasure him in full sight of the beach while he held tight to the deck railing and shouted his pleasure.

"Look, if you're worried that I might fall for you…" She shook her head, hoping she could be convincing. "Don't. I find you attractive. It's just sex."

From the first stirring of physical attraction, she'd accepted that they had no future. Even before she started posing as his first cousin, he'd regarded her with suspicion and she doubted he'd ever fully trust her. In so many ways, from their upbringings to their temperaments, they were completely incompatible. Never in her wildest daydreams could she imagine he'd walk into a public venue and be proud to call her his date much less his girlfriend.

But their chemistry couldn't be denied. That left sex. Great sex. Because after being kissed by Paul Watts, Lia knew the guy would be fantastic in bed. She shivered in anticipation of his strong hands running over her naked body. Just imagining how he would slide his finger through the slippery wetness between her thighs caused her body to clench in pleasure.

"Just sex," he echoed, murmuring the two words in a contemplative tone. "And in a week you'll be gone."

While her heart bucked painfully in her chest, Lia nodded. "That's the plan."

"Nobody could possibly fall for someone that fast." He raked her expression with hard green eyes. "I mean it's only a week."

"Absolutely." Damn the man could talk, but she was starting to see a glimmer of hope. "That's not enough time to get attached."

Lia wasn't sure which of them moved first, but the next thing she knew, he'd cupped the back of her neck in his hand and her fingers had tunneled into his hair. Then they were lip-locked and moaning beneath the onslaught of desire and need.

"That's more like it," Lia murmured a long while later after he released her lips and trailed kisses down her throat. "Damn, you are good at that."

"At what?"

He brought his teeth together on the place where her neck and shoulder joined. Pleasure shot through her at the tantalizing pain of his bite. She groaned as his tongue flicked over the spot, soothing the sting. Desire tore through her. Lia couldn't recall ever feeling so alive or invigorated.

"Kissing," she said. "I thought maybe you were too focused on chasing bad guys to ever make time for a love
life."

"So you thought I was inexperienced when it came to
women?"

He didn't wait for her to reply before seizing her mouth
for another hard, demanding kiss that left her weak-kneed
and flushed from head to toe. His fingers dug into her hip
as she rocked into him, before he sent his palm coasting
downward over her butt. When he lifted her against his
growing erection, Lia panted in frustration at the pressure
building in her.

His lips moved over the shell of her ear, awakening a
million goose bumps. Adrift in pleasure, she didn't expect
the sharp nip on her earlobe or the way fireworks detonated
in her loins, setting her on fire.

"Have you thought about us together?" he asked, his
voice a low purr that sent a riot of tingles along her nerves.

She nodded.

"Is this how it went?"

"Sometimes." She could scarcely speak above a whisper.

"Have you imagined me bending you over and taking
you from behind."

The image was only one of a hundred different scenarios
she'd toyed with. "Yes."

For a microsecond his whole body went perfectly still.
"My mouth between your thighs, driving you crazy?"

"Yes." This time she moaned the word.

His teeth raked down her neck. "I think about your
mouth on me."

"Yes," she pleaded. "Oh, yes."

"Wicked girl." He sounded so pleased by her response.

She sighed in relief when his hand slid between her
thighs, fingers applying the perfect pressure over the spot
where she ached. While she rocked against his palm, his

tongue plunged into her mouth over and over. Mindless, her arousal gaining intensity, she rubbed her clit against his hand. With the barrier of her clothes between them, equal parts frustration and delight prompted the incoherent sounds coming from her throat. At last she could take it no more.

"Damn it, Paul," she panted, her desperation giving her voice a shrill edge.

He lifted his head and regarded her from beneath his thick dark lashes. "What?"

Even as she struggled to find the words to tell him what she wanted, he sent his fingers skimming beneath the waistband of her yoga pants and followed the neat landing strip to where she burned. The pleasure was so overwhelming that she huffed out a laugh to relieve some of the strain of keeping her delight bottled up.

"I was just thinking that I should've waxed an arrow to point the way for you."

It was the first thing that popped into her head and one corner of his lips kicked up in a mocking salute.

"Baby, I know exactly where I'm going." Even before he finished speaking, he stroked through her hot core.

The move left her just enough breath for an awestruck curse. "Damn."

"You're incredible," he murmured, raking his teeth over her lower lip. "I can't believe how wet you are. That's so damn sexy."

He stroked his fingers through her slippery wetness, whispering his admiration, letting her know how much he appreciated her. Moaning, she shifted her hips, wanting his fingers inside her. The building pressure was almost too much to bear.

"Please," she panted, gathering a handful of his silky blond hair and tugging. "Make me come."

"My pleasure."

She shuddered in anticipation as he dropped to his knees and dragged her yoga pants and panties down her thighs. A moment later he leaned forward and drew his tongue along the seam that hid her sex from him. Lia's muscles failed her and she would've collapsed without his supportive grip.

"Hold on," he warned, a smile in his voice as his tongue speared into the heart of her.

An old commercial played through her head as Paul drove her excitement still higher. *How many licks does it take to get Lia off? One. Two. Three.* Just that fast she found herself coming. The speed and intensity of her climax blew her mind.

"Paul…" She threw her head back and welcomed the orgasm that blasted through her. Curses fell from her lips at the intensity of the pleasure.

"Wow," he murmured, trailing kisses across her abdomen as her muscles quaked with aftershocks. "You are a firecracker."

Not surprising since she'd had a week of foreplay to prime the pump. To her dismay, he reached down and slid her pants back into place before getting to his feet.

"Are we done?"

He raised his eyebrows at her scandalized tone, but long lashes hid the expression in his gaze. The roughness in his voice, however, gave him away as he breathed, "I hope not."

"Then kiss me again and let's take this thing horizontal."

He put his arm around her, hand sliding to cup her butt while he rubbed his erection against her hip. She savored the hard length of him poking at her and shimmied to add even more friction. The taste of herself on his lips made her eager to have her way with him in turn. Even though she hadn't yet gotten her hands on the bulge behind his zipper, she could tell he was well built.

A staccato horn beeped nearby as someone locked a car.

At the interruption of their thoroughly hot and promising embrace, Paul tore his mouth from hers. Female voices intruded on the sensual fog Lia had gotten caught up in. Paul's hands fell away from her body as he abruptly stepped back. His physical withdrawal left her shivering as if doused with cold water. Her eyes flew open in time to see shutters slam down over his expression. Only his heightened color and his unwillingness to look at her hinted at the passion he'd recently demonstrated.

A second later a knock sounded on the carriage house door and Lia almost whimpered in disappointment as she recognized Poppy's voice.

"Hey, Paul, are you there?"

A muscle jumped in his jaw as he shot a hard look at the door. "I have to answer that."

"Of course." She drew in a shaky breath as his gaze raked over her. Feeling exposed and raw in the aftermath of such all-consuming desire, Lia craved some privacy to recover her wits before facing the twins. "Can I borrow your bathroom?"

"In there." He pointed down the hallway and headed for the front door.

To her dismay, as soon as she met her gaze in the mirror, Lia found herself blinking back a rush of unexpected tears. She braced her hands on the sink and rode the wave of emotions until her breath steadied and she could smile without grimacing.

Although he'd been clear that lying to his family bothered him, Lia recognized that sneaking around added spice to their encounters. And she couldn't imagine Paul being susceptible to such a thing—doubtless he'd never allowed himself to be in a situation like theirs before. And he wasn't the only one.

During her years on the road, she'd had many men look at her lifestyle and view her as a short-term thing. Unlike her mother, who took frequent lovers, Lia needed some sort of a connection and rarely found it. What she'd just had with Paul was worth more than all her experiences combined and it left her wondering—if she'd found this before, would she have stayed put?

Lia loved her life on the road. Traveling around the country satisfied her restless nature and offered her the opportunity to experience places that people often missed because they either flew to their destinations or only visited tourist locations.

Her time stranded in Charleston had given Lia an opportunity to think about what she wanted for the future. Was she going to roam aimlessly for the rest of her life or should she put down roots somewhere? And what was her criteria for staying? She'd found much to like in Charleston, but did it feel like home? Was she drawn to the place or the people or both? Lia's inability to answer told her to move on.

She cracked the door to hear the conversation just in time to recall that she'd committed to spending the afternoon with the twins.

"She's going to tell our fortunes," Poppy was saying to Paul, referring to Lia's promise to bring out her tarot deck and read for them. "You have to come and have your cards read, too."

"It's all foolishness," Paul said, sounding exasperated.

"Come on," Dallas insisted. "I'm trying out some new recipes for Zoe and Ryan's wedding and there will be cocktails. It'll be fun."

"Please," Poppy wheedled. "You never hang out with us anymore."

"Fine. I'll be there."

"Awesome," Dallas said. "Half an hour."

"And leave your skepticism at the door," Poppy said. "The universe might have an important message for you."

Once Paul had ushered out his cousins and shut the door, Lia returned to the great room, a brave smile plastered on her face to hide her disappointment at the change in plans.

"She's right," Lia said, striding toward him. From his closed expression and rigid posture, she guessed the intimacy they'd shared five minutes earlier had been shattered by the twins' visit. "You should come with an open mind. The cards have a way of getting to the truth."

Paul stood with his hand on the doorknob and gazed down his nose at her. "Fortune-telling is all just educated guesses and made-up stuff."

"It can be," Lia agreed, thinking their differences couldn't be any clearer. "But sometimes if you open your heart, the answers will shine like the midday sun."

"Except I don't ask those sorts of questions."

Questions that might encourage him to lead with his heart and not his head. Lia knew nothing she could say would convince him otherwise so she pushed down her disappointment and vowed to only ask of him what she knew he could give.

Six

From Paul's perch on a barstool at the breakfast bar in the caretaker house kitchen, he could observe the shenanigans playing out at the dining room table without appearing to be engaged. He was working his way through the second of the three cocktails Dallas had prepared for them to taste. She'd dubbed this one Love Potion, and with two shots of vodka and one of bourbon mixed with both cranberry and cherry juice, it packed a punch.

Despite being identical twins, with their mother's blond hair and blue eyes, Dallas and Poppy had vastly distinct styles and temperaments. The oldest by ten minutes, Dallas had the Watts family head for business and more than her fair share of ambition. Since graduating college, she'd worked for some of the best restaurants in Charleston with the goal of opening her own place and currently worked as a private chef and caterer.

By contrast, Poppy was a stylist at a high-end salon in downtown Charleston and an active beauty blogger. She was free-spirited and headstrong, with striking pink hair and boundless energy, and whenever her family questioned her about doing something more serious than cutting hair, her quick answer was always a flippant one.

"Hey, Paul," Poppy called, breaking into his musings. "It's your turn."

He blinked several times to reorient his thoughts and noticed that he was the center of attention. "I'm not interested." He hoped his resolute tone would dissuade them from pestering him further, but their eager gazes remained fixed on him.

"Oh come on, we've both done it." Dallas shot Lia a look. "What are you afraid of?"

"Besides," Poppy chimed in. "It's not fair that you've heard all our dark secrets without spilling a few of your own."

"I don't…" Paul trailed off. He'd been about to deny having any dark secrets, but then realized since Lia had arrived, he had more each day. "You know this isn't my cup of tea."

"Ladies, leave him alone," Lia said, no disappointment or censure in her unruffled manner. She gathered up the cards from Poppy's reading and returned them to the stack.

"Obviously he's afraid to face the truth," Dallas said, displaying relentless determination.

For the last hour, while Lia had made credible-sounding predictions for the twins, Paul had grown increasingly skeptical of her glib performance. While her expertise had appeared genuine enough to thoroughly engage his cousins, in Paul's opinion the concept of being able to predict the future based on the turn of a card was nothing but nonsense. Still, as much as he'd wanted to scoff several times over the past hour, he'd held his tongue because Dallas and Poppy were thoroughly enjoying the experience. Or at least

they were making a show of doing so. Some of Lia's prog-
nostications had rattled both girls, although they'd laughed
and sipped their drinks to cover it up.

"There's no truth I'm afraid to face," Paul declared, his
gaze clashing with both his cousins' even as Lia kept her
focus on the tarot deck. He was mesmerized by her small
hands as she shuffled the deck to clear the energy. Why
didn't she chime in? Surely, she was dying to feed him a
load of rubbish to get a rise out of him. "I just see all of
this as a huge waste of time."

"Since when is having fun a waste of time?" Poppy
asked.

"When it comes to Paul," Dallas piped up, "since always."

"Come on, Paul." Poppy got up from where she was sitting across from Lia and gestured for him to replace her.
"What does it hurt to have Lia read for you?"

Seeing the two women weren't going to let him escape
without taking a turn in the hot seat as Lia had mockingly
called it, Paul finished the Love Potion cocktail and made
his way to the chair Poppy had vacated. Lia's hazel eyes
gleamed as she pushed the cards across the table toward
him. From the first two rounds, he knew she wanted him
to shuffle the cards. She explained that this would let the
cards absorb his energy.

"While you shuffle, think about something you want to
ask the cards about." Lia had issued this instruction with
both the earlier readings.

"Really," he insisted. "There's nothing."

Lia nodded. "Then just let your mind drift."

Paul handled the cards indifferently, demonstrating that
he viewed the whole activity as a grand waste of time, yet
while he shuffled the deck, mixing them thoroughly the
way he'd watched his cousins do, he found himself besieged
by memories of those delicious minutes with Lia in his car-

riage house. The taste of her. The way she'd given herself over to him. His name on her lips as she'd come.

His body tightened at the vivid images and he shifted uncomfortably on the chair before setting the cards on the silk cloth she'd spread on the dining table. "You know I don't buy into any of this stuff," he muttered with barely restrained impatience.

"You don't believe and that's okay." Lia had been staring at the cards in his hands, but now she lifted her gaze to meet his. The impact made his heart stumble. "But you never know. You might hear something interesting."

A tiny ember of curiosity flared as he wondered what she might tell him. He suspected it would give him insight into her motives. No doubt she'd try to guide him into some sort of behavior the way she had his cousins, telling Dallas that she'd soon be confronted with a difficult decision involving two men in her life and Poppy that she would undergo a transformative period that would shake up her status quo and possibly harm those around her.

Both of these vague but somewhat ominous predictions had puzzled the twins, but they'd eagerly embraced the readings as if they were a road map to their futures.

"Go ahead and cut the cards," Lia instructed. "Make three piles just like your cousins did."

Paul did as she told him and made three similarly sized piles. The ritual of handling the tarot cards had given the process a solemnity that made a strong impression on his cousins.

"Now pick one pile," Lia said.

His immediate instinct was to point to the one in the center, but as his finger was moving to indicate that stack, his gaze veered away.

"This one," he said, indicating the one to the right, unable to explain why he'd changed course.

With a reverent nod, Lia gathered up the deck, placing

the stack he had chosen on the top. Then she began to lay the cards out in a particular order facedown the way she had with his cousins. She'd called it a Celtic Cross and remarked that the layout was one of the most traditional.

"Ready?" she asked.

"Yes." He growled the word from between clenched teeth as he noticed a trace of excitement mingling with anxiety bubbling in his gut. Refusing to fall for Lia's theatrics, he ruthlessly tamped down the emotions.

As if drawn to the drama unfolding at the dining room table, his cousins raced over and took the empty seats on either side of him. Eyes bright with curious intensity, they leaned forward, their full plates and refilled crystal tumblers forgotten.

"We'll start with these two in the center," Lia intoned, indicating the crossed cards.

She pulled the bottom one out first and flipped it over, revealing an old man with a long gray beard and bowed back. He carried a lantern and leaned on a walking stick. The character reminded Paul of Gandalf the Grey from *The Lord of the Rings* trilogy.

"This is the Hermit reversed," Lia said. "It indicates what's currently influencing you. It's crossed by…" A dramatic pause followed as she turned over the next card. "The Fool. It is the first card of the Major Arcana and indicates the beginnings of a journey. The Fool can represent following your instincts despite what might seem the more sensible practice." Lia touched the Hermit card. "As you can see the Hermit is upside down. This indicates that your time of isolation is over. You are ready to rejoin your community."

Paul glanced from Lia to Poppy to Dallas and back to Lia as he absorbed her words. All three women were completely engrossed and he had to resist the urge to snort derisively. Let them have their fun. Nothing Lia said so far pertained to him. He didn't isolate himself. He worked long hours to make sure his clients' data was safe. As for starting a journey…he had no plans to travel anywhere.

Lia flipped over the card below the first two. "This position is the basis of the situation."

"That doesn't look like a very happy scene," Dallas said.

Paul peered at the image on the card and frowned. Two people slogging through the snow, their backs hunched, looking very much as if they were lost and having a very difficult time. Above them was a glowing church window with five circles.

"Many interpret the Five of Pentacles as a dire financial situation," Lia said. "But I often read it as someone who either can't see a helping hand being extended to them or is unable to accept the aid being offered."

As expected, none of this made any sense. Paul forced down his impatience. He wasn't in a situation where he had need of anyone's assistance. With the exception of Lia's appearance in their lives, everything in Paul's orbit ran as smooth as clockwork.

"What's in Paul's past?" Poppy asked, pointing to the card in the nine o'clock position.

Lia turned it over. "The Three of Wands, indicating someone who has achieved much and is now satisfied with all they've done." She lifted her gaze from the cards and regarded Paul. "I think that sums up your past perfectly. You've spent a lot of time working hard on your business and now you get to look forward to what's next. The position above is possible outcome." She flipped the card over.

"Whoa," Dallas murmured. "That's grim."

The card showed a woman standing blindfolded and bound in front of a semicircle of swords. The bleakness of the image made him suddenly glad that it wasn't a definite outcome. Even as that thought crossed his mind, he rejected it. This was nothing more than a foolish pastime. None of this meant anything.

"This is a potential outcome," Lia pointed out.

Poppy worried her lower lip. "It doesn't seem like Paul is destined for a happy ending."

"The key to this card is the blindfold," Lia said. "It symbolizes confusion and isolation. But notice that while her arms are bound, her legs are free. She could walk away from this dangerous situation at any point. Instead, she's choosing to stay where she is." Lia moved on. "This next position is near future. It shows some situation that you will soon have to face, but not with the same certainty as the outcome. However, it can influence how things turn out."

As she finished speaking, she flipped the card over and Paul's heart stopped dead at the sight of the two naked people on the card with the sun shining down and an angel hovering around them.

Poppy squealed with delight. "The Lovers."

"Well, well, well," Dallas said. "Paul, what aren't you telling us?"

To his dismay, he felt a rush of heat beneath his skin. It couldn't be possible. Lia must have managed some trick with the deck. There was no other explanation for why this card had shown up in this position after what had almost happened between them.

After what he wanted to happen between them.

"Looks like I'm going to get lucky," he remarked, retreating into humor to cover his discomfort.

"Good for you," Poppy said, making it sound like he'd been neglecting his sex life.

Dallas nodded her agreement. "Maybe you'll meet someone at Ryan's wedding who you'll click with."

Paul was standing up for his best friend at a small, private wedding in a few days. The speed with which Ryan had fallen for Zoe continued to bemuse Paul, but he had no hesitations about the two being perfect for each other.

"Unlikely," Paul said, "since I know everyone who'll

be there." Yet, even as he spoke Paul couldn't stop himself from glancing Lia's way. In truth, he'd already met someone who intrigued him.

"The Lovers card doesn't always mean the obvious," Lia said, injecting a calm note in the conversation. "In some instances it can be a choice between two things he loves."

"Do you have two things you love, Paul?" Dallas asked.

"The only thing he loves is working," Poppy put in.

He gave each of them a sour look before settling a heavy-lidded gaze on Lia. Since starting the reading, she'd mostly been actively avoiding looking his way, preferring to concentrate on the cards before her, but as soon as the Lovers card had appeared, a trace of color bloomed in her cheeks as if she, too, was thinking about what had happened between them.

"The card at the bottom of the staff indicates self," Lia said, resuming the reading. "The attitude you are contributing to the situation." She flipped the card over exposing a king sitting on a throne with a sword. "Yes," she murmured, "this makes sense. The King represents authority, power and judgment. He likes to rule the world with his keen mind and forceful personality."

"That sounds exactly like you," Dallas said.

"Totally," her sister echoed.

"This next card is your environment." Lia flipped the card over. The Two of Cups.

"I had that one, as well," Dallas said. "You said it stood for romance. Look, it's right next to the Lovers." She pointed to the proximity of the two cards. "It seems like Paul may be headed straight for love."

"What?" Paul muttered, unable to contain his displeasure. "Are you an expert now?"

While Dallas grinned at him in cheeky confidence, Lia shook her head.

"Or it could just mean that he's torn between two things

that are really important to him," she said. "Perhaps he needs to balance his time better between family and his love for chasing criminals."

Her interpretation sounded so reasonable, yet all this talk about romance, love and sex was making him itchy.

"What about the last two cards?" he demanded, impatient to have the whole reading done.

"This position is your hopes and fears." Lia pointed to the second-to-the-last position, and then shifted her finger to indicate the one above it. "And this is your final outcome."

"So what do they say?" Poppy asked, her blue eyes dancing with anticipation.

Lia turned the first card over. From Paul's vantage point, the image appeared to be a man dancing on top of a log, but he realized that he was looking at the card upside down and that the man was actually hanging by his feet.

"That doesn't look good," he said.

"It's not as bad as it looks," Lia countered. "The Hanged Man symbolizes peace and understanding. However, he believes the only way to maintain this state is by withdrawing from society. He's similar to the Hermit. He's serene because he's locked up his emotions for years."

"And the last one?" Paul demanded, ready to be done.

Lia flipped over the final card to reveal a single chalice, balanced on a palm and suspended over the ocean. "The Ace of Cups indicates a time of happiness and love. A gift of joy."

"So," Dallas began, "if I'm hearing this correctly, Paul has been alone too long and he's going to start a new relationship, but he's going to fight his feelings because he's locked up his emotions for so long that he's afraid of them, but in the end it's all going to work out and he'll be very happy."

While Dallas summarized the reading and Poppy nodded her agreement, Lia studied the cards. A frown line appeared between her brows. Had Lia twisted the reading to suit her needs in the hopes that he would believe himself falling for her? If so, she didn't look as pleased as Paul would've expected, given the strong romantic overtones of the cards.

Poppy turned her bright gaze on him. "I can't wait to meet the lucky woman."

Paul very deliberately kept his attention from straying to Lia as he replied, "This isn't a great time for me to focus on my personal life."

Dallas chuckled. "I like the way you believe you'll have a choice." She indicated the cards. "Looks to me like your future is clear. There's romance on your horizon and it's going to change everything."

As Dallas summed up her take on Paul's tarot spread, Lia gathered up the cards and put them away. While she'd been reading for the twins, he'd worn an indulgent half smile. Now, however, he'd retreated behind an impassive expression and only the slight dip in his eyebrows indicated that he was disgruntled.

Either the twins were accustomed to ignoring their cousin's bouts of irritation or they didn't notice that he was troubled. For Lia, Paul's displeasure was palpable. She tried shooting him a reassuring smile, but all that produced was a narrowing of his eyes.

It seemed impossible that she could be falling for someone as serious-minded as Paul Watts. Yet after what had happened between them in the carriage house, Lia recognized that without their growing emotional connection, the earth-shattering orgasm he'd given her wouldn't have been possible. She'd never known that sort of all-consuming passion.

In some ways it terrified her. She was accustomed to

being able to pick up and go whenever the mood hit her. She didn't have any emotional ties that limited her freedom. Traveling like a leaf on the wind of her whims was how she'd grown up. Her mother's idea of a perfect lifestyle seemed perfectly rational to Lia given what had happened to Jen Marsh.

No one got close when you moved all the time.

No attachments meant no heartbreak. Or that was how it was supposed to work.

"What did you think of your first tarot reading?" Lia asked as they strolled along that path that led away from the caretaker's house.

"You know I don't believe in any of that stuff."

"I get it." Lia knew his skepticism would continue to come between them if she reacted defensively. "You're a logical guy. It's not really your thing."

"All that business about a future romance and having to choose between two things that I love," Paul continued, his tone thoughtful rather than dismissive.

As she struggled to make sense of what was bothering him, Lia realized that Paul had seen enough truth in the reading to be unsettled by it. How was that possible? He was too much of a realist to do anything but reject all he'd seen and heard today.

"If you aren't ready for love then that's not likely to happen for you," she reassured him, despite having seen the opposite happen when the cards predicted romance. But if anyone could avoid his emotions or anything that distracted him from business, it was Paul. "Maybe the universe is just nudging you to work less and spend more quality time with family and friends." From the way he scowled at her, Lia should've kept the advice to herself. Awash in sudden frustration, she threw up her hands. "Look. What do I know? It's your life."

They walked in tense silence until the path was joined by one that stretched between the house and driveway. Lia started to turn away, but Paul touched his fingertips to her arm, stopping her.

"I know it's last-minute, but I was wondering if you'd like to come with me to Ryan and Zoe's wedding on Saturday."

Lia laid her fist over her rapidly thumping heart. "I thought you wanted me to keep a low profile."

"It's a small gathering of my close friends. None of them will spread gossip around Charleston about you."

His declaration struck her as naive and shortsighted.

"Given how your cousins reacted to the tarot card reading," she said, "there's more interest in your love life than you realize."

"If anyone asks, we'll just say you're a family friend in town for a short visit."

Lia studied his impassive expression, knowing she shouldn't read too much into his offer. Her instincts warned her that spending more time with Paul was a mistake, but the temptation was so strong.

"Let me guess," she said, concealing her jumbled emotions behind mockery. "You were so busy catching bad guys that you forgot to invite anyone and you don't want to go to the wedding alone."

His crushing glare confirmed her hypothesis, but his fingers skimmed down her arm and trailed over the back of her hand. The urge to drag him back to the carriage house and finish what they'd started made her shiver.

"Why do you have to make everything so difficult?" he demanded, his impatient tone at odds with the fire dancing in his eyes.

"Funny," she snorted. "I was thinking the same thing about you."

The air around them sizzled as Lia turned her hand and

placed her palm against Paul's. She barely bit back a groan as he intertwined their fingers. For several silent seconds they stared at each other until Lia's phone chimed, indicating she'd received a text. It took a supreme effort of will to break eye contact with Paul. Glancing down at the screen, she noted that Ethan had sent her a message.

"Something wrong?" Paul quizzed.

"Ethan was going to give me a ride to my camper so I could pick up a costume, and then we were going to go truck shopping, but he has to go into a late meeting so he can't make it." Lia considered her options as she continued, "The nurses are throwing a birthday party for one of the children at the hospital on Saturday and I promised to surprise her with a visit from Elsa."

"I can take you."

"You don't have to do that," she murmured, turning him down despite the craving to spend more time in his company. "Ethan—"

"Forget about Ethan."

His firm command sent a ripple of pleasure cascading through her body. Before meeting Paul, she never imagined herself attracted to someone so authoritative and formidable. He was as set in his ways as a granite boulder while she glided past, a butterfly borne on the winds of chance. The lack of compatibility in their natures offered no reason why they should have the slightest hint of chemistry, yet the pull between them couldn't be denied.

"I don't want to bother you," she protested.

"It's too late for that," he growled, the sound sinking into her bones, turning them to mush. "Text Ethan and tell him I'll take care of you."

Lia shivered at his words, every cell in her body sparkling with delight. "Really, it's okay. I can ask one of the twins…"

"Is there a reason why you suddenly want to be rid of me?"

"I don't want to be rid of you," she retorted in exasperation.

Paul frowned. "Is there a reason why you prefer going out with Ethan over me?"

"It's not that I prefer Ethan's company."

"Then what is it?" Paul persisted.

"The thing is, I think you view me as a tad eccentric—"

"A tad," he agreed, a teasing note in his voice.

Despite his attempt at levity, she remained earnest. "It's just that taking you to where I live is intimate."

All emotion vanished from his expression. "More intimate than what we did earlier?"

"For me, yes. Misty is my safe place. No matter what else changes in my life, she's a constant, my refuge." And being away from the camper, disconnected from the nomadic lifestyle for so many months, had caused a shift in her identity that left her feeling vulnerable and a bit lost.

"And I'm not welcome in your safe place."

"No, I mean…" She scrambled to explain without causing further damage to their fragile rapport.

"But Ethan is?"

"It's different with him," Lia said.

"Different how?"

"We're friends."

"Friends." His jaw worked as if he was grinding the word to dust.

"What I'm trying to say is that I've known him for months and we've talked about a lot of things."

"Are these the sorts of things you don't feel comfortable sharing with me?"

Lia thought about the differences between the two men. Ethan was more like a brother who accepted her oddities. Paul was a shining beacon of all things correct, perfect and gorgeous. From the start he'd been vocal about all her flaws and limitations. Lately she'd glimpsed grudging admiration for how she'd helped his grandfather. At the same time, Lia suspected if Paul hadn't been so suspicious of her from the start, she might never have registered on his radar.

"Ethan sees me. He accepts who I am."

"And you don't think I do?"

When his fingers tightened, Lia realized they were still holding hands. Suddenly aware that they could be discovered by one of his family at any second, Lia tried to tug free.

"You have a bad opinion of me," he declared, looking stunned.

"I don't," she countered.

"On the other hand, you have a high opinion of Ethan."

"Look." Deciding it was fruitless to dance around the truth any longer, Lia stripped all finesse out of her justification. "Ethan isn't likely to judge me for living in a camper."

"But you think I would." Paul released her hand and stepped back. "Let me point out that you are the one jumping to conclusions about me. Which is ironic, considering I spent the last hour watching you read tarot cards and didn't utter a single disparaging remark."

"You're right. I... I'm..."

"Sorry?" He crossed his arms over his chest. "You should be. I've been pretty openminded about all the alternative treatments you've used on Grady. Meditation. Sound baths. Aromatherapy. I've never met anyone who believes in the sorts of things you do, but I've never tried to interfere with anything you've suggested."

"You're right," she repeated. Lia bowed her head and accepted the scolding. "I'm not being fair to you. I know the things I'm into are completely foreign to you and you've been great about all the weirdness." She paused and looked into his eyes, then said, "If you're still willing to take me to pick up the Elsa costume, I'm happy to go for the ride."

"Afterward we'll go truck shopping," he declared, his tone brooking no further discussion. "And then I'll take you to dinner."

"That would be very nice," she said in a small voice, offering him a tentative smile. "Give me ten minutes to put the deck back in my room and get my purse."

He nodded in satisfaction, but his expression had yet to relax. "I'll meet you by the driveway."

Seven

While Paul waited for Lia, he paced from his SUV to the edge of the driveway and back, made restless by his heightened emotional state. Gone were the days when he could summon icy calm and a clear head at will. Just being near Lia disrupted the status quo. The factual logic that had served him all his life was being defeated by things he couldn't see, touch or prove existed. He was actually buying into all her metaphysical nonsense. His tarot reading had struck far too close to home. He'd like to put it down to sleight-of-hand card tricks and guesswork, but she hadn't touched the tarot deck after he'd handled it.

He'd always viewed his suspicious nature as a fundamental part of him like his height and eye color. Innate and something he couldn't change even if he wanted to. He could see how his skepticism created distance from others, but he'd accepted this as a matter of course. He had faith in those who were important to him. His family. Close friends. The rest of the world could go to hell.

But lately he was growing increasingly aware of how his distrust impacted Lia. She lacked the sort of armor those he usually dealt with wore. Her openness and upbeat take on the world displayed vulnerability that charmed everyone she met.

Which made her resistance to letting him see her camper all the more striking.

She didn't trust him.

The revelation stung.

Worse was her blind faith in Ethan. Had she forgotten which brother had landed her in their current predicament? Ethan, not Paul, had been the one who'd perpetuated Grady's incorrect belief that Lia was his long-lost granddaughter. More than any other member of the Watts family, Ethan was the one she should be most wary of.

"Ready?"

Paul had been so lost in thought that he hadn't noticed Lia's approach. She'd done more than grab her purse at the house. While he'd wrestled with his demons, she'd changed into a loose-fitting black-and-white-striped T-shirt dress and white sneakers. With her hair in a loose topknot and dark glasses hiding her eyes, she gave off a cool, casual vibe at complete odds with the turmoil raging in him.

Longing rippled through him. He itched to reach across the distance separating them and haul her into his arms. Instead, stunned by the willpower it took to keep his hands off her, he gripped the passenger-side door handle as if it was a lifeline and gestured her into the SUV. No matter how temptation swelled in him, this wasn't the time or place to cross that line. Why was it so hard to do the right thing around her?

Forty minutes later, Paul drove through the security gate of a boat and RV storage lot and stopped his SUV beside a small vintage trailer painted white and mint green. From

Lia's doting expression, he gathered this must be the famous Misty.

"It won't take me but a second to grab the costume," Lia said, her hand on the door handle. "Do you want to wait here?"

After their earlier quarrel, he intended to prove that he wasn't the judgmental jerk she'd branded him. "No." And then hearing how abrupt that sounded, he added in a more conciliatory tone, "I'd like to see what she looks like inside." He'd picked up Lia's habit of referring to the vintage camper by the feminine pronoun.

"Okay." She drew the word out as she exited the SUV.

Paul noted the matching mint-colored curtains framing the windows as Lia unlocked the camper and stepped inside. He followed her in, surprised that the ceiling height accommodated his six-foot-one-inch frame without him having to stoop.

"This is tiny," he declared, at once shocked by the camper's limited footprint and impressed by how Lia had made efficient use of every inch of it. "How do you live in such a small space?"

"Simply." She flashed him a wry grin and gestured at the boxes piled up in the sitting area toward the back. "It's not usually this cluttered. Normally I store all the costumes in my truck."

"Do you like living with so little?" Paul asked, shifting uneasily in the narrow aisle between closet and kitchen. He became all too aware of the inviting sleeping nook behind him with its extravagance of soft pillows.

"I find it calming." She gave him a quick tour, narrating the camper's history while assessing his reaction the whole time. "What do you think?"

"It's cozy," he ventured, glancing around. "And it suits you."

Into less than one hundred and fifty square feet, she'd

fit a kitchen and bathroom, full-size bed, dinette and a decent-sized closet. Vintage pastel fabrics softened the white walls, tin-tile ceiling and wood-look vinyl flooring. The appliances were the same mint green as the exterior and appeared original to the 1960s' vibe.

"Thank you."

"For what?"

"Being openminded." Her infectious smile bloomed for the first time since Dallas had interrupted them at the carriage house. "You know, we aren't likely to get interrupted anytime soon." While he processed what she'd said, she blew out an exasperated breath. "Are you just going to stare at me?" Giving his shirt a sassy tug, she finished, "Or are you going to take me in your arms and rock my world?"

Relief flooded him. They were going to be okay. Paul wrapped his arm around her waist and hauled her up against him. The breath swept out of her in a soft, satisfying huff. He expected her to get all clingy and press herself against him, but instead she wrapped her arms around his waist and rested her cheek on his chest.

"What are you doing?" Paul asked.

She flexed her arm muscles, embracing him more snugly. "Giving you a hug."

"Why?"

"I want you to know that I like you." Without lifting her cheek from the front of his shirt, she canted her head and gazed up at him. "Before you kiss me. Before I go all weak-kneed and gooey inside. I want you to know I like you. You. Not your money. Or the power your family wields in this town. I'm a simple girl with simple needs. One of them being a gorgeous, sexy man who makes love to her as if she's the most desirable woman he's ever known."

It was both a request and a plea for him to treat her well. But her declaration tempered Paul's all-consuming drive to possess her. He eased his grip, second-guessing everything.

"Why is that important before I kiss you?"

"I don't think this time we'll be able to stop there," she said. "And after whatever happens you'll be even less willing to trust me."

"It's not that I don't trust you…" It was more that he didn't trust himself around her. The feelings she aroused messed with his head.

"You trust that I'm good for your grandfather. But I don't think you'll ever trust that I could be good for you."

With his gaze locked on her lips, he rasped, "That's not true."

But he recognized the reason for her apprehension. He approached decisions with logic; she believed a deck of cards could predict what was to come. She took leaps of faith with little regard for her own safety. He rarely made a move without knowing in advance what the outcome would be. Yet at the moment he felt driven beyond wisdom and sense by his need for her.

"You won't believe that I don't want anything from you," she persisted. "Even when nothing I've done gives you any reason to suspect me."

It should've bothered him that she had him all figured out. Well, maybe not all figured out. But her grasp on what made him tick surpassed what he understood about her.

"I don't have all the answers," he admitted. "You're not like anyone I've ever known before and frankly, you scare the hell out of me."

Her eyes widened. "I don't see how."

"You've brought magic into my life." He braced his hip against her kitchen counter as his admission caused something inside him to snap. Light-headed and reeling, he closed his eyes.

"You don't believe in magic," she murmured.

"I believe in you."

He dropped his head and let his breath flow over her lips

before easing forward to taste her. Anticipating a powerful jolt of desire, he was unprepared for the way his entire body lit up like he'd backed into a high-voltage generator marked *Danger*.

Drinking deep of her sweet, sinful mouth, Paul savored a kiss that reminded him of a quality bourbon, warm and complex. Heat spiraled through his veins. Her moan gave him the signal to take the kiss deeper. Lost in the liquid slide of their dancing tongues, Paul sucked on her lower lip and smiled as an eager groan broke from her throat. Their teeth clicked and he slanted his head to adjust the angle of the kiss so he could continue to devour her unhindered.

Lia's questing fingers dove beneath his shirt and an electrical storm flashed behind his closed eyes. He crackled with wild thrumming energy.

He came up for air long enough to whisper, "This is going to complicate things."

"Oh." The anguish in her murmur made him hate that he'd voiced his concerns. But then she kept going and it was her throaty yes that sealed both their fates.

He breathed in her laughter, capturing it in his lungs before crushing his mouth to hers. A needy whimper broke from her as she ground herself against him, her movement becoming more frantic by the second. She rocked her hips, as if she'd given herself over to what her body needed and to hell with pride or consequences.

Paul couldn't get enough of this woman. The chemistry between them was born of Lia's romantic optimism and his surrender to everything caring and earnest about her. Even knowing this stolen moment couldn't last and despite recognizing her sweetness might shatter his defenses and leave him open and exposed, Paul could no more stop or pause than he could fly.

He lowered his lips to hers once more. As her tongue, hungry and seeking, stole into his mouth, setting him on fire, he reached up and released her hair from its clip. Threading his fingers through the espresso waterfall of silky strands, he savored the spill of softness against his skin. He breathed in her vanilla scent as she roped her arms around his neck and murmured her appreciation. The sound popped a circuit in his brain, turning his thoughts into white noise that drowned out all things rational.

They tumbled onto her bed, hands skimming beneath the fabric of their clothes to the hot skin beneath. Groaning and panting, they deepened their kisses. Clothing fell away. Paul cupped Lia's breast and pulled her tight nipple into his mouth. With a wordless cry, she arched her back and shifted her hips in entreaty. He wanted to take his time, to put his mouth between her thighs and taste her arousal, but his hunger for her burned too hot. His hands shook as he slid on a condom and shifted her until she straddled him.

Her blissful expression transfixed him. Then she tossed her head back and lowered herself onto his erection. Engulfed by the heat of her, Paul forgot how to breathe. No woman he'd ever known had blindsided him like Lia. She aroused impulsive cravings that couldn't be denied and he'd long since lost the will to resist.

When her orgasm slammed into her, Paul felt the impact shake his soul. In the aftermath, he skimmed his palms over her flushed skin until her lashes lifted. Her eyes glowed with naked joy and absolute trust. At the sight, something rattled loose in his chest, stopping his heart.

"I…"

With a tender smile she set her fingertips against his lips. "Come for me. Please. I need you so much."

Keeping them locked together, Paul flipped Lia onto her back and began driving into her tight heat. With an ardent moan she drove her fingers into his hair and met his deep thrusts with a hunger and enthusiasm that turned his desire into something reckless and unstoppable. He locked his lips to hers and surged into her over and over, feasting on her pleas. She was on the verge of coming again when his climax built to a point of no return.

With her legs wrapped around his hips, her teeth grazing his neck, he held off until a series of tremors detonated through her body and she yielded a soft, keening cry of pleasure. Only then did he let himself be caught in the shattering brilliance of his orgasm.

Contentment settled over Paul as he buried his face in Lia's silky hair and waited for his breath to level out. Trailing his fingertips across her delicate shoulders and down her slender back, he stared at the tin ceiling, then turned his head and took in the cozy pillows they'd knocked to the floor with their passion. Reality intruded, banishing the hazy glow of satisfaction.

They'd agreed she would stay for two weeks. Seven days had already passed. The proof that she would soon depart was all around them. The truth in his heart was that Paul wasn't ready to let her go.

With the wedding Paul had invited her to only two days away, Lia took inventory of her closet and found nothing suitable for an evening wedding featuring a Charleston socialite and a multimillionaire. Dallas had described the private event as a "simple affair," but Lia guessed Charleston "simple" wasn't a barefoot bride in her momma's backyard with a barbecue picnic to follow. No, this wedding would be elegant and classy with a guest list that included the town's elite.

Lia wanted something that would let her blend in with the rest of the Southern women in attendance, but had no idea what that would be. Her best bet would be to reach out to Poppy and Dallas to see if they had recommendations. Once Lia had shot each woman a text, explaining her dilemma, their immediate and enthusiastic response left her second-guessing her decision. In just a few days she'd be bidding them goodbye. Growing closer to the twins was only going to make leaving harder. Not for her. She was all too accustomed to parting ways with those she'd grown fond of.

On the other hand, the Watts family was a tight-knit group who'd been devastated when Ava left. Of course, Grady's daughter had spent her whole life embraced by her family and naturally when she'd fled Charleston, her absence left a void. By the time the story came out that Lia wasn't actually Ava's daughter, they would only have known her for a couple weeks. The loss wouldn't be as profound.

While Lia was pondering her eventual break with the Watts family, she'd received a flurry of group texts. Dallas listed the names of several boutiques in downtown Charleston while Poppy chimed in with her opinion on each one. Lia read the messages with a growing sense of turmoil. At last she jumped in and asked if either one would be available later that afternoon to come shopping with her and give her some tips. An enthusiastic yes from both women left her overwhelmed with fondness and riddled with guilt.

At three o'clock Lia slid into the back seat of Dallas's large SUV while Poppy rode shotgun. The two women exchanged animated opinions as to what would be suitable for the wedding as Dallas drove.

At the first store the twins took her to, Lia could immediately see she was in the wrong place. The clothes had a sexy vibe that she might have explored if her goal was to stand out. When she said as much, the twins exchanged a puzzled look.

"But you've got the perfect body to rock all of this," Dallas said, indicating a short red-orange number with a plunging neckline.

"I don't see why you wouldn't want to show off what you've got," Poppy contributed.

"That's not the first impression I want to make," Lia said carefully. "I was thinking that I wanted to blend in."

"But that's so boring," Poppy cried.

"I think boring is just fine when it comes to a wedding," Lia countered.

"But we're already here. At least try on two things," Dallas said. "Even if you don't buy anything, it'll be fun to try some stuff on."

"Dallas and I will each pick something for you and you can see which you like better."

Poppy's enthusiasm quashed any further protest. What would it hurt for her to indulge the twins? But even as Lia nodded her acceptance, she reflected on their growing camaraderie. Usually her nomadic lifestyle kept her from diving too deep into friendship, but the twins were engaging and endearing. From the first they'd made Lia feel like a part of their inner circle. The fact that she didn't belong, combined with her part in the deception, shadowed Lia's enjoyment of the outing. Still, the twins were a formidable distraction when they combined their persuasive powers and soon Lia surrendered to their enthusiasm.

They didn't allow her to do any browsing of her own and Lia could see that they'd played this game often with each other. Although they were identical twins, their personalities and styles couldn't have been more different. Where Dallas preferred pastel tones and floaty, ruffled dresses that moved as she walked, Poppy adopted a more casual style with bright fabrics that hugged her body and showed off all her assets.

Selections made, the twins herded Lia toward the dressing room. She entered the enclosed space and surveyed each outfit. The first was a strapless bedazzled dress in cobalt blue. While it was beautiful and would no doubt look great with her coloring, it screamed *look at me*. The second dress—a body-skimming red halter with high side split—was no better. If she walked into the party wearing this, everyone would see her and want to know who she was.

Still, Lia had agreed to try both on. She stepped out in the cobalt blue dress first.

"What do you think?" she asked, turning before the three-way mirror.

"I think all Paul's friends will be drooling over you," Dallas said.

That was the last thing Lia was looking for. She didn't want anyone singling her out.

"It's beautiful," she said. "But not exactly what I'm looking for. I feel a little too…" She tugged up the neckline, and then down on the hem. "I would feel a little too exposed in the dress."

"Try the red one on," Poppy said.

Lia returned to the dressing room and swapped dresses. Although the red halter was a little better, she still felt like she was trying too hard to send a message. She came out and had mixed reactions. While Poppy nodded vigorously, Dallas shook her head.

"The color is good on you and it really shows off the muscle tone in your arms, but that slit…"

"Agreed," Lia said. "Let's try somewhere else."

King Street was lined with boutiques and Lia soon learned that at some point, the twins had shopped them all. At the next store they went to the dresses were more in Dallas's style, with lace and ruffle details in pastel fabrics that made Lia look as if she was trying too hard to be someone she wasn't.

"I'm looking for something between these two stores," Lia said, worrying that she was never going to be able to find anything that suited her.

"I have a place in mind," Dallas said.

Lia changed back into her regular clothes and the three women departed for yet another boutique. As soon as they entered, Lia knew this was exactly where she needed to be. This time, instead of letting the twins choose, Lia intended to be part of the search for something she liked. There was a lot for her to pick from, but she settled on one dress in particular.

The gorgeous long-sleeved, ankle-length sheath fit her perfectly. A subtle sparkle ran through the blush-colored fabric that helped define her slender curves without drawing too much attention.

"This one," Lia said, exiting the dressing room to show off her pick.

"It's elegant and understated," Poppy said, but her expression reflected doubt. "Are you sure you don't want something with more pizzazz?"

"Elegant and refined is what I was going for," Lia said, gazing at her reflection in the mirror. "Unfortunately, I can't afford this dress. But you get the idea of what I'm going for."

"You shouldn't worry about the expense," Dallas said, highlighting the stark difference between how the twins lived and Lia's reality.

Despite the fact that both women held down jobs and paid their own expenses, they came from a wealthy family and this gave them a financial edge. Where Lia lived simply and sometimes had to scrape the bottom of her piggy bank when something unexpected happened, she knew all the twins had to do was dip into their extensive reserves.

"It's too much money to spend on something I can't imagine having the chance to wear again," Lia said, pretending not to see the look the twins exchanged.

Since the first day she'd met them, Lia had been dropping hints that she'd soon be leaving Charleston to get back on the road, preparing everyone for the moment when the testing mistake was revealed. Each time she mentioned leaving, one or more of the Wattses deflected her assertion, making it perfectly clear they didn't want her to go. Even though she recognized their affection for her was based on their belief that she was Ava's daughter, Lia had begun to dread the moment when she was no longer part of this family.

She'd always downplayed her need for an emotional support network. Her mother had instilled self-reliance in Lia from an early age. But looking at this way of life through the eyes of the Watts family, she'd started to see its limitations.

Bidding a determined farewell to the blush sheath, Lia settled on a markdown dress in black that skimmed her slim figure and highlighted her shoulders. Both Poppy and Dallas approved the sophisticated style, but best of all, the price was just inside her comfort zone. It wasn't the dress of her dreams but it would definitely do, and she couldn't wait to see Paul's expression when he saw her in it.

Ethan was heading home after another long day at Watts Shipping when he spied the open door to his father's large corner office and stepped inside. Instead of finding his father behind his large mahogany desk, Miles Watts stood near the windows, a drink in his hand, his gaze aimed toward the Cooper River, his mind far beyond the space he occupied.

"Wasn't Mom expecting you home hours ago?" Ethan asked, struck as always by how much Paul resembled his father with their matching tall frames, the family's distinct green eyes and wavy blond hair.

"No," Miles replied, shifting his gaze to his younger son. "She had book club tonight."

"I'm surprised you didn't take the opportunity to head to Chapins."

Chapins was a favorite of the Watts men. An upscale cigar lounge in the heart of downtown Charleston, it offered a large selection of rare and vintage brands.

"I had too much to do here," Miles said, gesturing toward his desk with the crystal tumbler. "Are you heading out?"

"I thought I'd swing by the gym before heading home." But instead of bidding his dad good-night, he advanced into the room. "Is everything okay? You seem distracted."

"Your mom brought one of her lemon pound cakes over to Grady today. You know how he loves her baking."

Ethan smiled. "We all do."

Miles nodded. "She ran into Taylor English while she was there."

While it wasn't unusual for Grady's attorney to visit him, something about the encounter had obviously prompted Ethan's mother to comment on it.

"And?" Ethan asked.

"And nothing." His father threw Ethan a dry look. "You know she wouldn't discuss her business with your grandfather."

"But Taylor must've said something that got you thinking, otherwise you wouldn't mention it."

"It wasn't what she told your mother, it was the questions she was asking about Lia, her background and if Paul had checked her out."

Ethan began to feel uneasy, but kept his tone neutral. "What did Mom tell her?"

"That she assumed Paul had vetted her." Miles glanced toward his son for confirmation before continuing. "But Taylor had all sorts of questions."

"Like what?"

"She pointed out the holes in Lia's adoption story. Would

a court really give a baby to a woman who moved around so much? Isn't there a whole process that happens where she'd have to be evaluated for stability?"

"I'm sure that happened," Ethan interjected, wishing they'd concocted a more run-of-the-mill backstory instead of using Lia's actual past.

Ethan's father didn't look convinced. "Why would Taylor ask so many questions about Lia unless she suspected something was wrong?"

"You know what kind of lawyer Taylor is. She's thorough."

"But why would she need to be thorough? The testing service determined Lia is Ava's daughter. I don't understand why Taylor would question that." His father's eyes narrowed. "Unless she doesn't think the testing service is reliable. Your mother wondered if we should have our own DNA test run."

Although his father had just presented him with the perfect opportunity to explain about the mistake, Ethan hesitated to put an end to their scheme. They'd agreed to a couple weeks. Paul was acting as best man at Ryan and Zoe's wedding the next afternoon and had invited Lia to join him. Both deserved a heads-up before Ethan broke the news that Lia wasn't family.

"Is Taylor right to ask questions?" Miles demanded after Ethan took too long deciding how to answer. And then when Ethan continued to grapple with his conscience, his father cursed. "What is really going on with Lia?"

"Nothing."

Miles crossed his arms and glared. "Do not lie to me."

Ethan sucked in a deep breath and let it ease from his lungs. "Okay, here's the thing…" As he explained the situation, claiming complete responsibility for the scheme, his father stared at him in dismay.

"Damn it, Ethan," Miles raged as he kneaded the back

of his neck. "This is the craziest stunt you've ever pulled. What were you thinking?"

"I did it for Grady," Ethan said, refusing to be treated like a reckless teenager. "And for Paul. Haven't you noticed that things between him and Grady have improved?"

Miles gave a reluctant nod. "And I'm glad, but you can't seriously be planning to pass Lia off as family forever."

"The plan was only supposed to last until Grady improved and he has. Everything will be over in a few days."

"Over how?"

Ethan's concern eased as he realized his father was willing to hear him out before deciding to blow the whistle. "We plan to announce that the testing service got it wrong and she's not Ava's daughter."

"That is going to devastate Dad."

"I know he'll be upset," Ethan said. "But I'm convinced that we would've lost him if he hadn't believed Lia was Ava's daughter. And he's stronger now. I think he'll be okay when he finds out the truth."

"You *hope* he'll be okay," Miles corrected. "Just be ready for the consequences, because if there are any setbacks in Grady's health, that's on Paul and you."

"Not Paul. Just me. By the time Paul found out what was going on we were too far in."

Miles leveled a keen stare on his younger son. "One last thing. You really need to tell your grandfather the whole truth."

Ethan shook his head. "I considered that, but decided that if Grady found out we tricked him on top of losing Ava's daughter, it would be a bigger blow."

"The problem with the whole DNA testing angle," Miles said, "is that Grady will believe Ava's daughter is still out there."

"I've been thinking about that." Ethan opened his brief-case and pulled out the test kit he'd ordered in the days after he'd concocted his scheme to pass Lia off as Grady's grand-daughter. "Maybe you could help me find her for real."

Eight

The morning of his best friend's wedding, Paul spent a few hours at the office, but found he couldn't concentrate. That had been happening all too often in the days since that long afternoon in Lia's camper. Despite the unusual surroundings, or maybe because of them, Paul knew the time with Lia was indelibly etched in his memories. They'd made love for hours, forgoing new truck shopping and skipping dinner. Only after their exertions made their hunger for food more urgent than their appetite for each other did they get dressed and grab a couple burgers at a fast-food restaurant.

He hadn't been exaggerating: giving in to their attraction was going to complicate things. She wasn't like any woman he'd ever known and he hadn't crossed the line with her lightly. This left him with a dilemma. Sneaking around with her compounded his discomfort about the lies they were perpetrating. But the thought of giving her up left him in an ill-tempered funk.

Following the compulsion to see her, Paul left his office

and drove to his grandfather's estate. The sound of feminine laughter reached his ears as he exited his SUV, luring him toward the pool. Expecting to find his cousins clad in their customary bikinis, lazily floating on rafts in the turquoise water, he was besieged by wonder and a trace of amusement at what greeted him instead.

His cousins and Lia balanced on paddleboards in the middle of the pool, engaged in yoga moves. While both Dallas and Poppy wore bathing suits, Lia was dressed in her daily uniform of black yoga pants and a graphic T-shirt that flattered her lean curves and drew attention to her high, firm breasts. Given that both his cousins had wet hair and were wobbling dangerously on the ever-shifting boards while trying to hold a standing yoga pose, Paul assumed it must be much harder than Lia was making it look.

She moved fluidly on the board, shifting from one pose to another with barely a ripple in the pool. Her confidence fascinated him. At every turn she surprised him with a whole range of unexpected talents from cake decorating to accompanying Grady's drumming on the harmonica to assorted art projects geared toward children that now adorned Grady's bedroom.

With each day that passed, she endeared herself to his entire family more and more, and even Paul's high level of skepticism had failed him. Lia was a whirling dervish of energy and optimism and it was hard to remain detached, especially when every time they occupied the same room, she became the focal point of his awareness. His determined distrust had given way beneath the pressure of the undeniable energy between them. The maddening chemistry was more than sexual. The hunger to be near her was a fire that burned throughout his entire body.

He found her stories of life on the road fascinating. Her kindness toward his grandfather wasn't an act. Every minute Paul spent in her company boosted his optimism and lightened his mood. The tiniest brush of his hand against hers sent a shower of sparks through him. Dozens of times he'd caught himself on the verge of touching her in front of his family. Whenever they occupied the same room, he had to struggle to keep his gaze from lingering on her.

Spying Grady in the shade of the pool house, Paul approached and sat down beside his grandfather's wheelchair. Grady reached out and gave Paul's arm an affectionate squeeze. With the return of his grandfather's love and approval, Paul had no more need to arm himself against the grief that had caused him to guard against personal relationships. Another positive change in his life he could attribute to Lia. Was there no end to her uplifting influence? Did he really want there to be?

Once again Paul was struck by concern for what the future might hold after Lia's departure. While Grady grew more robust with each passing day, finding out that Lia wasn't his granddaughter was certain to hit him hard. Would his depression return?

"What are they doing?" he asked, crossing his ankle over his knee as the afternoon's humid air made its way beneath the collar of his navy polo.

"Yoga," Grady sang, bright amusement in the gaze he flicked toward his grandson.

"Why are they doing it on paddleboards in the middle of the pool?"

"Harder."

Seeing Grady's fond smile, Paul felt a familiar stab of guilt they were perpetrating a fraud on the old man. His grandfather loved Lia because he believed she was his long-lost granddaughter. That she wasn't ate at Paul more every day.

"I can see that. The twins look like they're struggling."

Even as he spoke, Poppy lost her balance, but before she tumbled into the pool, she dropped to her knees and clutched the edges of the board. She laughed in relief while Dallas and Lia called out their encouragement.

Paul guessed this wasn't Lia's first time doing this because she was rock-solid on the board. "It's good to see you outside," Paul said, tearing his gaze away from her. "How are you feeling today?"

"I'm feeling strong." Grady spoke the words with triumph.

"You're getting better every day," Paul murmured. "That's wonderful."

The two men sat in companionable silence and watched the three women for another half hour, until Lia brought the session to a halt.

"Nice work, ladies," she called, towing the paddleboards toward the storage room at the back of the pool house while his cousins toweled off.

Paul went to help her, eager for a couple seconds alone, somewhere out of the way so he didn't have to guard his expression. He took in the light sheen of moisture coating her skin, tempting him to ride his palms over her sunwarmed arms and around her waist. If he dipped his head and slid his tongue along her neck, he knew she would taste salty. His mouth watered at the memory of her silky flesh beneath his lips.

"You've done that before," Paul said, letting her precede him into the large room crammed with pool toys.

"My mother teaches yoga. I've been doing it since I could stand," Lia said. "You should try it. Besides increasing flexibility and muscle tone, it can reduce stress."

He paused in the act of stacking the boards against the back wall. "Do I seem stressed to you?"

"I was thinking maybe you'd like to improve your flexibility," she teased, shooting him a wry grin.

Paul nodded, letting her score the point without retaliating. She wouldn't be the first person who'd described him as intractable. It's what enabled him to keep pursuing criminals when the trail went cold. At the same time, he recognized being obstinate had created problems in his relationship with his family.

"Grady seems to be doing better every day," he remarked, reaching for her hand. As their fingers meshed, his entire body sighed with delight at the contact. "It's hard to believe that less than two weeks ago we were all worried he wasn't going to last until the end of the month."

"You know he's really proud of you."

His gut twisted at her words. "I don't know that."

"Well, he is," she said, her thumb stroking across his knuckles.

"Even though I didn't join the family business?"

"It makes him happy that you're passionate about what you do." Lia's warm smile eased the tightness in Paul's chest. "And that you help people by making the world safer."

"Thank you," Paul said, tugging her closer.

Entreaty flickered in her eyes, quickly masked by her long dark lashes. His blood heated as he detected an unsteadiness in her breathing. Damn, he badly wanted to kiss her. The need to claim her soft mouth overwhelmed him. Not even the worry that they might be caught could temper the wild emotions she aroused.

Acting before he could convince himself that it was madness, Paul backed Lia toward the wall. A surprised whoosh of air escaped her as her spine connected with the hard surface. He skimmed his fingers down her arms, pinned her wrists to the wall on either side of her hips.

Curses momentarily drowned out his thoughts. "We should get back to the pool before someone comes looking for us."

Releasing his grip on her, Paul flattened his palms against the wall and started to push away, but her reflexes proved faster than his. Before he could escape, she'd locked her hands around his back and tugged him even closer.

"Kiss me first." Her lips curved in a sassy grin that was equal parts sexy and sweet. "Unless you don't want to."

He almost laughed at her words. Not only did he *want* to kiss her, he *needed* to kiss her. Needed it like the air he breathed and the food he ate. She was the most irritating, frustrating female he'd ever known. Thoughts of her distracted him all the time. It took effort to concentrate on his job and for that he couldn't forgive her. Worse, he was ravenous for her in a way that couldn't be denied and with each day his willpower weakened.

Her eagerness was a temptation he couldn't resist and Paul found himself swept into the kiss. Into her warmth and sweetness and enthusiasm. He took what she gave. Unable to stop. Unwilling to stop.

Paul wasn't sure what brought him back from the brink, but soon he lifted his lips from hers and trailed kisses across her cheek.

"I can't stop thinking about being with you again," he murmured, surprising himself with the admission. "But you have that birthday party at the hospital this afternoon, don't you?"

Her chest rose and fell as she stared at him, her beautiful hazel eyes wide and utterly trusting. "You remembered."

Paul stepped back and raked his fingers through his hair. "Do you mind if I tag along?"

"You're always welcome to be my knight-errant."

Even as warmth pooled in his gut, the urge to warn her to be careful of him rose. The things he wanted to do to her weren't romantic or chivalrous. Her love of dressing up as a princess drove home the intrinsic sentimental nature of her true soul.

In fairy tales, princesses got rescued from towers, endless sleep and villains who intended them harm. Paul was no Prince Charming. In fact, he'd acted more like a beast with Lia. And even if his initial disdain had given way to grudging admiration, he didn't deserve her trust.

"That's fine as long as I don't have to wear tights," he grumbled and neither her surprised laughter nor her affectionate hug improved his mood.

On a normal visit to the children's ward at the hospital, Lia would've lost herself in the part of Elsa, the Snow Queen. Bringing joy to children, especially ones who needed to escape reality for a little while, gave her own spirits an enormous boost. But Paul's solemn gaze on her the entire time made her all too aware of the heat and confusion between them.

Every stolen moment with him pushed her further into uncharted territory. She'd never known the sort of urgent craving he aroused in her. In the past, she'd always viewed sex as a pleasurable way to connect with someone she cared about. What she experienced with Paul turned every other encounter into a foggy memory. The crystal-pure clarity of his fingers gliding over her skin. The keen pleasure of his weight pressing her into the mattress. His deep kisses and soul-stirring moans as he slid into her. All of it was etched into her soul never to be forgotten.

Yet all too soon she'd be leaving Charleston, never to see him again. Lia wasn't sure what to do about her growing resistance to the idea of resuming her travels. Never before had she faced a compulsion to stay put. But her growing attachment to Paul was a big part of that. Normally Lia would blindly follow her heart, but this time she recognized that trusting her instincts was impossible. She'd mired herself in a scheme that had only one outcome. Once the genetic test was revealed to be flawed, no member of the Watts family would want her to stick around.

Not even Paul. Despite her longing for a relationship

to developing with him, she feared that if she remained in Charleston, eventually her past would come between them. He'd dedicated his career to hunting criminals. She could imagine his fury when he discovered her grandfather was in prison. And learning what had put him there would confirm Paul's initial opinion of her as an opportunist.

Part of her recognized he was probably still digging into her background. She'd be wise to tell him the truth and face his displeasure before her growing feelings for him made heartbreak inevitable, but as they walked back to the estate, Lia lost her nerve. She was gambling that he wouldn't turn up anything with less than a week until she left Charleston. Better that she stay silent so that his memories of her remained unsullied.

They parted company at the driveway and Lia headed for the house. Upon entering her bedroom, she spied something that hadn't been there when she'd left. A garment bag, twin to the one from the boutique hanging on the armoire door, lay across her bed, along with an envelope. Puzzled, Lia set aside her long ice-blue gloves, opened the envelope and read the note.

We know you loved this dress and wanted you to have it.—Dallas & Poppy.

Overwhelmed by the twins' generosity, Lia slowly unfastened the bag's zipper to reveal the stunning blush gown she'd fallen in love with. Guilt clawed at her. She shouldn't accept the gift. The twins had purchased the expensive dress believing she was their real cousin. Yet to refuse would force awkward explanations.

Lia wanted to scream in frustration. Why did everyone have to be so kind to her? The deception would've been so much simpler if she'd been greeted with the same sort of suspicion that Paul had demonstrated.

After shooting the twins an effusive thank-you text, Lia jumped in the shower. As she applied her makeup and experimented with several hairstyles, she tried to ignore her anxiety over what she might encounter at the upcoming event. Pretending to be Ava's daughter had grown easier these last few days. Not that her subterfuge rode any easier on her conscience, but once she'd answered the tricky questions surrounding her childhood to everyone's satisfaction, she'd been able to lower her guard somewhat.

But attending this wedding with Paul meant she would be under scrutiny once more. Although he'd promised his circle of friends wouldn't ask too many questions about her, Lia suspected that they'd be wildly speculative about any woman he'd bring. Once again, the opportunity to spend more time in his company was a temptation she couldn't resist. Hopefully it wouldn't backfire on them.

The dress fit as perfectly as when she'd tried it on in the shop, reviving Lia's confidence. Tonight she would demonstrate to Paul that she could at least appear as if she fit into his social circle, even if she'd be completely out of her element. As long as she smiled a lot, said little and stuck like glue to Paul's side, she should be fine.

Lia arrived in the formal living room five minutes before she was scheduled to meet Paul only to discover that he'd beaten her there. She had a fraction of a second to appreciate the way his charcoal-gray suit fit his imposing figure and to indulge in a little delighted swoon before he glanced up from his phone and swept a heated gaze over her.

The possessive approval Lia saw there stripped her of her ability to speak or move. As often as she'd donned a costume and played the role of a princess, she'd never truly felt like one before. But now, as she basked in Paul's admiration, she understood what it meant to be treasured.

"You look gorgeous," Paul said, walking over to her. Clearly cautious over the possibility that anyone could stumble on them, he limited his contact to a brief squeeze of her fingers, but even that fleeting touch sent Lia's pulse into overdrive. "I'll have to stay close tonight or my friends will try to lure you away."

"Oh." His low murmur set the butterflies fluttering in her stomach. "No." She shook her head as the full import of his words struck her.

"No?" He looked taken aback.

She shook her head and rushed to explain. "I didn't think I'd stand out in this dress."

Paul's posture relaxed once more. A sensual smile curved his chiseled lips. "You stand out no matter what you wear."

With her skin flushing at his compliment, Lia slid a little deeper into infatuation. Even so, she recognized that the easing of Paul's earlier distrust gave his approval greater significance. Still, there was no fighting the inevitable. She was falling hard for his man.

He took her by the elbow and propelled her toward the door, his confidence muffling her concern. "Relax, you'll be fine."

"That's easy for you to say," she muttered grimly. "This is your world." And she didn't belong.

Twenty minutes later, Lia's mood had lightened. During the short drive to one of the most impressive mansions in Charleston's historic district Paul had shared Ryan and Zoe's inspirational path to love.

Long before the pair met, Zoe had been in the middle of a scandalous divorce. To appear the wounded party and avoid having to pay her alimony, her husband had publicly accused Zoe of infidelity. Eventually the truth of her innocence came out, but by then her reputation was ruined and her finances were in tatters.

Devastated and bitter, Zoe had joined a revenge bargain with two strangers, women who'd also been wronged by powerful men. To deflect suspicion, each woman was tasked with taking down a man she had no connection to.

In Zoe's case, her target had been Ryan and she was supposed to hurt him by damaging his sister's political career.

Zoe hadn't counted on the romance that bloomed with Ryan or the difficulty in extricating herself from the vengeance pact. In the end, because Zoe hadn't been directly responsible for the resulting scandal that harmed Ryan's family, he'd chosen to put aside his anger, unable to imagine a future without her in it.

Paul obviously approved of the union despite its rocky beginning, leading Lia to hope he could set aside his stubborn and judgmental nature when faced with true happiness.

As soon as they went inside, the soothing strains of a string quartet enveloped them. Lush floral arrangements in warm shades of peach and pink decorated every room on the main floor. Lia inhaled the richly scented air as they strolled through the various rooms on their way to the rear garden where the ceremony would be taking place.

Paul introduced her to several people before his best man duties called him away. He left her with Zoe's former brother-in-law the race car driver Harrison Crosby and his fiancée, London McCaffrey. Lia appreciated the couple's easy acceptance of her company as they sipped preceremony champagne before making their way to the area in the garden where the chairs had been set up for the wedding.

The ceremony was short but beautiful. The bride wore a romantic confection of tulle embellished with lace flowers. Her groom stood beside Paul in a charcoal suit and pink bow tie, looking positively gobsmacked as she walked up the aisle toward him. They were emotional as they exchanged vows, bringing both smiles and tears to the thirty or so guests who'd come to celebrate with them.

Lia was still dabbing tears from her eyes when Paul came to find her after the ceremony.

"Are you okay?" he asked, arching an eyebrow at her.

"It was a beautiful wedding," she whispered. "They're so obviously in love."

"They came through a lot to get here," he murmured, his gaze following the bride and groom as they greeted friends and accepted congratulations. "I think it's made them stronger as a couple."

Struck by both his sentiment and the show of obvious affection for his friends, Lia exclaimed, "Paul Watts, you are a romantic!"

He frowned at her accusation. "I wouldn't say that."

"Don't deny it." A happy glow enveloped her. "Here I expected you to have a suspicious view of the whole love-and-marriage thing and you go all mushy on me."

"I'm not mushy."

She ignored his growled denial. "I never imagined you'd be a fan of love and such."

"Calling me a fan is a little over-the-top," he protested, taking her by the elbow and turning her toward the house where the reception dinner and after-party were taking place. "And why is it so surprising that I believe in love?"

"Love requires a leap of faith," she explained, having mulled this topic often in the last few days. "You're so logical."

He looked thoughtful as he considered her point. "It's also about trust," he said, indicating he'd also given the matter some consideration. "Trust of yourself and of the other person."

"But you're not exactly the trusting sort," she reminded him.

"That's not completely accurate when it comes to family and friends."

His single-minded, fierce protectiveness of those closest to him was sexy as hell. She was used to being alone and never considered what it might be like with someone to count on. Lately, however, Lia had pondered the immense sense of security those closest to Paul must feel. She'd never doubted that he was someone who could be counted on to aid and protect, but until now hadn't considered what being the beneficiary of such attention might be like.

That afternoon in her camper, encircled by his strong arms, she'd experienced a sense of well-being unlike anything she'd ever known. At the time she'd put the sensation down to their lovemaking and her joy at being inside the familiar refuge of her camper.

But maybe it had been just as much about gaining Paul's trust. Watching him with his family had offered her insight into his protective nature. He wanted nothing but the best for those he loved. When he'd begun to open up to her in small ways, she'd been thrilled to be gifted with this show of faith.

"So what you're saying," she clarified, "is that once given, your trust is complete?" The power of that took her breath away. "What if someone does something that goes against your principles?"

She was thinking about how Ethan had plotted to introduce her as Grady's granddaughter and the hit Paul was taking to his integrity in going along with the scheme. Yet the animosity between the brothers originated with Ethan. Paul obviously loved his brother and hated their estrangement.

"As much as I wish everything was black-and-white, it's never that simple." Paul stopped beside their assigned places at the dinner table and drew out her chair. "Now, can we drop all this serious talk and have some fun?"

With a nod, Lia abandoned the topic and focused her attention on enjoying the delicious reception dinner Dallas had prepared and marveling at the change in Paul as he socialized with his close friends, trading good-natured quips and contributing his share of funny stories that stretched back to their grade school days.

The depth and breadth of connection these people shared highlighted Lia's isolation. An ache grew in her chest that she recognized as longing. She wanted to belong. To feel the snug embrace of camaraderie. To be in on the private jokes and accepted into the club.

But this was an exclusive group of people, and not just because they'd been friends since childhood. Each one possessed an easy confidence born of privilege. In contrast was Lia as she sat beside Paul, listening attentively while speaking little, a huge fraud in the dress she couldn't afford.

As the waitstaff set plates of wedding cake before all the guests, Lia excused herself and headed to the bathroom. On the way back to the dining room, Dallas appeared in her path. As Lia gushed over the delicious dinner, she immediately sensed that Paul's cousin wasn't paying the least amount of attention to her compliments.

"Is something wrong?" Lia asked, uneasiness sliding across her nerve endings at the older twin's somber expression.

"You and Paul…" Dallas began, her voice scarcely rising above a whisper. "I saw what happened between you when you were putting the paddleboards away."

Cheeks flaming, Lia thought back to those stolen moments. It was her fault that they'd been caught. She'd begged him to kiss her.

"You two were…" Dallas looked horrified. "Kissing."

Lia threw up her hands as if to ward off the undeclared accusation. "It's not what you think—"

"You're first cousins."

"We're not." Stricken by Dallas's accusation, Lia blurted out the denial without considering the wisdom of spilling the truth before she'd spoken to Paul and Ethan about it.

Dallas frowned. "I don't understand."

Lia clutched her evening bag to her chest, struggling with the dilemma she found herself in. "There's a problem with my DNA test results," she declared in a breathless rush, sick of all the lies. "Ethan and Paul know, but you can't tell anyone else."

"What sort of a problem?"

"I'm not your long-lost cousin." Lia crossed her fingers and hoped that Ethan and Paul wouldn't be angry with her for jumping the gun. "We just found out that there was a huge mix-up."

Dallas looked appalled. "Why haven't you told anyone?"

"Because Grady has rallied since he thought I was his granddaughter and we've been waiting for him to be fully on the path to recovery before saying anything."

"He's going to be so upset," Dallas said. "He's been obsessed with finding Ava's daughter."

Lia hung her head. "We know."

"I can't believe Paul would let this go on."

"He's not happy about it, believe me." Lia grabbed Dallas's hand. "Please don't tell anyone. We've agreed that I'm only going to stay another few days."

"And then what?"

"Then we come clean about the mistake and I get back on the road."

Dallas stared at her in silence while emotions flitted across her face. "I don't understand any of this," she complained at last. "Why do you have to leave?"

"I was never going to stay," Lia reminded her, repeating what she'd been saying all along. "I like traveling the country too much to stay put anywhere."

"But Grady loves you. We all do."

"He loves his granddaughter," Lia said, her heart aching at the thought of moving on. Never before had she grieved for her lack of family ties. "I'm not her."

"What about Paul?"

"What about him?"

"You're obviously the woman from his reading. The one he's supposed to fall in love with."

"No." Lia ignored her pounding heart. "He's not in love with me. Attracted maybe, but we're too different to ever work."

"I think you might be exactly what he needs."

"Are you listening to yourself?" The laugh Lia huffed out fell flat. "A moment ago you were worried he and I were doing something creepy and wrong."

"That's when I thought you were our cousin," Dallas said. "Now that I know you're not, I heartily approve of you two."

"There is no *us two*," Lia corrected, her desperation growing by the second. "Please don't speak about this to anyone. Not even Poppy."

"But we tell each other everything."

"I know, but for now the fewer people who know, the better. And everything will come out in a matter of days." Seeing Dallas was still waffling, Lia gripped her hand. "Please."

"Fine," Dallas groused. "But you really should think about staying. For Paul's sake. And yours."

As Lia returned to Paul, she debated whether to tell him about her conversation with Dallas. She hated to let secrets and subterfuge get between them, but worried that he would keep his distance if he discovered that his cousin had caught them. With her time in Charleston growing short, she selfishly wanted to soak up his company and if he thought his cousin knew about their deception, that would preoccupy him to the exclusion of all else. She would just have to ensure that they were more careful around his family.

"Is everything okay?" Paul asked, his green eyes roaming her expression.

"Fine." Lia slid into her seat and hid her disquiet beneath a weary smile. "Just a little tired."

"Do you want me to take you home?"

Home. The word sent a spike of electricity through her. She knew he meant his grandfather's estate, but her home was a nineteen-foot camper parked north of the city. A few days from now she'd be hitting the road once more.

"Or maybe back to your house," she said, pushing aside all thoughts of leaving and the disquiet it aroused. "I'd love to spend some time alone with you."

"It's like you read my mind," he murmured. "Let's go."

Nine

The morning after Ryan and Zoe's wedding, Paul was up at dawn, retracing the walk along the beach he and Lia had taken the previous night before he'd dropped her off at the Watts estate. Her mood after leaving the wedding had been reflective, but when he'd asked her what was on her mind, she'd stopped his questions with a passionate kiss.

They'd made love for hours while the moon rose and spilled its pale light across his bedroom floor. He marveled how being in her company kept him grounded in the moment, his thoughts drifting over her soft skin, his focus locked on her fervent cries and the way her body shuddered in climax beneath him.

He'd been loath to take her back to his grandfather's house. Although they'd been together for hours, the time passed too quickly. He wanted to keep her in his bed. To wake up to her sweet face and bury his nose in her fragrant hair. Alone atop the tangled sheets that smelled of her perfume and their lovemaking, he'd spent the rest of a sleepless night staring at the ceiling and probing the dissatisfaction that dominated his mood.

What became crystal clear was that he didn't want Lia to leave. Not that night. Not in a few days. Maybe never.

Now as he looked out at the water this morning, he flashed back to the tarot card reading. The reversed Hermit card, indicating his time of being alone was over. The Lovers in his near future. The final outcome card promising happiness and joy. But there had also been the possible outcome card of the bound woman who Lia said represented confusion and isolation. He had a choice to make. Either maintain his current priorities by giving all his time and energy to his business or take a more balanced approach and open himself to the potential of love.

Appalled at himself for remembering all that New Age nonsense much less giving it the slightest bit of credibility, Paul returned home, showered and then sat down in his home office to lose himself in work. Although he had staff to follow through with the day-to-day business of protecting their clients' data, Paul liked to keep his skill level up to date. As fast as they plugged one hole, the criminals found another to get through.

The morning passed in a blur. He'd left his phone in the kitchen to avoid the temptation to call Lia. Around noon his stomach began to growl so he went into the kitchen to make some lunch.

Ethan had messaged him, asking how the wedding had gone and inviting him for an afternoon of fishing. The offer delighted Paul. It had been a long time since he'd hung out with his brother and he missed the fun times they'd had.

After a quick text exchange to accept, Paul headed west to James Island. Ethan lived in a sprawling four-year-old custom-built house that backed up onto Ellis Creek and offered direct access to Ashley River and Charleston Harbor. With its white siding and navy shutters, reclaimed heart pine floors, white woodwork throughout including kitchen cabinets and built-ins, the home had a more traditional style than Paul expected from Ethan.

A mix of antiques and new furniture filled the rooms, offering a comfortable but conservative feel. Only one room had a purely masculine vibe and that was the entertainment room on the lower level. The room's dark brown walls and red ceiling were the backdrop for a large projection screen, sports-related art and pool table with red felt.

It was in this room Paul found his brother waiting. Because Ethan liked to entertain, the room's location on the creek side of the garage with direct access from the driveway meant that Ethan's friends could come and go from the party spot without traipsing through his entire house.

"So I've been thinking," Paul began, accepting the beer his brother handed him from the beverage cooler built into the wet bar.

"When are you not thinking?" Ethan countered. He flopped onto the leather sectional and took a long pull from his bottle.

Ignoring his brother's jab, Paul rolled the bottle between his hands and paced. "Grady is progressing, but he's far from back to full health."

Ethan's eyebrow rose. "And?"

"We're due to tell everyone there's been the mix-up with Lia's genetic test in a few days and I'm just worried it's too soon and that he'll regress." For the hundredth time Paul wished Lia hadn't had such a profound effect on Grady's health. If she'd never come to stay at the estate, Paul could continue to pretend that he was perfectly content, never knowing how right he felt in her company, never knowing the all-consuming hunger or the raw joy of making love to her. She'd twisted his perceptions and made him question beliefs that ruled his life. Yet he couldn't get over the sense that she was the missing piece that made him whole.

"So you want her to stay longer?" Ethan asked, his eyes narrowing.

"Grady is happy." Paul spoke with deliberate care. "Because he thinks his granddaughter is back."

"I thought you were worried that he'd get too attached."

Paul let out a frustrated sigh, hating that he found himself trapped between a rock and a hard place. "That ship sailed the moment we didn't tell Grady the truth." He paused and drank his beer, picturing his grandfather by the pool the day before, the amused fondness in his gaze as he watched what he thought to be his three granddaughters.

"I don't know," Ethan muttered, sounding more like Paul than Paul at the moment. "The longer we let this go the more we risk the truth coming out. Grady might never forgive us if he thinks we tricked him."

Paul couldn't believe the way the tables had turned. Usually he was the one sounding the alarm. "He'll never know."

"He'll never know?" Ethan echoed, looking doubtful. "What's gotten into you?"

"What do you mean?"

"You were dead set against her pretending to be Ava's daughter at all. Next you'll be suggesting she should stay permanently."

Ethan's remark was a hit Paul didn't see coming.

"Now that's a really bad idea." Paul trusted that he could keep his attraction hidden for another week or two, but pretending she was his first cousin wasn't a long-term solution. In fact, it was more like endless hell. "We can't keep lying to the whole family about her being Ava's daughter."

"About that…" Ethan stared out the windows that overlooked his expansive back lawn. "We're no longer lying to the *whole* family."

Ethan's statement was a streaking comet along Paul's nerve endings. "What does that mean?"

"It means that Mom ran into Taylor English the other day and she had a lot of questions about how Lia's mom came to adopt her."

"Do you think Taylor suspects that Lia's not Ava's daughter?"

"Maybe. I don't know. Mom shared her concerns with Dad and he was worried. So…" A muscle flexed in Ethan's jaw. "I told Dad the truth."

"Damn it, Ethan."

"He suggested running another DNA test," his brother retorted in a reasonable tone that Paul found irritating. "And I was able to explain what we're doing and why. It took some convincing, but I reminded Dad that Grady was on the verge of slipping away from us before he started believing his granddaughter had returned."

Paul sputtered through a string of curses, until the revelation of what Ethan had not said sank in. "He knows we lied about Lia, but he hasn't told anyone?"

"He hasn't told Grady," Ethan said, his precise wording catching Paul's attention. "But I'm guessing he told Mom."

"And his sister?"

"I don't think so," Ethan said. "Can you imagine Aunt Lenora keeping that secret to herself? She might be able to avoid letting it slip with Uncle Wiley, but she talks to the twins about everything."

"Okay." Paul rubbed his temple where a dull ache had developed. "So, you explained the plan to Dad and he was willing to keep Lia's true identity a secret?"

"For a few days." Ethan finished his beer and set it aside. "So you can see why it's probably not a good idea to ask Lia to stay longer."

"Just one more week can't hurt," Paul said, convinced he couldn't make a decision about Lia in a few days. "I'll talk to Dad."

Ethan looked doubtful. "You should also check with Lia. She's pretty keen to get back on the road."

"Speaking of that," Paul said. "I think we should revisit how much we're paying her."

Ethan studied him for a long moment before nodding. "Okay. But I thought you believed she was only in it for the money."

Paul made a dismissive gesture. "That was before I got to know her better."

"How much better?" Ethan demanded, his eyes narrowing.

"Well enough," Paul retorted, unwilling to expound on the time he'd spent in Lia's company. He pivoted the conversation back to something he was comfortable discussing. "She can't leave town without a truck to pull her camper. I've been thinking that our grandfather's health is worth a whole lot more than a brand-new truck, don't you?"

"Okay. Let's get her a truck with all the bells and whistles." Ethan got off the couch and headed for the beverage cooler. "Just don't be surprised when she decides against sticking around longer after she has the means to leave."

Ethan's warning plunged deep into the heart of what had been bothering Paul for days. He didn't want Lia to disappear out of his life. The free-spirited nomad had entangled him in her quirky web of metaphysical nonsense and selfless generosity. Where he kept to himself and focused on business, she told fortunes, spread joy and showered positive energy on everyone she met.

He had yet to decide if being complete opposites would work for or against their romantic future. Since meeting her, Paul had begun noticing the concerns of those around him. He'd spent more time with his family in the last week than he had in the last few months. While he'd done so initially in order to keep an eye on Lia, as his suspicions about her faded, he'd realized how much he enjoyed interacting with his family.

"Do you think the lack of a vehicle is the only thing keeping her in Charleston?" Paul asked.

"That's always been the impression she's given me." Ethan paused and regarded Paul with raised eyebrows. "Has she indicated that she's ready to give up the road?"

"No." And that was the problem. "But you've known her longer. I thought perhaps she'd mentioned what it would take for her to settle down."

Ethan hit him with an odd look. "Why are you so interested?"

"It's just…"

Asking Ethan for romantic advice was harder than he expected. Paul didn't have a lot of practice putting his feelings into words. Nor was he good at sharing what was bothering him. That he wanted to try was another example of Lia's influence.

"Are you asking because you're attracted to her?" Ethan asked.

Feeling cornered, Paul kept his expression neutral. "She's pretending to be our first cousin." Yet he couldn't deny that it was getting harder and harder to avoid letting his feelings for her show.

"She's not our first cousin, though," Ethan countered. "And once the truth comes out the situation will get even more complicated. She's not going to want to stick around."

"No one will blame her for the testing service getting it wrong. Let's just see if she'll delay leaving for another week." Seeing his brother's worried expression, Paul added, "For Grady's sake."

"I'll talk to her," Ethan said. "But you need to be clear about what you want. Lia isn't someone you can toy with until an exciting project comes along that takes all your focus and energy."

"What are you saying?" Paul demanded, bristling at his brother's criticism.

"That if you're leading her on, you can do a lot of damage in a very short period of time."

Even though Ethan had invited his brother to go fishing, by the time their conversation concluded neither one was in the mood to take the boat out. Instead, after Paul left, Ethan wandered into his home office and contemplated the second genetic testing kit he'd ordered, but hadn't yet used.

As much as he wanted to satisfy the ever-intensifying craving to connect with his biological family, he recognized the revelations could come at a cost. Not only did he risk upsetting the people who loved him, but also he could be opening himself up to disappointment and heartbreak. Ethan couldn't explain his pessimism over the outcome, but recognized that not taking the test left him no better or worse off than he was at the moment.

And after watching Paul struggle with his fears and desires concerning Lia, Ethan was even more wary of throwing himself into an emotional maelstrom.

When he'd introduced Lia to his family as Ava's daughter, the last thing Ethan had imagined was that Paul would complicate the situation by developing feelings for her. Paul was too logic-driven to appreciate Lia's spiritual nature and too skeptical to ever trust her motives for helping them. Then again, physical attraction was a powerful thing and could lead to an emotional connection. Even in someone as jaded and pragmatic as Paul.

While Ethan enjoyed seeing his guarded older brother thrown off-balance, concern for Lia tempered Ethan's satisfaction. Although she claimed that traveling around so much kept her from getting too attached to those she met, Ethan sensed that this time was different. If Lia fell for

Paul the way he appeared to be falling for her, she'd throw her heart and soul at him and if Paul didn't wise up, she might end up hurt.

Turning away from the complicated and messy ramifications of his actions, Ethan focused on the trio of good things that had resulted. Grady's improved health. The healing rift between Paul and his grandfather. And one that Ethan hadn't expected, but found himself grateful for—the renewed connection with his brother.

Ethan hadn't realized the cost of pushing Paul away until the scheme with Lia had brought them together again. Setting his fingertips on the genetic testing kit, Ethan shoved it away. Maybe it was time to appreciate the family who loved him and not chase something that might not be out there.

The Sunday morning after Ryan and Zoe's wedding dawned as clear and golden as so many others Lia had experienced in her sumptuous bedroom. Despite her late return to the estate, she was awake with the sun. On a typical morning, she would bound out of bed and begin her day with yoga on the terrace overlooking the lush garden. But today didn't feel typical. Her mind raced, but her body felt sluggish. She curled herself around a pillow and clung to the glow from the previous night with Paul.

Three short days from now the news would break that she wasn't Grady's granddaughter, freeing her from the lies and obligations keeping her in Charleston. In the beginning, with Paul treating her like a criminal, Lia had dreaded the deception and longed for the moment when she could get back on the road. The sheer size and elegance of the Watts estate, not to mention the rules and traditions that operated within its walls, had been overwhelming. She wasn't used to being around people so much and missed the long hours of solitude to meditate or read or daydream.

CAT SCHIELD   151

But one thing that all her traveling to new towns had instilled in Lia was adaptability. Her acquaintances and jobs
were constantly changing. So she'd learned how to function
within the tight-knit Watts clan with their frequent visits to
check on Grady, outgoing natures, busybody ways. And to
her surprise, she'd started to enjoy the fun-loving twins, the
kind mothering of Lenora and Constance and even Paul's
unsettling presence.

Confronted with the reality that she would soon be leaving it all behind, sadness sat like a large stone in her stomach, weighing her down. Yet she couldn't deny there was
relief, as well. Living with the lie that she was Grady's
granddaughter made her anxious and her attraction to Paul
complicated everything.

With her emotions seesawing with each breath she took,
Lia struggled to maintain her usual equanimity as she ate
with Grady on the back terrace. She knew his family cred-
ited her with his daily improvement, but Lia put the credit
squarely on his shoulders. His determination was only
matched by his enthusiasm to try anything she'd suggested.
The singing that had worked in the beginning hadn't been
the only method to help him communicate. She'd created
a notebook of common words and phrases that he could
point to, which sped up conversations and eased frustration all around.

Grady had improved to the point that he intended to join
the family for dinner that night. Leaving him to rest, Lia
took a taxi to a nearby discount auto sales lot where she'd
identified a truck that she hoped might be a good fit. The
price was higher than she'd anticipated paying, but she
was running out of time to find something that could pull
Misty. Unfortunately, when she got to the lot, she discovered that the vehicle had already been sold, and nothing
else they had would work.

She was on the verge of heading back to the estate when

Ethan called her. When she explained what she was up to, he offered to act as her chauffeur.

"How was the wedding?" he asked as she slid into the passenger seat of his bright blue Mercedes twenty minutes later.

"It was beautiful. The ceremony was so heartfelt and romantic. I cried." She sighed at the memory. "Silly, isn't it? I don't even know Ryan and Zoe, but all I could think was how they belonged together."

A lump formed in Lia's throat as she recalled the way Ryan had looked at his bride. The love between them was like a stone tossed into a pond, rippling out from the couple to touch all the guests. She trembled as she recalled a moment during the vows when Paul's gaze had found hers amongst the well-wishers. The fleeting connection had sent a shock wave through Lia from head to toe.

"They really do," Ethan agreed. "It's as if everything that they went through created a one-of-a-kind connection between them."

Lia nodded. "That's what Paul said, as well."

"Paul said that?" Ethan blinked in surprise.

"I know, right?" She laughed. "It doesn't seem like him at all."

Ethan considered that for a moment. "I think his emotions go deeper than he lets on. He just needs someone he cares about to start breaking down his walls."

Lia didn't know how to respond, so she fidgeted with her phone. "While I was waiting for you to pick me up, I found a couple options at a dealer west of town."

"We can check those out, but I have a friend who owns a dealership and can get you a deal on something brand-new."

"I can't afford brand-new," Lia insisted.

"Paul and I discussed that and we'd like to help you out."

"That wasn't part of our original deal," she murmured

ungraciously, as she revisited her mixed feelings about accepting the dress from the twins.

Obviously neither Paul nor Ethan understood that she didn't welcome the handout. While part of her acknowledged they perceived their offer as helpful, Lia resented being treated like a charity case.

"Well, we'd like to alter our original deal."

"Alter it how?"

"We were wondering if you could stick around another week."

For days she'd been bracing herself to leave on the date they'd agreed on. Lia contemplated Ethan's offer with a mixture of relief and dismay. As much as she wanted more time with Paul, this increased the risk that someone besides Dallas might suspect something was going on between them.

"Are you sure that's a good idea?" she asked. "Grady is doing so much better. I don't think there's any chance that his health will be impacted when he finds out I'm not Ava's daughter."

"I agree with you," Ethan said. "This was all Paul's idea."

Tears sprang to Lia's eyes, forcing her to turn her gaze to the passing landscape. She knew better than to read too much into what Ethan said. Paul might only be thinking of his grandfather's welfare and not have more personal motives.

"Is something wrong?"

She grasped for some explanation that would convince Ethan of the folly of her staying longer and recalled her conversation with Dallas the night before. Given how tight the twins were, how long could they count on Dallas to keep their secret?

"Something happened last night," she said.

"You don't say."

His tone was so sly that Lia blinked her eyes dry and turned to look at him. Something about his knowing grin sent a spike of anxiety straight through her.

Did he know? She and Paul were playing a dangerous game.

"Dallas knows I'm not your cousin," she blurted out, hoping to distract him.

"Oh."

"Just *oh*?" She'd braced herself to deal with his dismay. "Why aren't you more upset?"

"I guess that means the jig is up."

"Not yet," Lia replied, her frustration rising at his casual manner. Living in fear of being found out for nearly two weeks had taken a toll on her nerves. "I talked her out of telling anyone by promising it would only be a few more days before we tell Grady. So you see why we can't keep going with this."

"I'll talk to her," Ethan said. "Maybe if I explain and let her tell Poppy we can go a little longer."

"What if I don't want to stay?" Lia murmured.

"Is this because Paul didn't ask you himself?"

"Don't be ridiculous." But even as she denied it, heat surged into Lia's cheeks.

"I knew it," Ethan said, looking concerned. "I knew something was going on between you two."

"It's not like that." Even as she spoke, Lia could see that protesting was a waste of breath.

"It's exactly like that. Paul is attracted to you. And it looks as if his feelings are reciprocated."

"Well, yes. But it's just…" She'd almost said *sex*. "It's nothing serious."

"Are you sure?"

Lia fidgeted with her phone. "We're not in the least compatible."

"Here's where you're making assumptions. Has it occurred to you that he doesn't need someone who's like him, but someone who balances him? Someone who's lively and impulsive and knows exactly how to get him out of his head?"

The picture Ethan painted was tempting. Being the yin to Paul's yang appealed to Lia in every way. And it worked in the confines of their secret relationship. Taking things public would bring a whole new series of challenges.

"It might be good for him short-term," she said. "But in the end what he needs is a serious girlfriend. Someone who matches his ambition and his background. Someone he can be proud of."

"You don't think he can be proud of you?" Ethan asked, sounding surprised.

"Look at me." Lia gestured at her denim shorts and graphic T-shirt with its yoga-inspired pun. "I don't bring anything to the table."

"You shouldn't underestimate yourself," Ethan said. "I think you are one of the kindest, most delightful people I've ever met."

Lia forced a laugh. "Paul would say eccentric, impractical and frivolous."

"Maybe that's exactly what he needs."

"It would never work between us long-term," Lia said, musing that in her own way, she was as skittish about emotional entanglements as Paul.

Where he closed himself down and focused on work, she flitted from town to town, never really investing herself in any significant relationships. She was a butterfly. He was a rock. They couldn't possibly work.

"You matter to him," Ethan argued. "I just don't think he's figured out what to do about the way he's feeling. Give him time to adjust. He's never fallen in love before."

Ethan's words electrified Lia, stopping her heart. She pressed her shaking hands between her thighs, terrified that if she bought into Ethan's claim that she would only end up getting hurt. Yet even as she forced herself to be practical, her heart clamored for her to stay in Charleston and be with Paul. Be with him for how long?

"Do you know if he's still investigating me?" she asked, noting that the question surprised Ethan.

"He hasn't said anything. Why do you ask?"

As fast as she was falling for Paul, she needed to know if what was in her past would cause Paul to reject her.

"Paul has made it perfectly clear that he thinks I agreed to pretend to be your cousin because I'm up to no good."

"I'm pretty sure he's changed his mind on that score."

"Maybe." In fact, Lia wanted that to be true because she hated to think that his doubts shadowed the moments she'd spent in his arms. "But I'm afraid he might discover something about me that he won't like."

Ethan frowned. "What sort of something?"

Lia gathered a bracing breath and began to explain about the man who'd swindled people out of hundreds of millions of dollars. Peter Thompson.

Her grandfather.

Ten

When Paul entered Grady's spacious living room prior to the family dinner, he discovered he was the last to arrive. In a matter of seconds he noted the placement of all his relatives throughout the room and had taken two steps toward Lia, following the instinct to be close to her, when his mother intercepted him.

"How was Ryan and Zoe's wedding?" Constance asked, seeming oblivious to the fact that she'd just stopped him from a huge blunder.

"Very nice."

"I never thought she and Tristan Crosby were well matched," his mother continued. "She seems much happier with Ryan."

"They're both happy," Paul declared.

"I don't suppose I'll be helping to plan any weddings in the near future," Constance muttered, casting meaningful glances from Paul to Ethan.

"Isn't wedding planning usually left up to the bride and

her family?" he countered, skillfully turning the conversation to less fraught waters. "You wouldn't want to step on anyone's toes."

"When have I ever overstepped?" Constance asked with studied innocence.

"Never."

But the truth was, Paul's mother was known for getting her way with the various charity events she helped organize. Was it any wonder both her sons had such strong leadership skills? They'd learned how to be in charge from a master.

Dinner was announced before Paul had a chance to do more than wave at his cousins and offer a smile to his aunt and uncle. Paul found himself seated between his father and Dallas, relegated to the opposite side of the table from Lia.

As always, Grady sat at the head. Tonight he was flanked by Lia and Lenora. Grady was in high spirits. Although he still struggled to speak, his eyes twinkled as he observed his family's interaction. The stark contrast in his vitality two weeks earlier lent an even greater festivity to the meal.

From his family's effusive remarks, Paul gathered the food was delicious, but he noticed little of what he tasted. He was preoccupied with Lia and pretending to maintain his interest in the twins' chatter or his father's concern about the imbalance in imports and exports due to the recent tariffs.

As dessert was served, Grady clinked his glass to gain everyone's attention. With each day, he gained more control over his words, but sometimes still relied on singing to produce certain sounds. Having gained everyone's attention, he began in a singsong rhythm.

Reaching for Lia's hand, Grady fixed his gaze on her. "I changed my will to include Lia."

Suspicion ran like poison through Paul's veins while Lia sat in stunned silence, wide eyes glued to Grady's face.

Around the table, there were exclamations of approval. Paul locked gazes with his brother and saw his own concern mirrored there.

"This is quite sudden," Constance murmured with a slight frown. "I mean…" She seemed at a loss as she glanced from one son to the other.

Paul shook his head in an effort to communicate that this wasn't the moment to come clean. If they explained about the testing mistake on the heels of Grady's bombshell announcement, everyone would want to know why the delay in bringing up the issue. They couldn't afford any of the family asking questions that would clue Grady in to their scheme.

"You shouldn't have done that," Lia said, shaking her head. Her dismay seemed genuine. "It's… I don't…"

Her gaze darted Paul's way and just as quickly fled, leaving him unsure that she'd manipulated Grady into changing his will.

"You don't know me," she argued, her panic visibly threatening to choke her.

Grady shook his head, squeezed her hand and gave her a lopsided, reassuring smile. "You're my granddaughter," he announced in definitive tones, suggesting what was done was done.

As everyone finished off the red velvet cake, it was pretty obvious that Grady was fading. Although no one summoned her, Rosie appeared and wheeled him out of the room. Lia followed, but before she could escape upstairs, Paul drew her through the living room and out onto the side terrace.

Lia looked shell-shocked and near tears as she scanned his expression with near-frantic eyes. Paul balled his hands into fists to stop himself from taking her into his arms and soothing away her distress. He had so much to say, but didn't know where to start.

"This is a huge mess," Paul declared, his gut tight with conflicting emotion.

Before Lia could respond, Ethan appeared on the terrace. Her gaze went straight to him and clung like he was her lifeline.

"I had no idea he intended to change his will." Lia's voice was filled with anguish.

"You're sure he didn't mention it at all?" Paul demanded. "Because with a little warning we could've headed off his decision and saved us all a lot of grief."

Seeing her woeful expression, Ethan threw a protective arm around her shoulders and shot Paul a hard look that warned him to back off. "I'm sure if Lia knew she would've told us."

When Lia slumped against his brother's side, Paul felt like he'd been slapped.

"What are we going to do about this?" Irritation gave his voice a bite.

"Tell the truth," Lia said, sending a speaking glance Ethan's way. "The sooner the better."

But once they did Lia wouldn't have a reason to stay in Charleston any longer. He stared at Lia while the conversation at Ethan's house ran through his mind. The thought of her leaving made him ache.

"Let's give it a few days," Paul said. "If we explain about the testing service right now, the timing will look suspicious."

"I agree." Ethan nodded. "The damage is already done. A couple more days won't matter."

Lia grimaced. "I'm not sure that's true."

A significant look passed between Lia and Ethan, turning Paul into an unnecessary third wheel. What happened to the closeness he'd shared with Lia these last few days?

"Am I missing something?" Paul demanded.

"It's more complicated than you know," Lia admitted.

"More complicated how?"

"Why don't you and I grab a drink and I'll fill you in," Ethan said. Then, ignoring Paul's growing impatience, Ethan directed his next words to Lia. "I'll call you in the morning."

"Thank you."

Lia headed for the outside stairs that led to the second-floor terrace and was out of sight before Paul recovered from the bolt of jealousy that shot through him at the easy affection between Ethan and Lia. His resentment even overshadowed the shock of what their grandfather had done.

"What the hell?" Ethan demanded, as they left the house and crunched in the gravel side by side along the garden path on the way to their cars. "Why did you take your frustration out on Lia like that? None of this is her fault."

Paul grappled with dismay and self-loathing at the way he'd taken his shock and jealousy out on Lia. Although his first reaction to her being included in the will had been suspicion, he knew better. Instead he'd acted like she'd manipulated Grady, forcing Ethan to come to her defense.

But instead of owning his mistake, Paul lashed out. "I told you passing off a perfect stranger as Ava's daughter was going to blow up in our faces."

"Fine. You were right as always." Ethan's expression shifted into stubborn lines. "Look, fighting isn't going to do us any good. We need to figure out what to do."

"It's obvious we need to come clean to Grady immediately," Paul declared. "I'll tell him."

"We should both tell him," Ethan said. "It was my idea to let Grady believe she was his granddaughter. You should talk to Lia." Ethan's expression softened with pity. "Although after how you behaved just now, I'm not sure she's ever going to forgive you."

* * *

After leaving Paul and Ethan, Lia escaped to the solitude of her bedroom, intent on digesting the evening's events, and ran straight into more trouble. Dallas stood with her back to the windows, her arms crossed over her chest, wearing a scowl of open hostility. As soon as Lia closed the door for privacy, she rushed to reassure the younger woman.

"Please believe that I never meant for any of this to happen," Lia said, hating the way Dallas's eyes narrowed in suspicion. "I had no idea your grandfather was going to do that."

"This whole thing has gone too far," Dallas said, her voice an angry lash. "You need to tell everyone the truth."

"I agree," Lia assured her. "Ethan and Paul are talking about the best way to handle that right now."

"I really liked you." Dallas turned the declaration into an accusation. "I was so happy you were our cousin."

"The only family I ever had was my mother and since I turned eighteen and struck out on my own, I barely know where she is half the time." The sharp ache in Lia's chest made her next words almost impossible to get out. "You have no idea how much I wanted to be part of your family."

"But you're not." Some of Lia's anguish must have penetrated Dallas's outrage because her next words were gentler. "And that really sucks."

"I'm sorry I upset you, but I never meant for anyone to get hurt," Lia protested, overpowered by loss.

"You should've thought about that before you lied."

Dallas left the bedroom without another word and Lia threw herself facedown on the bed. For several minutes she wallowed in misery while her eyes burned with unshed tears. She'd deserved to be called out for her lies. Lia just wished it didn't hurt so much.

As Lia pondered her next course of action she realized it was time for her to leave Charleston. Earlier that day she'd purchased a truck. Not the fancy brand-new vehicle Ethan had insisted he and Paul wanted to buy for her, but one within her budget. After some determined negotiating, she emptied her savings account and left the lot the proud owner of a five-year-old model similar to the one that had been totaled six months earlier, but with fewer miles on it and a working air conditioner.

The purchase compelled her to confront what she'd been avoiding since the wedding. In the days before the romantic event, as she'd recognized her feelings for Paul were developing into love, she'd toyed with giving up her vagabond ways to be with him. Tonight she'd come to grips with reality. No matter how strong her attachment to Paul, his stark accusation demonstrated that without trust he couldn't love her with the openness and honesty she needed. Settling for anything less would lead to heartbreak.

Halfway through her packing, Lia noticed her duffel held more than when she'd arrived. The fact that she'd begun to collect unessential items revealed a shift in her attitude. There was nothing extravagant or indulgent in the miscellaneous clothes and accessories she'd let the twins encourage her to buy, but the purchases suited the life she'd been living in Charleston.

After stacking her costume boxes and overflowing duffel by the door, Lia crossed the hall and gently knocked on Grady's door. She owed him the truth and an apology before she left.

Later, she would call Ethan and say goodbye. Although she was angry with Ethan and herself for the ruse, he'd been a good friend to her. And he'd worry if she just vanished.

That left Paul. Her heart clenched in regret. Would he even care that she was leaving? She'd been a fool to imagine that she'd won him over, that his poor opinion of her had changed, could change. Instead, his suspicions had merely lain dormant, waiting for something terrible to happen.

No, she couldn't face him again. Couldn't confront the suspicion in his eyes and be devastated by his stubborn refusal to believe that she'd had no interest in financial gain. Now that she was leaving, Lia was overwhelmed with relief that she'd never face Paul's dismay about her grandfather.

When Grady called for her to enter, Lia stepped into the room and crossed to where he sat in bed. Setting aside the book he'd been reading, he smiled at her with such joy that a lump formed in her throat. She might not be his granddaughter, but she loved him and was ashamed that she'd ever lied to him.

At that moment, Lia knew that no matter what the brothers decided over drinks tonight, she had to speak the real truth. Not the story they'd concocted about the mistake with the DNA matching, but the fact that there'd never been a genetic test.

Dropping to her knees beside his bed, Lia touched his arm. "I want you to know that these last couple weeks have been some of the happiest of my life." Her voice faltered, but she cleared her throat and kept going. "You have made me feel welcome and nothing I can say or do could ever repay your kindness."

Grady frowned down at her, obviously perplexed. "What's wrong?"

She couldn't get over how much progress he'd made with his speech, and hated that she was leaving before she could help him make more.

"I'm so sorry." Lia closed her eyes to block out his face for this next part. "The thing is, I'm not your granddaughter."

Grady gripped her hand. "What?"

Lia's heart broke as she continued. "I feel terrible. It's all been a huge misunderstanding. The genetic testing…" She stumbled on her words, needing a moment to collect herself. "We made that up because you were so convinced

that I was your granddaughter and you got better because
of it. You'd been looking for Ava's daughter for so long,
and we just wanted you to be happy. And then you changed
your will. And now it's all just a big confusing mess." The
words flowed out of her in a great rush. She didn't realize
she was crying until Grady's knuckles brushed her cheek
and she saw how they came away damp. "I know you must
be so upset and I never meant to cause you pain."

She'd surveyed him as she spoke and saw that he was
confused and shocked, but her confession hadn't devastated
him. In fact, the way he kept patting her hand conveyed he
was more concerned that she was so upset.

"We were going to tell you in a few days because you've
been doing so much better. Before now we were afraid
you'd stop trying to get well again. I know I shouldn't have
gone along with it, but Ethan was so desperate and then
Paul was forced to keep our secret because he didn't want
to put your recovery at risk. It wasn't his fault. And please
don't blame Ethan. Your family has been so warm and
welcoming. But then you included me in your will and
I'm not really your granddaughter." Lia paused to get her
ragged breathing under control and peered at Grady. "You
are going to be okay, aren't you? Please tell me I haven't
made things worse."

"I'm fine."

"Oh good." She squeezed his hand. "I'm glad because
I need to leave Charleston and I couldn't go if I thought
you might relapse."

"No." Grady shook his head. "Stay."

"I can't. When your family find out I lied about being
Ava's daughter, they will all hate me."

"Not everyone," Grady said. "Not me."

The sight of his earnest smile blurred as fresh tears
formed in Lia's eyes. If the only opinion that mattered belonged to the patriarch of the Watts family, Lia knew she'd

stay and work hard to earn everyone's trust. But she was really running from Paul's reaction, recognizing that he could never trust her because of what lurked in her past.

"The thing is," she whispered, barely able to speak past the raw tightness in her throat. "There's also this issue with my grandfather being a thief and a liar. He's a terrible person and because we're related everyone will think I'm a terrible person, too. Even though I've never met him."

Lia paused to gulp in air, unable to believe she'd blurted out the truth about her grandfather on top of all the other revelations.

"And since I'm confessing everything... I'm in love with Paul and he doesn't love me, so it's too painful for me to stay." Lia pushed to her feet and dropped a fleeting kiss on Grady's cheek. "I want you to know that being a part of your family was the best thing that ever happened to me."

Eleven

Paul barely slept and was on his third cup of coffee when his phone chimed, letting him know he'd received a text. His stomach muscles clenched in reaction. Had Lia finally replied to his messages from the previous night? Her lack of response from the first one had prompted him to send another apology late in the night, asking if they could talk. That she hadn't acknowledged that one either was eating him alive.

A hundred times since last night he'd pledged if she gave him another chance, he would never doubt her again. But as the hours ticked by, he grew less confident that she would give him a hearing.

Glancing at the screen, he discovered the text was from Dallas and not Lia. With the bleak landscape of his future stretched before him, he cued up his messaging app and read his cousin's text.

I did something terrible and now Lia's gone.

Before he could reach out to Dallas about her ominous message, a call from Ethan lit up his smartphone.

"I just talked to Lia," Ethan said, sounding grim.

"She called you?" The words tasted like sawdust. Could he blame her for choosing the brother who'd had her back the night before? "Is she okay? I just got a text from Dallas saying that Lia is gone. Did she say where?"

The night before, he and Ethan had discussed how to handle the revelation that Lia wasn't Ava's daughter and decided to stick to their original story about the testing service getting things wrong instead of telling Grady the truth. She'd been a reluctant coconspirator and shouldn't have to face Grady's anger.

"She's at her camper," Ethan said.

"What's she doing there?"

"I don't think she felt comfortable staying at the estate any longer," Ethan said. "She told Grady the whole story last night."

Paul cursed, remembering how she'd pushed for the truth to come out. "How did he take it? Is he okay?"

"She said he was shocked, but okay when she left. I'm heading over there now."

"Why did she do that?" Paul mused. "We had it handled."

"Maybe because she has more integrity than both of us put together."

Ethan's ironic tone recalled all the accusations Paul had lobbed at her. He knew his brother was right. While they'd all lied, Lia had been the only one who'd done so without selfish motives. She'd declared time and again that she only wanted to help. And that's what she'd done.

Whereas he'd been inspired to sacrifice his own integrity by the desperate need to keep his grandfather alive and the return of Grady's approval. When had guilt stopped eating at him? Somewhere around the first time he'd kissed Lia. After that, he'd been less conflicted about lying to his grandfather and more disturbed by how she affected him.

"Here's the other thing," Ethan continued. "The reason she's at her camper is because she's preparing to leave Charleston."

"Leave?" Paul's chest tightened, robbing him of breath. "When?"

Ethan's tone was hoarse with sympathy as he answered. "She might already be gone."

Blind panic rose at the thought, and after arranging to meet Ethan at the estate in an hour, Paul hung up on his brother. With clumsy fingers he immediately dialed Lia's number, praying that this time she'd answer.

"Ethan says you're leaving," he declared the instant she engaged the call.

"Yes." She sounded shaken, but determined. "I have to."

"No, you don't."

"Grady knows I'm not Ava's daughter."

"I'll make him understand that none of this was your fault."

"But it was my fault. I never should've pretended to be something I'm not." The catch in her voice tore at Paul's heart. "It'll be better once I'm gone. Your family can put it behind you," she finished.

"Don't worry about my family," he said, feeling ragged and unsteady. "Ethan and I will sort everything out. Please don't go. I know Grady won't want you to leave town. He loves you."

Even as he spoke the words, Paul winced. Why hadn't he told her how miserable he would be if she left? Using Grady as an excuse was cowardly.

"Not me. He loves his granddaughter." Her bleak tones told him any attempt to convince her was wasted breath.

"I'm really sorry if I created trouble for you and Ethan by telling Grady the truth," Lia said, a somber warble in her voice.

"Don't worry about Ethan and me. We can take a punch." He stripped all humor out of his voice before saying, "I'm heading to the estate now. Afterward I think you and I need to talk."

"There's nothing more to say."

Oh, there was plenty to say. It just depended on whether he had the guts to declare how he felt about her. "Please don't leave Charleston."

"I have to go," she declared, her urgent need to run coming through loud and clear. "Don't you understand?"

Paul shook his head. He did, but that didn't mean he'd stop trying to persuade her to stay. "Promise me you won't leave town without seeing me first."

"I'll only promise I won't leave today."

That didn't leave him much time. "I'll come by after I see Grady. Where can I find you?"

"I'll be at my camper."

Disconnecting the call with things so unresolved between them was one of the hardest things Paul had ever done, but he trusted her when she promised to stick around until he could get there.

When he arrived at the estate, Paul met his brother near the pool and together they found their grandfather in the library on the first floor. The room was at the back of the house with dual access to the outside terraces. White bookshelves, trim and wainscoting offset the red walls, giving the room a lived-in, cozy feel. Little had changed since his grandmother's death nearly fifty years earlier except for the addition of children's books and thrillers beside the classic novels Delilah Watts had loved.

As soon as they entered the room, Grady spoke. "You lied to me."

"It was all my idea," Ethan explained. "Don't be mad at Paul or Lia. We just wanted you to get better, and from the moment you believed that Lia was your granddaughter, you did."

"It wasn't just Ethan," Paul chimed in, refusing to let his brother shoulder the full blame. "I went along with the ruse, as well. We really did believe it was for your own good."

Grady scowled. "I changed my will."

"We didn't expect that," Ethan admitted, speaking before Paul could. "Our plan had been to tell you this week that the testing service had made a mistake."

"But then you put Lia in your will and everything blew up," Paul added.

"And just so you know, none of this was her idea," Ethan said. "I tricked her that day at the hospital."

"She only went along with it because she wanted to help you." Awash in misery, Paul willed his grandfather to believe that Lia was genuine. "That's all she's ever done."

"I know," Grady said, his words coming with slow, deliberate care. "I don't blame her."

"Does she know that?" Paul asked. "Because she's leaving town. Running away from Charleston. From us." *From me.*

"I told her." Grady shook his head. "She's afraid."

"Of what?"

"Of you."

Paul recoiled from Grady's censure. "I'd never do anything to hurt her."

"Last night—" Ethan began.

"I screwed up." Paul interrupted, glaring at his brother. "And then I made it worse because I got mad when you jumped to her rescue." His irritation faded as he realized how stupid his defense sounded. "I'm an idiot for not believing in her. And she's leaving town because of it." Paul dropped into a chair and let his head fall into his hands. "How do I convince her to stay?"

"Have you told her you're in love with her?" Ethan asked in exasperated tones. "From what I've heard women really go for that."

"I'm not…" he began instinctively, shocked at his brother's revelation. Paul glanced from him to Grady and saw curiosity rather than surprise on his grandfather's lean face.

"Not what?" Ethan demanded. "Not in love? Not sure she'd trust you with her heart? I don't know that I'd blame her."

Paul struggled to wrap his head around what truth lay in his heart. Is this what love felt like? An obsessive hunger to be around her all the time? To revel in blazing joy and suffer terrifying despair in the space of minutes?

And while Lia's generous spirit and upbeat sincerity had gotten beneath his skin, Paul didn't know how to surrender to a relationship that challenged his black-and-white views. Lia's belief in all things metaphysical, her flighty, impulsive need to live a nomadic existence, her lack of substantial ties to people and place ran contrary to what was important to him.

"You're right," Paul said, aching at the thought that she intended to leave him. What could he say or do to convince her to give up her nomadic ways and stay in one place? With him. "I love her, but I messed up big time. She won't stay for me."

Grady shook his head. "She loves you."

For a second Paul couldn't breathe. He shifted his gaze from his grandfather's fond smile to Ethan's exasperated expression. Hope rose.

"Are you sure?" The level of desperation in his voice shook him.

"She's been falling in love with you from the first," his brother said. "I have no idea why. You've been a complete jerk."

"The whole time," Paul agreed, unable to imagine how she'd managed to see something of value in him.

When he wasn't pummeling her with distrust, he'd been battling the unsettling emotions that turned him inside out. He wasn't the least bit lovable. And then he realized the familiar path down which his thoughts had taken him. Damn it. He was still questioning her judgment. Maybe the time had come for him to accept that he had much to learn from her.

"How do I fix this?" he asked the room at large.

"You could start by telling her that you can't live without her," his brother said. "And that you have her back. Then remind her that we all love her and everyone believes she only had Grady's best interests at heart."

"What if I can't convince her?"

Ethan ejected a curse. "When did you become the guy who gives up? Is that what you do when your clients have a data breech?"

"No."

"So why with something that is so much more important than all the hackers you chase put together are you just quitting?"

The question, combined with Grady's disgusted expression, caused Paul's gut to twist in shame. He hated that Ethan was right. Was he really going to let her go? Without a fight? What was wrong with him?

All at once everything became so clear to him. He loved her. She loved him. He just needed to figure out a way to convince her they were meant for each other. In a flash he knew exactly what it would take to convince Lia that he was the man for her. The brilliance of it made him grin.

"I have to go."

"Wait." The single word came from Grady. He pulled something out of his pocket and held it out to Paul. "Give this to Lia."

Feeling slightly light-headed, Paul opened the small box and saw a familiar diamond ring tucked into the black velvet. "This is Grandma's ring," he murmured in awe.

Grady's lopsided smile bloomed as he nodded. "Make her my granddaughter."

Clutching the small box, Paul left the library and raced downstairs.

The trip from the estate to where Lia was keeping her camper felt as if it took forever, but it was only a forty-minute drive. He took advantage of the time to rehearse what he intended to say to her. He started with *I love you* and ended with *Will you spend the rest of your life with me?* What came in between would be all the reasons why she made his life better. Her laugh. Her giving nature. Her sweetness. Her free-spirited ways. Her beauty.

He didn't deserve her. But from now on, he'd work damn hard to.

When he reached the spot where her camper had last been parked, he saw it was gone. He gripped the steering wheel in dismay, unable to believe she'd leave after promising to wait for him. Several seconds ticked by while he brought his doubts back under control.

Lia hadn't left. She'd given her word and she was the type of woman who kept her promises. He turned around and headed toward the shop to find out where the camper had been moved to. To his relief, as he rounded the final corner, he spied it near the water station. She was filling the tanks with water in preparation for starting out.

He parked his SUV so that it blocked her truck and hopped out. Finding himself oddly out of breath, he strode toward her. There was wariness, not welcome, in her hazel eyes as he stopped before her.

"You can't leave," he began, suddenly awkward. Incapacitated by growing panic, he stood looking at her with a pounding heart.

"You have to be kidding," she said, shutting off the water and replacing the hose. "Now that this whole ridiculous scheme is over and everyone knows I'm not Ava's daughter, no one will want me to stay."

"I do." He came over and took her hands in his. "Stay in Charleston with me."

She shook her head and wouldn't meet his gaze. "Why?"

"Because I love you."

Her conversation with Ethan hadn't prepared her for Paul's actual declaration. His open and earnest manner as much as the words he spoke stunned her. Paul loved her. Her heart sang with joy. For days she'd been arguing with herself, seeking ways to make her relationship with Paul work.

If she was too quirky for Charleston society, she could dress differently and learn to discuss what was important to Paul's friends. Giving up the road wouldn't be a hardship if it meant waking up every morning beside the sexy cybersecurity specialist. Already he'd had a grounding influence on her. She'd even imagined herself going to school and becoming an occupational therapist, helping others the way she had Grady.

But then she remembered all that stood between them. She'd deceived his family. Her grandfather had swindled investors out of millions. Their vastly different natures. Any one of those things would create challenges. All three together were insurmountable.

"I don't know…"

"You don't know?" Paul's outrage clearly indicated he

was under the misguided assumption that all he had to do was declare himself and she'd fall at his feet in gratitude. Lia's annoyance gave her the fortitude to resist the romantic longing building in her.

"Ethan said that you've never been in love before," she explained, determined to do the smart thing. "And that you're conflicted."

"Maybe I was before. But that's not how I feel anymore."

"And tomorrow?" she persisted. "When something comes up about my past that triggers your suspicions again?"

He frowned. "What's going to come up?"

"I don't know." She waved her hands around. "My mother could show up and shock you with her passion for taking nude photos of herself. Or you could judge me because I have no idea who my father is." She sucked in a shaky breath and braced herself for his reaction. "Or maybe the fact that my grandfather is Peter Thompson."

His obvious shock at the familiar name confirmed what he'd thought about her all along and sparked her greatest fear. He'd always perceived her as the fruit of a poisonous tree. Still, she couldn't deny a certain amount of relief at getting everything out in the open.

"That's right," she continued. "I'm the granddaughter of one of the country's most notorious swindlers. His Ponzi scheme defrauded investors of hundreds of millions of dollars. The scandal rocked Seattle and devastated my family. It's why my mother changed her name and lives off the grid. It's why I do what I to help people. I'm related to a liar and a thief who harmed thousands. You were right about me all along."

Paul captured her hands and squeezed gently. "I wasn't right about you at all. That was the problem. I judged you before I knew what a kind, loving, selfless person you are."

"My grandfather is a criminal," Lia said, compelled to point out the obvious.

"A fact that has nothing to do with who you are."

As tempting as it was to accept his breezy dismissal of her background, Lia couldn't believe he'd just let it go. "But it's a scandal that could come to light. I can't imagine your family will appreciate that."

"If it does, we'll deal with it," Paul declared. "You are exactly what I need in my life. Someone to remind me to laugh and to stop working and to enjoy myself. You've made me feel again. Or for the first time. And now that you've opened me up, I need you so I will stay this way."

"But you said it yourself, we're completely different. How long before I start to drive you crazy?"

"Immediately." He laughed and his happiness made her heart pound. "Don't you get it? I'm thrilled that you do. Isn't that what your tarot cards said? For too long I've been burying myself in work. Isolating myself from the people I love and the world at large. You brought me back from the wilderness."

She couldn't believe he remembered the reading much less had taken it so to heart. "Does that mean you believe a little?"

"I'm starting to believe a lot. And that's all because of you."

"But what if I don't want to settle down in one place?"

"I can do my job from wherever," he said. "If you get itchy feet, we'll load up your little camper and take it on the road. Have laptop will travel," he joked, but to Lia's surprise and delight, it looked as if he meant it.

Still, if he'd taught her anything these last few weeks it was caution. "It sounds like a fairy-tale ending," she said. "But I'm not a princess, I just play one for kids who are stuck in the hospital."

"I have an idea." He turned utterly serious. "You read

tarot cards for me and my cousins, but you never did one
for yourself."

"I don't generally do my own readings."

"Because you can't?"

"Because I don't want to see what's coming."

"How about for just this once, you take a look. If the
cards tell you to get back on the road without me, then
you'll know."

She laughed, unable to believe what she was hearing.
Paul Watts was going to let his future be shaped by something he claimed not to believe in? "If you truly wanted
me to stay, I would think you'd be trying to convince me
yourself instead of depending on the cards."

"I haven't stopped trying to convince you. And I think
the tarot cards will show you that you belong here. With
me. Come on. It'll be fun."

Lia wanted to argue, but the obstinate set of Paul's jaw
kept her silent.

"Fine," she said, heading toward the camper. "Let's do
this."

In the hours since she'd said goodbye to Grady, she'd
restored Misty to her preferred organized state. As she
pulled out the tarot deck and sat down at the snug dinette,
she noticed the way Paul glanced around, his gaze lingering on the bed where they'd made love the first time. Her
heart skipped as stony determination settled over his features. That this man wanted her, loved her, weakened Lia's
resolve to make a clearheaded decision. She'd followed her
intuition all her life, impulsively jumping into action, but
some of Paul's deliberate, logic-driven methodology had
rubbed off on her.

Beneath Paul's intense regard, Lia shuffled the cards
while asking a simple question. Should she stay in Charleston and be with Paul? Instead of laying out the Celtic Cross
spread all at once with the cards facedown the way she'd

done in the earlier readings, Lia slowly placed each card faceup, considering the meaning as she went.

The reading started out ordinarily enough with the Fool, signifying the beginning of a journey, covered by the Two of Swords, which had a picture of a blindfolded woman, with arms crossed over her chest, holding two swords. The defensive imagery was clear enough that even Paul blinked in startled understanding.

"The basis of the situation is the Four of Cups," she narrated. "Indicating a situation where someone is apathetic about the same dull situation."

"Meaning it's time for you to leave Charleston?"

Or that she wasn't as enthusiastic to get back on the road as she once might have been. In truth, as she'd prepared the camper to leave, she'd noticed a dullness in her movements, a depression at the idea of leaving behind a city she'd grown to love.

"Possibly," she answered, laying down the card symbolizing the recent past. "The Lovers." Since that interpretation was also incredibly obvious, she moved on to possible outcome. "Eight of Cups." The card showed a man walking away from what had been a happy situation. Lia's heart sank as the message began to materialize.

"The King of Swords," Paul said when he saw the next card. "Is that me in your future?"

Obviously, he'd been paying attention during the readings she'd done for his cousins because there'd been all sorts of kings in their spreads that Lia had interpreted as the significant appearance of strong men in the lives.

"I believe so," Lia said cautiously. In the self position she drew the Six of Swords. It showed a couple traveling across the water in a boat, indicating a journey. The fact that it was reversed suggested the travel would be unsatisfying. "In my environment," she continued, placing another from the sword suit.

"That doesn't look good," Paul remarked, gazing at the Nine of Swords which depicted a woman crying against a backdrop of swords. "In fact, she looks pretty unhappy. Seems like your leaving is going to upset people."

Refusing to give him the satisfaction of agreeing, Lia placed the next card. "Hopes and fears." Her reaction to the card's significance must have shown on her face because Paul eyed her intently.

"What does it mean?"

Lia ground her teeth and debated whether to share that the card indicated the end of a journey or explain the more commonly held understanding that the Eight of Wands quite literally read as arrows of love.

"Action taken in love affairs," she grumbled. "Proposals made and accepted."

Although Lia didn't glance at Paul, she could feel the smugness radiating from him.

"And the outcome card?"

She froze, afraid to see what her future held. So much of the reading confirmed Paul's belief that she needed to stay and give their relationship a chance. How many times had she told people to trust in what the universe was telling them through the tarot deck? To turn her back on such clear mystic advice meant denying what she believed in.

And why?

Because she was afraid to take a risk with Paul.

"Lia?" Paul's gentle prompt brought a lump to her throat. "What's the last card?"

"I'm afraid to find out," she admitted. "In this moment, right here and now, I haven't made a decision that will impact the rest of my life. I'm at a crossroads where I can see my life going either way and there's a certain amount of peace in that."

"Schrödinger's cat," he declared, in all his adorable nerdiness. "Until you see the outcome you are both staying in

Charleston and taking a chance on us while also content to drive off and never look back." Paul plucked the last card from the top of the deck and placed it facedown in its position. "Forget the cards and trust your heart."

That heart was hammering so hard against her ribs that Lia could barely breathe. Loving him consumed her, but she couldn't shake the anxiety that one day he'd wake up and regret asking her to stay.

"It's not my heart I need to trust," she told him, pointing to the King of Swords card that represented him in the near-future position. "You rule your world with the strength of your personality and intellect."

Paul indicated the card that represented her. The Fool. A free spirit. Impulsive. Naive. Trusting that a leap of faith will bring joy and happiness.

"It's why I need someone like you in my life. We've known each other two weeks and I've changed so much in that short period of time. If you leave, I'll just go back to being lonely and isolated, only now that state will make me miserable." He then pointed to the Eight of Cups in her potential outcome position. "Don't leave behind what promises to be a wonderful life with me here."

"But your family," she protested. "I lied to all of them about being Ava's daughter. How can I ever look them in the eye again?"

"Actually, several of them already knew," Paul said. "Ethan told Dad and we suspect he told Mom."

"Dallas confronted me last night and she was really upset that Grady wrote me into his will," Lia admitted, hope fading even as she noted the gentleness that softened the strong lines of Paul's handsome face. "I think she hates me."

"She doesn't. She texted me this morning after she realized you left and knows she handled things badly. My whole family loves you. And I love you. The only question that remains is whether you love us enough to become a permanent member of the Watts clan."

Her breath stopped. "What do you mean by permanent?"

"I mean…" He grinned at her as he slid out of the dinette. Dropping to one knee beside her, Paul popped open the ring box Grady had given him. "Ophelia Marsh, will you do me the honor of becoming my wife?"

The formal words filled her with joy. "I adore you, Paul Watts," she murmured around the thick lump in her throat. "But…" Panic rose; she wanted so badly to belong that she could barely keep it together. "Your family has to approve."

"This is my grandmother's ring," he told her, pulling the circle of white gold and glittering diamonds free of the velvet padding. "Grady gave it to me to give to you. He wants you to be a part of our family. We all do."

Lia stared at the ring, the legacy of an earlier generation's love and fidelity, and something shifted inside her, settling into place, making her whole for the first time in her life. She held out her left hand and let Paul slide the ring onto her finger.

She framed his face with her hands and smiled. "Nothing would make me happier than to spend the rest of my life with you."

As Paul leaned forward to kiss her, he reached out and turned over the outcome card. Lia caught a glimpse of the image an instant before his lips met hers.

The Sun.

Joy. Happiness. Optimism. Energy. Wonder. The card promised all these and more.

Brilliant light exploded behind her closed eyelids as she gloried in the perfection of his kiss and reveled in all the boundless possibilities the future held. As opposites they'd been attracted to each other. Through their differences they'd learned, struggled and eventually changed. Like yin and yang they belonged together, two halves that made up a whole. Their journey had been a blend of destiny and deliberate choices. And as many challenges as they might encounter in the years ahead, Lia trusted they would overcome them together.

Epilogue

In the midst of the party to celebrate their engagement, Paul took Lia's hand and drew her away from the well-wishers. Since arriving at his grandfather's estate, they'd been swarmed by family and friends all eager to congratulate them. It was their first major social event as a couple and he'd been worried how she'd handle all the attention, but her dazzling smile demonstrated that she was gaining confidence by the hour.

Much had happened in the weeks since he'd proposed. Grateful for all she'd done for him, Grady had left Lia in his will, but since she wasn't Ava's daughter, he'd changed the amount intended for her. On the matter of Lia's background, they'd chosen to reveal her family connection to the infamous Peter Thompson. By controlling the way the story came out, they'd gotten ahead of the gossip. Still, when faced with so much unwanted media attention, Paul half expected Lia to bolt for the open road. Instead, supported by the entire Watts family, she'd weathered the news event with grace.

Craving a few minutes alone with Lia, Paul guided her onto the back terrace and into a dark corner away from prying eyes. He didn't expect they'd have more than a few minutes alone before they were discovered. He desperately needed to kiss her. As if her own desires matched his, Lia melted into his embrace, sliding her fingers into his hair and applying pressure to coax his lips to hers.

The scent of her perfume reminded him of the first time they'd met. He realized now that he'd started falling for her in that moment. His tactics for scaring her off would've worked if Ethan hadn't concocted his scheme to pass her off as Grady's granddaughter. Realizing just how close he'd come to losing her made Paul tighten his arms around Lia's slim waist.

"I thought we were done sneaking around," she teased with a breathless laugh when they finally came up for air.

"With a family as large as mine, if we want privacy we're going to have to get creative."

She hummed with pleasure as his lips traveled down her neck. "I like getting creative with you."

The sound of a door opening a short distance away made Paul groan. A second later he heard Ethan's voice.

"Here's where you two disappeared off to."

"Go away," Paul growled, not ready for his interlude with Lia to end. "We're busy."

Ethan ignored his brother's attempts to send him packing and stepped closer. "I thought you both might be interested in learning that we've received a hit from the testing service."

Paul's breath caught as the momentous news hit him like a sharp jab to his gut. Lia clutched his arm as she, too, reacted. Their eyes met and in that moment of connection the rest of the world fell away. Paul reveled in the deep bond developing between them. No matter what happened in the future, Paul knew Lia would be beside him, offering support and performing the occasional tarot card reading.

He grinned down at her. "I love you."

"I love you, too," Lia echoed, her sweet smile setting his heart on fire.

"Did you two hear what I said?" Ethan demanded, his exasperation coming through loud and clear. "We found Ava's daughter."

* * * * *

COMING SOON!

We really hope you enjoyed reading this book. If you're looking for more romance, be sure to head to the shops when new books are available on

Thursday 17th October

MILLS & BOON

THE HEART OF ROMANCE

A ROMANCE FOR EVERY KIND OF READER

MODERN
Prepare to be swept off your feet by sophisticated, sexy and seductive heroes, in some of the world's most glamourous and romantic locations, where power and passion collide.
8 stories per month.

HISTORICAL
Escape with historical heroes from time gone by. Whether your passion is for wicked Regency Rakes, muscled Vikings or rugged Highlanders, awaken the romance of the past.
6 stories per month.

MEDICAL
Set your pulse racing with dedicated, delectable doctors in the high-pressure world of medicine, where emotions run high and passion, comfort and love are the best medicine.
6 stories per month.

True Love
Celebrate true love with tender stories of heartfelt romance, from the rush of falling in love to the joy a new baby can bring, and a focus on the emotional heart of a relationship.
8 stories per month.

Desire
Indulge in secrets and scandal, intense drama and plenty of sizzling hot action with powerful and passionate heroes who have it all: wealth, status, good looks…everything but the right woman.
6 stories per month.

HEROES
Experience all the excitement of a gripping thriller, with an intense romance at its heart. Resourceful, true-to-life women and strong, fearless men face danger and desire - a killer combination!
8 stories per month.

DARE
Sensual love stories featuring smart, sassy heroines you'd want as a best friend, and compelling intense heroes who are worthy of them.
4 stories per month.

To see which titles are coming soon, please visit

millsandboon.co.uk/nextmonth

MILLS & BOON
MODERN
Power and Passion

Prepare to be swept off your feet by sophisticated, sexy and seductive heroes, in some of the world's most glamourous and romantic locations, where power and passion collide.